Carmella McKenzie

HABERDASHERY

Acorn Independent Press

Contents

Chapter One — CUTTING OUT A PATTERN 7

Chapter Two — TACKING IT ALL TOGETHER 20

Chapter Three — CROSS STITCH 34

Chapter Four — CHAIN STITCH................................. 47

Chapter Five — RUNNING STITCH........................... 59

Chapter Six — DARNING... 71

Chapter Seven — OVERLOCK....................................... 83

Chapter Eight — KNIT 1 PURL 1 96

Chapter Nine — BLANKET STITCH 109

Chapter Ten — PATCHWORK.................................. 122

Chapter Eleven — HERRINGBONE STITCH.............. 134

Chapter Twelve — A TEAR IN THE FABRIC.............. 146

Chapter Thirteen — SEED STITCH 159

Chapter Fourteen — BROKEN CHAIN STITCH............. 171

Chapter Fifteen — UNRAVELLING............................... 183

Chapter Sixteen — SPLIT BACKSTITCH 197

Chapter Seventeen — SINGLE KNOTTED STITCH 209

Chapter Eighteen — BARRIER STITCH 222

Chapter Nineteen — LOCK STITCH 234

Chapter Twenty — WEB STITCH 247

Chapter Twenty-One   FORBIDDEN KNOT 260

Chapter Twenty-Two   SATIN STITCH 273

Chapter Twenty-Three   KNOTTED LOOP STITCH............ 285

Chapter Twenty-Four   UNPICKING AND
                        RE-ATTACHING 297

Chapter Twenty-Five   CLEAN FINISHING........................ 309

Epilogue   SEWN UP 321

Acknowledgement

With very grateful thanks to my sister Alison, and her ruthless eradication of what she calls 'weak words'. Without her support and suggestions, I would have found writing this book, very difficult.

Also, to the two Davids, for reading right to the end, when it would not exactly be their first choice in subject. Well done chaps!

To Leila and everyone at Acorn for their help in seeing me through my first foray into the world of self-publishing.

Chapter One

CUTTING OUT A PATTERN

*A template from which the parts are traced
before being cut out and assembled*

Hannah stared at her reflection; getting a bit chubby again, not looking her best and, if not careful, the years would pass her by before she realised. Something had to be done before it was too late, and she owed it to Jack to take more care of herself.

Hannah had always been curvaceous; that's what Michael, her husband, correction, *ex*-husband had liked about her. 'My cuddly, little homemaker,' he'd called her. Well, she'd made a home alright, a home that was now gone. Sighing, she adjusted the button on her skirt; too much baking had been done lately.

Michael had always loved her cooking. The skills that Hannah brought to her marriage had been learnt from her mother, an old-fashioned housewife who firmly believed a woman's place was in the home. Subsequently, she instilled in her daughter a love of 'home'. This involved a strategic battle plan for housework, washing, ironing and cooking.

From quite a young age, Hannah could prepare a sumptuous feast for the table, along with a baking regime to keep tins and Tupperware full at all times. She could also sew and made most of her own clothes. A small rebellion had ensued during her teenage years when she wanted to dress like her friends, but as her weight crept up, the visits to the fashion outlets they frequented led to increasingly embarrassing situations, and the paper patterns came out again. Hannah spent her evenings hunched over the sewing machine, trying to make her larger-sized outfits more fashionable, or at least, using the colours that were touted in magazines and TV as being trendy.

Leaving school after her GCSEs, she went to work for an up and coming estate agency where her job was to photograph properties and arrange appointments. Her manager was delighted with her efficiency, but aspired to a more 'hip' look for his staff, and Hannah was only sent on accompanied viewings if there was absolutely nobody else available, or if it was an elderly couple that the others weren't interested in. Michael joined the staff six months later. Hannah heard the whispers about him still living at home and being a bit of 'a mummy's boy', even though he was in his mid-20s. She thought he was lovely. Dark, copper-coloured hair and twinkling brown eyes that appraised her at times before giving her a wink.

Surely, he couldn't be interested in her? She was now 19 and still with no boyfriend. Her 18th birthday, celebrated with people from school, had been an embarrassment, them all bringing somebody.

One day, coming to work in a new dress she'd made from a size 16 pattern, generously cut, along with a tub of warm flapjacks baked early that morning, she was delighted when Michael fell on them with gusto.

'These are the best ever,' he announced, brushing crumbs off his suit, and Hannah had to stop herself from helping him. 'Did you make them?'

Nodding shyly, she pushed the tub forward. 'I had a bit of time this morning and had all the ingredients.'

Pulling a tissue from the box on the table, he used it to carefully wrap some more of the flapjacks. 'I'll take these to eat when I'm out this morning. You look different, is that a new dress?'

'Oh, this? Yes, I made it myself.'

'You made that as well? What a treasure you are, Hannah, you'll make some man very happy one day. See you later.'

He dashed off, leaving Hannah staring longingly after him, not noticing her hand dipping into the flapjack box at least another three times. She got into the habit of bringing something in once a week, twice, and then eventually, three or four times a week. Michael made a beeline for her desk every morning.

'What's my girl got for me today then?' If there was nothing, he would put on a sad, puppy dog expression, which made her giggle and promise a treat for tomorrow.

My girl, I wish. Hannah spent a little more time on her hair and make-up and tried, on and off, to lose a few pounds.

Michael had gone through a few girlfriends but nobody he was serious about. Living with his elderly mother curtailed his sexual adventures. As selfish as he was, he wouldn't disrespect her by treating his room like a knocking shop. He had a very comfortable life, was fed well, laundry done, and no rent to pay. His mother told him she was well provided for and wanted him to save his money to set up with, 'a nice girl' one day and have a family. That suited him fine. Fatherhood did appeal to him, creating a new generation in his name, as long as it didn't upset his life too much.

'Mother,' he said to her one night, 'how would you feel *if* I wanted to get married, about me, *us*, setting up home here for a bit before we find a house of our own?'

Doreen nearly dropped her knitting in excitement. 'Have you got a girl then, one I don't know about?' Then she frowned slightly. It would have to be someone she approved of. If they were going to live under *her* roof, the girl would have to know her place. She knew what her son liked and needed and didn't particularly want to hand over control.

'I've got my eye on someone,' Michael said. He'd realised with some surprise that he was beginning to feel quite fond of Hannah. His mother wouldn't be around forever and the house would be his anyway. He could picture Hannah slipping easily in as a replacement for all his needs, as well as providing sex on tap whenever he wanted it. She wasn't *that* bad, he told himself, even as he cringed slightly, remembering some of the remarks from other staff that he'd laughed along with. If she lost a bit of weight, she'd be quite passable, although he liked women with a bit of flesh, 'something to get hold of'. A few kind words and she'd be putty in his hands. Making his mind up to ask her out for a drink, he smiled at his mother.

'I could murder a cup of hot chocolate, Mum, would you mind?'

* * *

Hannah carefully boxed up the baklavas she'd made the night before. They had been a little tricky but he was worth it. Having sampled quite a few of them, she'd gone to bed feeling slightly nauseous, but still had her peanut butter on toast for breakfast. The salty peanuts would neutralise all the sweetness, she convinced herself. Glancing in the mirror, she thought her face looked a little bloated. Was that another chin? With her dress designs, lumps and bumps could be disguised, but a few pounds needed to come off again. Reluctantly, she stopped herself having a third slice of toast and decided to walk on to one further bus stop, which should burn off a few calories.

Michael ate and praised her baklavas. 'Listen, Hannah, how about a drink together after work? We never really get a chance to chat, are you free this evening?'

Was she free? Was this real? 'Er, a drink would be lovely, thank you.'

A horrible feeling washed over her, was she being set up as a joke? No, surely, he wouldn't be that cruel. When 5p.m. came and he was waiting, she breathed a sigh of relief. Some of the others looked a little surprised at the two of them walking out together but she ignored their stares and breathed in as she went past. Michael got himself a pint and a glass of wine for her. She'd asked for one with half lemonade, but he'd scoffed and told her to 'lighten up'.

After asking a few questions about her life, most of the evening was taken up with him talking about himself and his future ambitions. He was going to apply for the assistant manager's post that was coming up. Although he hadn't been there as long as some of the others, he had made his mark with sales numbers, albeit with his rather ruthless bending of the truth at times. Getting a better idea of his living arrangements, Hannah managed to slip into the conversation how much she enjoyed looking after a home and to having her own, one day, *with the right man.*

He walked her to the bus stop and, to her great surprise, kissed her, accompanied by a quick fondle of her breasts. Not having kissed anybody before, she thought she did okay and he seemed pleased. Although he had his car, a lift home was not offered. Maybe it was too soon for that, she thought, and he did live in the other direction after all.

Undressing that night, she studied herself despondently. Michael would obviously want to do more than fondle her breasts. Although not experienced, Hannah was not without knowledge, devouring historical romantic blockbusters, where the heroes were always dark and handsome and took their women with practised and knowing skills, which made the heroines gasp and scream with pleasure. Where their skimpy lace underclothes were torn off or lovingly removed, sadly, her armour-plated underwear would put Michael right off.

Hannah decided to go on the grapefruit diet she'd torn from a magazine. Ten pounds in ten days, it promised. Baking would be done only for Michael. For his sake, she would endure ten miserable days.

* * *

Two days later, Hannah nearly fainted at work. Michael, seeing her tear-stained face, bought her some flowers and a box of chocolates, asking her, what the matter was. She mumbled some excuse and he nodded, with a 'you don't have to tell me' look. *Women's things*, he thought. What she needed was another night out. The pictures on Friday and then a curry, he announced. Hannah wasn't a huge fan of curry – it usually gave her heartburn – but eagerly agreed. She could always fill up with rice and naan bread.

Deciding the grapefruit diet didn't suit her metabolism at all, she made pasties for herself and her parents in the evening, with a couple of extra ones for the next day. Her mother was overjoyed that Hannah had a 'proper date' at last.

'Why don't you bring your young man here for a nice home-cooked meal?'

'It's a bit soon, I'm not sure if he's really my young man yet, but he does like my baking.'

Her mother nodded sagely. 'It's true, the old saying. The way to a man's heart *is* through his stomach. You get a few good meals into him and you've got him, mark my words. I mean, look at your father, a more content man you'd never find.'

Her father, who usually let these conversations go over his head, looked carefully at his daughter. When did she get quite so large? 'Hmm, this boyfriend thing's all very well but aren't you a bit concerned that our daughter of 19 is beginning to look like a woman in her 50s?' There was a deathly silence. 'I'm only thinking of her health,' he continued feebly.

Hannah pushed the rest of her pasty away and scuttled out of the room, crying noisily.

'You're a complete fool, Ronald.' Hannah's mother swatted her husband around the head with a napkin. 'Our Hannah has more to offer a man than some of these stick insects that are about. I'm going up to see her, get this table cleared, *stupid* oaf!' *The silly old fool, he never thinks, that's the trouble with marrying an older man.*

He wasn't that much older, only 11 years, but a life in the army had conditioned him to a way of thinking that seemed very old-fashioned at times. He took early retirement after six years of being 'Major Rawlings', and with his pension, could afford to now enjoy his garden and his family without having to work.

* * *

In the morning, a red-faced Hannah boxed up the pasties. She'd taken great pleasure in telling her father that she'd lost a pound and she didn't want to hear his opinions anymore. There was some lovely material she'd been saving, so a new dress was called for. Knowing what suited her, she was making her own patterns now. By cutting a little extra here and there or leaving out the occasional dart, she could dress more flatteringly. Before going to bed the night before, the material was spread out on the dining table, lightly pressed with the pattern pinned into place, ready for cutting, which her mother said she would do while Hannah was at work.

'You look happier,' Michael said to Hannah as she was dunking a ginger in her morning cuppa.

Splash.

'Oh, you made me jump, I dropped my biscuit.' Fumbling for it with a spoon, she watched it sink to oblivion in the bottom of her mug. *Damn,* she hated soggy biscuit at the bottom of her drink. Oh well, she'd have to make a fresh one. 'I do feel better, thanks. I was just a bit out of sorts yesterday. I'll be fine for tomorrow, that is, if you still…'

'Of course we're still on, silly. I just didn't want to take you for a curry if you weren't up for it. You don't want a gippy tum on top of the other.' He winked knowingly at her.

The other, what's he talking about? 'Er, no, definitely not. Umm, my last bus is at 10.20p.m., will we be finished by then?'

'I'm not sure, depends on how fast you eat.' He roared with laughter and she, a little unsure, joined in. 'Don't worry, if it gets late, I'll run you home.'

Her heart skipped a beat. 'But it's out of your way.'

'Your way, my way.' He winked at her again. 'Did you bring anything in for me today, sweetheart?'

Sweetheart. She melted and produced the pasties. 'I made some for our tea last night. They've got the best steak in them, I don't like cheap cuts.'

'Never thought you would, you're not that sort of girl. Cheap, I mean. See you later.'

He didn't think she was cheap, that was good, wasn't it? Washing her cup out and rinsing the dregs of her ginger biscuit down the plughole, she started daydreaming about what it would actually be like living in a house and looking after him. Would he want her to keep working? If she did work full-time, it would be a struggle to keep the house as nice as she would like. Would he want a family? Did she? Not right away but, yes, everyone did, didn't they?

'Hannah! Your phone's been ringing on and off for five minutes.' A terse voice from the office broke her reverie.

'Sorry, I've got it.' She missed the call by a split second but luckily, it rang again immediately. After making an appointment, she told herself not to be ridiculous; it was only their second date, for goodness sake.

The dress was completed that evening. Slightly lower cut than usual, she wondered if it was a bit too daring, but she had bought a new bra, which gave her a better shape, and there was no harm in showing a bit off, was there? The material skimmed over her rounded stomach and hips, ending just below her knees. At least her legs weren't too chunky and her calves were quite shapely really. The sleeves were elbow length as Hannah thought her arms were a bit flabby. Honestly, with all the mixing and beating she did, they deserved to be as firm as the kitchen worktop. It just wasn't fair. One of the girls at the office always had something out of Hannah's treat tins *and* had a burger with fries almost every lunchtime. How could she be so slim? Convinced that there was a problem with her glands, Hannah knew nothing could be done about it. Her mother was large and so was she, so that was the end of it.

* * *

Michael stared down her cleavage as she answered a phone call at work. *That was some pair!* He hoped to have a better feel and hopefully a look on the way back to hers tonight. It was the least she could do after he forked out for the cinema and a meal. Although careful with his money, except what *he* wanted it for, this situation was an investment as far as he was concerned. Hannah would suit him in almost every department; apart from the fact she was a bit bigger than he'd have liked, he couldn't fault her and felt sure his mother would heartily approve. Finishing work, they went for a drink first. Michael got her a glass of wine without asking, but she took that as a compliment.

'You look great by the way,' he said as he put her drink down. 'One of yours?'

'Yes, I sort of designed it as well.' She coloured slightly.

'Really?' He didn't know what that involved but obviously, she was pleased about it. 'That's very impressive, maybe that could be a side-line for you?'

'Oh, I don't think so.' She gulped her wine. 'I'm happy just doing it for myself.' *Rather than trying to buy off the peg.*

'One day perhaps, when you have a family, you could set up at home?'

A family, with him? 'Mmm, it's possible.'

In the cinema, Michael's hand caressed her thigh, his fingers pushing under the hem of her dress. He hadn't suggested any popcorn and Hannah caught the enticing odour of the tubs around her. Pushing the thought of the imminent curry aside, she rested her hand on his, trying to stop it going any further up her leg. The cinema was not the place for this sort of carry-on. She would have to nip to the ladies and take off the waist elasticated thing she was wearing that pulled her in a bit. She didn't want him finding it if he got that far later.

The film wasn't really her choice either. She'd mumbled something about wanting to see the new chick-flick but he hadn't listened. This was a shoot-em-up with lots of shouting and swearing, but he enjoyed it and so she agreed after when he said, 'That was good, wasn't it?'

The curry was torture; far too hot, she guzzled water all the way through. The plan to fill up on rice and naans was foiled by Michael telling her to 'eat up', whilst shovelling curry into his mouth. Managing to persuade him to let her have ice cream after made her feel a bit better. Paying the bill, he gave a wolfish smile.

'I'll drive you home, I know a quiet spot we can stop for a bit and get to know each other better.'

'I umm, I'll just be a minute.' Bolting into the ladies, she divested herself of the (even tighter after the meal) cummerbund and stuffed it into her bag. What to do about the bra? The thought of him struggling with a double layer of hooks and eyes at the back was a non-starter, so that had to go as well. The dress would support her well enough in the car and taking the large, wire-supporting, extra-strength appliance off gave her a sense of abandonment and wickedness. She was a woman, just like the ones in the books she enjoyed so much, the ones she lost herself in. Even if Michael wasn't a Regency

Duke, which would have gone down very well, she still fancied the pants off him.

Michael pulled off the road, switching off the engine. 'Now then, I've been wondering what's under that dress all day.' He pressed his lips to hers and his hand on her breast. Instantly, he pulled his head back. 'You naughty, naughty girl, there's nothing on under this dress and there are buttons down the front, how perfect.' Quickly, he undid them and his hand snaked in. Her breasts were large, warm and squashy, just how he liked them. Kissing her some more, he kneaded and pinched her nipples. He was turning her in the seat with his other hand, pushing her dress up. Encountering a roll of flesh, he hesitated a second, then explored below it.

Hannah was very uncomfortable and the handle of the door was sticking into her back, but the kissing was very nice. The nipple pinching she could have done without, however, she was experiencing that lower-down, fluttering feeling that she'd read about. When Michael pulled her hand to the front of his trousers, she felt 'the rod of steel' she'd also read about, but this had always happened in more comfort than squashed in the front of a car.

'Michael,' she gasped, 'it's a bit cramped in here.'

Reluctantly, he pulled away. Red in the face and quite breathless, he sighed. 'Yes, I can't get at you properly, I need more space. Could you get the house to yourself?'

'I don't think so, my parents never go anywhere together, what about yours?'

'Same thing, but it's just my mother and she does go to a lunch club one Sunday a month, this coming Sunday, in fact. She's out for about two hours, could you manage that?'

Could she? 'Yes, if you're sure it would be okay.'

'Be outside your house at a 11.45a.m. so you can jump right in the car, we don't want to waste any time. I'll meet your parents another day.'

He must be serious about her if he was happy to meet her parents, Hannah thought happily. Trying not to think about being naked in front of him, she gave him directions to her house and let him kiss and fumble a bit more before saying she ought to go in.

Reading another chapter of her current book before going to sleep, she wished she could wear something like a silky chemise, and imagined being picked up, carried to the bed and laid gently down before being taken in a masterful fashion...

Chapter Two

TACKING IT ALL TOGETHER

To temporarily hold in place until it can be
permanently sewn

On Saturday, Hannah was in such a state, she refused
to cook.

'Whatever is the matter with you?' her mother asked.
'Cooking always makes you feel better.'

'Not today it won't. I'm out for, umm, lunch tomorrow
and I need to think.'

'*Think*, what's to think about? Is it something to do
with this man you're seeing? When will I get to meet
him?'

'I don't know. I shall be in the bathroom for at least
the next hour, okay?' Hannah disappeared up the stairs
and her father rustled his paper irritably.

'In the bathroom for an *hour*, what's it in aid of,
hmmm? Not here for lunch tomorrow indeed, I shall
miss her Yorkshires, they're better than yours m'dear.
She's putting herself on a plate instead of a meal, *that's*
what's going on.'

'*Ronald*,' his wife was incensed, 'what a thing to say.
How could you think that?'

'Just remembering what it was like,' he mumbled
from behind his paper. *I remember what it was like
when you did it for me.*

'Stop grinning like a buffoon, man, and go and make a cup of coffee.' *Is he right?* Margaret couldn't lecture her daughter; Hannah was old enough to make her own decisions, but a broken heart? She didn't want to deal with that.

Hannah lay in the hottest water she could tolerate; hopefully, she would sweat off a pound or two. A mudpack covered her face and her legs had been shaved to within an inch of their lives. *Am I doing the right thing?* She was halfway in love with Michael, he was the first man who'd ever paid her a compliment or seemed attracted to her. She would make him *so* happy if he gave her the chance. There would be no better home life he could have and she'd be so proud to be by his side.

Her current book was propped up on the soap rack and she was riveted by yet another four-poster interlude in which the Duke was causing his woman to melt in his embrace. *Will I melt tomorrow?* In her room, all the clothes were pulled out and laid on the bed. Everything there was beautifully made, but not alluring. Did it matter? The fact that they were going to have sex was pretty definite and clothes would come off anyway. At least, she presumed they would. Perhaps she should choose something that wouldn't crease or at least could be taken off quickly. What a minefield this all was.

Eventually, she picked a gypsy-style skirt with a loose top she'd embroidered herself and was very fond of. It was quite slimming and the generous, elasticated waist wouldn't show any tight red lines on her skin, which was her best feature. Creamy and unblemished, it needed little enhancement and was as smooth as silk. There may be a little too much of it in places, but at least it was nice to touch.

That evening, she ignored her parents' pointed stares and forced herself to have just an apple and a handful of raisins. Keeping her mind occupied, she embroidered the rest of a cushion cover, read some of her book and went to bed dreaming of Michael, dukes and Regency fashions, which, in her sleep-infused, muddled brain, transformed into huge, billowing skirts.

* * *

Michael was waiting in the car as promised. At last, he'd be able to cop a proper handful, but realising he still needed to chat her up properly, he would have to curb his impatience and go through the niceties. Hinting to his mother that she may meet 'the girlfriend' this afternoon, he would also have to keep his eye on the clock. Hannah could not be seen coming out of his bedroom, looking dishevelled.

'Hi gorgeous, you look nice,' he said as she opened the car door at the agreed time.

'We'd better go; my parents are hovering, hoping to catch a glimpse of you,' she said breathlessly.

He needed no second bidding; there was no time for that today. Twenty minutes later, he pulled up outside a neat semi with a small, tidy front garden. Pristine white nets met with Hannah's approval, along with shiny brass attachments on the front door. Not too sure about the selection of gnomes in the garden, she wondered what it would be like inside. There was no time to admire the interior as Michael was guiding her upstairs.

'I hope you're as hot for me as I am for you,' he gasped as they reached his room. He started kissing her immediately and she could feel his hands creeping under her blouse. 'Let's get this off, shall we?' His fingers moved to the back.

'Let me do that,' she squeaked, and undid the collection of hooks with a practised movement. Her breasts fell into his hands and he thought he'd gone to heaven.

In a few moments, she stood self-conscious and topless. Noticing her nervous look, Michael slowed down a little and took her hands. 'You are sure about this, aren't you?'

'Oh yes, it's just... my first time.'

'That makes you really special to me, come here, sweetie.' Laying her down on the bed, he took a quick look at the clock, started kissing her earnestly and stroking her thighs. Hannah did begin to feel the fluttering again and helped him ease herself out of her skirt and pants, then watched nervously as he took his trousers off. Thank goodness it wasn't as *big* as her imagination had dictated. *Those books must exaggerate.* When it eventually happened, it did hurt a bit, but he cuddled her afterwards and seemed pleased. She hadn't exactly shattered or melted, as her heroines did, and Michael's face had looked very peculiar when he shouted out and collapsed on her.

'That was great, and it was good for you, wasn't it?' Without waiting for an answer, he jumped off the bed, grabbing his trousers. 'We'd better get dressed in case Mum gets back early.'

Mum did get back early, but thankfully, not early enough. Her son and his girlfriend were sitting in the lounge with a cup of tea and some of her lemon drizzle cake that she'd made 'just in case'.

'Mum, this is Hannah, she's been looking forward to meeting you.' Michael had one of his pleading looks and she never could deny him.

'Hello Hannah, I believe you work with my son?'

Over tea and a chat, Mrs Rawlings studied the girl; a bit hefty, but quite pretty and well spoken. Hannah enthused over the glass cabinet full of fussy figurines, which she guessed were the woman's pride and joy. Praising the lemon cake, she mentioned how much she enjoyed cooking and said how she could never get the 'drizzle' to stop running down the cake too quickly. Mrs Rawlings puffed up and decided the girl would do very well. Under further interrogation, she learned of Hannah's home skills and love of dressmaking. The embroidered blouse was much admired and photo albums were brought out. Michael's father had died some years ago. The boy had been a late and surprise addition to the family; they had given up on having a child. Mrs Rawlings was almost 40 when she had Michael, and treated him like a precious object to be coddled and protected

Michael was bored and said he needed to run Hannah home. Having done so, he kissed her again with a quick feel and made arrangements to meet her parents in a few days, when Hannah would cook a nice meal.

'Curry?' he asked hopefully.

'Oh no, sorry, it would give dad indigestion. I'll do that for you another time.'

He drove home to hear his mother praise his choice and decided there was no point in wasting a lot of time. He asked for the mail order catalogue and found a nice little ring at a very reasonable price. Hannah wouldn't care; she didn't seem to wear much jewellery anyway. If he got the assistant manager's job, which he was pretty sure of, he'd ask her then.

Her parents liked him. Her father approved of his ambitions and attitude to the job. Michael was very polite and asked all the right questions. It was a nice house, he thought, worth more than his mother's, and he presumed it would all be Hannah's one day. He listened to Mr Worth going on about the garden, the greenhouse and his tomatoes, and asked if he could take a look. Feigning great interest in everything, he mumbled thanks when cuttings were promised, and listened in total bemusement to the man's crop rotation plan, in a garden the size of half a tennis court.

For God's sake, does it really matter if spuds are grown in the same place or not? And what a fuddy, old couple they are. The mum's not so bad but her father's come out of the ark.

'What a nice, young man,' her father said, as Michael, with great relief, drove away.

* * *

Michael got the assistant manager's job, as he knew he would. Taking Hannah out for a meal, he produced the ring.

'Oh, Michael it's beautiful.' Hannah's eyes filled with tears. 'Yes, I'd love to marry you. How far on were you thinking? We need to save for a deposit.'

'Well, I thought, if you don't mind of course,' he added quickly, 'we could move in with my mum for a while. She's elderly and would be lonely without me. If we did that, we could save our money for something better later, and the other reason is, I may have to run another branch, which could mean moving anyway.'

'Oh, I see, I didn't realise.' Hannah was a little disappointed. Although she got on well with Mrs Rawlings, she'd looked forward to running her own home. But she mustn't be selfish, she told herself, it would all be for the betterment of their lives later, and she could still help with the cooking and do her dressmaking as she'd always done.

'I thought we needn't wait too long,' Michael continued. 'Neither of us has a big family so we could book the register office with a hotel lunch after. You'd want to make your own dress I suppose?'

Would I? Yes, I think I would. It would be the most beautiful thing she'd ever made. Already in her mind's eye, she could picture beading and embroidery. 'I'd need a few months.'

He realised how important the dress would be to her. 'Okay, what about four months from now? I don't really want to wait for you, but if you need that time…'

'Four months, I promise it'll be ready.'

After showing her ring off at home and receiving congratulations, Hannah started sketching her ideas. An empire line, she thought, dropping from below her bust would be the most flattering; ivory, rather than white, with a layer of gauze, which she would bead. She showed it to her mother.

'It's lovely, dear, but you said it was the register office? Isn't it a bit much for a small wedding? Is it what you really want? You know Dad and I would pay for the wedding you've always wanted. We always thought you'd get married in the church you were christened at. I know we don't go so much now, but I'm sure it wouldn't be a problem.'

'I don't think Michael wants a lot of fuss,' Hannah said quietly. There was a lump in her throat as she looked at her sketches.

'You leave Michael to us, we'll have a word with him,' her mother said firmly. 'Maybe he thinks we don't have the money for a proper wedding and he's being thoughtful. We've always had that money put away for this time. Your father wants to walk you down the aisle and that's what's going to happen. You make that dress and you'll look beautiful, like you should do on your wedding day. Even if it is a small affair, we can still do it properly. I'm sure Mrs Rawlings would prefer it as well.'

Mrs Rawlings didn't particularly care. When Michael had told her of their plans, she wondered if the girl was pregnant. Why the rush? Register office! It smacked a bit of desperation to her mind. Then her son informed her a few days later that the plans had changed. Hannah's parents were paying and they wanted her to have a special day. Oh well, maybe she wasn't pregnant. Tutting to herself at such goings-on, she then realised she could have a new outfit and a splendid hat. She wouldn't let her boy down and there were a few relatives they could scrape up for the day to bolster their side. She decided to wangle an invite to Hannah's next meal arrangements and meet Mr and Mrs Worth. There were ideas she could put forward, in a subtle way of course, and have some influence on this important day for her son.

The whole of the spare room was taken over for the dress. The basic shape had been cut out and tacked, and was hanging in layers of protective cellophane. The gauze had been marked with Hannah's own design for beading. Hundreds of tiny pearls were being painstakingly attached with the finest silver thread curling and winding its way between them. Hannah was rarely in bed before one in the morning and was too busy to bake. Subsequently, the pounds were falling off her.

* * *

Two months later and nearly two stone lighter, Hannah was fitting into a size 14. People at work were complimenting her and Michael was most appreciative.

'You're looking really sexy, but don't lose anymore. I like a bit to cuddle and for God's sake, don't lose any off the top.'

Their sex life was a hit and miss affair. They snatched odd times when one of the houses was free and the rest of the time involved uncomfortable trysts in the back of the car. Hannah was getting apprehensive about what would happen after they were married.

'You know when we're actually living at your house, with your mother?'

'Yeah, what about it?'

'You know, in bed… It's a bit embarrassing with her being, well, next to us.'

'Mum's out like a light. Nothing wakes her up, don't worry about it. If I thought we couldn't do it, I *would* be looking for somewhere else to live. Now stop fussing and get your knickers off.' A short time later, Hannah again felt a little unsatisfied. Maybe it would be better when they were both more relaxed. Michael couldn't seem to get enough of her, so he must be pleased with what they were doing.

'Am I seeing you tomorrow?' he asked, playing with her nipple.

'Do you mind if I don't? I really need to work on the dress. I've still got a whole section that needs beading.'

'That bloody dress! It seems an awful lot of fuss for something you're only going to wear once.' He had a sulk on.

'I know, but I'll only get *married* once and I do want to look really perfect for you.' Hannah was beginning to learn how to get around these moods.

He shrugged. 'Still seems an awful lot of fuss, but if it makes you happy. You will look good I guess, with the weight you've lost.'

'And you'll look so handsome,' she continued. 'Everybody will say how lucky I am to be marrying such a man.'

Michael preened. 'If you think so, go on then, make your dress beautiful. I was actually wondering whether to go away this weekend. Some of the lads are going to an away match and staying over. That would give you a lot of free time,' he said craftily.

Hannah cringed at the mention of 'the lads'. Every time she and Michael had bumped into any of them, she'd always felt they were sniggering behind her back, and had even been suspicious on more than one occasion that Michael was joining in. She'd told herself not to be daft, he wouldn't do that to her. Wasn't he telling her now how great she was looking?

'Of course you should go.' Actually, Hannah was a little relieved to have time to herself. She had wanted to go to the larger town a few miles away for trimmings and bits. The town where they lived was limited in choice and she so loved to feel the fabrics and threads before she bought them. 'You work so hard, Michael, you deserve a treat.'

He had the grace to feel a little guilty, knowing they would be visiting some topless bars and strip clubs. Well, he could look on it as an early 'stag do'. He'd buy Hannah a nice box of chocolates as a surprise.

* * *

On Saturday, Hannah was ready to go. Her mother had planned to accompany her, but then said she felt a bit tired and had a headache, so would Hannah mind going on her own? Relieved her mother had refused the offer of her staying to 'look after her', Hannah took her bag with some swatches of her material and a sample of the beading and caught the bus to accessory heaven.

It was a pleasure-filled morning. Choosing a few lengths of material in the weekly market for future projects took a lot of the time and she hadn't started on her wedding requirements. Treating herself to a salad bowl, she felt very noble and thought she deserved a piece of coffee walnut cake. Heading towards the large department store that had the haberdashery department she liked, saw with mounting horror the closed signs over all the windows. *No! It can't be.* Furiously blinking back tears, she sat down on the nearby bench, looking dazed.

'What's the matter, my dear?' An older lady already sitting there looked at her in concern. 'Can I help?'

'No, nobody can help,' Hannah almost sobbed and then, shocked, remembered her manners. 'I'm sorry, it's just that I'm so disappointed. The store there is closed you see.'

The lady nodded. 'They've gone into administration, not enough call for their sort of products.'

'I had a call for them,' cried Hannah. 'I need trimmings, buttons, thread, feathers and all sorts of bits, and where will I get all my beads?'

'What do you need all that for?' the lady asked.

Hannah looked at her properly. She was quite a bit older but seemed to have a timeless quality about her, a *very* kind face, and the softest looking eyes. If Hannah had a grandmother, that's what she'd want her to look like. 'I'm getting married in a few months and I'm making my own dress. I brought all the bits with me to get things…' she tailed off.

'May I see?'

There was no harm in it. Hannah carefully took the pieces out and handed them over for inspection.

'Ivory, yes, I can see how that would suit your colouring. This is your own design?' She was peering at the beaded gauze. 'The stitching is exquisite. You are a very talented young lady. I hope you work in some sort of dressmaking field.'

'Oh no, I work at an estate agency. My fiancé is the assistant manager.'

'Fancy that. I hope he realises what a lucky man he is.'

Is he? I'm the lucky one, thought Hannah.

'I think I can help you.' The lady handed the swatches back.

'Help me, how?'

'I have a small shop that may be of interest to you. I'm certain it would have all the things you need.'

'A shop here? Why don't I know about it?' Hannah wondered if the woman was quite right in the head, she looked as if she was in a bit of a dream.

'It's a little difficult to find. I'm sorry, dear, please let me introduce myself. I'm Fae, and you are?'

'Hannah, Hannah Worth, umm, soon to be Hannah Rawlings.' She went pink as she'd only practised saying it to herself a few times. 'Fae, that sounds Irish, is that where you're from?'

'It does sound a bit Irish. Now, would you like to come with me?'

'Where is your shop?'

'It's not far, how much time do you have before your bus?'

My bus? I didn't... 'I didn't say I came on the bus.'

'Oh, I think you did, dear. Anyway, I have a million trimmings and all the beads you could possibly want. Coming?'

Hannah couldn't resist. Even if she was a bit batty, the woman seemed harmless. Fae looked back, smiling as she saw Hannah follow, and led the way through the main centre, around the back of some warehouse buildings and came to a cobbled lane behind an old church.

'Just down here, dear.'

'I can't see a...' As Hannah spoke, she blinked, as an old-fashioned shop front came into view, bow-fronted windows with small panes of glass and a sign hanging outwards from the wall.

FAE DOROTHY GRIM
Haberdashery Needs

It was like something out of Dickens; Hannah expected to see a little matchstick girl at any minute. 'I'm not sure if this is going to be...' She stopped, enthralled by the window display. Dozens of tiny fairy lights twined their way around spools of thread, embroidery cottons and ribbons. Buttons of all shapes and colours spilled out of tiny drawers. Swatches of patchwork pieces adorned the shelves, along with lace, trims, feathers and pots of beads.

'It's stunning,' gasped Hannah. 'Like a treasure cave.'

'There's a lot more to see and I'm sure you'd like a cup of tea and a piece of ginger cake. I know I would.' Fae opened the door to a tinkling sound, like the laughter of small children and, as Hannah entered, a sun's ray shone through the door showing all the...dust motes? It looked like glitter dancing in the light. The inside of the shop was even better than the window. Although small, it was crammed with enticing bits and pieces. Hannah felt like she was in a dream, picking up this trim or that thread and exclaiming with delight.

'Here we are, my dear.' Fae came from the back with a steaming pot of tea and delicious-looking ginger cake.

How did she do that so quickly? 'You shouldn't have troubled yourself on my account.' Hannah eyed the cake.

'I didn't, it was for my own account. I always like a piece of cake around this time,' Fae laughed, the same tinkling sound as the doorbell. 'Now, come and sit down and tell me all about yourself.'

Chapter Three

CROSS STITCH

A stitch formed by two crossing each other

'There's not much to tell, I'm nothing special.' Hannah took the offered cup of tea gratefully.

'What about your family? They must be looking forward to your wedding.'

'It's just me with mum and dad. I never had a brother or sister, I would have liked that.' Fae saw a wistful look creep over Hannah's face. 'There are a few aunts, uncles and cousins, but we're not really close. They'll come on the day I suppose; everybody likes a wedding, don't they?'

'What about this man of yours and his family, does he have one?' Fae absently picked up a cross-stitch she was working on.

'He hasn't said much. Again, it's just him and his mother; we're going to live with her to start with.' Hannah took a piece of cake; it was delicious, with ginger such as she'd never tasted before.

'Well, I hope that works out for you,' said Fae, 'and I hope after you're married, you'll keep up with your sewing. You have a real talent and a love for everything in here,' she gestured to her stock. 'The old skills should be kept alive by people like yourself.'

'So much is mass produced now but I love going to exhibitions by the WI and such, they do some lovely things and there's stuff on the TV, it does create interest.'

Hannah accepted another cup of tea. 'It gives me a feeling of satisfaction when I've done something and finished it, like my dress. I'm enjoying every minute of the work; it is time-consuming though.'

'I'm sure your dress will be beautiful and I hope it brings you good luck in your life.' Fae said the words sincerely but she had an ominous feeling that she would be needed in the years to come. They had hunches, her people, and she had been chosen to monitor this young woman. 'Now you had better select all the bits you want to take with you today. We don't know when you may be passing this way again.'

'Oh, I think I'll be back here regularly, it's just the best shop I've ever been in.' Hannah rummaged happily for a while as Fae watched thoughtfully. She knew it would be some time before she saw Hannah again and much would change in her life. There would be a lot of heartbreak before the path to real happiness was taken.

Everything was packaged up in a pretty box. As Fae tied a ribbon to secure it, Hannah could have sworn she saw the box shimmering. 'It must come to more than that?' she queried when told the price.

'No, that's correct dear. A lot of it was end-of-line stock; you're doing me a favour.'

'There were some very unusual colours, I don't think I've ever seen any quite like them. That's a shame if they're being discontinued, but thank you.' Hannah took the box, which most definitely shimmered as it changed hands. 'It was a pleasure to meet you Fae and your shop really saved my dress, I'm so grateful. I have to go for my bus now but I hope I'll see you soon.'

'I'll just walk up to the end of the road and make sure you know the way; we are a little hidden away here.' Fae smiled.

At the junction, Hannah said goodbye and then turned a minute later to give a wave. Fae had disappeared from sight already and she couldn't see the shop either, but a mist had come down and she had no coat, so she hurried on through to the main street, which was bathed in sunshine, how very strange. On the bus, Hannah hugged the box of precious bits she'd chosen and absent-mindedly brushed glitter from her skirt.

* * *

Michael had the mother of all hangovers. He and the lads had left on Friday evening, deciding not to waste a second of the weekend. They hit Soho and stumbled back to the hotel at four in the morning. He wasn't sure if he could face the match now he felt so ill. What exactly had happened last night? His memory was very fuzzy. Lots of topless girls, which had been most enjoyable, and then after that, it became a bit of a blur. There was a vague recollection of a lap dancer who'd got very close. It was coming back to him, a tiny waist and breasts the size of rugby balls. He groaned. What had he done? Not even wanting to open his eyes, he rolled away from the light penetrating the thin curtains and came up against a warm body.

Whaaat? A mass of peroxide-blonde hair and a face smudged with make-up came into focus in front of him. *Oh my God.* Easing himself away, the bed creaked and the eyes opened.

'Morning handsome; that was some night.'

'W… was it? I mean, yeah sure, it was great.' Michael really felt sick and what was worse, he didn't even know if he'd had a good time or not. His clothes were strewn all over the room, which stank of stale booze.

The peroxide blonde got out of bed in all her naked glory. 'You can put your tongue back in now, I'm not staying any longer. We agreed a hundred, right?'

Gulp.

'A hundred. Er, just a sec.' A hundred was nearly all the cash he had, apart from small change. He had a feeling that his so-called friends had something to do with this. Well, they could jolly well cough up and help him out. He counted the money, feeling very self-conscious and aware that the part of him that had obviously been active last night was now shrivelling up under her scrutiny. He had one minute's delight watching those magnificent breasts while she dressed, saw her out with a mumbled thank you, and then rushed to the bathroom to be violently sick. Hannah must never, never know about this. Okay, he argued, he was entitled to a last-minute bachelor blast, but she wouldn't see it that way. He couldn't even remember the girl's name, if he'd ever known it. Christ, he felt rough. A rapping on his door made his head pound even more painfully.

'Come along, Mikey.' He could hear them outside. 'We've got some hair of the dog for you.'

I'll kill them! Then he grinned ruefully, it was just a bit of fun after all.

* * *

Hannah arrived home to find the house empty and a scrawled note on the table from her father saying mum was in the hospital but she was not to panic, it wasn't too serious. *Hospital? I shouldn't have left her.*

The special box was left forgotten on a chair, where it glowed softly as Hannah flew back out of the door for a bus, or a taxi, if she saw one first. Luckily, she did, and was at the hospital in 15 minutes, enquiring at the desk where her mother could be found. Her father was in the corridor outside the room in which her mother had been made comfortable. He held out his arms and Hannah was enfolded.

'What's the matter with mum? What happened? I need to see her.'

'The doctor's with her at the moment, they're just checking her over. Her headache got really bad so I called our doctor and he phoned for an ambulance. It seems as if she's had a stroke.'

'Oh no!' cried Hannah.

'Don't worry, they think it's a minor one and they'll just keep her in overnight. It'll probably mean some medication but there's no reason this should happen again if she follows advice. It's been a scare, but it should be alright.'

Hannah looked at her father. His face was grey but there was hope in his eyes. The doctor came out.

'Mr Worth, you can come in now, and this is… your daughter?'

'How is my mother?'

'Go and speak to her,' he gestured, and Hannah went to the bedside where her mother suddenly looked very small and a little agitated.

'Hannah, darling, they want to keep me in tonight but I feel fine now, really I do.'

'Let's hear what the doctor has to say, m'dear.' Her father went to the other side of the bed.

The doctor smiled. 'Mrs Worth has, as I told you, suffered a mini stroke. They are quite common but now she's here, I suggest we keep her overnight and after a check in the morning, she should be able to go home. It'll give us a chance to sort out the best after-care and have a talk about possible lifestyle changes.'

'What sort of changes?' Hannah was thinking bungalow, bed rest and all sorts of things.

'Maybe a change in diet and a light exercise programme, a short walk every day, that sort of thing. Sometimes, this can be a warning, so we do everything to make sure it doesn't occur again and, with the right care, there's no reason why it should. Mrs Worth's blood pressure is a little high, but she *is* stressed. We'll check that overnight and address that problem quite easily if needed. You really mustn't worry.' He looked at the both of them.

'I suggest that Hannah and I nip home and pick up a few things for you; you'll feel better with your personal bits and pieces,' said her father, holding his wife's hand.

Mrs Worth grabbed her daughter's arm. 'Hannah, listen to me. Your father can bring my things back; you'll know what I need. I want you to stay at home and get on with your wedding dress.'

'But Mum...' Hannah started.

'No dear. I shall be as right as rain tomorrow and this wedding means everything to me. You do the dress now while you've got peace and quiet and I'll see how you're getting on tomorrow. Oh, did you get all the bits you needed?'

'Yes, and more, it was really quite extraordinary. I don't quite understand how it happened but I'll show you tomorrow. You have a good night's sleep, Mum.' Hannah hugged her mother; they thanked the doctor and walked out of the hospital.

'Don't be upset, Hannah, Mum's fine.' Her father could see her red face and knew she was trying not to cry. He had been quite shaken by it. With the age difference between them, he'd always imagined that *he* would be the one with health problems, not his wife.

'It's just a bit of a shock, that's all, she's always been so well, hardly ever ill.'

Hannah sorted her mother's things; a nice nightdress, not that horrible hospital robe, soap bag, the book she was currently reading, along with her glasses and a pair of slippers. About to pop a container of cookies in, she remembered what the doctor had said about the change in diet and instead, just included a bottle of lemon barley and two nice peaches from the fruit bowl. Maybe the baking would have to be rationed a bit more. Well, it would be good for her as well now she'd lost some weight. She would have to put her mind to exciting salads and less pudding.

When her father returned to the hospital, Hannah remembered her box. Taking it upstairs to the workroom, she carefully spread the purchases out and studied them again with delight. The thread had a shimmer she couldn't remember ever having seen before, and the beads had a lustrous sheen and warmth that made them feel as if they were alive. She laid the bodice pieces of her dress on the table and wondered if she had time to do a design around the neckline. Perhaps a cup of tea was needed first to calm down a bit. Putting a handful of beads and thread onto the material, she cleared the rest of the space and went downstairs. Sitting in a comfortable chair with her tea, her eyes felt very heavy. It had been a tiring day. She would just close them for five minutes...

Upstairs, there was the faintest sound of tinkling laughter and a glow of light shining under the crack of the door.

'Hannah.' Her father was shaking her gently. 'Hannah, it's 9p.m.'

She looked at him blearily. 'It can't be, I only closed my eyes for five minutes, I was dreaming about my dress design.'

'There's a cup of tea here, stone cold, I'll make us a fresh one,' he said.

'Oh, thanks Dad, was Mum alright?'

'Absolutely fine. They've moved her into a ward with some other ladies and she's busy telling them all about you and the wedding. I was quite superfluous, so I came home.'

Hannah smiled for the first time since she'd got home. 'I'll drink my tea this time before I go back up. I'm going to do a bit of work before bed. What's happening in the morning?'

'They've told me to phone after 11, so hopefully, your mother will be home for lunch. Er, perhaps we shouldn't have such a large roast as usual.' He looked a little despondent.

'No,' Hannah said firmly, 'smaller portions but just as tasty, and fresh fruit salad for dessert.'

'Can't wait,' muttered her father as she went upstairs.

As she moved to the table where she'd left the material, she blinked. The beads and shimmering thread were laid out in a beautiful and very unusual design. The thread was actually through the eye of a needle, which was paused in the process of stitching the beads into position. *I don't remember doing that.* It did look a bit like her dream so maybe she had started it. *I was so tired, I can't be sure.* Looking more closely, it *was* the design she'd dreamt of. She must have started it before making her cup of tea. Picking up the needle, she automatically attached the next bead. Her fingers flew over the stitching, the design growing and glowing as she sewed. It was the most stunning thing she'd ever done. There was no way she'd allow herself to put weight on before the wedding. She held the bodice up in front of her. The glow reflected off her skin, making her and the material almost merge into one. Looking at her gauze overlay, she wasn't sure it would pale in comparison. As she lifted it and shook it out, a silver cloud of dust filled the air before disappearing. Holding it against the bodice, they melded together beautifully, and her original beads showed the same lustre as the new ones. *I never noticed that before, I thought these new ones were better.*

It needed something else, but what? Hannah looked at her sketches. There was one she remembered but it looked slightly different; she didn't recall having added that trim to the sleeves and hem. The box drew her eye; she'd emptied it, hadn't she? Going back to it, she noticed tissue at the bottom. *I didn't see that just now.* Lifting it out, it opened and a coil of beautiful lace trim fell out. *I don't remember picking that either.* The lace was inlaid with the same shimmering thread, and beads made up part of the design. It was a perfect match for the dress. Excitedly she assembled the bodice, sleeves and trims on her tailor's dummy and pinned it all together. It's far too beautiful for me to wear, she thought sadly. Lifting it off carefully, she slipped it down over her head. Looking in the mirror, she tried to imagine her hair done and her face made up. Then, she tried to picture Michael beside her. His face was elusive, and creeping into her imagination was the idea of the Duke in her latest 'bodice ripper'; dark and brooding, with raven-coloured hair and chiselled features.

For goodness sake, she told herself crossly, *get in the real world.* At last, there was Michael in her mind's eye. Feeling sure he would be impressed with the dress, she removed it carefully and, before she went to bed that night, tacked the whole top together, ready to machine and hand stitch the next day.

* * *

Mrs Worth was collected in the morning by her husband and Hannah. Armed with foolscap notes containing after-care and warning signs, she let them fuss over her for all of five minutes.

'I'm not an invalid; I'm perfectly alright now, so please stop worrying. I will take their advice, and Ronald, you can come for a short walk with me after lunch. What are we having, Hannah?'

'A roast, as usual, but smaller portions, and I've dry roasted the potatoes, no fat. A fruit salad for afters, it'll do me good as well, Mum.' Hannah smiled.

'Well yes, but don't finish the dress and then lose a lot of weight. Did you do some last night?' her mother asked eagerly.

'Mum, it's looking amazing; I can't wait to show you. It's different to how you last saw it; I think I was inspired by the new shop.'

'New shop?'

'Yes, that's what I said I'd tell you about. Wait till we've eaten.'

Just as they finished lunch, the phone rang. 'Hannah, it's me, Michael, did you miss me?'

Uh, not really. 'Of course I did, but I've been very busy. I found this fantastic new shop...'

'Yes, good, listen. I think I had a dodgy curry with the boys last night. I've just got home and Mum thinks I should go to bed. If you don't mind, I'll see you at work tomorrow?'

Michael looked around the empty house. His mum had gone out for lunch and he did feel ill, but it was from drink, not curry. He also felt too guilty to see Hannah today. By tomorrow, it would all be a distant memory, 'a lads' mistake'; what she didn't know about wouldn't hurt her. It was a one-off, not to be repeated. She didn't deserve it and he would make it up to her. Hadn't he bought her the biggest box of chocolates?

'Okay Michael, I hope you feel better. Can I just tell you about Mum…?'

'Sorry babe, got to go, think I'm going to puke. Love you.'

Click.

Hannah stood with the receiver in her hand then slowly replaced it in the cradle. *He's not feeling well; I can tell him tomorrow.* She felt an emptiness, which had nothing to do with her small lunch portion; she didn't even want to reach for a biscuit, which was her habit in times of uncertainty.

'Was that Michael, did he have a good time? I hope you didn't go worrying him about me,' her mother piped up from the front room.

'No Mum. I'll tell him later, he's a bit tired so I can carry on with my work today. Let me tell you about yesterday.'

Over a cup of tea, Hannah told her all about finding the store, which had closed, and her chance encounter with Fae. Trying to describe the shop, she couldn't find the words, but if she closed her eyes, it was as if she were there, surrounded by all the beautiful things.

'I must show you everything, I'll bring it downstairs.'

'You will not!' Her mother was insistent. 'I shall come upstairs where it's all clean and look properly. Then Ron and I will go for a little walk and after that, if you'd like, I'll help with any bits you'd like me to do.'

Upstairs, Mrs Worth stared at the work in progress. Tentatively, she fingered the embroidery around the bodice. 'Hannah, this is the best thing I've ever seen you do, wherever did you get the idea for this? And these beads and thread, they're out of this world. It must have cost you a fortune.'

'No, I was surprised.' Hannah explained about the 'end-of-line' stock, 'and I think I must have dreamt up this design. I was sewing it so quickly last night as well. I want to put this trim on the bottom of the dress and shape the hem a little more, make it a bit pointy?'

'Well, it's certainly different to the first drawing, but I think that will be perfect. If you slip it on, I'll pin the main part and mark it in chalk for you to cut, then when I come back, I'll help you to attach the trim and we'll be nearly there.'

True to her word, after her walk, Hannah's mother helped to assemble the final pieces and only stopped when Ron insisted that she go to bed and read quietly after her night in hospital.

'Dad's right, you go now. Thanks so much for all this. I'll carry on for a little bit and finish this hem.' Hannah sewed happily for an hour or so and then felt her eyes droop again. It had been an exhausting weekend. Resting them for a few minutes, she fell asleep with the needle in her hand.

Mrs Worth was reading her magazine in bed. *Has Hannah got the radio on? Whatever is that funny little laughing noise?* She shrugged and went back to 'Pru's problem page'.

Hannah woke and realised she'd been asleep for forty minutes. *Forty winks,* she smiled to herself. The needle was still in her hand, but it was only about five centimetres from the end of the stitching. *I'm sure I had loads more to do.* Obviously wrong again, she must be stressed with the worry about her mum. Finishing the last little bit, she snipped off the thread, gently shook the dress out and lowered it over the ever-patient dummy. A dummy she'd had to alter the size of and make smaller as she'd lost weight.

The dress was magnificent. It glowed and sparkled from every angle, and looked nothing like she'd ever seen before. It was a magical dress, fit for a princess, she thought. Fit for her? Why not? It was her creation and Michael would adore it.

Chapter Four

CHAIN STITCH

An embroidery or crochet stitch
resembling a chain

Hannah arrived at work to find an enormous box of chocolates on her desk. Normally, she wouldn't have been able to wait to open it up and pick out all her favourites. Now, the thought of chocolate sickened her. Michael was already on an early viewing and when he did return, he shuffled sheepishly over to her.

'Hey Hannah, sorry about yesterday, is everything alright?'

'Not really, Michael, Mum was in the hospital Saturday night because she'd had a stroke.' Hannah knew she had made it sound far worse than it was, but she was cross with his attitude over the phone, and his 'illness' had been totally self-inflicted as far as she was concerned.

'Oh God, is she okay? Look, I'm really sorry. If there's anything I can do to help…' He prayed that there wasn't but he *was* sorry. Mrs Worth wasn't a bad old stick and he didn't like to see Hannah upset.

Hannah thought she had been a bit harsh and softened slightly. 'It's fine, it was only a mini stroke and Dad did have the sense to call the doctor. She's home and just needs to make a few adjustments. Did you have a good weekend?'

'Er, yes, just the usual "lad stuff", you know. Actually, I'll catch up with you later; it's warm in here, isn't it?'

'You're very red around the back of your neck, whatever's the matter?' Hannah thought he was acting very strangely and being evasive. What *was* the usual 'lad stuff'? Maybe she didn't need to know.

'It's just the heat, like I said. Anyway, do you like the chocolates? Take them home and share them with your mum.' He noticed a rather pinched expression on her face. 'Perhaps you'd better spend some time with her. We'll catch up in a day or two, shall we? You can get on with your dress and stuff.'

'My dress is f… yes, perhaps that would be best, thank you. A few days maybe just to make sure she really is on the mend.'

He breathed a sigh of relief. Everything would settle down. When he left for his next appointment, Hannah opened the chocolates, took one and invited the others in the office to help themselves. It didn't take long for the box to be emptied and she took it straight out to the bins at the back. Funny, she hadn't missed eating them at all.

Michael came back in a foul mood later that day.

'What's the matter now?' she asked.

'The sale I was going to close on, that's the matter; the old cottage four miles away? I thought it was going to a developer, they'd already shown interest in it. Wanted to knock it down of course for more housing. Apparently, some old biddy put in an offer and the solicitor accepted it. Now the developer's mad and we lost the commission.'

'Ivy Cottage, is that the one? I thought it was so pretty.' Hannah had noticed the brochure when it came in. The owner had died some time ago and the sale was being dealt with by a local solicitor. There was no family and the money was going to charity. It was just the sort of place where Hannah would have liked to live; a storybook cottage with an old-fashioned porch, pretty mullioned windows and a large, tangled garden, profuse with meadow flowers. It had got a bit dilapidated but nothing too serious and could easily be put right.

Michael was still seething. 'Bought it cheap as well, worming her way around the solicitor. The land was worth 10 times what the cottage was, it's a travesty.'

'Oh Michael, it's just one sale,' said Hannah crossly. 'And if the lady's happy with it, so am I. It was too nice a place to knock down. Who was she?'

'I don't know and I don't care. She's probably going to sell it on herself and make a fat profit. That daft solicitor let her talk him round. Said he'd never met anybody like her and felt so happy selling it to her. He's obviously as addled as she is. Anyway, I'm going to try and salvage something from the day. I'll have to sweet talk the developers now and find something else for them.'

Sometimes, Hannah didn't like the way he conducted business. *That's how you become an assistant manager, I suppose, but I don't want to be like that.*

She was surprised when she got home to find her mother had made a big pan of fresh vegetable stew.

'Mum, I would have cooked.'

'Hannah, please, I've told you, I'm not an invalid. I've been reading up on healthy eating and I enjoyed doing it. We'll have one small bread roll with it; I may let your father have two, with the low-fat spread.'

'If you're sure, but don't overdo it, will you?' Her mother gave her a withering look. 'Okay.' Hannah held her hands up in surrender.

'Are you going out tonight? You haven't seen Michael for a couple of days.' Her mother stirred the stew, it did smell delicious.

'I saw him at work and he said… well, I mean, he's got a few things to catch up on, so we'll go out later in the week.' After that lecture, she wouldn't dare let on to her mother that she was at home to keep watch. 'I'll spend this evening tidying up all my sewing bits; they're all over the place up there. There won't be a lot of space at Michael's house, not for a sewing room anyway.'

'You can keep the machine and use the spare room here anytime you want,' her mother said. 'It'll be a nice excuse for you to pop in and see us, and you can still do embroidery and smaller things over there. Goodness me, it's going to be your home after all, you won't be a lodger; some adjustments will have to be made.'

'Yes, I suppose so; I'll sort out a small selection of stuff to begin with.'

Upstairs, Hannah once again admired her dress and then started looking through her sewing boxes. Her eye kept being drawn to the new box, which was on the floor next to her patchwork hamper. *How did it get down there?* As she went to retrieve it, she wondered about the patchwork. The hamper was full of different shapes she'd already cut out from her material off-cuts. The beads in her new box were twinkling and glowing, and she picked a pair of brilliant blue round ones that looked like eyes. An image flashed across her mind. *Patchwork teddy bears.* She could make those easily at Michael's house. What she needed wouldn't take up much room and they would go to the hospital charity shop for fundraising. Yes, that's what she'd do. Feeling happier, she packed a box with all the bits she would need for a dozen or so teddies.

* * *

It was two weeks before the wedding. Michael had been kind and courteous since that first day back and had sent a large bouquet to Mrs Worth. His mother had offered to take over the arrangements for the wedding day, but Hannah's mother stood firm. She did mollify Mrs Rawlings slightly by suggesting that she liaise with the hotel about seating for her side of the family. Hannah's relations could fit on one table of eight, so they were no problem. Mrs Rawlings immediately rustled up a few more so they could have two tables for her side. An enormous hat had been purchased, which she showed her son and nobody else. He stared at it in horror but didn't dare say a word against it. She'd persuaded him to buy a new suit. He did, begrudgingly but then realised he could use it for work and, when he was the manager, which he had his sights set on, it would be perfect. Hannah would be a good wife to him, he knew that, and she got on with his mum okay. It would be nice to have their own place, but the house would be his and that would mean a lot of spare money for a nice car and some holidays.

Hannah was also doing some thinking. It wasn't ideal, starting married life with a mother-in-law, however kind and well-meaning she was. Hopefully, they would have a place of their own in the near future, a place where they might have a family. She was a little disappointed that they weren't having a honeymoon, not a proper one. Michael had suggested the Bank Holiday weekend for the wedding so they wouldn't be at work on Monday at least. They were going to Pembrokeshire for the weekend, staying in a bed and breakfast so they could go out in the evening for a meal. When he said he wondered what Welsh curry was like, her heart sank, and she was determined that she would most definitely choose one of the restaurants while they were away.

The other thing he'd discussed worried her more. As assistant manager and possibly soon to be the manager, he didn't think it was a good idea for them both to be working in the same office. He thought she ought to look for something else. After all, it didn't really matter what she did, he would be the main earner and it would be embarrassing if there was any disciplinary action to be taken.

What can I do? There aren't that many jobs going around here. Disciplinary action indeed! She was one of the most conscientious people in that office, but if one of them had to go, it had to be her; it didn't seem like she would progress to anything there. She had no particular ambition and didn't want to train for anything, only really being good at sewing. Maybe she could advertise dressmaking and alterations while she was looking for something else? She had her room to use at home so it wouldn't inconvenience anyone. Feeling a little more positive, she drafted up some ideas for flyers.

* * *

The day of the wedding was bright and sunny. Thank goodness, thought Hannah, I don't have to cover the dress up. Her mother had helped her do her hair and make-up. A face stared back from the mirror that Hannah hardly recognised. Due to the weight that she'd lost, it had planes and contours she didn't know existed. Her eyes were shining and her skin, always flawless, glowed along with her dress. As she came down the stairs, her father's eyes filled up.

'My darling girl, you've always been beautiful to me but today has surpassed all my expectations. I shall be the proudest man in that church with you by my side.'

'Oh Ronald, it should be Michael who is the proud one,' Margaret scolded. 'We're both very proud of you Hannah, and I know the saying is we're gaining a son, but we wouldn't lose you for anything.'

'Oh Mum, you'll make me cry and I don't want to spoil my make-up. Do you really think Michael will appreciate all this?'

'If he doesn't, he's got fewer brain cells than that tailor's dummy upstairs. Now come along. Your Uncle Stuart is driving me to the church and the car is outside for you and Dad. I'll see you there.' She kissed her daughter gently so as not to smudge anything and went out where Uncle Stuart was waiting patiently, not being allowed to see the dress until Hannah arrived at the church. The last time he'd seen his niece, he thought she was a bit of a pudding and wondered how she'd look as she walked up the aisle.

Michael's mother was assisting him with his bow tie. 'You're even more handsome than your father was; that Hannah doesn't know how lucky she is. A lovely home to walk right into as well. I started married life in a small, rented flat.'

He didn't say that Hannah would probably prefer that, but they'd both reap the benefits when they had the two houses they could cash in on. He didn't want to appear mercenary but his own mother had him late in life and was beginning to show signs of frailty. Hannah's mother had just had a scare and her father wouldn't want to stay there on his own, surely? He was already thinking of one of the prestigious houses on the outskirts. Somewhere he'd be able to entertain business clients, like the developer he'd managed to pacify by finding another site. Michael had big plans and ambitions, and pictured himself in charge of a chain of property sales and management. Hannah would need to spruce herself up a bit, not so much of this homemade stuff she liked. More tailored suits and dresses from the big stores.

He hoped she'd look good today; he was a bit worried about her making her own wedding dress. Why couldn't she just buy one?

'Your cousin is ready to take you to the church, Mrs Rawlings,' Neil, Michael's best man, called up the stairs. She came down carefully, making sure the large brim of her hat didn't catch the wall. She had chosen a dress with a voluminous, cape-style jacket that swayed and flapped as she descended.

'Wow,' said Neil as the door closed after her. 'She looks like a ship in full sail.'

'Don't talk to me about it,' sighed Michael. 'Can you picture her and Hannah beside each other?'

'Actually, Hannah's looking quite tasty these days,' Neil smirked, 'and still got a great pair of knockers.'

'That's my future wife you're talking about; you keep your eyes off.' Michael was secretly pleased; Hannah *was* looking good, and hopefully would stay that way.

'Your ball and chain you mean. Come on, mate, let's get you to church, poor sod.'

As Hannah entered the church on her father's arm, she sensed, rather than heard, the gasps of surprise. She looked stunning, and the dress fitted her like a glove. She'd lost a few more pounds and worried it may be a bit loose, but it was perfect. She saw Michael's mother opening and closing her mouth like a goldfish. *What the hell has she got on her head? It looks like a flying saucer.* The lady next to her was cricking her neck to avoid having her eye taken out by the edge of it. As she got closer, Michael, who was now quite nervous, turned. Neil had already been gawking.

God, she looks amazing. Did she make that? He actually swelled with pride as she stopped beside him and gave a shy smile. Giving her hand a squeeze, he whispered quietly to her, 'You look absolutely beautiful; you look like you're shining.'

The dress was shimmering, and flashes of light reflected off some of the beads. At the back of the church in the shadows, Fae stood silently and unobserved. *It's turned out perfectly; that should make him appreciate what he's got.* She smiled secretly to herself and gently swatted away the golden dust around her. *Not now, go away; you've seen what you needed to.* Fae slipped away from the church, back to Ivy Cottage before the end of the service.

Hannah felt as if she were in a dream. Michael had never looked at her so lovingly, and he stuttered over his vows like a nervous schoolboy. His mother's loud 'tuts' could be heard clearly. When he slipped the ring onto her finger, she felt so happy; glancing around, she saw her mother's smiling face and her father's proud one.

'You may kiss the bride,' she heard the vicar say and Michael did so, very gently, as if he was afraid she would break.

Many photographs and congratulations later, they made their way to the hotel, Hannah and Michael leaving first in the car.

'Hannah, I can't get over how you look, did you really make that dress yourself?'

'Yes, I did, thank you. You look very smart as well, but where did your mum get that hat?'

He groaned. 'That bloody hat! I couldn't say anything. I can't wait to get at you tonight you know, you will change before we leave, won't you?'

'Oh yes, I don't want this damaged. Mum will take it home.'

'Mrs Rawlings, how does it feel?'

'It'll take a bit of getting used to, but it feels good, thank you, Mr Rawlings.'

Hannah picked at her meal, too overwhelmed with the day to feel hungry. She'd never remember the names of all these people, but Michael said they hardly ever saw them so not to worry. Neil made a typical best man speech with awful jokes and innuendoes, which she didn't like, but gritted her teeth and smiled. Her father embarrassed her by telling some of her childhood misdemeanours, but finished up by saying what a fine son-in-law Michael was going to make, which made his mother beam with pleasure. To Mrs Rawlings senior's great annoyance, she'd had to remove her hat for the meal as she was far too close to Mr Worth, and after she knocked him a few times and heard the titters from her family on the opposite table, it was quietly taken off.

At last, after the final dance, Hannah and her mother went to the room they'd booked for the day so she could change. Michael's packed bag for their trip was already there.

'I'll make sure the dress is stored nicely. It's such a shame it only got to be seen today. Can you adapt it in any way?'

'I hadn't thought past the wedding, maybe. I don't want to sell it so I'll think about it later. Thank you, both of you, for giving me such a wonderful day.'

'You're our daughter, what else would we do? Now you two go away and have a good time. Pembrokeshire is lovely and you don't need to spend all your time in bed, you've already got to know each other, haven't you?'

'Mum!'

'Oh don't "Mum" me, I'm not daft. As long as you're happy, that's all I care about.'

Uncle Stuart drove them to the station. As he wasn't driving, Michael was by now quite tipsy and a bit loud. Hannah hoped he'd fall asleep on the train so she could re-live the day in her mind with peace and quiet. Her luck was in; he was snoring within 10 minutes of departure. Hannah stared out of the window, watching the scenery and thinking. After a while, she pulled a book from her bag. 'At the Duke's Pleasure' showed the typical dark-haired, brooding man on the cover with a woman swooning in his arms. Opening it at her marked page, it coincidentally was describing the wedding that had been brought about by his indiscretion. He was about to take his new bride to bed, which he had wanted to do when they'd got caught.

Hannah drank in the words like a person dying of thirst. The Duke was very gentle and, of course, experienced. He explored every inch of his naked bride's body, bringing her to heights of pleasure before the main act. She felt a hand groping across the table.

'Hey, are we nearly there? There's a part of me getting very impatient.' Michael leered at her drunkenly and grabbed at his crotch.

'Michael, not on the train.' Hannah went beetroot red, although nobody was that close or seemed to be taking any notice. She was almost tempted to show him what she was reading, hoping he'd take the hint, but she knew that was a waste of time.

'I'll go and get some coffee from the buffet car,' she said. *Strong and black, I think.*

They checked into the B&B, which Hannah thought was a bit downmarket for a honeymoon. The man on the desk showed them to the room, giving Michael a most unsubtle wink as he closed the door. The room was okay, she thought, a bit old-fashioned and the net curtain had seen better days. Michael tested the bed.

'Come on, Hannah, I've waited all day for this, the first time we've actually got a whole night together. Get your kit off and get over here.'

It *was* her wedding night when all was said and done. 'Okay, let me get ready, I won't be long.' She cleaned her make-up off and undressed in the bathroom. A squirt of her scent and she put on the silky robe she'd bought.

Michael grabbed her immediately; there was no exploration of her body or pleasuring of any kind. 'God, I'm sorry, Hannah, I just need you now.' It was all over in one minute. He rolled off her, gave her a kiss that left a lot to be desired and squeezed her breast. 'I'll make it up to you in a minute when we do it again.' Then he promptly fell asleep and started snoring once more.

Hannah lay looking at the ceiling. She had to remind herself again that she was in the real world. Grooms got drunk; maybe many honeymoon nights were like this. It would be okay tomorrow, she felt sure of it. Leaving her bedside light on, she reached for her book...

Chapter Five

RUNNING STITCH

Small, even stitches, which run back and forth
without overlapping

Michael was sheepish in the morning. He even got up and made her a cup of tea from the meagre facilities they'd been given. 'I'm really sorry, it wasn't a good night for you, was it? I drank too much but I feel alright now, shall I make it up to you?' His hand crept under the duvet.

'No, Michael, it's okay. Let's wait until tonight, please? It's a lovely day and I'd like to see some of the area while we're here.'

'Oh, right.' He sounded unenthusiastic. 'Well let's have breakfast then and we'll find out what's to be done around here.'

Breakfast was a typical B&B landlady's special, which Michael shovelled down with copious amounts of coffee. 'I shan't drink today, babe,' he winked at her. 'You won't have any complaints about the service tonight.'

Hannah cringed, but softened when she saw the twinkle in his eye. Feeling in her pocket, she pulled out a small piece of lace trim, leftover from the wedding dress and, running her fingers over it, saw it reflecting and shimmering in her hand. 'I'm really happy we got married, Michael, we'll be good together, won't we?'

'Course we will. Pass the toast, there's a good girl. We've paid for it so don't let's waste it. Now to make up for your disappointment last night, you choose what we do today.'

'Really? Oh, Michael, I'd love to see Picton Castle.'

His face fell but he nobly (he thought) tried to look keen. 'Picton Castle it is then. Perhaps... we could have a curry tonight?'

'Of course we can.' She reached for his hand across the table.

Picton Castle was 13th century, but with changing ownership and modernisation, had a mostly Georgian interior. Hannah was enthralled by the tour of the staterooms. Although not the home of a duke, she could well imagine the ladies of the time in their beautiful gowns and the dashing men in tight breeches and frock coats. I was definitely born 200 years too late, she thought.

'Did you know there are 44 acres of gardens here? Gardens, can you imagine the housing that could be built on that?' Michael's voice shattered her illusions.

'Yes,' she shuddered. 'I really would like to look around some of it.'

'I might sit in the café for a bit, if you don't mind, flowers don't do much for me.'

She sighed. 'That's fine but I may be a while.' Leaving him with a cool drink, dozing on a bench in the shade, she wandered around the formal walled gardens. Again, she imagined a lady stepping out for fresh air during a ball and being pursued by the handsome hero. As she rounded a path in the rose gardens, she blinked and stared at the couple in front of her. The man was tall, nearly six foot, she guessed, maybe a year or two older than her. He was holding the hand of a young, blonde woman, who was gazing lovingly at him. He was the most handsome man Hannah had ever seen, black-haired and chisel-featured, straight off the cover of one of her books. A bit young perhaps, but still...

She realised she was gawping and, embarrassed, stepped to one side so they could walk past. The lady gave her a smile.

'Thank you, isn't it beautiful here? It puts our garden to shame, although we haven't really started on it yet.'

'It is lovely, yes,' Hannah mumbled, hoping she wasn't red-faced.

'Are you on holiday? We're actually on our honeymoon, doing a tour of Wales.' She went a little pink and smiled up at the gorgeous man.

'Er, yes, just for a day or two. Congratulations to you both, have a lovely, umm, honeymoon.' Hannah couldn't bear to try and explain why *her* new husband wasn't looking adoringly at her like the man was with his new wife. 'I'll, er, leave you to it, bye.' She hurried up the path and heard the end of their conversation.

'Can we do the bluebell walk, Christopher?'

A deep, resonant voice replied, 'Whatever you want to do my darling is fine with me.'

Glancing back as she went through the arch, she saw his head bend to his wife's and realised he was going to kiss her. Her face flamed and she rushed around the corner to catch her breath.

Waiting half an hour to calm down, she went to collect Michael, hoping and praying she wouldn't see them again, but not able to get the man's face out of her mind.

'Michael, shall we head back now?' She shook him out of his doze.

'Mmm, that's wonderful, do that again.'

'Michael!'

'Eh? Oh, Hannah, I was er, just dreaming about you. How were the gardens?'

'Fabulous, but I think we ought to make tracks now.'

He didn't need to be asked again. 'Yep, sure, you see one flower, you've seen them all, right?'

'Something like that, yes. I'd like time for a shower before we go out to eat.'

'Sounds good, maybe I can help you?' She felt a sharp pinch to her bottom.

'I really need to wash my hair and dry it... maybe next time?'

'It looks alright to me,' he grumbled. 'I've got later to look forward to, I suppose.'

Hannah dodged another pinch. She felt sure if 'Christopher' looked at her, she would melt, but Michael's leering countenance didn't quite have the same effect.

'What's the matter with you?' Michael demanded. 'You've hardly said a word. You chose that castle so what was wrong with it?'

They'd driven for an hour with him chatting away and Hannah giving monosyllabic replies. *This isn't fair on him, I must snap out of this.* 'I'm sorry, Michael. The castle was lovely but I just had a bit of a headache, the sun I think.'

'A *headache*?' He nearly swerved off the road. 'You can't have a headache, not when I'm on a promise.'

She started to laugh, he was so ridiculous at times. 'It's gone now, don't panic. I'll be fine.' *I'll be fine.*

* * *

Hannah made an effort to be more attentive for the rest of their stay. It was the evenings that were a bit of a let-down. Michael *was* good looking and she did fancy him. It was just... well, just that he didn't set her on fire. Maybe that was the way of it, she thought. You could write anything in a book and imagine anything in your mind; it didn't make it so.

I need to get real, she thought, so she held his hand when they were walking and reached for him in bed that night. It *was* better and he did spend more time on her. The world didn't shatter, but he cuddled her for five minutes before falling asleep. *This is our marriage and we both need to make it work.*

* * *

As they drove home on Monday night, she told him about her idea of dressmaking from home.

'Do you think that will bring enough money in?' he frowned. 'I know we're living cheap at Mum's, but we don't want to drop our standard.'

'I didn't know we had a standard, we don't really spend a lot. I could stay at the office for a few months, or maybe go part-time and see if it takes off.'

'Part-time would be good,' he swiftly agreed. 'Wean yourself out of there and you could look for something else in the meantime. I'm not sure if there'll be much room at ours, Mum does like to keep it tidy. She wouldn't want material and all your stuff cluttering up the place.'

Hannah looked out of the window so that he didn't see her hurt look. *He's the one who doesn't want me in the same office.* 'I'm going to use the room at my house, I'll just do small things at yours and it'll all be tidied away.'

He must have sensed something. 'It's not mine, it's ours now. I know it's not ideal but we will have our own home one day. Let me find out where I'm going in this job or if we may have to move, okay?'

She turned and smiled at him. 'Yes, we'll all get along well, I'm sure. Your mother has to make adjustments as well as us; it won't be easy for her either.'

'She'll get used to it; did your parents drop your stuff over while we were away?'

Hannah had already ferried a few things to Michael's house. She had been allocated a wardrobe in the box room with a few shelves, and Michael had cleared a drawer in his room.

His mother had the larger bay-windowed bedroom at the front and it would have made more sense to swap, but she wouldn't dare suggest it, and it *was* Mrs Rawlings' house after all.

'I think so, they said they would. It's only another suitcase and my sewing box. If I'm using my room there, I can still keep things and exchange clothes occasionally.'

He patted her knee. 'It'll be nice to be in our own bed, eh?'

'Er, yes.' Michael's bed only just qualified as a double and, although she liked a cuddle, also wanted her own space. It was another thing she'd have to get used to. As soon as they had their own home, she would insist on the largest bed possible. *A four-poster would be nice.*

Mrs Rawlings was waiting up for them. 'Well, you're back earlier than I thought. There's a casserole in the oven if you're hungry. Don't expect it regularly, we'll have to sort out who's cooking and when, but you must feed a working man.' She patted her son on the cheek.

What about me? I'm working as well. Hannah rummaged in her bag. 'I thought you might like this, it's similar to your figurines.' She handed her mother-in-law a Welsh shepherdess holding a lamb, made in delicate bone china.

'It's nice enough, I suppose,' she sniffed. 'Of course, the ones in the cabinet are Royal Doulton, but I'll find somewhere for this.' It was placed at the rear of the sideboard. 'Michael, dear, I'll put the kettle on; you must be gasping for a *proper* cup of tea.' She disappeared in the direction of the kitchen.

'Nice try, Hannah, she does like it really, I can tell.'

'If you say so, and what does she mean "a proper cup of tea"? What does she think we drank in Wales, leek juice?'

Michael choked back a laugh. 'Put your claws in, I don't want to feel those when we go to bed later.' He gave her one of his leering smiles.

'Would it be alright if I have a bath?' asked Hannah.

Mrs Rawlings came in with a tray. 'A bath? Can't you have a shower? It's far more economical. I have to think about costs you know.' Hannah thought her face resembled a wet haddock's.

Michael jumped in. 'Now that there are three of us, Mum, don't forget we'll be contributing.'

The wet haddock turned into a beaming smile. 'Of course, you will be, son.' *Well, I'll take her money anyway.* She poured tea, muttering to herself. 'Help yourself to casserole if you want some. I'll dish yours up while she's in the bathroom, Michael.'

Hannah sat, stony-faced. *Oh God, will I survive this?* 'I'll take my tea up and unpack some things,' Hannah said as sweetly as she could. The minute she was upstairs, she cried a little, silently, then mopped up her tears, found her book and lost herself in her Duke's arms for a while.

* * *

After three weeks, Hannah's nerves were as sharp as piano wire. She tried so hard but everything she did was wrong. If she cleared the table, Mrs Rawlings wanted it stacked for washing 'just so'. Seeing as Hannah did the washing up, what did it matter? Everything had its place, and God forbid an item found its way into the wrong drawer or cupboard. Washing was done on a Monday and on the occasion when she found Hannah rinsing one of Michael's shirts, she snatched it away, muttering that 'girls these days don't know how to starch a collar'.

To make matters worse, Michael informed her that she would be working mornings only from now on, and only for a few more weeks. He said she could use the afternoons to try to find another job or get started on her sewing business. She took to wandering around the town occasionally, looking in the job centre window or going to see her parents.

'Are you alright, Hannah? You look very pale.' Her mother was studying her. 'You can talk to me, you know? Is marriage not what you thought it would be?'

Hannah burst into tears and her mother let her cry it out. 'I'm sorry, Mum, it's not marriage exactly; it's just not very good with Mrs Rawlings. I know it's an upheaval for her as well but she doesn't give way in anything. I don't feel like part of the family.'

'She's never had a daughter, only a son *and a very spoiled one*. She has to learn to share and that's not easy. That house has been run the way she wants it for years and she probably has to feel needed, not pushed to the side-lines now you're there.'

'I suppose so,' Hannah sniffed. 'I didn't see it from that point of view. How can I get on her good side?'

'Well, praise what she does, of course, compliment her on her cooking and house skills. You're as good as she is but she doesn't need to know that. Maybe make her a coffee or whatever she has in the evening and say something like "I hope this is how you like it, I've watched how you do it", flatter her.' *That should turn the old bag around.* Mrs Worth was furious but she wouldn't let Hannah know that. She would have welcomed Michael into their house like a son and expected the same show of courtesy and warmth for her daughter.

'I'll try, Mum, thanks. I'll go upstairs for a while, I want to cut a blouse out and tack it ready for sewing next time.'

'Have you done anything with your flyers yet?' her mother asked.

'No, I must sort something soon.'

'Well, your father and I both think you should put a proper ad in the paper, maybe with a picture of your wedding dress. Don't just chase repairs and alterations, you can design, Hannah, we've seen that, *and* you cut your own patterns. Make up a sample book of fabrics and drawings you can take to people, or they can come here.'

'This is your house, Mum, that's not fair.'

'It's still yours as well and we'd be pleased to help. You have a talent and it shouldn't be wasted. Giving up your job will be the kick-start you need and it would get you out from under Mrs Rawlings' feet. Get everything prepared and your father will help you with your ad; he's actually quite good at things like that, but don't tell him I said so.' Mrs Worth smiled.

'Maybe I could do that... I'll be upstairs for a while.' Hannah felt the happiest she'd been for three weeks.

Upstairs, she pulled out all her swatches of material that had been kept from previously made items or stock that she had plans for in the future. It *would* make a nice selection for people to get some ideas of what could be done. Her mother's suggestion of a picture of the wedding dress was inspired, and she would take photos of other things that she'd produced. Along with her sketches, it would be a good portfolio. The dress was hanging again in its cellophane, ready to be stored. Hannah couldn't resist another proper look. *Was it only just over three weeks ago?* The dress shimmered and rustled, and looked like a breeze was blowing across the material. As she ran her hands over it, she thought she could hear a faint tinkling sound. This beautiful dress will set me up for what I really want to do, she thought.

That evening, she did as her mother had suggested. Just before 8.30p.m. which was Mrs Rawlings' time, Hannah slipped into the kitchen and made a cup of hot chocolate. She'd hidden a small pot of cream in the fridge and stirred some in with a tiny bit of extra sugar.

'Mrs Rawlings, I hope you don't mind, but I thought you looked a bit tired. You cooked such a nice tea tonight and you've mended that tear in Michael's pocket. I've made your chocolate for you, I do hope I've done it the way you like it. It's probably not as good as yours but you deserved to put your feet up tonight.'

Hannah, of course, had cleared all the tea things away, and washed and dried the dishes. The first time she'd asked Michael to dry, he'd looked at her as if she had two heads, and his mother had snatched up the tea cloth in a fury and said if Hannah was 'too busy' then to leave them until the morning. That would change when they had their own place, Hannah had bristled with indignation.

'Oh, well, I don't know I'm sure.' Mrs Rawlings' face looked like a smacked backside. 'I like it made in a particular way, but you're right, I am a little fatigued, maybe just for once.'

She took a sip gingerly, and the look of surprise on her face nearly made Hannah laugh. She took another sip.

'I have watched you do it,' Hannah volunteered.

'Ah, of course, that's why it's... perfect. Very nice, thank you, dear, oh, and you'd better start calling me Doreen I think; Mrs Rawlings is a bit of a mouthful.'

'Thank you... Doreen,' Hannah sent a silent prayer of thanks to her mother. It might be a long road but she had taken the first step. In bed that evening, as Michael pulled her towards him, she started to tell him about her advertisement.

'Yeah, fine, whatever. I still think it would be better if you got a proper job instead of fiddling about. It's okay while we're living here I suppose, but we need to save. Now, let me at you before it gets too late.'

'Actually, I've got a bit of a stomach pain, probably my monthly, perhaps...'

'Oh right.' He pulled away as if he'd been scorched. 'Let me know when the coast is clear, eh?' He was snoring within two minutes.

Hannah spent another night looking at the ceiling, wondering exactly where they were going. We need to save, he'd said, why was he looking at new cars then? She was determined to make her business a success. Maybe she should take a visit to that lovely haberdashery shop and stock up. It would be nice to see Fae again as well; she was such a lovely lady.

* * *

Mrs Worth had put the word around to all her friends and neighbours, and within two days, Hannah was inundated with enquiries. Most of it was for alterations or repairs, but it was a start. She spent every afternoon in her sewing room and her evenings buttering up Doreen. She was exhausted. Michael seemed to think she was jollying away her time nattering to her parents and drinking tea. He had to swallow a bit when she showed him what she had earned in the first two weeks.

'That's just the start, Michael. When I actually start designing for people, it'll be worth a lot more. My advertisement is going in next week for four days. Mum is doing the bookings and enquiries so *Doreen* won't be bothered with the phone ringing.' Hannah had felt very guilty about her mother doing this work, but Mrs Worth had stressed it was not physical in any way, her mind was perfectly sharp, and they did have an answer phone so she wouldn't be a slave to it.

Doreen seemed to think it was a lot of nonsense when one could buy perfectly good clothes at Fashion for All, the main store in their town. 'Giving people ideas above their station, *designer* clothes,' she huffed. Hannah was learning to ignore these remarks and to not let them upset her.

She was so busy, there was no time for the haberdashery shop and, as it happened, a small stall opened at the indoor market, which stocked fabric and thread along with basic trimmings, enough to get her well on the way. Her advertisement caused a rush of initial phone calls and she found herself having to go out several evenings with all her samples, to see people. After the first time asking Michael if he would give her a lift at least one way and having Doreen leap down her throat with 'a working man needs a good tea and some rest time', she never asked again. Putting some money aside every week, she planned to have driving lessons as soon as possible. Her father took her out a few times and got her started on the basics. For the first time in her marriage, she kept something a secret and didn't mention it to Michael, and certainly not his mother.

Chapter Six

DARNING

A technique for repairing holes or worn areas

FIVE YEARS LATER

'Who are you and what are you doing in my house? I'll call the police.'

Hannah sighed. 'Doreen, it's me, Hannah, you remember? I'm married to Michael.'

'Michael?'

'Your son; look at him, here.' She picked the photo up showing Doreen standing beside Michael on his wedding day.

'Ah, Michael, always such a *good* boy. Who are you and why are *you* here?'

'Sit down, Doreen; I've come to make you a nice cup of tea.'

'Well, why didn't you say that before?' Doreen sat quietly.

Hannah went into the kitchen and pressed her head against the door of the freezer. How had her life come to this?

* * *

The first year of her marriage plodded along in much the same vein as the first month. Hannah and Doreen reached a form of truce, only rubbing each other up the wrong way occasionally. Her sewing kept her very busy, with a few special orders between the bread and butter jobs. Michael seemed vague when asked about them having a home of their own, always saying the manager's job wasn't far off; decisions could be made then. Hannah had made another wedding dress for one of the girls at the office – the office where *she* didn't work anymore. Passing her driving test without Michael knowing anything about it, when she announced to him that she could now go on the insurance, he went very tight-lipped.

'I don't know why you kept it such a big secret, were you afraid you'd fail? How much did all that cost then?'

'It's an investment for my business, Michael; you're always saying how important that is. I can go further now for work and you don't need the car every evening.'

'Well no,' he spluttered, 'but I expect my wife to spend time with me when I come home from work.'

'I try to be here most evenings and *you* have meetings or such when I'm here keeping your mother company.'

He flushed. 'That's different, I have to entertain clients. Property developers are busy people; I have to fit in with them. You don't understand, I need to make contacts.'

'I understand alright, don't worry.'

* * *

She was so busy, she forgot about the little haberdashery shop, as she could get most of what she wanted from the market stall. Borrowing her father's car made it easier and her portfolio grew as her reputation spread. It was around this time that she noticed Doreen was becoming a little forgetful. Small things at first; the door would be left unlocked, a pint of milk put inside the oven instead of the fridge, and the same questions being asked time after time. Michael either ignored it or refused to accept it until, on one occasion, his mother left the gas on without pressing the ignition. Luckily, Hannah realised, switched everything off and opened all the windows, averting a possible tragedy.

'I don't want my mother in a home, Hannah.' She thought how caring he was until... 'The house is in her name so it would have to pay for her care. There would be nothing left for me – us, I mean, of course. She wouldn't want this. We'll have to work it out.'

'We?' Hannah's voice had an edge to it.

'Well, I'll do what I can, of course, but sweetheart, I work full-time, the breadwinner, while you...'

'While I'm "messing about" sewing a few dresses. Go on, why don't you just say it?'

'Hannah, that's not fair. I'm not saying you should do it all by yourself,' he said feebly. 'If she gets really bad, we can think again, but the money from this house will give us such a good start, a house for a family, that's what you want, isn't it?'

'Apart from her mind, your mother's in perfect health, she could be like this for years.'

'Look, we can use the money we're paying for our keep to maybe get some part-time help, to give you a break and time for your... work. Can we just give it a trial? Please, Hannah; it would be such a weight off my mind.'

Yes, very convenient, you can live your life just as you please, Hannah thought furiously. He was right in some respects, she did want a family, and a home that was theirs. 'I'll see how it goes,' she said slowly, 'but I want somebody here for at least four hours a day.'

'That won't be cheap,' he grumbled, and saw the look on her face, 'but cheaper than a home, I suppose. You find someone, just somebody responsible. It doesn't have to be a nurse or anything, does it?'

'No,' she sighed. It was a shock for both of them. Doreen was only in her early 70s and neither of them had expected anything like this.

* * *

His mother became steadily worse and couldn't be left alone at all. The brunt of it fell to Hannah, and she started baking again to fill some of the time. The house was always well stocked with cakes, scones and tray-bakes of gooey loveliness. The pounds started to creep back on and she altered a few of her clothes. It was gradual and not too noticeable for the first year, but after five, she was a few sizes larger; Doreen had a sweet tooth and could always be placated with a cup of tea and something nice from the pantry.

Mrs Worth offered to help but Hannah flatly refused. She allowed her mum to visit but not to do anything. She'd had one or two mild 'attacks', or at least that's how the family referred to them, but while she took her medication, they didn't seem too much of a worry. That, on top of Doreen's condition, took its toll on Hannah, and Michael didn't even seem to notice.

* * *

At breakfast the next morning, she put her foot down. 'I've got an appointment to see somebody who wants dresses made for a cruise. It's tonight at seven so I need you home, Michael.'

'Tonight? I was, er… going to have drinks with the boys.'

'Boys? For God's sake, you're men now with responsibilities, you especially, she's *your* mother. There will be tea for both of you in the oven; I need to leave at 6.30p.m. If you're not here, I shall ring social services and tell them I can't cope.'

'Don't do that, whatever's the matter with you? I'll be here. Look, Hannah, I know it's hard and I do appreciate it, but I'm trying to get a better life for us and I need support too.'

'And you get it, every day. You've never once, not once, offered to look after her for a whole day at the weekend so I could do something I wanted.'

'What on earth do *you* want to do?'

Hannah nearly screamed. 'Just go for a walk without having to check my watch, get my hair cut instead of doing it myself, sit in the park and read my book without being asked every five minutes who I am.'

'You've got your nose in one of your damn books nearly every night!'

'Yes, because it's the only time I can read more than one page.' She thought longingly of the days when she could enjoy her historical romances, getting lost in the story and imagining herself being accosted in the Duke's carriage on her way home from the ball.

'Why don't you read to Mum? She might enjoy that.'

Hannah would never, ever share her Dukes with anybody. She had tried reading other books to her but Doreen was too fidgety and showed little or no interest. 'I've tried that, I did tell you but, as usual, you don't listen.' She had recently discovered a whole series of books centred around a large family, set in Regency times, and was steadily working her way through the second one. They were quite explicit in places and made her blush while she was reading them. Why oh why had she not been born then? To sit doing needlework would be the greatest pleasure for her, and the *nights...*

'Of course I listen to you, I just forgot. I've got a lot on my mind. Robin's talking about taking early retirement; this could be my chance, Hannah.'

With difficulty, she brought herself back to the conversation. Robin was the manager of the now three sales and property management agencies. 'So, you really think you'll get the manager's job?'

'I will. This will put us in a different league, I'll be earning a lot more money, you won't need to work; you'll have time to look after Mum.'

'Don't you understand? I *like* my work. We can use the money to get more help; we could afford a mortgage then and get proper supervision for your mother. I may have my *own* mother to think about in the future, have you thought about *that*?'

'Look, let's see what happens, I should know within a month or two. I promise I'll be here tonight, but I'll have to be out "networking" a bit more in the next few weeks.'

Networking! She'd noticed some of these expressions creeping into his conversations lately. Where had they suddenly sprung from? 'Make sure you're here and we'll take it from there.'

Mrs Figgins, the next-door neighbour, had said she would pop over if Michael was late but Hannah wasn't going to tell him that. If he thought he could get away with it, he'd stay out. 'Give the devil your little finger and he'll take the arm,' her mother was fond of saying. Well, Michael wouldn't just take the arm, he'd take the whole damn lot. Hannah had done a lot of little mending and alteration jobs for Mrs Figgins, so didn't feel guilty about asking on the odd occasion.

As it happened, Michael *was* home on time and even offered the car to Hannah. He was up to something she thought, being extra nice to her. She gave a wave to Mrs Figgins to let her know all was well and set off. She was rather excited, as the person who had called gave the address of Ivy Cottage. She wondered if it was the same 'old biddy' that had enraged Michael at the time he was trying to sell it, and rather hoped it was. Pulling up outside, she sat for a while in the car and admired the garden. It was a real old-fashioned chocolate-box cover. Trailing roses over a porch, and honeysuckle, giving off a beautiful scent, climbed over the fence. The rest of the garden was full of what Hannah supposed were cottage flowers. No neat rows of bedding plants but a profusion of soft colours, slightly chaotic, but achieving a pleasant, wild look. Bees and butterflies were in abundance in the late evening sunshine. It was idyllic. Far enough from the road to mute the traffic noise, actually, Hannah thought in surprise, she couldn't hear it at all.

There was a delicious gingery smell wafting from the open door as she struggled up the path with armfuls of booklets and material swatches.

'Hello? I'm sorry I can't knock; my arms are full.'

'Come in through, my dear, I'm at the back.'

That voice sounds familiar. Walking through the hall of the cottage, she could smell beeswax and ginger. The sun, which was just beginning to set, shone its rays over the oak wood and Hannah could see what looked like golden dust motes. *I've seen that before, I'm sure.*

'In here, dear.'

Walking into what appeared to be a dining room she saw the table set with tea cups, plates of scones and cake, which was giving off the aroma of ginger. The lady stood smiling and Hannah recognised her but couldn't remember the name.

'Oh hello... umm.'

'It's Fae, dear; it has been over five years.'

'You don't look a day older, Fae. I didn't mean to sound like you *should* look old; you look really well, I'm so sorry I never got back to the shop.'

'Don't worry, dear; the shop will be there if you need it. Anyway, have some tea and a scone and tell me what's been happening to you.'

'Goodness, I hardly know where to start.'

'I saw the picture of your wedding dress in the advertisement, why don't you start with that? It's the reason you found me in the first place, isn't it?' *The poor girl doesn't look very happy at all.*

'Oh yes, the dress was amazing.' In between cups of tea, the delicious scones and feather-light ginger cake, Hannah went through a potted history of her life. Every time she tried to ask Fae a personal question, the subject was changed and it came back to her own story.

'I am sorry about your mother-in-law, it's very sad when peoples' memories drift away on the wind.'

'That's a really nice way of putting it; it doesn't make it seem so… clinical. It's like the memories are still there, just out of reach. Oh,' Hannah looked at her watch, 'it's nearly eight, I had no idea we'd been talking so long. We'd better get on to the reason I'm here. You're going on a cruise, Fae?'

Fae waved her hand. 'Maybe, don't worry about it all. I have the fabrics and everything you need from my shop, also drawings of what I'd like and all my measurements.'

'Would you not make them yourself, you must be a good needlewoman?'

'Oh, I'd much rather you did it, dear, I'm far too old and busy to be doing all that. Now, have another cup of tea. Everything is ready for you to take when you go. I am just enjoying a chat and your company at the moment.'

'I wish everybody was as organised as you. It would make my job so much easier. Do you have a number I can call you back on for fittings?'

'I don't have one of those things dear, I... borrowed one to make the appointment, with your mother, wasn't it? Why don't you come back in say, three weeks? Would that give you time enough?'

'I think so, but what if you're out?'

'I shall be here when you come, three weeks today then, yes?'

'Okay, yes,' smiled Hannah. Spending another pleasant hour with more tea and another piece of cake, she collected the large package of materials to take home. She had a quick peek.

'These fabrics are exquisite, Fae; I've never seen anything like them.' Running her fingers over them, she felt excited, they would sew up beautifully; she could hardly wait to start.

Arriving home at 10p.m., Michael was watching television and looking very harassed. 'Well I hope you had a good night, it's been horrendous here. I had to put my mother to bed three times, she kept getting up again.'

'Only *three* times?' Hannah asked sweetly. 'You got off lightly. Tell me something, on the evenings that you *are* here, don't you notice what's going on?'

He quickly changed tack. 'You're so organised, Hannah, everything runs so smoothly, problems just disappear. Do you feel like a hot chocolate and a bite?'

Meaning, how would you like to make it. 'No, I don't think so, I've got this order to sort out, you go ahead if you like; I'll be a while.'

'Mum's asleep, I thought...'

'I know what you thought, you'll have to wait. If you're at a loose end, there are several things that need doing.'

'No! I'll... er, look at some proposals for work until you're ready. I had no time to do anything for myself this evening.' He was defensive again.

'How strange, I don't know how I fill *my* time.'

'No need for sarcasm,' he grumbled as she went into the dining room.

They hardly ever sat around the table anymore. Doreen had to be fed most of the time and that was easier if she had the TV to distract her. Michael had taken to calling in for breakfast at the café near the office, and when he and Hannah did eat together, it was in the kitchen, grabbing time before his mother demanded attention. As the dining room was not needed anymore, Hannah had taken it over for her work. Keeping the door locked as a precaution against Doreen coming in and getting hold of scissors or ruining something, it was her one haven in the house. Laying out some of the fabric, she was again taken aback at the beauty of it. What material was it? It felt like chiffon or silk but was a bit thicker. She smiled to herself to think of Fae in chiffon on a cruise. It poured through her hands like water and settled itself on the table. Studying the drawings carefully, she could see they were unusual, but similar to the designs she already had in her mind. Also in the bag were buttons, thread, ribbons, and everything she could possibly need. A brand new pair of scissors and pack of needles were tied with a bow and a little gift card; 'Just to get you started x.' How kind Fae was, she thought, as she pinned the sketches to her board and covered the fabric with a sheet.

Michael stuck his head around the door. 'I'm going to shower, don't be long. It's been over a week, you know?'

Why don't you make up a chart for that as well as your sales? 'I won't be long, and I'll shower after you.' Locking the door, she had a quick look around the kitchen. Doreen and Michael's plates were still on the side, not even scraped off. Sighing, she did that and put them to soak until the next morning. Checking the laundry basket and seeing that was also full, she put a load on to wash, looked in on Doreen, who was soundly asleep, and waited for Michael to finish in the bathroom. As he came out, she grabbed her dressing gown.

'Don't put that thing on,' he said. 'It's such a passion killer. I hardly see what you look like these days.'

'It's just in case your mother wakes, I don't want her to see me naked, thank you very much.' That was her excuse. She hadn't let Michael see her for some time. Ashamed of the weight she'd put on, looking in the bathroom mirror, she poked at the roll of fat that was now hanging over her panty line. There was also a bit of an overhang in the bra department as well. All the pretty ones that she'd bought had been pushed to the back of the drawer and the old ones had been dug out. I'd never get in my wedding dress now, she thought sadly. She had no incentive to look good anymore. That last remark aside, Michael didn't seem to care how she looked. They never went out anywhere together and she didn't have to dress for work. Apart from seeing her clients, who in the main weren't interested in *her*, the only people she saw were her parents.

It had been so nice talking to Fae tonight; somebody who was actually interested in her and how *she* was feeling. What a mystery the lady was; she never seemed to answer a question about herself and had been very vague about the cruise.

Hannah showered quickly, wrapped herself in the commodious dressing gown, and switched the bedroom light off before dropping it by the side of the bed and crawling in under the sheets.

'About time, it's like you don't want to do it anymore,' Michael whined, as he grabbed and fondled a breast.

Hannah tried to make peace. 'I'm sorry, it's difficult when we're both so busy and tired. Let's hope you get the manager's job and we can find a bit more time for ourselves if we have some more help.' She put her hand down tentatively and discovered he was more than willing.

'Ah, that's better.' He rolled on top of her. 'Ready for it, are you?' He pushed into her whether she was ready or not and she, trying to hurry things along, sighed and moaned appropriately for the few minutes it took. 'That was good for you too?'

'It was lovely, Michael.'

'That's my girl.' A quick kiss and he rolled over, snoring within five minutes.

Hannah gingerly eased herself up the bed and switched on her night light. He didn't stir. Reaching for her book, she imagined herself in the wilds of Scotland, being pursued by the dark-haired, handsome man she was destined to marry. *He* would certainly make sure she was ready for it; no need for any fake sighing for his benefit.

Chapter Seven

OVERLOCK

Strengthen and prevent fraying of an
edge by over-sewing

Hannah went into Doreen's room the next morning and
found her mother-in-law huddled on the floor, crying
and wailing. 'They're looking at me, they're watching
me.'

'They've gone now, Doreen, here's a cup of tea for
you.' She settled her into a chair, changed the soiled linen
and incontinence pad, and felt like crying and wailing
herself. Michael hadn't put his mother into the special
pants for night-time; did he not take anything in? Trying
to get Doreen to the shower was another battle; it was
surprising how much strength the woman had when she
was in one of her contrary moods. Swinging her arm, the
woman managed to hit Hannah right in the eye, making
her reel and see stars for a minute.

Right, that's it, thought Hannah. When she finally
managed to get Doreen cleaned, dressed, fed and settled
in front of the TV, she called social services. A very
sympathetic-sounding woman said she could call the
next day for a chat. Hannah wouldn't say a word to
Michael until after the visit.

'Soldiers!' *What?* Hannah nearly jumped out of the
chair, were they being invaded? 'Soldiers!' shrieked
Doreen, and Hannah realised it was on the screen. Quickly

changing the channel to something less intimidating, she had a hysterical fit of laughter. It was either laugh or cry and she'd done too much of the latter lately. Recovering, she tried to look at her mother-in-law kindly. 'Her mind has slipped away on the wind.' It certainly had, sucked up in a tornado more like. Even wishing Doreen back to the way she'd been when they first married, Hannah thought, was far preferable to this.

When Helen, the part-time carer, arrived after lunch, Hannah said she would be working in the dining room if there was an emergency, but she really had a lot of work to do, so wouldn't stop and chat. Helen was a lovely girl, but having heard the ins and outs of her family doings for the last couple of weeks, Hannah needed a rest. Helen didn't mind; Mrs Rawlings often dozed in the afternoon, so she could watch afternoon films and flick through magazines. Being only a glorified baby-sitter suited her, and there were always nice things to eat that had been freshly baked.

Hannah started making a pattern from Fae's drawings. It was so easy for a rather complicated-looking outfit. The pieces were pinned and she began to cut. The scissors almost took over; she had never cut so well or so quickly, it was as if they knew where to go. Within an hour, the garment had been cut, pinned and tacked together, and she was studying it on the hanger.

Looking again at the drawing, it was hard to see how it would be functional. The fabric was truly beautiful, the colours changing in a similar way to shot silk as it moved and caught the light. Colours that Hannah found hard to describe, any other person would probably say 'green', for example, but it was so much more than that. At one moment, it would bring to mind the deepest green of the sea and then would shift to a clear green, like apple juice, a minute later, an emerald. Also, the whole appearance of the garment would change from the look of a day dress, through to evening, and then something one could wear just sitting in the garden on a summer's day. She'd never seen anything like it and was determined to ask Fae about her designs and if she could show her how it was done. Surely, she could do something similar, but not exactly like these.

The house was suspiciously quiet. Against her better judgement, she had a look to see how Doreen was doing. Helen was nowhere to be seen but then Hannah noticed her outside the window, on her phone. Doreen was quiet but she was sitting on a chair, gleefully picking strips of wallpaper off the wall. She had obviously been there for a while as about half of the paper had been destroyed and every bit she'd picked off was scattered around the room like confetti.

Helen came back in and stood shocked and then looked embarrassed. 'Oh dear, I was only outside for a few minutes. She was asleep and I didn't want to wake her up with my phone call. I'll, er, tidy it up.'

'Don't bother,' Hannah sighed. 'I want Michael to see it when he comes home. Doreen,' she took the woman's hand gently, 'that's lovely but I think you'd like a cup of tea now and some toast?'

'Toast with jam?'

'I'll do it.' Helen scurried out to the kitchen.

'*I'll* do the toast!' Hannah shouted. 'You take Doreen to the bathroom and change her if she needs it.' It was one job Hannah hated and it *was* supposed to be her free afternoon, time to herself. She was even more determined to get proper help or a placement sorted and damn the house. They'd have to manage, other people did, and it wasn't as if Michael was badly paid, and *she* brought money in as well.

When Michael came home, he looked at the room with dismay. 'What the hell happened here?'

'Your mother, that's what happened, when Helen, the *help* that you told me to get, was too busy making a phone call to keep an eye on her.'

'Oh well, it needed decorating anyway. You should have made Helen tidy it up.'

'I wanted you to see what it's like. This is just one little thing that can happen every day. You always come back to everything tidied up. If you popped in at lunchtime occasionally, you'd get a totally different picture. I've had enough, Michael, I really have.' She pointed at her face. 'I've got the beginnings of a black eye from this morning. I wasn't going to say anything, I just wanted some advice, but there's a lady coming from social services tomorrow and I'm going to tell her we can't cope.'

He went white. 'You can't do that, the house will have to be sold.'

'So, let it be sold, we'll get our own place. I want my life back, Michael. I want *our* life and *our* family, don't you?'

'Listen,' he had to buy some time, 'I've remembered something but it needs to be checked. Will you trust me and give me two weeks? Please, Hannah, just two weeks and everything will be alright, I promise you.'

He looks sly, what's he up to? 'I'm still seeing the woman tomorrow, two weeks and then we make a decision.'

As soon as Hannah was settling Doreen in bed, Michael started rifling through his mother's papers. He found what he wanted; there was no way he would lose this house and he thought he knew how he could do it.

* * *

The next morning in the café while he was having breakfast, he made a call.

'Good morning, Evans and Garbett Solicitors, how can I help?'

'Morning darling, can you tell Mr Garbett that Michael Rawlings needs to speak to him urgently, can he ring me as soon as he's free? He has my number.'

'Of course, Mr Rawlings.'

The call came within 20 minutes and Michael arranged to go and see him right away. Telling the office he had a meeting with a client, he checked he had the papers needed and left.

'Michael, er, nice to see you again. What can I do for you?' Mr Garbett was a little nervous, but maybe this was a genuine enquiry.

'You can do me one huge favour, which, by the way, you owe me. Need I remind you of the fat fee you made out of that land deal, the deal,' Michael leant across the table, 'that would never have happened if I hadn't put those other buyers off with the scare story about contamination.'

Norris Garbett ran his fingers around the collar of his shirt, loosening it from the feeling of being choked. 'Of course, we'll help each other, one good turn and all that. What is it you want me to do?'

'I want you to draw up a document signing my mother's house over to me and leaving it in trust for any future children I may have, which will be signed by her and witnessed by you.'

'Well that's no problem at all, hardly a huge favour,' he said, relieved.

'Ah, there's a "but" involved,' Michael smirked. 'It needs to be backdated... how long have you been in this firm?'

'Umm... umm, 11 years.' The colour had drained from his face.

'Perfect, she did it on my 18th birthday, almost eleven years ago, you remember, don't you? It would be awful if rumours of unscrupulous dealings about this firm started.'

He had Norris by the short and curlies and the man knew it. 'You will need something to back this up,' he said feebly.

Michael threw the papers down on the table. 'I was such a good son; I started paying the house insurance, that's in my name. My mother *insisted* on paying all the other bills. Wasn't she kind? I can copy her signature, get it done as soon as, I'll be back and then I can show it to my wife as a lovely surprise.' His plan was to tell Hannah he'd remembered his mother saying something about it, checked with the solicitor and 'Hey presto' the document was produced. Mother could go into a home and they could stay in the house... *his* house.

* * *

Helen returned, very sheepishly, the next day and offered to take Mrs Rawlings for a walk to give Hannah some peace. Thankfully, they had the use of a wheelchair, which they settled her in, and Helen set off. Hannah opened all the windows, not a good idea when Doreen was around, and enjoyed an hour with no interruptions.

Fae's first outfit was ready for a fitting so she tackled the second one. A similar fabric, but blue... no, blue was too simple to describe it. It was the sky, the sea, a sapphire, a cornflower; it changed constantly. This design had overlaps of material that were reversible or removable, completely changing the look in an instant.

Again, the scissors flew through it and it was pinned and tacked like the first one. At this rate, she'd have nothing to do for two of the three weeks.

Deciding to wash her hair before they came back, she nipped into the shower. Drying herself, she looked in the mirror as usual. *I really must try to get some of this weight off again.* A lot of her nice clothes were stored at her parents' house and she would love to be able to wear them again. As she rubbed her breasts, she winced, as they felt very tender. Were they swollen as well? That was a symptom of... *Oh my God, it can't be, we're not ready.*

In the bedroom drawer were her pills and diary. She noticed the forgotten odd one; many nights she was so tired and didn't have a spare second of time to think about anything in the morning. Checking her diary, she realised she'd missed her monthly and the last one was nine weeks ago. Nine weeks! There'd been no sickness, no symptoms of any kind. This couldn't have come at a worse time, or could it? There was now a perfect reason to explain why she couldn't cope. Social services and Michael would *have* to listen. Whatever cock-eyed scheme he had in mind, it hadn't equated for this. Hannah didn't wish Doreen into a home but the current set up wasn't practical, and if there was a baby to look after...

Helen came back looking fraught and Hannah for once was not sympathetic.

'It's been hard work,' grumbled Helen. 'She kept screeching to people that she was being taken away and that I wanted to kill her. I think *most* of them realised that wasn't the case. She did quieten down in the park when we went to see the ducks.'

Hannah relented slightly. 'I'll make a nice pot of tea and sandwiches, if you'd like to get her freshened up and settled in her chair?' Every week that went by, Doreen was becoming a little less mobile, but could still put on a show of strength, evidenced by Hannah's black eye.

'That would be nice,' Helen said gratefully. As she went past the dining room door, which was still open, she noticed the two outfits. 'Oh, what beautiful material, wherever did you get that?'

'It's an order,' Hannah said. 'The lady supplied it herself.'

'It's so unusual, it almost looks as if it's changing colour, like magic. I'd love something made out of that.'

'Maybe she got it abroad? I'll have to ask her.' Hannah locked the door and went to see to the refreshments.

After Helen left and Doreen was napping, Hannah looked again at the dresses. They were quite extraordinary. They *did* change colour, very subtlety, but change, they most definitely did. Even the shape and style looked different from one minute to the next. It was most puzzling. There were large pieces of fabric left over, which Hannah had bagged up to return to Fae. Maybe she could have them for an adjustment on the price. Her mind began to whirl, imagining beautiful, little dresses for a baby girl. There was a soft, pinkish colour for the third outfit; that would be perfect. The colour shimmered and changed from peach pink to salmon with blue or orange undertones. With some of that trim from her wedding dress, the baby would look like a fairy princess.

Hang on, it could be a boy!

Pink thoughts disappeared and were replaced by blue and green tiny waistcoats and dungarees. Maybe even a tie for Michael? Would he be pleased about a baby? It was what they both wanted, wasn't it? It had been talked about in the past and then shelved, with Doreen's problems. Those problems hadn't helped their marriage; maybe this would bring them closer again and help to strengthen the tearing edges of their relationship. Perhaps she would take a test first, just to make sure before telling him, or anybody else.

Ding-dong went the doorbell. Hannah had forgotten the woman from the social was coming. Trying not to look as happy and excited as she felt, she welcomed her in.

'Doreen's napping at the moment. I have a baby alarm so I can hear when she wakes.'

Over tea and scones, Hannah explained the whole situation, when the problems had started and how her mother-in-law had deteriorated. 'I just don't feel I can manage any longer and, if I can tell you in confidence, I think I may be pregnant, and with a baby on the way…'

'I quite understand,' the woman said kindly. 'It's just a question of finding a suitable placement for her and, of course, the funding has to be assessed. Her pension will cover some of it. Is the house hers or does it belong to you?' *That's an awful black eye she's got, I wonder how that happened?*

'You'd need to check all the details with my husband, but I believe it belongs to her. I do realise it may have to be sold,' Hannah said quickly. 'What sort of money are we talking about?'

'Well it varies depending on the home.' She mentioned a sum that made Hannah's head spin. 'I can give you a list of some that have vacancies if you'd like to see them?'

'Yes, please. Umm, what happens if the money runs out?'

The woman laughed. 'Don't worry, we don't send them to the workhouse. It'll all be explained in full detail to you before anything is arranged. I take it your husband is in agreement with this? It is *his* mother we're talking about.'

'Of course, this is just an initial enquiry. I'll tell him what you've said and if we go to see the homes, we can get a better idea.'

'Is there… anything else you need to talk about?' The woman was staring at her.

'No I don't think so.' Hannah was puzzled and then realised. 'Oh, my eye? That was Doreen, I'm afraid, she packs a mean right-hander.'

The woman left her card and some pamphlets. There were lots of pictures showing elderly people in retirement homes playing cards, doing jigsaws or having a bingo session. Well, that wouldn't be Doreen. The 'nursing home' pictures of lounges with TVs and lots of chairs were more like it. Hannah tried to push the feelings of guilt aside; she'd done more than her fair share, now she had to persuade Michael. She heard Doreen mumbling over the baby alarm, so would have to get her up now or the woman would never sleep tonight.

Michael came home whistling and presented Hannah with a bunch of flowers.

'Thank you.' They were a bit ostentatious for her choice but it *was* a nice surprise. 'What's this in aid of?'

He looked hurt. 'Can't I buy flowers for my wife? It's just to say sorry, I know things have been difficult, but they will improve. I said I needed to check something out and I'll tell you soon. Also, Robin said today, he's definitely retiring in three months and more or less said the job will be mine. Did you see the social today?'

Hannah was surprised he remembered. 'Yes, I thought we'd talk about it after tea, there are some leaflets there about homes, we could go and have a look,' she said hesitantly, expecting an explosion.

'That's fine; we'll go on Sunday and take Mum. Sooner we get this sorted, the better. What's for tea?'

'Lasagne. I'll feed Mum first and then hopefully she'll sit in front of the TV for a bit.' Hannah couldn't quite believe what she was hearing. He'd been so against it, whatever was it that he was 'checking out'?

'I'll open a bottle of wine, you need relaxing. That's some shiner you've got, I hope old Figgins next door doesn't think *I* did it?' He crept up behind her and his hands came around to her breasts. 'Christ, these feel even bigger, enjoying that, are you?' he asked, pleased to hear her soft moan.

'They're just a bit tender, sorry.'

'Oh no, it's not that time of the month, is it?'

Not wanting to spoil his good mood, or to tell him until she was sure, Hannah answered quickly, 'Maybe a day or two yet, I'm okay at the moment.'

'Cracking! You get mum fed and I'll shower before tea.' Giving her a loud smack of a kiss along with another smack on her bottom, he rushed upstairs, not even giving his mother a glance.

Doreen looked accusingly at his retreating form. 'Who's that, is he stealing my things again?'

'Nobody's stealing your things, I've got some nice lasagne for your tea, you like that.'

'Who are you? You've got a horrible face.'

Hannah sighed.

* * *

On Sunday, having made some appointments, they managed, with great difficulty, to get Doreen into the car. She screamed and held onto the edge of the door until Mrs Figgins came out to see what was going on.

'Oh dear, taking her out for a nice drive, are you?'

'Trying to,' said Hannah. 'Look, Doreen, it's your friend, Olive Figgins.'

'Horrible woman, get her away from me.' Doreen cowered in the car and Michael shut the door.

'I'm so sorry,' Hannah apologised, 'she doesn't know what she's saying.'

'No, I know, it's so sad and such a worry for you both.'

Not for much longer, Michael thought gleefully. 'Come on, Hannah, hurry up.'

The first home was not suitable at all. 'This is a retirement home for gentlefolk,' the sour-faced owner sniffed. 'Mrs Rawlings needs *specialised* care. Might I suggest you try Furze House at Badgers Bottom?'

Michael chortled like a schoolboy, much to Hannah's embarrassment. 'That is on our list, but thank you so much for your time.' Thankfully, Doreen had nodded off in the car so they didn't have the same struggle.

'Far too expensive anyway,' said Michael, 'and too stuck up for Mother.'

Furze House sat back from the road, surrounded by lovely gardens. It was a bit of a sorry state and the staff seemed very overworked, but they obviously cared about their residents, calling them all by name.

'Awful smell of cabbage,' Michael whispered to her, 'like school dinners.'

'Could we see the vacant room?' Hannah asked.

'Of course,' the supervisor said. 'It is a very popular home because of the reasonable costs, so it won't be vacant for long. We would need to know soon if you want it for your mother.'

'If it's suitable, we'll make a provisional booking today and confirm within a week,' Michael said.

'We will?' Hannah was amazed. This meant they'd have to start looking for their own place. Worst way, they could stay with her parents for a while.

He winked at her. 'I told you not to worry; it's all in hand.'

The room was clean and empty. 'We find our residents usually like to have familiar things around them,' said the supervisor. 'Photographs, a favourite chair maybe. Does she watch television?'

'She sits in front of it,' Hannah replied.

'We try and get everybody into the lounges during the day. They can watch there, or listen to music, and it's much easier for us to keep an eye on them.'

'This is fine, we don't need to look anywhere else. Mum will be very content here, I'm sure, don't you think, Hannah?' Michael was quite emphatic.

'Well, yes. It does seem nice.'

Mrs Rawlings was signed, sealed and almost delivered.

Chapter Eight

KNIT 1 PURL 1

Single rib stitch

Hannah sat upstairs, staring at the pregnancy test stick. It was positive. She'd known it would be, it was just getting definite confirmation that was important. Resting her hand on her already swollen abdomen, she wondered how things were getting on in there. *Hello little one, I'm going to take really good care of you and I'm going to start by eating more healthily.*

That was easy today; she was at her parents' house. Helen was looking after Doreen, who had been very fractious for two days since her car trip. Michael was still in a buoyant mood and had promised some good news when he came home tonight. He was adamant that Doreen would be in the home within a week. Hannah couldn't see it. Unless all the fees could be paid after the house was sold, how could it be done? She didn't really know how it all worked and Michael had told her 'to leave it to him'.

'Hannah, lunch is ready,' her mother called. It would be a big salad with some cold meat or fish, just what she needed. The baking would be cut down now and she would take herself in hand. This baby would have the best start in life that she could give it.

'Are you alright? You were upstairs a while, you're looking a bit flushed.' Her mother was looking at her quizzically.

'Oh Mum, I shouldn't say really, Michael should know first but I... I'm pregnant.'

'Oh, I'm so pleased.' Her mother gave her a hug. 'Ron, come here quickly.'

'What is it, are you ill, m'dear?'

'I'm not *ill*, it's Hannah.'

'Hannah's ill?' He looked confused. 'Looks hale and hearty enough to me.'

'Be quiet, you great fool, you're going to be a grandfather, but it's a secret.'

He beamed. 'A grandfather, well I'll be. Why is it a secret? It'll show... well, soon enough, can't keep that hidden.'

'Just till I've told Michael, which will be tonight, so keep quiet till then, please Dad?'

'I'm delighted and pleased for Michael's sake as well, I was beginning to wonder.'

'Dad!'

'It's going to be a bit crowded, and difficult with Doreen's condition. How are you going to manage?' Mrs Worth didn't like to think of a baby in the midst of that confusion.

'Doreen will probably go into a home, Michael's sorting it all and he's promised me everything's going to be alright. I don't know what'll happen exactly.'

'Well, there's always room for you here in an emergency,' Mrs Worth said, 'if you're waiting in a chain or anything like that.'

'The job he's in, he can sort a house easily enough, m'dear, don't fret yourself; mustn't get stressed.'

'Oh, be quiet and sit down for lunch. Now, Hannah, how long do we have to wait for this baby?

* * *

Michael looked at the document in his hand and grinned. It had been so easy; he knew his deals would pay off when he needed them. Phoning Furze House with the confirmation of his mother's room, he then made an appointment with the council.

Reginald Blakesop eyed the cocky, young man across the table with dislike. Removing his glasses, he pinched the bridge of his nose. 'So, what you are saying, Mr Rawlings, is that your mother has nothing but her pension to contribute to her care.'

'That's exactly what I'm saying. My wife and I were sure the house had to be sold but then her solicitor contacted me when he was putting her papers in order. The house is mine, no doubt about it, all signed, as you can see.'

'Your mother has no policies or insurances for such contingencies?'

'Alas no, always as strong as an ox, my mother, never thought she could possibly be incapacitated, so to speak.'

Mr Blakesop shuffled his papers angrily. 'I see there is a small pension from her late husband, but there is still a considerable amount to be funded. We may have to ask you for a small top-up each month.'

'I'm sure if it's not excessive, we could manage.' *Hannah's sewing money will take care of that!* 'My mother will have to go in as soon as possible, she's already attacked my wife and it would be terrible if the council dragged their feet on this,' Michael said slyly.

The poor man went a deep shade of puce. 'Yes, yes, I get the point you're making.' He stamped 'approval' on the paper so hard, the table shook. 'Our department will get the paperwork drawn up for you to read and sign. We'll email it to you.'

'Please send it to my business address, my wife has enough to worry about, I'll take care of it all.'

As Michael left, Reginald watched him with growing anger. He looked at the copy of the document and the solicitor's name. Norris Garbett, *huh*, a slippery character if ever there was one. Those two made a good pair. He felt sure something fishy was going on here, but he had no way of proving it.

Michael wanted Hannah to get his mother settled quickly that night as he had something important to talk to her about.

'I've got something to tell you as well,' she said. *You could offer to help.*

Another sewing order, I suppose. 'This will make a big difference to us, hurry up, there's a good girl. I'll pour us some wine.'

'Oh no, no wine for me, just a lemonade please.'

Crossly, he poured out the lemonade. He'd wanted to loosen her up a bit, and with the news he was giving her, had expected a good time tonight. He was even going to offer to let her choose the décor of the house when they changed it all. Hannah did have a good eye for that sort of thing and he wasn't really fussed. As long as he came home to a tidy house and his meal, he was content. There was always a neatly-pressed, clean shirt every morning and, when he did have breakfast at home, it was a fry-up with all the works. Once his mother was gone, Hannah would relax a bit and they could have some fun together.

Michael had recently taken up squash. It was a good way of meeting 'the right sort of people', and it meant he had a legitimate reason for staying out later two nights a week. He couldn't bear the house with his mother the way she was now. Once she'd gone, he and Hannah would be able to go out again and, hopefully, she would lose some of that weight and look more like the girl he'd married. A couple of times when he'd been invited to business dinners, he made the excuse that his wife had to look after his mother or that she had clients she needed to see for her business. He didn't like to admit, even to himself, that he was a little ashamed of her. When he compared her to some of the other wives, who dressed so well and could talk knowledgably about the property market, he tried to remember the last time he'd had a proper conversation with her. The fact that he'd more or less pushed her out of the office and then more recently, spent as much time away from the house as he could, never entered his head as being his fault.

'At last,' he said, when she came down looking frazzled, 'I'm starving.'

Hannah felt like screaming. 'There are meals in the freezer so you'll have to wait. I have been rather busy today.'

'Okay, okay, don't get your knickers in a twist. Listen, how do you fancy Chinese? I'll ring and order if you like, sweet and sour chicken as usual for you?'

That rather took the wind out of her sails. *Chinese? That would be nice, almost a celebration meal.* 'I'm sorry I snapped, that would be lovely, I've got some good news for you.'

'Yes, you said; let me get the food ordered.' She heard him shouting into the phone as if the poor assistant was actually in China and not just down the high street. 'It's going to be about 20 minutes, they're not busy at the moment, so let me tell you my news first.'

She listened with increasing disbelief to his story. 'I remembered mother saying something some years back but I'd forgotten all about it. Then there was all this talk about the house and I spoke to the solicitor about her papers and affairs and he found the document; she signed the house over as a surprise present for my 18th. I *own* the house, Hannah, it's mine; it can't be used to pay for her care.'

'But it's so much money, it doesn't seem fair,' Hannah protested.

'Rubbish,' he scoffed. 'Mum's paid in all these years; it's her turn now. We may have to pay a small top-up but that won't be a problem.'

Hannah wondered how Mrs Rawlings could have paid in anything at all; the woman had never worked, as far as she was aware. It all seemed to be legal though and Michael said the council had accepted it.

'So, I rang Furze House and she's moving in on Saturday. We just have to sort what she's going to take with her. Her clothes, obviously, and those awful china ornaments can go,' he shuddered. 'You can decorate the house as you please and we'll get some new, modern furniture. I want it looking good so we can invite some of my colleagues when you... um, when you're ready. We can be an up and coming power couple, you'll see.' He sat back, looking proud of himself. 'Now, what was your bit of news?'

'I... I.'

The doorbell rang. 'That's the food, get the plates, Hannah. Oh, have you got a tenner? I'm a bit short of cash. Save your news for after the meal.'

Sighing, she got her purse and sorted plates on trays. The television was already on and she wanted Michael to be listening properly when she told him. She patted her stomach. *The Chinese is a little treat for tonight; I'll start eating properly tomorrow.*

The meal was eaten, accompanied by raucous laughter from Michael, who was watching some awful comedian who Hannah didn't find funny at all. As he made no effort, she cleared the plates and made them both a coffee.

'Can I talk to you now; you're not watching this next programme, are you?'

Reluctantly he turned off the TV. 'What's so important?'

'I'm pregnant; we're going to have a baby.'

Total silence.

'I'm thrilled; I thought you would be pleased.'

'I… oh God, yes, of course I'm pleased, it was just a shock.' Michael was gob-smacked. He thought Hannah was on the pill. All his plans of them being an about town couple, holding dinner parties and being seen in the right places, flew out of the window. A baby, noisy, and smelly; he hadn't wanted to replace his mother with another totally dependent person. 'I didn't think we were actually trying? Not with mother to look after.'

'No, it was a surprise to me, but it can happen. The timing would have been awkward but it's all worked out for the best, hasn't it?' She beamed. 'We've got about seven months to get the house ready now. We had talked about a family.'

'Yeees, I just didn't think it would be quite so soon. What is it, do you know and are you sure?'

'The test showed positive and I'm seeing the doctor this week. Of course I don't know what it is, does that matter?'

Does it matter, thought Michael? A son, most men wanted a son; a boy he could kick a football around with when it was older of course. Or a girl, Daddy's girl; it would be alright but it didn't have quite the same appeal. 'No, I suppose not,' he mumbled. 'I was looking forward to us having time to ourselves for a bit, that's all.'

'We've got a few months and then the three of us will have all the time in the world,' Hannah said happily. 'I'll get your mum's room done first when she moves and then we can have the bigger bedroom. Our room, I'll do up for the baby. Neutral colours I think, we can always add little touches for a boy or girl. I can knit a matinee jacket!' she announced. 'I haven't done knitting for ages and I've got ideas for baby clothes…'

'Great, I can't wait.' She didn't realise he was being sarcastic. 'I hope you won't ignore me now with all this *baby* business; I thought we'd celebrate my news tonight.' He then had a terrible thought. 'We can still… do it, can't we?'

The look of horror on his face almost made her laugh. 'I think most people do, I'll check with the doctor, if and when we have to be careful. I've got a million questions for him; do you want to come with me?'

'No! I mean no, I don't think so. I'm not one of these modern men who wants to be involved all the way through. You'll be better without me there.'

Although she felt hurt, Hannah did tend to agree with him.

* * *

A few days later, having seen the doctor and getting his confirmation, she had to set her mind to concentrating on Doreen. Most of the clothes had been packed, along with family photos and the knick-knacks from her bedroom. 'More awful ornaments', as Michael described them. The figurines were going to follow; when she had started to remove one to wrap in tissue, Doreen had let out a piercing scream and had such a look of terror on her face, Hannah had felt so sorry for her. Helen was coming on the Saturday morning to help and then she and Hannah's parents would bring the rest of Doreen's things to put in her room before she went there for the first time.

Michael was adamant that his mother wouldn't know if they were there or not. 'She was away with the fairies,' he said.

For some inexplicable reason, that remark made Hannah furious. 'That's a terrible thing to say and I hope you intend to visit her sometimes, she's your mother, for God's sake!'

'I'll visit; I'm out that way quite often, I can pop in then.' He'd hoped he could start with once a fortnight and then let it dwindle to maybe once a month? He had no intention of sitting there in the lounge like some of the families he saw, with their parents silent or, even worse, making strange noises. He would slip the staff a hefty tip now and again to make sure they mentioned to Hannah that he'd popped in. He knew she would visit; a complete waste of her time, he thought.

* * *

On Saturday, Hannah stood with a look of complete shock on her face when Michael told her he had an important viewing to go to.

'I know; I tried to tell them. I can drop you and Mum there then I'll have to shoot off. You'll be better at settling her and you can come back with your parents, that'll be nice, won't it?'

'There was no one else *you* as the "soon to be *manager*" could send?'

'It's a very important contract, Hannah, I *have* to do it.'

Of course you do, another responsibility to shove onto me!

They did get Doreen delivered safely and, with loud apologies to the staff, Michael sped off.

'I'm so sorry.' Hannah was very upset.

'It's quite alright; sons get very funny about their mothers coming to a place like this, they can't accept it,' said the supervisor. 'You're the one she trusts, I can see it.'

'It doesn't feel like that at times,' sighed Hannah.

'Let's get her in and we'll all have a nice cup of tea.'

When Hannah did leave later with her parents and Helen, she tried to ignore her mother's disapproving look. Whatever she felt about Michael's behaviour, she kept to herself. The house seemed very quiet and empty. Helen said goodbye and wished Hannah good luck for the future. Mrs Worth made more tea, even though her daughter told her not to.

'For heaven's sake, Hannah, I can make a cup of tea; I keep telling everybody I'm not an invalid.'

'Sorry Mum, and thank you for your help today.'

'It seems to me you'll need a lot of help when the baby comes, Michael's obviously so busy.'

'Once he *is* the manager, he'll be able to delegate a bit more.' Hannah wasn't sure if she was trying to convince her mother or herself.

Her father said he'd pop around and help to strip the rest of the wallpaper. 'I can get that off in a jiffy with my steamer,' he announced proudly.

'It's a bit... busy, isn't it?' her mother said politely.

'That's one word for it,' Hannah agreed. Large, pink, blowsy cabbage roses climbed up trellises in the front room and the dining room was very dark, with red, heavy, flocked paper, which Michael always said made it look like an Indian restaurant. Hannah wanted it all painted plain colours and she would create interest with fabric for the curtains and cushions.

'We'd better use that that wipe-clean paint in case the baby becomes an artist,' she smiled.

'We'll go to town and choose it,' her mother suggested. 'I'll treat you to lunch and perhaps we could go to that little shop you told me about, I need some buttons and thread anyway.'

'I'm seeing the owner next week for her fittings, I'll ask if she's going to be there.' Hannah thought how lovely it would be to see the shop again and hoped it hadn't been changed too much since her last visit.

* * *

A few days later, Hannah went for her first scan, not even bothering to mention it to Michael. Her dad was busy steaming paper and she promised to bring him a pasty back for his efforts.

'Didn't the father want to be here?' asked the nurse while getting Hannah ready.

'He couldn't make it, I'm afraid.' *This is a special moment just between you and me, little one.*

'Never mind, hopefully, we can give you a photograph of your scan.'

'Can you really? That would be wonderful.'

'Now, the doctor thinks you're about 12 weeks, is that right?' The girl was spreading gel over Hannah's abdomen and placed the ultrasound sensor on her skin.

'I think that's pretty accurate.' Hannah was peering at the screen at what just looked like interference.

'Do you hear that?' the girl asked. 'That's baby's heartbeat.'

A feeling of wonder and unconditional love washed over Hannah as she lay mesmerised at the sound of the little person alive inside her.

'There's the head, can you see?'

Again, she peered at the screen to where the girl was pointing. It became clearer. 'Oh... oh,' she breathed.

The girl laughed. 'I can tell it's your first one, everything looks fine, I'll just get doctor to check.'

The lady doctor, who looked very tired, agreed that all was well. She patted Hannah on the arm before she left. 'We'll see you again in a few months, Mrs Rawlings, take care of yourself and make sure you get your blood pressure checked regularly.'

Yes, I know I'm overweight, Hannah thought miserably.

As she came out of the hospital, she turned the corner quickly and collided with a tall, dark-haired man; a tall, dark-haired, *gorgeous* man.

'I'm so sorry,' she gasped. *He looks familiar, but where from?*

'It's my fault, I wasn't paying attention.' The voice was deep and resonant, and Hannah suddenly realised he looked as if he'd been crying...

'It's... none of my business, but are you alright? That's a silly question I know when we're at a hospital, but you look very upset.'

He was silent for a moment and then sighed. 'It's my wife; she's having radiotherapy for cancer.' He stopped and composed himself. 'The first lot of chemo didn't work.'

'Oh.' Hannah only had a vague knowledge about cancer treatments but a lot of people recovered, didn't they? 'I... hope she'll be alright.'

The man was staring into the distance, not really seeing Hannah at all. 'How do you explain to a five-year-old that one day, Mummy might not come home?'

'Is it that bad?' Hannah whispered. How absolutely terrible. She tried to imagine what it would have been like to lose her own mother when she was so young.

He was still talking as if she wasn't there. 'She got pregnant on our honeymoon, we were so thrilled, so many plans for our daughter that she won't see now.'

Hannah thought her heart would break; she rested her hand on his arm. 'Maybe everything will be alright, you have to hope.'

He noticed her again. 'You're very kind,' he murmured, 'thank you.' At that moment, an older lady came around the corner.

'Christopher, there you are, Claire's asking for you.' She looked very strained and upset as well. The man rushed away without another word.

Christopher? Where had she heard that before? Picton Castle, that was it, the lovely, young girl who'd spoken to her in the garden. She was so ill? Hannah crept back to her car, her happiness overshadowed by what she'd just heard.

Chapter Nine

BLANKET STITCH

A stitch used on the edges of material too
thick to be hemmed

The grainy photograph of the baby was propped in front of Hannah's sewing machine. When she showed it to Michael, he had said it looked like a slug and would rather wait and see when it was born. She planned to take the picture and show it to Fae that evening. Her father had finished stripping the paper in the front bedroom and had glossed all the woodwork, ready for the pale apricot paint and curtain material that Hannah planned to get on the shopping trip with her mum. The room she was most looking forward to decorating was the baby's, but she and Michael had to move out of it first.

Fae's outfits were all packaged and ready. Hannah had planned to go early and hoped that Fae would be there. If not, she was sure it would be alright to sit in that lovely garden and wait. A meal had been left with a note to Michael. She had no intention of rushing back; it wasn't as if he always hurried home from work. Anyway, he'd said he had an extra night for squash, some tournament or another. When he finally got in, he would throw his sweaty gear in the wash basket and see it magically appear clean and pressed in his drawer to be used again, with never a word of appreciation.

Checking the scales that morning, she noted that they read three pounds lighter. Her aim was to stay near enough the same and then her loss in weight would be compensated by the increase during the pregnancy. When everything settled down after the birth, she should be back to her marriage weight and could wear all those nice things stored away at her parents' house.

Pulling up outside Ivy Cottage, she thought again how perfect it was, and walking up the path, the sound of birdsong filled the air. It was so musical, not like those awful squawking crows around her house. Just standing for a moment, she listened. That was a blackbird's song, unmistakable; and a woodpecker could be heard and seen on a large oak tree. *What was that?* Three birds flew out of the cottage window. Hannah thought for a moment they were escaped budgies, two blue and one very vibrant green, or were they large butterflies? She blinked; they must have been butterflies, she didn't know an awful lot about the varieties.

Tapping on the door, there was no reply, so she walked around to the back. Wandering down the path, she saw Fae by some beehives collecting honey. She wasn't wearing any of the protective clothing Hannah associated with that pursuit and there were hundreds of bees around her.

Not wanting to agitate them in any way, Hannah stood like a statue until Fae came up the path with a basket of honeycombs.

'Hello dear, I'm so glad you're early, we can have some of this delicious honey with my fresh bread.'

'Fae, how on earth... I mean, why don't you wear all the special clothes; the bees must sting you?'

Fae looked back in surprise at the hives. 'Sting me, why ever would they do that? I leave plenty for them, they're my friends.'

'What, all of them?' Hannah blurted out.

Again, Fae looked surprised. 'Of course, I know them all. Oh look, Percy's got himself caught in my cardigan.' Hannah watched astounded as the bee sat quietly whilst Fae untangled him. Then, 'Percy' sat on her hand for a moment before buzzing around her basket as if inspecting the combs before heading back to the hives. 'There, he's happy now. Let's get the kettle on and you can tell me your news.'

'My news?' *Did it show?*

'I'm sure you must have some news to tell me, dear, I haven't seen you for three weeks.'

'Oh… yes, of course. Can I give you a hand?' Hannah asked.

'If you'd like to slice some of that bread on the table and get the plates, I'll do the tea. Take it out into the garden; it's such a lovely afternoon.'

The warm bread smelt delicious. Strangely, the oven felt stone cold when Hannah reached over for some plates; it was so pristine and looked like it had never been used. The kettle whistled within seconds and Fae busied herself with the teapot.

'Break off some of that honeycomb, dear, you may take some home as well if you like.'

'I would, thank you; I know my parents would love to try it. That reminds me, my mother and I would like to come to the shop one day next week, will you be there?'

'What day would you prefer?' Fae asked vaguely.

'Perhaps Thursday, it would be early afternoon I think.'

'I'll be there,' Fae smiled.

Once settled in the garden and the delicious bread and honey eaten – just some fruit for me later, thought Hannah – she decided it was time to tell Fae her news.

'Do you sell knitting wool in your shop, Fae? I can't remember seeing any.'

'The shop has everything you need, dear. What were you thinking of knitting?' Fae glowed inside.

Hannah reached into her bag and pulled out the picture from her scan. 'I'm pregnant, Fae, due in about six months. I want to knit some matinee jackets and bits.'

Fae studied the picture with pleasure. 'You can see the head quite clearly can't you, and there's a little hand I think? I'm so pleased for you, dear; this child will bring you great happiness. You don't want to know the sex?'

'I want it to be a surprise,' Hannah said.

'Then you'll want to avoid the traditional pink and blue I take it?' Fae's eyes twinkled. 'I know exactly what you will like, and I'll have it there on Thursday for you.'

'You need to try on the outfits, Fae, and I wanted to ask you about the material. It's so unusual, where on earth did you get it?'

Fae waved her hand in her usual vague manner. 'On my travels, somewhere, I can't be sure, but I have some other fabric I know would suit you.'

'You have it here?'

'Here, the shop, wherever.'

She says some very strange things sometimes, Hannah felt a lot of things were strange where Fae was concerned.

'Anyway, I think I should see how my designs have turned out, shall we?' Fae stood and turned in the direction of the cottage.

Fae came down in the green outfit she'd dressed in upstairs. As before, the colour shimmered and changed while Hannah looked. A cloud of the golden dust that she had got rather used to swirled around and accentuated the fabric even more.

'This is perfect, Hannah dear.' Fae turned so the dress could be seen from all angles. 'The others will be absolutely perfect as well, no alterations needed.'

Hannah knew she had worked from the measurements Fae had given her but was amazed that the dress looked to be a perfect fit.

'I'll put the others on if you'd like to see, but I know they'll be fine as well. It wouldn't take you very long. If you're not in a hurry, why don't you finish them here on my machine?'

'I don't think I'd have time, Fae, they'll take a while.' Hannah couldn't believe that Fae could think that could be done in an evening.

'Why don't you make a start on the pink one there and I'll make another pot of tea. I think you'll find the machine's all set up in the room across the passage.'

'Well, alright then.'

To her surprise, it was a very old-fashioned treadle sewing machine, like the one her mother had when Hannah was a little girl. A luminescent pink thread was already on the spool. As she placed the first seam ready to sew, golden dust swirled around and the machine hummed gently as if singing. The fabric moved lightly and the stitches formed; as she became more confident, it flew along. When Fae called her for her cup of tea, she realised with a start that the garment was finished.

That's impossible; I couldn't possibly have sewn it that quickly. Staring at it and not understanding, she moved it to one side and went out to the kitchen.

'Getting on alright, dear?' Fae was pouring.

'Yes, I can't quite believe how I did it.' Hannah took the cup and sat down. 'That's a beautiful sewing machine as well; a collector's piece I would think.'

'I wouldn't know,' Fae smiled at her. 'It's just my machine, which has served me well for... a very long time.'

'Are you sure you don't want to try the pink one on before I do the other two? I believe I would have time; that one was done so quickly.'

'No, that's fine, I'll bring the other two down; you enjoy your tea for a moment.' Fae was back within two minutes. 'All set up for the next one and the pink one looks wonderful, dear, I can't thank you enough.'

'It's my pleasure, Fae. I was going to ask about the leftover material...'

'It's yours to do whatever you like with. Finish those two for me now and I'll show you the other material I have.'

* * *

Michael had an interesting day. Robin more or less gave him a date on which he would become the manager and also asked him to set up a 'think tank' for marketing prestigious properties. Also, there was a very smart, young girl working at their nearest rival and it would be well worth head-hunting her.

'Her name is Shelby Young and she's already pulled off some deals that would make your head spin, Michael. She's got her finger right on the pulse and if you want an assistant manager when you move up, she's the one for the job. If I were you, I'd instigate a meeting. You won't be disappointed, very pleasing to the eye as well.' Robin tapped the side of his nose in a secretive way.

Michael took himself off in his lunch hour to suss out Shelby in the office half a mile away. It was impossible for him to actually go in, he was too well known in property circles, so he waited in the coffee shop opposite, where he had a good view from his window seat. Having had a fairly good description from Robin, after waiting nearly half an hour and getting a bit fed up watching the comings and goings, he suddenly sat up as his attention was taken by a tall, slender girl coming out of the door. Glancing at the traffic, she crossed the road in the direction of the coffee shop.

She was wearing a smart suit with a short skirt and white blouse and looked the business, Michael thought. Masses of blonde hair, and those lips! Plump and lush, what would they be like to kiss? He shouldn't think such things, but there was no harm, he was only thinking... Was she just getting a take-out coffee? No, she ordered and looked around for a free table. Michael pretended to be reading his paper.

Shelby Young knew exactly what she was doing. She'd been aware of Michael Rawlings for some time and had checked him out thoroughly. Soon to be a manager with a vacancy for an assistant, that's what she wanted. It would take too long in her current position and she was impatient. Rumours abounded in the business that he wasn't always as honest as he should be. So what? Shelby had no problem with that; she'd bent the truth for a sale when necessary. Spotting him from her desk, she watched as he settled himself at a seat in the window. Good, he was hoping to see her. *I'll make sure he sees me alright.*

'Well, hello Mr Rawlings, this is a surprise seeing you in this neck of the woods, may I join you?'

Michael looked up from his paper and there she was. A smile played about her mouth and a knowing look that said she knew exactly what he doing in the coffee shop. No point in playing games.

'Shelby, isn't it? Please sit down.' Sitting opposite, she shrugged off her jacket and her breasts strained against the white cotton blouse. Large for her tiny figure, perfect, in his opinion. He tried not to stare. 'So, you know who I am.' It was a statement rather than a question.

'Of course, as you do me.' She lifted the spoon out of her coffee and licked the froth off it seductively.

Jesus. 'I guessed it was you from a description. Do you know why I'm here?'

'I rather hope you've heard how... good, I am, and you want to offer me a job.'

'You get right to the point, don't you?'

She leant across the table, fixing him with a look that had floored many a man. 'Always,' she breathed, 'no point in wasting time, for either of us.'

The tell-tale flush was creeping around the back of his neck. 'There will be a vacancy for an assistant manager.' Sounding flustered, he checked himself. He was the one who was supposed to be in control here. 'How much notice do you need to give?'

She leant back, crossing her legs slowly.

Is that a stocking top? I must be dreaming.

'When would you... want me?' Again, the froth was licked off the spoon. Michael was lost in that moment; there was no going back for him.

'Within a month. Perhaps we could have lunch and talk it through some time?' He tried not to sound too eager.

'I never eat lunch,' she said. 'What was it Michael Douglas said in that film? "Lunch is for wimps." I'd much rather have a drink after work, if you think you could spare the time.'

I'll make the time, oh God, I'll make the time. 'Let me check my schedule. Umm, I could miss squash tomorrow?'

'Oh no, don't do that. I like a man who keeps himself in shape… if you know what I mean.'

Michael unconsciously breathed in. There was a few pounds surplus, which was Hannah's fault; she was always pushing extra food at him. The fact he never refused it passed him by. Shelby was still talking. He was watching those fabulous lips and not really listening, what was she saying?

'I go to the gym regularly, I like to be in the best possible shape myself and I run three times a week. Do you run, Michael?'

'Er, no, not at the moment, I don't really have the time. It's so easy to let these things slip, isn't it?' He tried to give a casual laugh, which came out more as a strangled squawk. *Run?* Good grief, the last time he'd run was during football games at school. 'Which, umm, gym do you go to?'

'The one at the new centre outside of town. I'm surprised we haven't noticed each other.' She batted her eyelids.

'I… I haven't signed up there yet, it's just the squash at the moment. It's on my list of "to do things", of course.'

'Of course, I can see you like to take care of yourself, Mikey. Is it alright if I call you Mikey?' Her eyes looked him over suggestively.

He was going to have to get out of here. 'If not tomorrow then how about the day after, shall we meet straight after work?'

'That would be fine with me.' She suggested an upmarket wine bar and sauntered back across the road like the cat who'd got the cream.

* * *

Hannah reluctantly left Fae's after finishing the dresses. It was hard to believe but there they were, all hanging up. Fae was delighted and gave Hannah all the offcuts, along with a large piece of material she said would be beautiful for the baby. It was the same type as the dress material but the colour was even more unusual.

'I remember how lovely the colour of your wedding dress was,' Fae had said. This was a cream but again, so much more. Mother-of-pearl came to Hannah's mind, as she saw every colour reflecting in the folds as it moved. Then it had the palest yellow sheen, like a delicate narcissus or the cream from the top of the milk. It was everything; she saw something different every time she looked at it. Fae had tried to pay Hannah for the sewing but she'd insisted the fabric was payment enough. When she got home and unpacked, a fat envelope fell out, marked 'for the baby', which had a generous amount of money in it.

'You were gone long enough,' Michael said, but he didn't sound too upset, she thought with surprise.

'I did the finishing at her house and she's given me…'

'I hope she didn't knock anything off the price because you did it there, it's still your time.' Then he looked a bit shifty. 'I'll be late home the day after tomorrow, we've er, got a think-tank meeting.'

Think-tank? Where do these things come from, doesn't he realise how daft he sounds? 'Shall I leave you a meal for when you *do* get back?'

'Don't worry, I'll grab something.' *A right handful, if I'm lucky.*

'What are you grinning about?'

'Nothing, look, I'll make you a nice cup of coffee while you sort out all that cra… stuff.'

Hannah nearly dropped the armful of material. *He* was going to make her a cup of coffee? She didn't really want one, having had so much tea, but wouldn't let this chance pass. Deciding not to mention the baby money now, it would go into a special account for his or her future. The christening robe would be made from this beautiful fabric; that would please Fae. The notion of asking her to be a godmother crossed Hannah's mind, but then was dismissed. She had only known the woman a short time and just because she was kind, didn't mean she wanted to embroil herself in their lives.

Michael was rather 'ardent' that night in bed, although mindful of the baby, and said afterwards maybe it would be better safe than sorry and abstain for a while. 'It is your first one; we don't want to take any chances.'

'Well, if you're sure, I did check with the doctor.'

'They don't know everything, unless you can't do without it?' he smirked.

'No that's fine, if you don't mind.'

'You and the baby are more important. I shall be very busy for the foreseeable anyway. I'll be tired when I do get home. I can play with these occasionally.' He mauled her breasts. 'They're bigger again, having a baby has advantages.'

'Maybe for you, they're getting a bit uncomfortable.'

'Sorry!' He dropped them like a hot brick. 'I'd better leave them alone, night.'

Was she relieved? A little, if she was honest with herself. She did love Michael, she *did*, but marriage wasn't all she'd imagined it to be. Okay, they didn't have the best start, moving in with Doreen and then having to cope with all *her* problems. It would get better now. They would soon be moving into the bigger room and then she would get cracking on the downstairs. It would be a different house and a new start. There was the baby to look forward to as well; they would be a proper family. Give it a few months and they'd be fine.

Shelby Young was musing over her day. Men! They were all the same. The slightest interest and they were all over you. Shelby had been interested in house designs since she was at school. Her father, who had run a mile once he found out his girlfriend was pregnant, re-appeared in his daughter's life when she was 15. A successful developer by then, he had read a story in the local paper about a school prize award for a project on property development and recognised his daughter's name. The girl had won recognition for her innovative campaign on the plans for an out of town shopping centre, shooting down objections with well-thought and concise arguments. He was impressed.

After some bridge building, which involved large amounts of money and a new house for her and her mother, he promised to help. Up until she finished school, she spent all her spare time shadowing him and learning the business. A job was offered, but she said she'd like to try being a success on her own first.

The estate agency was the first step. The manager there made the mistake at first of confusing her name with her abilities. 'Young' she might be, but a pushover she was not. Unfortunately, there was no progress in that firm for the near future and she turned her eye to the other main agency. Michael Rawlings was the man there, the future. That was her way in. She found out everything about him, his way of business and his home life. The wife she dismissed instantly, no one of any consequence; she hadn't even made much of an impact when *she* worked with him.

There were rumours about his underhand methods. Shelby had no problem with that but she knew it would be his undoing. He wasn't careful enough, whereas she could be. She had to get her foot in the door. Words were overheard by his outgoing boss, Robin, and he'd taken the bait.

If he thought she was going to be an easy lay, he had a big surprise coming. Oh yes, the promise was there and she'd keep him dangling until she got what she wanted. Then, he would be hers to mould as she wished. He'd be licked into shape in more ways than one. Smiling, she smothered her face with expensive night cream and went to bed.

Chapter Ten

PATCHWORK

*Work in which small shapes in different designs
and colours are sewn together*

Christopher sat with Claire, neither of them speaking.
The radiotherapy had not worked; there was nothing
else apart from a miracle. Christopher didn't believe in
miracles and he most certainly did not believe in a god
at that moment.

Six months.

That was the prognosis. Without saying, they both
knew what it meant; six months if she was lucky, but
anytime between now and then. Holding her hand, the
skin was almost translucent now and she was so thin.
The wedding ring had been taken off a while ago and
she wore it on a chain around her neck. A ring that had
meant so much, a lifetime shared, dreams and adventures
to fulfil, a family...

'Mummeeee, can you read me a story?' Their
daughter, Arianne, was peeping around the door. Too
young to understand how serious the situation was, but
still aware something wasn't right. Daddy and Grandma
looked sad all the time and Grandma cried when she
thought nobody could see her. Mummy was very tired
and spent a lot of time at the hospital. Daddy said the
doctors and nurses were trying to make her better, so
why wasn't she?

'I'll do it, Arianne,' said Christopher, but Claire put her hand on his arm.

'Let me,' and then quietly, 'while I can.'

He helped her up and watched as she walked slowly to their daughter's bedroom. His heart broke again, as it had done many times in the last few months. He didn't think it would ever mend itself. How they would have managed without Claire's mother, he would never know. She would look after Arianne at a moment's notice and there were always meals in the freezer. The school timetable was checked regularly and anything needed was sorted without fuss or inconvenience.

Work had been more than sympathetic. He'd been able to do a lot from home and if he wasn't able to go in one day, they understood. Their support would not be forgotten and he would never let himself be tempted by another offer as long as he was still wanted there.

Trying to be strong for Claire, and not ashamed of the fact that he'd shed tears, he just didn't do it in front of her. People were kind; that young woman in the car park of the hospital had been, he seemed to remember, but they couldn't help. Nobody could help. Claire would be gone and, after a while, people would expect him to get on with his life. Move on, what an awful expression. Even Claire had told him, while he listened in horror, that one day, she would like to think he had somebody else in his life.

Somebody else. He almost swept the two cups off the table in frustration. How could she even think he would ever look at another woman?

'Not a *replacement* for me, but somebody for you and for Arianne,' she'd said. 'A father can only do so much and my mother won't be around forever.'

Never. Arianne would neither want nor need anybody else. He would be the all-encompassing parent, her rock and her support.

'Promise me, Christopher.' Looking at the stubborn set to his jaw. 'Promise me you won't dismiss it out of hand; leave yourself open, just in case. It will make me happy.'

When he saw how distressed she was, he promised. 'I can't believe it will ever happen and I'm not going looking for it, but if it happens, so be it.' That was the best she could hope for.

It's not fair, he thought for the thousandth time. Life just wasn't fair and sometimes, it knocked you for six, but why did it have to be her when she was so young still and vibrant, with so much to live for and so much to give? Her own mother had said she wished it were her instead; she'd lived her life and would have swapped places in a heartbeat.

How could so much devastation be caused by one tiny, insignificant lump? When it was first noticed, nobody seemed particularly concerned and then everything collapsed. Malignant, intrusive, all the other horrible phrases they became so familiar with, followed by the nightmare treatment of chemotherapy, along with all the side effects. Claire, who had been so strong through it all, fell apart when she lost her hair and then, in her usual stoic way, laughed and joked about it so as not to upset Arianne. They chose wigs together, mother and daughter, normal ones and some humorous ones, which they would swap and make stories up about themselves. Now, she wore a scarf, even the weight of the wig seeming too much for her frail body.

Arianne would be six in three months' time and Claire was determined to be there for that day. Christopher looked at the scrapbook that Claire was putting together for their daughter. Special photographs, tickets for things they had seen together and letters, *oh God, the letters,* personal messages to Arianne to be opened at various stages in her life. There was one for every birthday and extra special ones for exam times, driving tests, her 18th and... marriage, all the times when she wouldn't be there. He put his head in his hands and tried again not to cry. He felt her then, her hand on his shoulder.

'No tears please, Christopher, there have been too many.'

He pulled her gently to sit beside him and wrapped her in his arms, handling her like porcelain. 'I'm sorry, darling, just sit and let's be together.' He echoed her words with his thought... while we can.

* * *

Michael was on tenterhooks and, trying to be nice to Hannah, stayed and had breakfast. She'd done his usual fry-up and he didn't comment when she just had a bowl of cereal. Unable to look her in the eye when he left, he mumbled something about not knowing how long the meeting would be and they may go for drinks, so not to wait up. He'd spent extra time in the shower that morning and worn one of his best shirts, she noticed; obviously, he wanted to make a good impression at this meeting.

She passed her morning rubbing down the woodwork in the front room ready for painting. Her father always made a big fuss about how important it was to get the preparation for glossing right, but he was doing a lovely job. He'd offered a set of brushes to Michael with the hope he could interest his son-in-law with the finer points of finishing, but Michael always seemed to have something more important to do. Her parents were coming over this afternoon and she was going to cook tea for them all. Not wanting to feel disloyal, it was always more relaxing when

Michael was not around, as he tended to dominate the conversation and not really listen to, or ask them, anything about what they were doing or how they were feeling. It would be a pleasant, relaxing afternoon with a meal and she was going to enjoy preparing something nice but not too high in calories.

By the time the woodwork was finished, her back was aching and, propping a cushion behind it, Hannah sat in a comfy chair, feeling pleased with what she'd done. By her side was the sewing box with the patchwork for the teddies she'd brought with her when they got married. A few had been completed but with everything else going on and the setting up of her business, they'd been forgotten about because of all her other work. Having thought that Fae's order would take longer than it had, she now realised she had a few free weeks. Teddies were easy to do.

Within an hour, half a dozen were almost assembled. They were missing that little something to make them extra special. *The material off-cuts.* One or two squares of that would make them really stand out. Nobody would miss spotting them in the hospital shop with *that* fabric, Hannah thought happily, and just before her parents were due to arrive, several pieces of the shimmering and changing material had been added to each one. Then Hannah looked at the scraps of Fae's material. Why not one very special bear? It would be unique, for her baby. The patchwork shapes were cut out and pinned together as she saw her mum and dad coming up the path.

* * *

'Whatever's the matter with you today, Michael? You look as if you're waiting to confirm you've got the winning lottery number.' His boss, Robin, was looking at him quizzically.

'I'm sorry,' Michael jumped, 'just a few things on my mind.'

Robin laughed and slapped him on the back. 'It's okay, mate, don't worry. You're allowed a day off occasionally with all the business you bring in. What's with the smart shirt, you haven't got a meeting today that I don't know about, have you?'

'Er, no, I just grabbed one this morning without really noticing.' Michael looked around the office surreptitiously. 'Actually. Robin, I do need to let you know that I acted on your tip and approached Shelby Young.' The fact that it was her that had done the approaching was ignored. 'She's very keen to join us here.' Michael made sure to use 'us' and include Robin, even though he would be well off the scene before Shelby put her pretty foot in the door.

Robin stared and then gave a loud guffaw. 'You dirty dog! I knew that shirt meant something and that's why you've got your head up your arse. You're no good to us here today, you might as well push off.'

'I can't do that, where would I go? I'm not... I mean, we're not having our consultation meeting till six, there's no point in me going home now.'

'Consultation meeting, is that what it's called these days? Relax, put your answer phone on and do whatever you want to do. But, I'll expect a full debrief tomorrow.' He gave a lewd wink.

Oh God, I didn't handle that well, he can be such a gossip. 'Mum's the word, Robin, with Hannah... you know, up the spout and everything.'

'No worries, mate.'

Thankfully, Michael was able to slip away from the office later without running a gauntlet of looks and innuendos from his boss. Lightly applying some aftershave he'd rescued from the bathroom cabinet and sucking a mint to freshen his breath, he made his way to the wine bar. She wasn't there, not the type to be waiting for a man. He could have murdered a pint but thought he'd better look the part. Should he order a bottle? But he didn't know what she drank. The price of champagne made him shudder, and may look as if he was desperate. In the end, he got himself a glass of red and waited.

Shelby breezed in nearly 40 minutes late, nodding and smiling at a few people on her way to the table.

'Sooo sorry I'm late, Mikey, last-minute things, you know how it is.' She leant over and gave him an amiable kiss on the cheek as if he were someone she was friends with but no more than that.

'You were worth waiting for, drink?' She was wearing a classic 'little black dress', which fitted her like a second skin. The length of it, along with her high heels, made her legs look like they went on forever. Nothing else apart from a thin silver chain around her neck and enough dip in the front to give the hint of her ample breasts.

'Large glass of dry white, please.' She sat in the chair next to him, where she could keep an eye on who was coming in, never missing an opportunity for a contact or an update; her father had taught her the importance of that. Michael looked okay, she thought, not drop-dead gorgeous but not bad.

'So, Shelby, I don't know much about you apart from your work and, er, your gym hobby. Whereabouts do you live?' Michael asked as he brought back her wine.

'At the edge of town, in the Patterson complex.' She waited for the reaction.

'The Patterson complex!' Michael spluttered. 'How on earth can you afford to live there?' And then realising how crass he sounded, 'I mean, they are very upmarket, and you haven't made enough commission for one of those, surely?'

Taking a slow drink, she made him wait. 'It was a 21st birthday present from my father.' And then, for greater effect, took another drink. 'He built them.'

Michael was struck dumb for a moment. 'Your father? John Patterson is your *father*?' That man was one person Michael would love to do a deal with.

'He suddenly decided he'd be a father about 10 years ago and he's looked after me very well since.'

'Why aren't you working with him then, surely he'd have a job for you?'

'He offered, but I want to have some success on my own first, not just from his coat tails; later, maybe. What about you, Mikey, where do *you* want to go in life?'

'Well, as you know, I'm going to be the manager soon and we're looking to open some more branches, which will also need managers.' He looked pointedly at her. 'I want to concentrate on prestigious and expensive properties, a whole new agency in itself. The sort of thing... your father deals with.'

She almost laughed out loud, he was *so* transparent. 'If things go well, I could set up a meeting maybe.' *My father will eat you for breakfast.*

'That would be fantastic and, of course, it would be a partnership between us.' He let his hand rest on her thigh, which she noted but didn't move.

'I do like you, Mikey,' the words purred, 'but I hope you don't think I'm... easy. *If* I invite you back for coffee tonight, that's what I mean, just coffee.'

Damn it to hell. 'I *never* thought you were that sort of girl, but you could drive me slightly crazy, you do know that?'

Having practised in the mirror until she got it right, she arched a brow. 'Well, we wouldn't want that, would we? Maybe, just a little taster tonight to keep you interested.' Stroking the stem of her wine glass in a seductive manner, she moistened her lips with the tip of her tongue.

* * *

Hannah looked at the time; it was 8p.m. and no sign of Michael. She *had* kept a meal back for him but it would keep until tomorrow. Her father had glossed everything in the front room so she'd moved all the furniture away from the walls and left a note in the hall warning of the wet paint. *I might as well put my bear together.* Moving into the dining room, she machined the main parts of the patchwork together. The colours were so different in their own squares, but when put together, they all complimented each other, while still looking different. She used some of Fae's special buttons for the eyes and found enough stuffing to finish him or her. This bear would be everything to anybody. It sat by her machine and she could have sworn it was looking at her. It shimmered and glowed and seemed *alive.*

Don't be so daft, but she was really pleased with it. A wonderful first present for their baby, she thought. Something nobody else would ever have. She intended to take it and show it to Fae next week. After clearing away her bits and pieces and with no sign of Michael, she had a shower and went to bed with a new book.

This character was the heir to a dukedom, so she hoped by the last few chapters, he would be the new Duke. He was being persuaded to marry a childhood friend whom he still regarded as such and had no intention of denying himself his rake's life, along with his mistresses. Hannah sighed with pleasure. As in most of her stories, he would fall deeply in love with his bride to be, although fighting it all the way, until accepting he couldn't live without her and never look at another woman again. The picture on the front cover was the usual, a dark-haired, handsome man, standing head and shoulders above the girl in his arms. Wide, strong shoulders leading down to muscular, steel thighs...

She fell asleep again, dreaming of her ideal man.

* * *

Michael couldn't believe the flat and was pea-green with envy. *I can see myself in a place like this.* Shelby didn't have her car and he had only drunk one glass of wine so he offered to drive her home. They pulled into the gated complex, operated by a smart, older man who nodded respectfully at Shelby, whilst secretly thinking what a tart she was. Her flat was the penthouse; *of course, it would be.*

She explained that her father had given it to her, off plan, so it only really cost him the build, and his other sales had covered it 10 times over. 'He owns the other penthouse, but he doesn't use it, it's rented out to some Middle-Eastern businessman at the moment.' She thought of the gold necklace nestled in her safe. A 'gift' from the businessman to her, as a payment for acting as hostess for a soiree when he first moved in and, of course, the little extras they'd negotiated after his guests had left. Having had enormous pleasure from that interlude, she never looked on it as anything else than a business agreement. She was not for sale.

The flat was tastefully and expensively decorated. An entire wall of floor to ceiling windows looked out over the town and down onto the integral indoor pool with its vaulted glass ceiling and potted palm trees. Leather furniture, which looked and smelt of money, sat on rich, plush carpet, along with glass and chrome tables and large, modern paintings on the wall. It was a world Michael could only dream of.

A small but state-of-the-art kitchen was off to one side, and on the covered balcony area, there was a table that would seat 12 people easily.

'Do you entertain here?' he asked enviously.

'Sometimes, but I get a caterer in. I don't cook much for myself. I'm into clean food, raw stuff and smoothies, you know?'

'Oh yes, umm, absolutely.' *Clean food? What the hell was that?*

'Sit down, I can do coffee, decaff alright?'

'Fine, whatever.' He sank down into the softest leather imaginable. He wondered what the rest of the flat looked like, especially her bedroom; would he get a look at that tonight?

'If you need the bathroom, it's in the hall, third on the right.'

A good chance for a snoop around, the bathroom was out of this world, with a sunken bath and Jacuzzi, a shower big enough for two and a steam cabinet. What he would give to live here. Hannah and his little semi faded completely from his mind. Where was the bedroom? Peeping in through a couple of the doors, he found what he guessed was a spare room, an office that was worthy of investigation another time, and then, he found it. How big was that bed? It must be super king-size. Not much else but another door off the room was slightly open and that looked to be a dressing room.

'Like what you see?' She was standing behind him with two mugs of coffee.

He held his hands up in surrender. 'I couldn't resist, it's stunning, Shelby, just like you, and it's so minimal and tidy.'

'I don't have "stuff",' she said. 'I don't clutter my body and I don't clutter my life. I only allow things into my personal space that I... desire.'

He took the mugs and placed them carefully on a small hall table. Putting his arms around her, he pulled her sharply towards him and felt those magnificent breasts crush against his chest. 'Do you think you could desire me?'

She wouldn't break her rule. 'Yes, but not the bedroom, not yet. We can explore each other a little first, back in the other room.'

Not yet, I can live with that.

Chapter Eleven

HERRINGBONE STITCH

Columns with all the lines sloping one way and
all the lines in the next column sloping the
other way

Michael had been in a funny mood for days. As she was asleep when he came in from his meeting, she didn't see him until the morning, when he shot out early with hardly a word. That evening, he was later home than usual and told her there was a lot of extra work to prepare for his management position and it was easier to do it at the office rather than at home. He had also joined a gym; he told her it was important to look after your body. A little half-heartedly, he did ask if she had any interest in joining.

'I'm pregnant, I don't think it would be a good idea and I'll be so busy when the baby is born, it would be a waste of money.' This was said a little defensively, as she wondered how much *he* had paid to join without discussing it with her.

'No, of course, you must think of the baby, plenty of time for that later.' He then went on to say that he didn't want cooked breakfasts anymore, could she get muesli and yoghurt. Also, he would cut down on his main meals and have more salads.

'We should eat more natural foods; it would be good for you too. I've been looking on the internet, there're loads of healthy recipes and there's a new shop in town selling all this stuff, brown rice and… and other things.'

Brown rice? He always wanted egg-fried rice from the Chinese, what on earth had got into him? Hannah was a little upset by his remark that it would be good for her too. *I know I'm overweight but he's never complained before, and I have been losing weight.*

'I'll keep Sundays free as a family day, but I'll be at the gym most evenings. It's the only time I can go, you don't mind, do you?'

Did she? A bit, but it wouldn't make a terrible difference to her life. The pregnancy made her so tired, she often went to bed early anyway, and at least she couldn't pick at food if she was in bed. He said he would get a bite to eat at the gym in their health food bar, so she wouldn't have to feed him so many evenings. Sunday, a family day? Well, she'd have to make the most of that. The job would settle down and the gym may just be a passing phase. At least she could sew and read without feeling guilty when he remarked that she never paid him any attention.

Michael had left Shelby's in a dream. A good snogging and petting session had whetted his appetite for other things, and the more time he could spend at her place, the better. The man at the gate had let him out without so much as a nod. That'll change, he'll get used to seeing me, thought Michael.

Wonder how long this one will last, the gateman wondered.

Michael *had* joined the gym; that much was true. It was a chance of seeing more of Shelby and also getting himself in shape, to which she seemed to attach high importance. He did some research into 'clean food' and some of the other things she had mentioned so he'd know what she was talking about. It didn't sound very appetising, if he was honest, but some things were worth a sacrifice. The odd burger or two wouldn't hurt, as long as she didn't know about it. The same with Hannah; if she didn't know, it wouldn't hurt.

Michael was putting his life into compartments, wife and child, work, Shelby. He just had to juggle them carefully and not drop one. Shelby and work would cross over, of course, and the two of them would have to keep their distance in front of the staff. Only in a personal way, she *would* be his assistant manager, and that meant many conferences in his office, many late-night conferences maybe? Feelings of guilt he pushed aside, he'd heard many men say once a baby arrived, they went way down in the pecking order and their wives or girlfriends didn't have the time or were too tired to see to *their* needs.

He was extremely envious of Shelby's set up. A flat like that, just given to her, it was so unfair, he moaned to himself. He *had* to meet her father; one good deal with him would set him up for life. He had been a bit hasty marrying Hannah, he reckoned, forgetting all the little things she did for him. Now, just when he stood a chance of becoming someone special, he was going to be saddled with a child and a wife of whom he was secretly resentful.

While Michael was having these thoughts, Hannah had done all the washing and hung it out, hoping it would be dry by the time she and her mother came home. Michael always liked his work shirts, in particular, ironed and hung up so he wasn't down to the last one or two to choose from. If he was going to the gym every night as well now, she decided to buy him some more sports gear or there would difficulties sorting clean stuff out for him on a regular basis.

It was almost time to collect her mother for their bus trip to the larger town. Her father had arranged to collect them later so they needn't worry about how much shopping they had. Hannah did want to buy material for curtains and that could be quite heavy. A stop at the large hardware shop on the way home was planned to choose the paint she wanted. Having asked Michael if he had any preference and getting a mumbled reply of 'anything you want I'm sure will be fine' left her scope to choose what she wanted. There was a momentary temptation to paint the front room dark purple with silver woodwork and see if she got a reaction from that! Smiling at the thought, she got her bits together, remembering the special bear, and left the house.

She and her mother were soon in the town and looked around some of the larger stores first before getting some lunch. Suspecting that Fae may well have some of the famous ginger cake when they got there, Hannah declined a pudding but did spoil herself a little with a creamy jacket potato, loaded with tuna mayo. She'd bought Michael two matching sets of gym gear, along with some new trainers, bits and pieces for the baby and nothing for herself. All the paint and curtain material she regarded as her territory as she was free to choose so she didn't feel left out. *When I'm thin again, maybe I'll treat myself.*

'Well, we'd better get to this shop of yours,' her mother said. 'We still have the curtain material to buy, but we'll do that last, then wait for your father.'

'Okay, it's this way... I think.' It had been some time since Hannah was last there and the town centre had changed slightly with a new one-way system in place. The church was easy to spot of course, so she headed in that direction. 'I'm sure it was around here.' She was puzzled. Where was the cobbled lane? After walking the whole perimeter of the church, she gave up. 'I can't believe it, why can't I find it?' Asking a few people, they all shook their heads – 'No shop around here' or 'Aberdash what?'

'You can't phone her?' asked her mother.

'No,' Hannah replied miserably, 'she doesn't like phones. Let's go back to the main street, I might recognise something.'

Mrs Worth collapsed on a bench. 'I must sit for a minute.'

'Mum, are you alright?'

'Oh yes, that was rather a long walk with the bags, I only need to rest my feet for a while.' Just then, they heard a voice.

'Margaret, Margaret Worth?' A tall, rather severe-looking woman was marching towards them.

'Oh no, it's Beatrice Congdon from the reading group at the library,' her mother sighed. 'I'll never get away.'

'Fancy seeing you here.' Beatrice sat herself down. 'Doing a bit of shopping, are you?'

'Yes, with my…'

'That last book we were given, how are you getting on with it? I must say, I'm struggling with the parallel between the couple's dynamic and the relationship aesthetics of modern art.'

'Really? I didn't quite see it that way; it just seemed a nice story about two people opening an art gallery,' Hannah's mother said feebly. 'This is my daughter; we were just about to go…'

The book was produced with a flourish from Beatrice's cavernous handbag. 'Could I show you this bit from chapter 15, you have got that far, I hope?' As the woman rifled through the pages of her book, Hannah looked firstly at her watch and then pleadingly at her mother.

'You go on, dear, I'll sit here with Mrs Congdon and wait for you, my feet hurt anyway,' she said, with a note of resignation in her voice. 'See if you can find it on your own.'

Beatrice looked up, noticing Hannah, and glanced down at the book again as if she were a stranger intruding on their conversation. Her mother gave her an encouraging smile. 'Go on, it's alright. Leave your bags with me.'

Hannah turned away, annoyed, and then saw the road she was sure she'd taken last time. Beatrice Congdon's strident voice faded as she made her way to the top of the street. Turning the corner, all sounds seemed to fade as there in front of her was the cobbled street at the back of the church and, as she walked down it, the shop suddenly came into view. The window looked exactly as she remembered it and the bell tinkled with the sound of laughter as she opened the door.

'There you are dear, the kettle has just boiled. On your own, are you?' Fae stood, smiling.

'Yes, my mother has been... detained in the town by someone she knows from her book club. I came on my own because we were getting short of time. It was very strange, I just couldn't find the shop at all, we walked all around the church, and then, when I was back, I suddenly recognised the road,'

'You're here now; a cup of tea?'

'Thank you. Do you know what else was strange? Nobody I asked knew about the shop.'

'Well, it's not your everyday shop, people don't see it.' Fae disappeared into the back and returned with a tray of tea and the wonderful ginger cake. 'How are you feeling, dear, everything alright with the baby?'

'I think so, I'm having another check-up in two weeks, but I've had no sickness, so that's good.'

'Have you felt it move yet?' Fae passed a plate of cake and a cup, brimming with freshly-brewed tea,

'It's a little early for that, I was told about another month. Ooooh!' Hannah grasped her stomach. 'I... I think I felt it, like a fluttering, that's amazing, when we were just talking about it.' Hannah's face was suffused with joy and wonder. Golden dust swirled around her, and as she stirred her tea, the rattle of the teaspoon sounded like a baby laughing.

'Well now, isn't that just splendid.' Fae was beaming. 'You wanted some wool, didn't you? I've sorted a selection for you.' She passed Hannah a basket with several skeins of different colours.

Hannah picked one out and held it up to the light. 'It changes, like the material,' she said in wonder. It did indeed change. One moment blue, then green and turning to a shade of lilac before slowly becoming a green hue again. 'It's like, like those candles that change colour, it's just wonderful.' The next skein worked its way through rich cream, yellow, a soft gold, and a dusky sand colour.

'If you knitted up a few things in all of those, it would suit any baby,' Fae said tactfully. 'What colour did you think of for the room?'

'I'm not absolutely sure, something neutral that can be added to later. I've had a few ideas.'

'I have some lovely material here you may like for curtains and perhaps a cot blanket.' Fae gave her a swatch of material that Hannah fell in love with immediately. 'It's beautiful; butterflies aren't they, with little faces.' She peered more closely. 'They are butterflies, aren't they, or are they meant to be faeries?'

'Whatever you want them to be, dear, everybody sees something different,'

Hannah had the strangest feeling that the eyes in the little faces were looking at her, like the bear. 'Oh,' she said, 'I have something to show you.' She pulled the teddy from her shoulder bag and carefully unwrapped it.

'Oh my, isn't he just wonderful?' said Fae, holding it lovingly. 'You've made something very special there, dear, a bear to watch over somebody,'

'My baby, that's who I made it for.'

Fae smiled, a little sadly. 'I'm sure it will serve its purpose. Now then, is there anything else you need?'

Hannah spent a pleasant half hour picking out buttons, thread and some material for her patchwork, along with some more for curtains in the main bedroom.

'Don't forget to pop into the cottage any time you're passing,' Fae said, as she walked up the lane with Hannah, 'I'm nearly always there.'

'What about the shop? You must be here a lot of the time. I wish you had a phone.'

'I know when I'm needed at the shop. You just call in whenever you want somebody to talk to and don't forget, I will want to see the baby as well.'

As Hannah glanced back after saying goodbye, Fae had disappeared again, and the mist was curling up the lane so she couldn't see the shop either.

Mrs Worth was sitting in a dazed state when Hannah returned.

'Mum, are you alright?'

'I've got such a headache, don't panic, it's a Beatrice headache. Did you know, I've misunderstood so much of the book I've been reading; I was enjoying the lovely couple's trials and tribulations with their new gallery. But no, I should be participating and interacting, emphasising the ephemeral experience, whatever that is, oh, and I mustn't forget to accelerate interconnectivity across time and space. I must discuss this with your father, I'll sure he'll have something to say on the subject.'

They looked at each other and burst out laughing, imagining what he *would* say about such 'ruddy nonsense', as he would put it.

Mr Worth found his wife and daughter giggling like two schoolgirls. Afraid to ask, he picked up the bags and told them gruffly to get a move on as he was stopped in a 20-minute zone.

'I'm sorry I couldn't come to the shop with you, I see you did manage to find it then.' Hannah's mother peered into the bags once they were in the car. 'This is lovely material. Isn't it a little flowery, if it's going to be a boy...'

'They're not flowers, they're butterflies, I think,' said Hannah.

'Are they? I would have said flowers, oh well; I don't have my glasses on.'

What was it Fae had said? Everybody sees something different.

In the hardware store, Hannah chose soft apricot colour paint for the main bedroom and, after much discussion, she picked a pale lemon for the baby's room, which matched some of the butterfly wings in her fabric. Her father said they would never go wrong with magnolia, it was most under-rated, so she got that for the front room. It could be jazzed up with curtains and cushion covers. Hoping Michael would like it all, she then thought, if he couldn't be bothered even to discuss it, he could lump it. The first coat of magnolia and the apricot upstairs was done before her parents went home. Hannah looked at the clock; Michael wouldn't be home for a few hours yet.

* * *

Michael was at that moment looking at the ripped bodies around him in dismay. At least his shirt covered the lack of a six pack, but he was so sweaty and red-faced after thirty minutes on the treadmill, he even hoped Shelby didn't notice him until he'd cooled off a bit. He'd noticed *her* alright. Well, he'd noticed her arse first, in skin-tight Lycra, as she bent over the water fountain. God, it was a glorious sight. Her whole body was so taut and firm, nothing moved as she walked across the room. Nothing apart from her breasts, which were controlled by her sports top, but still gave a little bounce.

He remembered how they bounced when she writhed on his lap teasing him, pretending to be a lap dancer. He remembered how they felt... *For God's sake, think about something else*! An email she'd sent to him at work suggested they meet after a workout and go back to hers for a quinoa salad.

Quin... o... aaa. Was that how it was pronounced, and what in hell was it? He had nipped out at lunchtime for some fried chicken to sustain him, hoping he would work it off. Three hundred and twenty calories had been burnt, according to the machine. Was that good? He had no idea how many calories were in his chicken but had a bad feeling it was more than three hundred and twenty.

Another body crossed the gym, a man so muscle-bound, he walked like a crab. His head, neck and shoulders all melded into one. *God, I don't want to end up looking like that.*

Gingerly lifting a few weights and trying to look the part, he saw Shelby glance in his direction and give him one of her cool smiles. Without thinking, he let go of the bar to give her a wave and with horror, heard and felt the end hit the floor with a sickening judder. Many loud tuts and exclamations of 'dickhead' could be heard, and he muttered apologies, knowing his face was even redder.

By the end of the session, he was a little more familiar with the equipment and had signed up for a session with a personal trainer; a tall, blond Scandinavian man who looked like he'd been carved out of granite. Michael didn't like the way the blue Nordic eyes followed Shelby as she walked to the ladies' changing room.

Blue-eyed, granite man noticed Michael watching her as well.

'A fine body, ja? An example to us all, nej?'

'Ja, er, I mean yes.' *Keep your dirty Norse thoughts to yourself, Hans, or whatever your name is.*

Michael finally caught up with Shelby in reception, waiting while she blow-dried her hair in the changing room. She came towards him, looking as fresh as a daisy. He'd run the shower on cold for the last minute to tone the redness down and to cool his ardour for later.

'Nothing like a good workout, is there? I have my car so you'd better follow me.' She swept out of the door.

Of course, *of course*, she would have a sporty, little car, top of the range, by the look of it. Was that another present from Daddy? Michael followed in his five-year-old, sensible saloon, grinding his teeth and counting down the days to his manager's post, when he would most definitely upgrade. The thought that he should discuss this with Hannah crept into his mind for a nanosecond then was gone.

The gateman looked disdainfully as Michael's car followed the tart's vehicle into the complex. In his little office, he marked down visit number two. He'd made a bet with himself that it wouldn't get to double figures.

The salad was produced. Thank goodness she'd pronounced it first – *keen-wa* – he'd have to remember that.

'It's got all the amino acids,' she announced, 'and its gluten free.'

'Great, looks... wonderful.' Not much of a salad lover, this didn't fill him with enthusiasm. It put him in mind of frogspawn without the tadpoles inside; that was a blessing at least.

'Mineral water alright? I only allow myself alcohol twice a week.'

'Absolutely, I'm driving anyway, of course.' He hoped she didn't ration herself to twice a week for other things.

'So, you like the gym?' Noticing she had a slight quirk to her smile, he decided honesty would be the best policy.

'I am a bit out of condition, but I'll get there with the right... motivation.' He stopped her putting a third ladle full of the frogspawn salad on his plate. *Thank God there's some bread to go with it.*

'I noticed you booked a training session with Sven. He's marvellous and will really change your body in a few months if you do what he says. Oh, and if you get the chance of a massage then take it, he's got the most *wonderful* hands.'

Michael didn't like the sound of that at all and got through the meal picturing Sven being served up as Swedish meatballs, or at least a part of him.

Chapter Twelve

A TEAR IN THE FABRIC

A tear must be repaired quickly or the edges will fray and be difficult to join

FIVE MONTHS LATER

Hannah felt like a Zeppelin balloon and was very tired all the time. It was a big baby, she'd been told at the last scan, and her blood pressure was high. The doctors said it may be necessary for her to be admitted for rest and maybe early inducement if her blood pressure continued to rise.

'What do you mean resting in hospital, you're here all day, don't you rest enough?' Michael was a bit put out when Hannah gave him a sheet of paper with instructions for the washing machine, boiler and cooker.

'Obviously not,' she snapped. 'I don't think you realise how much I'm on my feet. If I hadn't had Dad's help, the house would never have been decorated. It's not as if you're here much.'

The house was, in fact, transformed. From the dark and heavy furnishings favoured by his mother, it was now fresh, light and airy. Plain walls were broken up with splashes of colour from curtains, cushions and pictures. Most of the artwork had come from charity shops, but Hannah had taken great care with what she picked and everything went together perfectly. Michael had grudgingly thanked Mr Worth when it was all finished and he was impressed with how it looked, but he couldn't help comparing it with the sleek, minimalist look of Shelby's apartment.

'I told you I was busy and I still keep Sundays free to spend with you.'

'Oh yes, the morning spent reading the papers, waiting for a roast lunch to appear on the table, and then dozing off in front of the football, a great day that is.'

'Well, you've never asked me to do anything,' he said defensively. 'All you have to do is say.'

'Well, you won't have to bother for a while, I'll be in the hospital. I hope you'll have some time to come and visit me and also go and see your mother, which is another thing that *I* do.'

'She doesn't even know who you are; I don't know why you bother. The last time I called in, she spat at me! I do appreciate the fact that you go,' he tried to placate her, 'but don't feel you have to, not on my account.'

'I don't do it on your account,' she grumbled, 'I feel sorry for her.'

'You're too kind-hearted. I'll take the washing to the laundrette once a week; it's not as if we're short of money now.'

'I don't know why you're still so busy. You've got an assistant manager, Miss Young or something, you told me.'

'Er, yes, but she's still finding her feet and needs some guidance. Most evenings I go to the gym; you can see the difference, can't you?'

Given that Hannah only got fleeting glimpses of Michael's body these days, she still had to admit that he was in better shape. She was usually dropping off to sleep when he got home and he was up before her in the mornings to make his power breakfast.

He'd come home one day with a juicer and a list of fruit, vegetables and supplements to make healthy drinks.

'They're all the rage,' he told her. 'You said you want to get back into shape after the birth, this'll help. It's fantastic, a full glass of carrot juice in two minutes.'

What he omitted to say was although the drink could be made in two minutes, the pulp and mess was all left in the kitchen and it took twenty-two minutes to clean all the wretched parts. Hannah could hardly bear to try it out, knowing what she'd have to deal with afterwards.

* * *

Shelby was delighted with the way Michael was shaping up. After three or four visits to her place and one very expensive meal out, where she relaxed her regime slightly, he got his reward. She was very... adventurous, he discovered, and had a drawer full of all manner of toys, as she called them. Michael was not exactly a prude but some of those objects rather shocked him. However, he entered into the spirit of things and began to enjoy himself.

The gateman had to swallow his annoyance after the tenth visit and was now giving Michael something that resembled a nod as he drove in.

Shelby was not disappointed in how things were going. Michael was good looking and presentable. Not in the financial league that she would have liked, but there was time. She could do worse than him. From her initial thoughts of just using him, she was surprised that she actually had strong feelings for him. Maybe he *was* the one. If so, she intended to make sure she got him. A wife was an encumbrance but that could be got over. The upcoming child was more of a problem. The thought of children made her feel ill. Nasty, noisy, dirty, little things that had no place in her flat. No, the wife could have full custody as far as she was concerned.

Michael was blissfully unaware of the direction Shelby's thoughts were going in. He was certainly enjoying himself and saw no reason why things should change. She was a means to an end. As long as he could do something with her father and as long as they both got something out of it, all well and good. She'd been nagging him to take her away for a night to some posh hotel and he'd been wondering how.

'Michael, you're not listening to me. Will you take me to the hospital, or do I have to ask dad, *again*?'

His prayers were answered. 'Of course I'll take you.' He put on a hurt expression. 'I'll ring work and tell them I'll be in later. You come first, you and the baby.'

We come first? Well, that is a first. 'Thanks, my bags are upstairs. Are you sure you'll be alright here on your own? I've filled the freezer.'

'Hannah, stop worrying, let's get you there. Go and get in the car.'

She'd packed several books, the teddy and a cross-stitch picture she was doing for the baby's room. It was one she'd seen at Fae's shop, showing all the letters of the alphabet with a corresponding animal. It would take a while, but she had plenty of time sitting around in hospital. She wouldn't be bed-ridden, as she'd feared; they would encourage her to take short walks, along with a light physio programme, while she was monitored.

There was a large plastic container of flapjacks and cookies with her case.

'I see you don't intend to starve,' Michael said crossly as he put it in the car.

'That's for the staff on the ward,' she replied, feeling hurt. 'I have actually lost weight; I know it doesn't look like it, but it's all baby.'

'If you say so, come on. I hope you've got everything you need; I can't run around fetching and carrying at the drop of a hat.'

Hannah sighed and wondered where she'd gone wrong or what had happened to change him so much. Had he changed? Or had he always been like that and she was too blind to see it?

* * *

One week later, Hannah was reading in the small garden at the hospital. She liked it there. Usually, she was on her own, and the bees and butterflies reminded her of the garden at Fae's cottage. Michael had been on dutiful visits once every two or three days, and the longest time he had spent there was one hour. He then informed her that he had to go away for two nights to attend a "managerial' boot camp'. Her parents, particularly her mother, came every day, which she was grateful for. Her blood pressure had remained stable but they checked that, along with the baby's heartbeat, regularly.

Hannah put her book aside for a while and just enjoyed the late summer sun. Two people came into the garden. A young girl of about five or six, Hannah guessed, with an older woman, her grandmother maybe? They both looked like they'd been crying and Hannah averted her eyes, not wanting to intrude on their grief. She was there for the happiest of reasons, but coming outside of the maternity unit brought her into contact with every other reason people were in the hospital.

The two people sat on a bench across the garden and Hannah was aware the girl was asking the woman a question and then heard footsteps, which stopped beside her.

'Hello,' a little voice said.

Looking up, she saw the girl more clearly, a pale, oval face with dark, almost black, hair and big, brown eyes, which were red-rimmed.

'Hello, what's your name?'

'I'm Arianne, are you growing a baby?'

Hannah noticed the older lady looking over questioningly, so she gave her a smile of reassurance. 'Yes, I am, and I think the baby will be here soon.'

'Is it a boy or a girl?'

'I don't know, it's going to be a surprise, but I don't mind which it is. Do you have any brothers or sisters?'

'No, it's just me.' She was quiet for a minute, chewing her lip. 'Grandma says I have to be very grown up and look after Daddy now.'

Hannah felt chilled. 'Why do you have to look after Daddy?'

'Mummy is very sick and we don't think she's coming home anymore. We're going to the shop in a minute so I can buy her a present; something to look after her when I'm not here, 'cause I'm not allowed to stay all the time.'

A bear to watch over somebody. Fae's words jumped straight into Hannah's head. The precious bear, the one for her baby, was in her bag beside her. She didn't hesitate for a second and pulled it out.

'Arianne, you'll have to ask your Grandma if it's alright, but I'd like to give you a present. This is a special magic bear that looks after people. You give this to your mummy and if... if Mummy *doesn't* come home, then you can have it and it will look after you and your daddy.'

Arianne took the bear, staring at it in wonder, and ran over to her Grandma. Hannah could see the woman start to shake her head and so she called over.

'Please, I'd like her to have it, really. I... I make them, I can make another.' She knew there would never be another bear like that one.

'Thank you so very much,' the woman spoke softly and in a broken voice, but the gratitude could be seen in her eyes.

Arianne ran back, jumped onto the bench and gave Hannah a kiss. 'Thank you. You're a nice lady and I love him already. Mummy will love him too.'

The bear shimmered in Arianne's hands and golden dust could be seen in the fading light of the afternoon. The baby moved.

'Arianne,' Hannah said gently, 'would you like to feel the baby?' The brown eyes opened like saucers. Hannah took the small hand and placed it where it would feel the baby's kicks.

A look of such amazement crossed her face and she pulled her hand back. 'Does that hurt?'

'No, it doesn't hurt; feel it again if you like.' The little hand pressed down.

'Grandma, the lady's baby is moving, I can feel it,' she said.

Grandma came over and took Arianne's hand. 'We must leave the lady now, say thank you to her again.'

'Thank you,' Arianne said solemnly. 'Bear says goodbye as well.' She made the bear wave a paw.

'You'll have to give him a name,' Hannah said, waving to the bear.

'I'll think of a special name. What are going to call your baby?'

'Do you know, I'm not really sure yet, I'll have to think of a special name too.'

'Thank you, Mrs... ?' the older lady queried.

'Rawlings, it was nothing.'

'To see her face light up like that, even for a moment, it means everything, trust me.'

Hannah watched them walk back into the hospital and she could have sworn she saw the bear's paw move again as they went through the door. How sad, she thought, and wondered what was so wrong with the child's mother that she may not come home again.

I hope she and her father will be alright.

✳ ✳ ✳

Michael's boot camp involved two nights away with Shelby in Brighton. It cost him a small fortune but she made it worth his while. Presenting herself to him the first night in some very alluring underwear, which involved a burlesque show she put on for him, he felt like a dish rag that had gone through the mangle by breakfast time.

'Come on, a nice bowl of yoghurt and fresh fruit will set you up for the day.'

I could murder a fry-up. 'It's a bit early for breakfast, isn't it?' He peered blearily at his watch.

'Yes, it's too early. We're going for a run along the front first. You did bring your gear like I told you, I hope!'

A silent groan. 'Okay, give me a minute.'

He felt her hand on his worn-out appendage. 'I'll wash your back and... other parts when we get back.' The woman was insatiable; he was out of bed in a second.

The rest of that day was an eye-opener. He was highly embarrassed when she dragged him into a sex shop, spending ages looking over the bits and pieces, and even more embarrassed when she threw over a leopard print thong with rubber teeth around the hole where his cock was supposed to make an appearance.

He was even more put out when she insisted they go to a gay club that night.

'Don't be so silly,' she said. 'It's Brighton, they know how to have proper fun here, and you'll be safe with me.' Would she be safe with him, he wondered, when he saw what she was wearing. A dress, if that covered its description, which she'd bought, no, *he'd* bought in the sex shop. It was a very tight, rubbery, latex affair with holes where her nipples poked out and were adorned with some feathery decoration. It was so short, the slightest bend forward showed everything in that thong she was hardly wearing. Having had one of her waxes before they left, the area on show was a smooth as a baby's bottom. *Baby! Don't think about that.*

Michael saw things that night he could hardly believe, but Shelby was all over him, highly excited by it all, so he had no complaints, even when he had to brush aside men who showed an interest in *him*! The rubber teeth did what they were supposed to do later and he made sure the thong went into her suitcase for future use. He couldn't imagine what would happen if that was found in his washing at home.

'This has been *so* great, Mikey, we must do it again soon.' She nibbled his ear as they pulled up outside her flat. 'You were a real stud.'

He almost felt ready again at her words. 'I'll see you Monday at work.' He was careful never to mention his family life after she'd flown into a rage one day when he let Hannah's name slip with something he was going to do at home.

'I don't want to share you,' she'd said, sulking. 'I know you're married but you've got me now, I give you everything you need in bed, don't I?'

In bed, yes, he couldn't argue with that, and she was so adventurous and inventive.

'I know you're going to be a father, but that happened before you met *me*, there're no excuses now.'

* * *

A week later, Hannah didn't feel so good, and after finding her blood pressure raised considerably, they decided to induce the baby.

She phoned Michael's office.

'Shelby Young, assistant manager, how may I help you?'

'Umm, oh hello, Shelby, is Michael there?'

'*Mr* Rawlings is out on a site visit, may I take a message?' The voice was decidedly unfriendly.

'It's his wife, Hannah. Could you please let him know they're starting me and the baby may come today?'

Shelby looked at the phone with distaste, *starting her?* What the hell was that supposed to mean? 'I'll tell him as soon as he returns, Mrs Rawlings.'

Not a 'hope all goes well', nothing, thought Hannah. She did have a mobile number for Michael but he'd made it plain that was only for the direst emergency. Well, he'd be bound to come back to the office soon and then he'd be here.

Four hours later, she was told the baby was distressed and they advised a caesarean section. By that time, her parents were there, but no Michael.

'Do you want me to go and find the fellow?' her father asked gruffly.

'No Dad, he'll be here, I'm sure. Mum needs you more.' Mrs Worth was indeed in a bit of a state. Worried about Hannah and the baby, they were reassured that all would be well, it was better safe than sorry and the baby needed to come out sooner rather than later.

Michael thought he'd better pop in and see how Hannah was doing after being away for the weekend. Sitting around, reading and drinking tea, he supposed. It was alright for some; everything had piled up at home. Shelby had given him a look of utter horror when he asked if she could possibly do some laundry for him.

'Darling, I don't do my *own* laundry, sorry.'

They were locking up the office. 'Shelby, I have to go to the laundrette and do some other stuff, I'll miss the gym tonight.' As he had done no washing for two weeks and had nothing clean for the gym, that was a given anyway.

Shelby gave a gasp and slapped her forehead very theatrically. 'Oh, my God, Mikey, I'm sooo sorry, I completely forgot, with all the work I was doing.'

'What did you forget?' *To pick up some lentils maybe?*

'Your wife phoned, something about them starting her? I didn't quite understand at the time, is it... the baby?' *I'm so good; I should be on the stage.*

Hannah was awake for the operation; they'd given her an epidural, which they explained meant she wouldn't feel anything. As they were preparing her in theatre, she wondered if Michael was there yet.

He screeched into the car park, cursing, and ran to the maternity unit. *Oh crap, her parents are here.* Mrs Worth sat with lips so compressed, they couldn't be seen, and Mr Worth was a bit red in the face.

'Here you are, m'boy, about time too, I would say.'

'Mr Worth, Mrs Worth, I'm so sorry, my, er, my assistant forgot to give me the message.'

'Most inefficient, some discipline needed in that office.' Mr Worth glared at him.

Michael had sudden lustful thoughts as to how he could 'discipline' Shelby and got all hot under the collar. 'I'll see to it. What was the big emergency anyway?'

Mrs Worth sighed and explained. 'They're having to do a section.'

'What, cut her open?' That did shock him; he didn't want anything to happen to her or the baby.

'Yes, and she's going to need some care and help for the first few weeks. I can be there in the daytime, but you'll need to put in some hours at home.' The look she gave him said it all.

'We'll discuss it when we know what's happening.' Michael was sweating. He'd have to come up with something.

Across the hospital, in the palliative care section, Christopher sat, holding his wife's hand. He had asked Claire's mother to take Arianne away, he knew it was time.

'You need to say goodbye to Mummy,' he said, trying to hold himself together. Arianne understood that Mummy was going to live with the angels, but it didn't stop her tears.

Placing the bear in her mother's arm, she kissed her, and then her father. 'Bye Daddy, I'll see you later?' For a moment, she looked panic-stricken, wondering if Daddy would come home.

'I'll see you at home sweetie, be good for Grandma now.'

'Don't forget to bring Mr Bear home with you; he's going to look after us.'

Hannah heard a wail and then was shown a bundle very quickly. 'It's a boy, Hannah,' said the surgeon. 'They're just going to check him over and clean him up, but it doesn't look like he's suffered any effects, you did very well.'

I didn't really do anything. She was feeling very tired now but happy. *Jack, I'd like to call him Jack.*

As Jack, the new life, was taking his first breaths, Claire was taking her last ones, and slipped away to the sound of her broken-hearted husband's sobs. The golden dust around the teddy dimmed and faded.

Chapter Thirteen

SEED STITCH

Creating layers that appear to have dimension

Hannah couldn't stop staring at Jack. She had produced this perfect, tiny person who already had his own personality and she watched Michael, sitting beside her, holding his son. Part of that was to appease his in-laws, who were still regarding him with displeasure. The boy was okay and he was glad it was a son, but not very interesting, in his opinion. It was just a squalling baby like others in the rooms around them. He felt rather proud, he had to admit. His son had weighed in at 9 lbs 10 oz, a bruiser. He didn't have any hair to speak of but what there was of it looked brownish and his eyes were blue.

When Hannah woke, he gave her a rather awkward kiss and let it be known that he was on time to see his son wheeled out of the theatre. Hannah looked awful, pasty-faced and swollen, although that would go by the morning, they'd been told. For producing such a huge baby, she didn't look like she'd lost a lot of weight, but he felt no urge to examine her more closely.

She was told she could go home in a day or two. Her parents had gone for a cuppa and gave her the chance to talk to Michael.

'I don't want my mother doing too much. I know she wants to help but I'll have to keep an eye on her. I hope you can be home a bit more in the evenings.' She saw the look on his face. 'Just for the first few weeks, most men take paternity leave; why can't you, or at least, use some holiday time?'

He couldn't really wriggle out of it. 'Look, I'll see what I can do. Maybe I can take two weeks off.' He brightened up as he had a thought. Shelby couldn't take holiday at the same time as he did, but she could have 'appointments' during the day, when it would be easier for him to slip out if Mrs Worth was around. It *would* only be for a couple of weeks, surely Shelby would understand. 'I'm *sure* I can take two weeks off.' He patted her hand. 'You're a bi... strong girl; you'll be over this in next to no time. It's not like a *proper* operation, is it?'

He's unbelievable. 'I guess not, at least I'm not *sitting* on my stitches.'

He shuddered. 'I like the name Jack,' he said, swiftly changing the subject. 'That wasn't one of the ones we'd talked about?'

Hannah found it hard to remember much of a conversation with him about names. She'd suggested a few, and got a grunt in reply. The only time there was a strong response was when she'd suggested Ashley. She'd always liked that since reading *Gone with the Wind*. He scoffed at that, saying it was far too girlish for *his* son's name.

'It just came to me when I saw him, he looked like a Jack.'

'You do say some daft things at times. Your parents are back, I'll nip off now and, er, get the house cleaned up properly for when you come back.'

Mrs Worth fixed him with a beady eye as he left but was reassured slightly when Hannah told him what he'd said. 'Maybe he won't want me around for the first two weeks then, it'll be a chance for the two of you to have some time together.'

'It would,' said Hannah thoughtfully, 'but I might suggest he goes to the gym or plays squash in the afternoons, seeing he's going to be home in the evenings. He enjoys it so much and it does seem to be doing him some good.'

Michael had driven straight to Shelby's from the hospital.

'Oh, she frowned, 'I didn't think you'd be able to tear yourself away, I was thinking of going out to a club.' She had thought nothing of the kind. Already showered and wearing one of his favourite underwear sets, she'd been sure he would come to her as soon as was possible. 'What is it then, the baby?'

'A boy, do you really want to go out?'

After she'd let him pleasure her and given him something to think about other than the baby, she came straight to the point. 'Okay, what does this mean for us now?'

He gulped and explained what he had in mind for the next two weeks. She glared at him.

'Two weeks? I can't disappear *every* day you know, *somebody* has to run the office.'

'Every other day?' he asked hopefully. 'I will make it up to you, I promise. I got you something.' He'd kept the gift back for such an occasion and took it out of his jacket pocket.

'What is it?' She grabbed at it eagerly. It had taken a lump out of his savings but Shelby didn't come cheap. It was a pair of rose-gold earrings with tiny diamonds. Apart from his car, it was the most expensive item he'd ever bought. 'They're nice.' Her voice was dismissive, but her mind was already calculating how much they were worth. 'Thank you, my darling Mikey.' She softened; he was obviously desperate to please her.

'I, er, do have a favour to ask you. My house is a bit of a mess. I was wondering if your cleaner would be able to spare a few hours to give it a going over.'

'Vanya? She's very busy, can't you do it yourself? It must be important to impress your wife with a clean house.'

'I'm sorry, it's not to *impress* her, but you're far more important to me than tidying up. The mother-in-law will be poking her nose around as well.'

Shelby tapped her teeth with a long, red-painted fingernail. 'I will ask her if she could go around tomorrow after she's been here. Can you leave a key?'

I'll put it under the plant pot by the door. What would I do without you?' He let his fingers trail down her body and linger until she smiled again.

* * *

Hannah was amazed when she walked into the house. It was spotless and smelt of polish. Michael put Jack, who was lying in his baby carrier, onto the floor and looked around, beaming.

'You thought I couldn't look after myself, didn't you?'

She peered into the kitchen, which looked like it hadn't been used at all. The worktops, sink and drainer were gleaming, and there wasn't even a dirty mug waiting to be washed.

'All the washing's been done as well,' he announced proudly. 'Some of it is hanging on the clothes horse, but even I can't get it dry in the rain.'

'I'm very impressed. Let's get a takeaway tonight, I don't want to dirty the lovely kitchen. If you could carry Jack upstairs, I'll see if he'll settle down for a sleep in his new cot.'

'Will do. Could we dirty it enough for you to make a nice cuppa?' Michael had been delighted when he'd come home from work and seen the house. Vanya had gone above and beyond and had left him a bill in proportion of that fact, but it was worth it. Brownie points had been earned so he could slip away for an afternoon in a day or two.

Michael hovered while she settled Jack. He'd sorted his time off and even seeing Shelby glowering at him while he received congratulations at work hadn't taken away the moment of pride at being a father. As Hannah started to remove Jack's nappy, he beat a hasty retreat.

'Tell you what, *I'll* make the tea while you do that.' He'd already had a quick inspection to make sure his boy was 'alright in that department', and was more than impressed with the size of the equipment so young in life.

Hannah guessed Michael wasn't going to be a hands-on father in nappy duties; hopefully, he would put him to bed occasionally. She'd cut down her workload of orders to give her time to settle into a routine with the baby, and just took work from a few of her regulars. One of the bridal boutiques had asked her to do alterations for them and, not wanting to lose that income, she still took those, but did them at her parents' house with no risk of any accidents.

Going downstairs, there was a cup of tea waiting with a couple of biscuits on the side.

'Thank you, but I am cutting down you know.'

'You need your strength at the moment, two won't hurt. Umm, when do you think your mum might come over? I would like to keep up with the gym... we did talk about it.'

'Let's have tomorrow together with Jack and I'll need you to get some things for me, so the day after? The gym must be good for you, you've shaped up. You should carry on with it, if it means that much to you.'

Michael felt his neck flush and swallowed the momentary guilt. 'I won't be out all afternoon, I promise. Make a list of everything you need.' *Maybe I could slip in a quick half hour while I'm shopping.* He saw Hannah wince as she moved slightly. 'Are you in pain?' he asked, alarmed.

'Bit sore still. I have to be careful for a few days.'

* * *

By the morning, Michael was already rather fed up with being a father. Jack had woken three times, his lusty cries shattering pleasant dreams. He *was* glad he'd taken two weeks off; he wouldn't be fit for work in the morning. Hannah had Jack in a basket by the side of the bed so she only had to reach over for him. Unfortunately, he was being bottle fed, so each time involved a trip down to the kitchen, which he felt obliged to do. He had stared at her in disbelief when she told him she couldn't breastfeed their baby.

'What? You're telling me, with the size of those, there's no milk in them, I don't believe it!'

'It's nothing to do with size. I'm very disappointed, it's what I wanted, but we tried over and over and in the end, they told me not to stress about it and do bottles. I got a batch of ready-made ones but that's what I need you to go shopping for please.'

'I don't know what to get,' he panicked.

'I've got it all written down; the shop will know exactly what it is.'

Michael hoped and prayed that none of his important clients would see him buying baby paraphernalia or if, God forbid, Shelby got wind of it.

When Michael had gone with the shopping list, Hannah sat gratefully in the chair with Jack sleeping beside her. 'This is the first time we've been completely on our own.' She stroked his cheek, which felt soft and warm. 'I'm sorry you didn't get your special bear but it was needed by somebody else and I think it's gone to a very good home. I'll be watching over you, Jack, you don't need to worry about anything.'

Michael went into the large mother and baby store that Hannah had told him would have everything they needed. How could such a small person need so much stuff? Half of the shop was taken up with pushchairs, prams and strange circular objects on wheels. Baby walkers, the label said, and then there were the clothes. Row upon row of outfits labelled for all sorts of different ages. He looked at one small romper marked 'new-born' and even he could see that was too small for Jack. There were a lot of pregnant women in the shop but Michael spied one attractive, young assistant and made a bee-line for her.

'I wonder if you could help me, er, Louise?' Nice breasts behind that name badge, he thought.

'Of course, a new father, are you?' Louise smiled.

'Ha-ha, is it that obvious? I have a list here.'

Louise took the list and guided him in the direction of the milk powders and equipment.

'You'll need a steriliser, which is on the list.' She explained the various products.

Michael was bored within minutes. 'Please, if my wife hasn't actually stipulated something specific, just put the most popular ones in the trolley.'

They moved onto nappies. Huge packets of disposable nappies piled up in his trolley.

'The size that's on your list, it must be a big baby?' Louise looked impressed.

'Ah well, you know what they say, big baby, big...' He winked and leered at her.

Louise didn't look impressed any longer. 'That's all the things on the list, is there anything else I can help you with?'

If it was any other time, your phone number. 'No that's alright, darling, thank you.' Maybe this shopping lark wasn't so bad, although the bill gave him a shock.

The woman at the till noticed him falter. 'Expensive little things aren't they, babies?'

'I never realised how much cra... stuff they needed,' he said miserably, glancing at the prices on some of the pushchairs.

As soon as he had everything hidden in the boot, he called Shelby on her mobile phone.

'Michael, this isn't a good time, I'm *very* busy.'

'Oh, I was hoping you could maybe grab an hour?'

'An hour? One *hour*, you have to be kidding. No. I can't, sorry.'

* * *

Michael deflated like a balloon. '*I'm* sorry; I shouldn't have expected you to just drop everything. I would be free tomorrow afternoon, could you possibly... squeeze some time?'

'Just a moment, goodbye Mr Pearce, so good of you to drop in... yes, we must have that drink. What was that, Michael?'

Mr Pearce, that's my client. 'What did Mr Pearce want?'

'Don't worry, I've seen to him. Tomorrow afternoon, you say, 2p.m. then.' The phone went dead.

Michael was furious. Not only had he been dismissed like an annoying punter on the phone, she'd been chatting up Mr Pearce. That shopping mall was *his*; she'd better not sink her claws into it. *I'll sort her out tomorrow alright.* With that, his thoughts became lecherous again and he didn't feel inclined to rush home so went to the wine bar, where at least he could chat up some of the women in there and make himself feel better.

Shelby put her mobile down with a smirk. Mr Pearce hadn't been in the office at all, she just wanted to wind Michael up. She'd give him one hour, what did he think she was? Dialling another number, she was gratified when it was answered immediately.

Shelby, how's my favourite daughter, making money I hope?'

'Working on it, Dad, trust me. How would you like to take me out to dinner tonight? I've got some inside news on a shopping mall.'

'That's my girl,' he chuckled. 'I'll pick you up at seven. How do you fancy La Belle Gastronomie?'

'I might need a new dress for that.'

'Put it on my account, sweetheart.'

'I have to pop out for an hour,' she announced to the office. 'An important appointment just cropped up.'

Hannah had a lovely afternoon with Jack. Although she appreciated Michael taking time off and going out for the shopping, she loved the house when it was quiet and Jack had slept peacefully for three hours. As he woke up, his face screwed up in hunger and he let out a cry loud enough to wake the street.

'Okay, little man, let's get you changed and dry first.' She had set up a changing mat in the dining room so she didn't have to go upstairs. As she was seeing to him, Michael came home, not in the best of moods.

'What's that god-awful smell, it makes me feel sick.'

'It's your son.' Hannah came out with the offending nappy in a plastic, scented bag. 'I've opened the window; we were all babies once, you know. Did you get everything?'

'Yes, I did, and the sooner he grows up and can pay his way, the better.' He saw the look on her face. 'I'm not serious, can't you take a joke?'

'I never know sometimes with you. Hold your son a moment, while I do his bottle.'

Jack lay in his arms, glowering up at his father, or at least, that was how it looked to Michael.

'Do you want to feed him? It would help you bond.'

'Alright, but I might go up and have a nap after that, I'm exhausted.' Once Jack latched onto the bottle, it wasn't so bad.

'He has to be winded now,' said Hannah. 'I'll do it if you like, just in case he drools over your shoulder.' She imagined the fuss he'd make about *that* if it happened.

'Right, I'll go upstairs for a rest; I brought everything into the hall.' A loud burp followed him as he went out of the room. *God, babies are disgusting.*

It wouldn't occur to him that I may want a rest, I suppose. Hannah had to smile. She would have liked to take Jack out but she wasn't really up to it and she didn't have the push-chair yet. Her mother had told her they'd bought one as a present and would bring it over tomorrow. Jack was already dropping off to sleep again so she laid him down and picked up her cross-stitch. She was up to 'G' and was just starting the colourful giraffe when she thought of Fae. As soon as she was able to drive, she would take Jack to the cottage and hoped that she would be there.

Shelby's father arrived in his Mercedes and was almost bowed to by the gateman. John Patterson always rewarded loyalty and the man had been a long-standing employee. After retiring, he'd had a string of bad luck and after requesting a meeting with his former employer, asked if there was any job he could do. Mr Patterson gave him the job at the complex and in turn, got reports on who his daughter was seeing. He didn't care what she did in her personal life, as long as there was no scandal. This Mr Rawlings was not at the top of his list of desirables and he needed to find out how keen Shelby was on him.

Having watched out for him, she came down in the lift, looking impeccable. She always dressed demurely, but with class, when she met with her father. Resentful still of the way he'd ignored her early years, she was mindful that he was making up for it and intent on getting what she could out of it.

John Patterson had no other children; not by choice, it just hadn't happened, even after three wives. Each one had cost him a pretty penny and he would now invest his future into this girl, who was already proving herself to him.

La Belle Gastronomie was fifteen miles away and normally had a two-month waiting list. But, as John Patterson's firm had converted the old, sprawling vicarage, he never needed a reservation. It was run now by a TV celebrity chef and was *the* place to eat. Ushered to their table by the maitre d', who then called an obsequious waiter to fawn and grovel, was much to Shelby's satisfaction.

John's usual wine was served and the waiter was waved away. 'Give us a while, we'll order later.' He looked at Shelby. 'Now then, when are you going to leave this tin pot estate agency and come and work for me?'

'In a while, Dad, I'm enjoying myself. It didn't take me long to find an assistant manager's post.'

'Was it the position or the actual manager that you fancied?' She looked up, shocked, but he was pouring her wine and looking at her as if it was the most natural question to ask. 'Let's not play games, Shelby, I've been around too long, you won't fool me. Just where are you going with this? The man's married and just become a father, I understand.'

She didn't even bother to ask how he knew. If her father wanted information, he got it. 'I like him and he likes me,' she said defiantly, then realised how childish she sounded. 'I do really like him and he thinks like we do. I'm sure you already know *that*, along with everything else.'

John Patterson smiled. 'I would never need a DNA test to accept the fact that you're mine, but listen to me carefully. If you want him, that's fine by me. But I don't want your name cited in any divorce and I don't want to hear any gossip. So, you either get him out of your system or make it clear to him that he has to choose. One year, that'll be enough time for you to be sure about him. Am I making myself understood?'

She narrowed her eyes. 'What gives you the right to dictate to me?'

'You want a slice of my pie, you eat what I give you. Now, decide what you want to eat tonight and tell me about this shopping mall.'

Chapter Fourteen

BROKEN CHAIN STITCH

The needle is inserted again outside the
previous stitch

Jack was one month old and Hannah decided to go and
see Fae, who had obviously borrowed a phone again
to ring Hannah's mother and enquire about the baby.
Letting it be known she was in every afternoon the
following week, she hoped they would be able to pop
round. Hannah wondered who was looking after the
haberdashery shop but that was Fae's business and if
she was going to be at home, it was a lovely excuse for
a visit.

She decided this time to take something *she* had made,
so a tin of moist fruitcake went into the large bag with
all Jack's bits and pieces. After a lot of discussion and
many negative points raised by Michael, he had finally
agreed to get her a small car. It was several years old
and a bit battered, but Hannah loved it. It was hers and
it meant she could take Jack out more. Her father had
taken it immediately to his friend, Eric Brooking, who
was a mechanic and had given it the once over. A set of
new tyres, a battery, along with windscreen wipers, and
her father told her it was now road worthy.

Michael had never been so pleased to get back to work.
To his relief, Shelby was apologetic about her terse phone

call and admitted to just getting his back up about Mr Pearce.

'I'm so worried that the baby will take all your attention now,' she pouted. 'If things get difficult, maybe I'll have to go to another office.' Looking down at the floor sadly, she waited

'I don't want to hear any more of that sort of talk,' he panicked. 'Shelby, darling, I know it's difficult at the moment, but it's you I want to be with; it's just Hannah and… Jack. I need time to sort it out.'

'I understand that. Listen, give it a few months, and then think about how you can do it. You're the boy's father; you can still see him and spend time with him.' *Somewhere else, not with me, thank you very much.*

Michael felt things were fast running out of his control. Deep down, he knew he couldn't keep juggling two lives like this, but he didn't want to lose Shelby. He didn't want to hurt Hannah either, but when he thought of his future, she really didn't fit into it. What on earth was he going to do?

Hannah pulled up outside Ivy Cottage and quickly assembled the pushchair for Jack. It was one that could be used right from new-born up to toddler and she was so grateful to her parents. The bag fitted underneath and he hardly stirred in the transfer from his car seat.

Fae was waiting by the front door. 'Hannah, dear, I'm so pleased you came, let's have a look at the little fellow.'

'Not so little,' laughed Hannah, 'but here he is, asleep at the moment.'

'Well, he's very handsome; I think he has a look of you about him. Come in, it's a bit chilly out here for him. The kitchen's nice and warm and I've moved one of the armchairs in for you.'

'Oh Fae, you shouldn't have gone to that trouble, and who's looking after the shop…?' Hannah was left talking to an empty doorway as Fae turned and walked through the cottage. *Oh well, she must have it organised.*

The kitchen *was* warm and full of delicious baking smells.

'Are you feeling alright now, dear? Your mother said you had a difficult time. You do look well, I must say.'

'I'm fine, it was a bit difficult for the first couple of weeks, but my husband took some time off, which was a help.' *Maybe two or three days of it was a bit of a help.*

'How splendid,' said Fae, trying to hide the doubt in her voice and wondering who Hannah was trying to convince. 'I have some scones and some more honeycomb, I know you enjoyed it last time, and there's some for you to take again. What a shame he's a bit too young to enjoy it, maybe later.'

'I've brought something as well.' Hannah produced the fruit cake, which Fae was delighted with and immediately made the tea, producing the warm, soft scones with honey. After they'd eaten and drunk their tea, Jack woke up.

'Would you like to feed him?' Hannah asked.

'Oh, I'd love to, thank you, dear. Shall I warm his milk?'

Hannah handed the bottle over and it was quickly passed back feeling as if it was the correct temperature. *How did she do that so quickly?* 'Why don't you sit in this comfy chair, Fae, and I'll pass him to you.' Fae took Jack as if he was the most precious object and beamed as he took the bottle beautifully. The golden dust was swirling around again. *Wherever does that come from?*

Finished, and back in his reclining seat, Jack didn't fall asleep or grizzle, as he sometimes did, but lay with his eyes open, and if Hannah didn't know better, she would have sworn he was studying his surroundings. *Maybe he is, maybe he's very advanced?*

'He's happy enough; warm and fed now,' said Fae. 'There are blackberries in the garden, if you'd like to pick them and take some home.'

'If you can spare them, I'd love some; shall I pick any for you?'

'Not for me. You take as many as you'd like. I'll sit and keep an eye on Jack, we're friends now, aren't we little fellow?' She passed Hannah the tin that the fruit cake came in. 'Fill this one up.'

As Hannah went down the garden path, a group of what looked like colourful butterflies flew into the kitchen.

'Tch.' Fae brushed them away from Jack. 'Not too close now, and a very quick look if you please. You know what curiosity did.' She didn't really blame them; babies were so fascinating, such innocence before they grew and sometimes developed greed or avarice, or worse.

Hannah was picking the plumpest and juiciest blackberries she'd ever seen. Careful not to pick too many, as she glanced back over where she'd already been, the branches looked full again. *How could I have missed all those?* In no time, her tin was full and the bushes still hung heavy with fruit. Walking back up through the garden, a cloud of butterflies drifted past her and she heard the faint sound of tinkling laughter.

Fae was talking quietly to Jack, who almost looked like he was smiling.

'Are there children around here, Fae? I thought I heard some.'

'Not that I know of, dear, but you know children, they get into all sorts of adventures. I see you got a nice lot of fruit.'

'Yes, thank you, I'll make you a pot of jam. Umm, Fae, I hope you don't mind me asking, but I don't see a car here. How do you get to your own shop and do your normal shopping? I would be happy to give you a lift if you ever have a heavy load to get.'

'That's very kind of you, dear, I'll remember that, thank you so much. Now I'll make another pot of tea before you have to go.'

Michael came back to the office looking very pleased with himself, and called Shelby in for a meeting.

'That shopping mall deal, Mr Pearce is off the scene, there's a much bigger developer interested, which will mean a bigger commission for me.'

'You mean us, don't you? The firm, that's what you meant.' She knew exactly who the developer was, a subsidiary company of her father's that he used when he didn't want his name involved. When Shelby had explained the deal, he could see what a little gold mine it was. He would make a pretty penny out of it and was happy to let Michael deal with it. If his daughter was going to end up with this Michael, the man would need every penny he could earn. If he ended up messing Shelby about, he would be swatted like a fly.

'That's what I meant,' he said crossly, omitting to mention the 'personal' cash in hand deal he was getting alongside the official one. 'Anyway, we should celebrate. Can I take you out tonight?'

'If *you're* able to get out, I'm free. How long can you spare me?' she asked a little sarcastically.

'Shelby, don't be like that, I always try to put you first, but I have responsibilities at the moment, you said you understood that.'

'I do, but I'm not sitting around like a spare part forever, Michael, I want to be a permanent fixture, and if you can't see that happening then please tell me now.'

He flew into a panic. 'Don't do this to me at work; I won't be able to concentrate. I do want you, you know that; just give me a while. Christ, the baby's only a month old. Let things settle down a bit.'

'Sure, I just want to know where I stand.'

'At the top, I can assure you. Now, are we on for tonight?'

She leant over the desk so he saw right down her cleavage. 'I think I could manage that.'

* * *

Two weeks later, Hannah took some pots of jam over to her parents, on her usual visit with Jack. She was sure she had seen the first real smile from him that morning and was hoping for a repeat performance this afternoon. Also in the car was a cake, for the staff of Furze House, who she had phoned earlier. Apologising for not visiting for a while, she asked how Doreen was. Informed that there was no real change, she decided to take Jack along with a photograph of Michael, which sometimes got a reaction. Doreen never seemed to know who Hannah was.

Her parents were, as always, delighted to see her. After they'd settled down, had a chat, and Mr Worth had gone to see to things in the vegetable patch, Margaret fixed a look on her daughter.

'Hannah, you're not happy, I can see it. What's the matter and how can it be fixed?'

About to protest, the words died on her lips and she looked back miserably. 'Things aren't brilliant at home. Michael's out nearly every evening and hardly sees Jack. He does do a bit on weekends but I always have to ask and he's not interested in… me at all.'

'Well, you can't get back to that right away, not after what you've had done.'

'No, but he doesn't even want to sit with me when we watch television and never even gives me a cuddle anymore. I must disgust him.'

Her mother looked shocked. 'Whatever are you talking about? There's nothing wrong with you.'

'Look at me, I'm huge.'

'Now you listen to me, my girl. You are *not* huge. You still have a bit of baby weight, that's to be expected, that'll go soon.'

'I'm *fat,* how could anybody fancy me?'

'You were overweight before you married and you lost that. I must admit, you put some on again, but you didn't gain much during pregnancy, you told me that yourself. You're wearing those loose maternity clothes that you don't need anymore. You just see yourself as fat, my darling, I've been reading about that in my magazine.'

Hannah thought about what her mother had said. She hadn't really studied herself in the mirror for a while; there was a memory of what she looked like pregnant and it wouldn't go away. It was true, she was wearing very loose clothes. *I wonder?*

'Mum, could you watch Jack while I sort some stuff out upstairs?'

Mrs Worth smiled as she watched her daughter go upstairs and then, frowning, thought what she'd like to do to that no-good son-in-law of theirs.

Hannah stood in her old bedroom and looked at some of the clothes she'd pulled out from storage. Not the ones worn around the time of her marriage, that was a bit hopeful, but some of the others. The lovely gypsy top was slipped on. She stared in amazement at the mirror, the blouse was swamping her. Quickly, that was put to one side for alterations. The dress that she'd made for her date with Michael, that fitted well and could probably be taken in after another month or two. The pile of clothes needing nips and tucks grew steadily. *Mum was right, I'm not that bad.*

Perhaps if she changed her image from blowsy mum to the girl he used to know and put on a bit of make-up, Michael might take more notice of her. A little voice at the back of her head telling her how superficial that was and he should accept her as she was rankled a bit, but she pushed it aside and decided to make an effort. Perhaps she should get a different hairstyle as well? It was looking a bit untidy.

One quick look at the wedding dress, which she did every so often; it was so beautiful and such a shame that it was never seen. What could be done with it? It would have to be something very special. *I'll know when the time is right.*

'Mum, thanks for making me take a look at myself, you were right, I just need to lick myself into shape a bit and I've got a pile of alterations to take home and work on. Could you give me the number of that lady who comes to the house to do hair?'

'Oh Hannah, I'll look after Jack while you have your hair done. Go to the salon in town and treat yourself.'

'Aren't they a bit trendy?'

'What are you, an old maid? You're a young woman, get yourself there.'

'Okay Mum.'

After a pleasant afternoon and a bag full of vegetables from the garden, Hannah and Jack drove to Badgers Bottom and Furze House. The staff came, in turn, to admire Jack, and presented Hannah with a romper suit and a 'baby's first mug'.

'Thank you for the cake, I'll put a piece on a plate for Doreen. She's having one of her better days so hopefully she won't throw it at you,' one of the girls said. 'I've put her in the side room on her own; the baby might be too much excitement for some of them, especially Mavis.'

Mavis was a lady who always carried a rag doll and believed it was her own baby. Hannah felt desperately sorry for her and, in fact, all the residents of the home. She hoped her parents would never go down the road that Doreen's mind had taken.

Doreen was sitting and humming to herself when Hannah took Jack to meet his other grandmother.

'Complete and utter waste of time,' Michael had said when she suggested they all go one Sunday. 'He could catch something horrible there, you shouldn't take him.'

'They're not sick,' Hannah snapped. 'If there was an outbreak of flu or something else unsavoury, the staff would let us know. It's her first grandson, it may be the only time she ever sees him.'

'You could stick a potato in front of her face and say it's a baby, it wouldn't make a blind bit of difference.'

'That's a terrible thing to say, whatever's the matter with you lately?'

He grumbled something about problems at work so Hannah didn't ask him again, just went by herself.

'Hello Doreen, it's me, Hannah. I have a surprise for you.'

Doreen peered up suspiciously and then smiled. 'Hello love, nice to see you.' As she often said this when it was obvious she didn't remember who Hannah was, it didn't mean any more than that she was in good humour.

Hannah tried something else, showing her the picture of Michael. There was a flash of recognition and then, nothing. She lifted Jack out of his carrier.

Doreen's face lit up with great excitement. 'Michael,' she cried, and tried to grab Jack.

The carer jumped forward. 'It's not Michael, this is your grandson and this is Hannah, she's married to Michael.'

Doreen looked very confused. 'Michael's married? How old is he?'

'He's thirty one now,' Hannah said gently.

'Twenty-six!' She shrieked. 'I've got a son of thirty one? Well, how old am I then?'

'You'll be seventy one, next birthday,' Hannah tried again. 'This is Jack, you're his grandmother.'

'No, no,' Doreen wailed and started rocking.

'I'm so sorry,' said the young girl, 'she wasn't too bad earlier.'

'It's alright, it was worth a try. At least I can tell Jack he did meet her, even if it was only once. I'll take him away now.'

Doreen grabbed her cup, which thankfully was plastic, and hurled it towards Hannah as she was leaving the room.

Michael was doing a half-hearted session at the gym. Shelby wasn't there and had 'other arrangements' that evening. He knew she was playing games with him and putting him under pressure. Why couldn't she be a bit more patient and understanding? He couldn't just walk out on a wife and new-born baby. Resenting the position she had put him in, he was trying to imagine life without her while he was on the rowing machine. The trouble was, he didn't want a life without her.

Sven passed him, muscles rippling, and giving him a pitying look as if to say 'is that the best you can do'. Michael gave up and spent time in the steam room before having a long shower. He would eat at home for a change, Hannah would rustle up something tasty fairly quickly. He'd have a quick look at his son and then enjoy a beer while watching the match that was on tonight. It would never occur to him that *she* might want to watch something.

He swaggered back into the house to find it empty. Her car was in the drive so where was she? Annoyed, he phoned her mobile.

'Hello Michael, I thought you were at the gym.'

'I packed up early and came home for tea, where are you?'

'Jack wasn't settling so I've taken him for a walk, we're in the park.'

'It's chilly out, how long will you be? I'm hungry now.'

'He's wrapped up well, I didn't expect you, so nothing's prepared. By the time I walk back, it'll be half an hour and then he'll have to be changed and put to bed. There's a casserole in the freezer, if you put that in the oven now, it'll be ready in an hour.'

'Right.' Fuming, he found the casserole and put it in. Grabbing some cheese and biscuits to keep him going, he sat in front of the TV. It wasn't too much to expect, was it? A meal when he got home? Disregarding the fact that he hadn't eaten a weekday meal at home for months, he sat grumbling and mentally listing her faults until she got back.

'Jack's fast asleep and he doesn't feel wet so I'll put him straight to bed. There's a film on channel...'

'Can I have mine on a tray when it's ready? I'm watching the match now. I've had a really bad day, I just want to relax.'

She stared at him in disbelief. No how was your day or, how's our son. Blinking back her tears, she took Jack upstairs. It wasn't worth a row; he'd be in a better mood after the casserole. It had nice herby dumplings, one of his favourites. Perhaps she should ask him a bit about *his* work; he hadn't been very forthcoming when asked before, but she'd try again.

Watching Jack's angelic face for a few minutes while he slept, she couldn't understand why Michael took so little interest in him. All men wanted a son, didn't they?

She waited until half-time and an advert break before serving up his tea. 'I saw your mother today.'

'That must have been riveting,' he grunted.

'She thought Jack was you and got very upset.'

'I told you it was a waste of time; any more of these dumplings? Some bread and butter would be nice to soak up some of this gravy as well.'

Sighing, she dished herself out a small bowlful and gave him two more of the dumplings along with a doorstep of bread, slathered with butter. 'What happened to the healthy eating?'

'I can have a free day occasionally, I work it off. My bag is by the washing machine.'

Biting her tongue, *again*, Hannah later unpacked the bag and put a wash on. She had a feeling of satisfaction and amusement as she shoved two baby-sick-covered outfits in with his precious sports gear.

Passing him a hot chocolate later, she asked, 'Are you coming up to bed?'

He looked cagey. 'Er, a bit later, I need to prepare some work for tomorrow. Thanks for the chocolate.'

'I was going to ask you about how it's going at work.'

'You don't need to bother yourself with that; you've got enough to think about here. Let me worry about work.'

Upstairs, she reached for her book, 'The Duke's Legacy', quickly forgetting Michael and his selfishness.

Chapter Fifteen

UNRAVELLING

Untangle, separate

THREE MONTHS LATER

Hannah snipped the last stitch of the blouse, allowing herself a satisfied smile. All the clothes she had taken from her old house to alter had been done and re-done as she lost more weight. She was now 20 pounds lighter than when she'd come out of the hospital.

She and Michael had reached a form of stalemate. They shared a bed but didn't sleep together. During the week, he came home late and told her little of what he was doing. Sundays were still spent at home but he often took Jack out for a walk or a drive so Hannah could have 'time to herself'.

This weekend would be make or break as far as she was concerned. Always keeping herself covered up at night, Michael hadn't seen her properly for months. It was his birthday on Saturday and Jack was going to stay with her parents. Hannah was going to surprise him with a two-night stay in London. They needed time to discover each other again; that's what she'd told her mother. Surprisingly, she'd also unburdened herself to Fae on a visit.

'My dear, you look troubled. It's not my business, of course, but I have a wise head on these shoulders if you need somebody to listen.' Fae had looked kindly at her. Hannah was quiet for a few minutes and Fae was afraid she wasn't going to open up at all.

'Fae, I don't mean to be personal, but were you ever married?'

'No never,' Fae said gently, 'but, as I said, I'm very wise.'

And then it had all come tumbling out. How grateful she felt at the beginning when somebody had taken an interest in her, the difficulties settling in with Doreen and no support from Michael. Then, the problems in the last few months, no, she admitted, it was more than months.

'We're living like brother and sister, but I'm sure even a brother would give me more consideration than he does. I don't like criticising Michael, but you've never met him, so it's a bit easier.'

Fae pursed her lips at the last remark. Never met him? No, not in the flesh, but she knew him alright, a most unworthy recipient of this lovely girl's affections.

'So, what I thought,' Hannah continued, 'was to book us a surprise weekend away for his birthday in a couple of weeks and maybe he'll remember why he liked me.'

Fae was as angry as she could allow herself to be. Remember why he liked her indeed. It wasn't her place or her mission to interfere, just to lend a helping hand or guidance when appropriate.

'Well, it seems like a good plan, dear, I hope he'll appreciate it.' Swallowing the bitter taste that came with these words, she knew Hannah was in for a very bad time of her life. 'I'm glad you feel you can talk to me, but please, don't put yourself down. You have no need to feel grateful that somebody is attracted to you. You're a very special person and whoever comes into your life will...' She corrected herself quickly. '... *should* be because they genuinely can see you for what you are. They would get as much out of the relationship as they're prepared to put in. Just remember, I'll always be here if you need me.'

'Fae, that's so good of you. Do you know, I'm glad that store closed because if it hadn't, I'd never have met you and you're such a good friend and so kind. I never knew either of my grandmothers but I feel like I've found one in you.'

'Oh, get away with you.' Fae almost blushed and a faint laughing sound blew around the room. 'Perhaps I could be… your honorary Godmother; I would feel happy if you looked at me in that way, dear.'

* * *

Hannah's mother had plenty to say when asked if she was alright to look after Jack for a couple of days.

'He doesn't deserve you, I'm sorry, but it needs saying. He's the most selfish man I've ever met. Your father and I gave him the benefit of the doubt when we first met him. He was completely spoiled by his mother but we both hoped getting married would buck his ideas up a bit.'

'It didn't help that we lived with Doreen for so long, he just carried on as if nothing had changed. I thought being a father would make things better between us. I know Jack wasn't exactly planned but he wasn't *un*planned either. We'd both expected to have a family at some time.' Hannah looked miserable.

'I hope this trip will be good for you both,' her mother sighed. 'You need to put your foot down a bit more and not be treated like his housekeeper.'

'I know, I just don't like arguing. Can I leave Jack with you for half an hour? I want to go and make an appointment for my hair and I think they do make-up as well.'

***

Shelby looked in the mirror and admired the highlights she'd had done. 'Jonathan, that's fabulous as usual, thank you.'

'Always a pleasure to do your hair, my darling. Maybe one day, you'll let me show you what else I'm good at.'

Shelby laughed. They always had friendly banter between them, but Jonathan was in a happy and steady relationship with a long-term boyfriend. 'I haven't booked it, but is there any chance of a manicure while I'm here? I don't have to rush back to the office.' That was one of the benefits of having Michael as a boss; he could always be persuaded to let her slip away for a while.

Jonathan came back with the diary. 'If you don't mind waiting for 15 minutes, we can fit you in. Why don't you go and sit down with a magazine and I'll have someone make you a coffee?'

Shelby sat happily with the latest glossy gossip selection when she overheard the rather plain-looking woman at the desk.

'I wonder if it would be possible to make an appointment?'

The painted doll-like figure at reception gave her a doubtful look. 'What exactly did you have in mind? The salon further down is more your thing, shampoo and set, is it?'

'Well,' Hannah said nervously, 'I was thinking of a completely different style and maybe a slight colour?'

The doll brightened up considerably. 'Jonathan, could you come and have a word with this lady?'

Shelby, flicking through her magazine, was half listening with amusement. Jonathan would have his work cut out there for sure.

'Hmm, the first thing I would do is cut off at least eight inches to give it some body and lift. It would frame your face better, with some layers. The colour's not too bad; just make it a shade lighter maybe?' Jonathan was always happy to grab a new client.

Eight inches off? 'Whatever you think,' she said firmly. 'I need a complete change; can I have my make-up done as well?'

'When would you like to come in?' asked the doll.

Hannah gave the date, a Friday, in three weeks' time. 'Could it be as late as possible in the afternoon?'

'A special night out, is it?'

'Well, actually, it's a big surprise for my husband. I've booked a weekend away and I want to collect him straight from work. It's his birthday, so I want to look really special.'

That reminds me, it's Michael's birthday in a couple of weeks; maybe I could plan something. Shelby was still half listening and studying the latest catwalk designs.

'We will work magic for you,' said Jonathan. 'Your husband will not recognise you. Katrina will book you in and I look forward to seeing you, Mrs...?'

'Rawlings, Hannah Rawlings, thank you so much.'

Crash!

Everybody jumped and turned to see the flustered woman picking up a broken coffee cup and rushing to the restroom.

'Oh dear,' Jonathan said, 'I will go and see if she's alright. See you soon, er, Hannah, wasn't it?'

Katrina made the appointment and offered Hannah a style book to take with her for some ideas. 'But the best thing to do is let Jonathan take charge, he'll know what suits you.'

In the ladies, Shelby was shaking with fury. That was *Hannah*? That plain-looking housewife was Michael's *wife*? Splashing her face with cold water, she took a deep breath. The door opened a crack.

'Shelby, my darling, are you alright?'

'I'm fine,' she snapped. 'Cancel that manicure, I'm not in the mood now.'

'Whatever you say, darling.' *Bitch*.

She had to do something, this could be a disaster. She'd only heard passing remarks about Hannah from one or two of the staff who remembered her. Mumsy, that was one description, and another painted her as 'plump, to be ever so polite'. Apparently, she'd lost weight for the wedding but put it on again. And horror of horrors, she'd *made* her own wedding dress. Who did that, for God's sake? No, this wouldn't do at all, sabotage was needed here. As she thought about it, a cruel smile crossed her face. An idea was forming, an idea that would light the fuse for an explosion.

Humble pie had to be eaten, so she apologised to Jonathan, explaining she'd had a message on her phone that upset her. Going to the desk, she smiled sweetly at Katrina.

'I was going to make an appointment at the time that lady asked about, I think it was the same day. What time would she finish? Could you squeeze me in at all?'

'I don't see how.' Katrina studied the diary. 'We may run over 15 minutes, she really wanted it to be at the end of the day so as to get to hubby's office at 5.30p.m. Hope he likes it, she'll certainly look better when she leaves than she does at the moment.'

Shelby thought what a dreadful receptionist the girl was, talking about clients, but it was for her own benefit this time.

'We could squeeze you in before she comes...'

'No, forget it, perhaps I'll come in the day before instead.' Shelby only wanted to know what time Hannah would be leaving. If things worked out as she planned, *Hannah* and Michael would get a very nasty shock.

When she got back to the office, to Michael's surprise, she made him a cup of tea, proper tea as well, not that herbal stuff that she liked, and whispered suggestions in his ear for that evening, which made him unable to concentrate for the rest of the afternoon.

Back at her parents' house, Hannah told her mother what Jonathan had said.

'You're going to cut your lovely hair?' her mother stared in dismay. 'Oh well, it's your hair, I suppose, it may be easier for you to look after. I hope you're doing the right thing.'

'Actually, I'm quite excited about it now. Look at some of these styles; with all the products that are available, I don't think it would be difficult to keep it looking good.'

They pored over the magazine and Mrs Worth realised what a difference it could make to her daughter and so, encouraged her. Her father came in from the garden.

'Hannah's going to get a new hairstyle, Ron, isn't that a good idea?'

'Why don't you let your mother give it a trim? Save you a fortune.'

'It's more than a trim, Dad, and I'm having it lightened a shade.'

Mr Worth looked very puzzled. 'I don't think I can contribute to this conversation. Shall I put the kettle on, m'dear?'

Hannah tried to think how many times in the years past that Michael had offered to put the kettle on, let alone make a cup of tea. Her orders were starting to come in again, people relied on her now, and she would put it to him that she was also contributing and deserved a bit more help in their marriage. Hannah was sure that after their weekend away, things would be better. He would know that she still loved him.

I do love him, don't I?

Pushing that niggling doubt aside she felt more positive.

* * *

'Michael, it's your birthday tomorrow, my parents have offered to take us out for a meal. I said yes, I'm sure you can fit us in for this occasion.'

Damn, I'll have to explain to Shelby. 'What about Jack though?' he asked, hopeful that Hannah wouldn't bring him along.

'Mrs Figgins will babysit. We won't be gone that long and he should sleep right through. I'll have my phone if there's a problem.'

'Fine.' Why was she still wearing those awful baggy clothes? She didn't care what she looked like these days, was it any wonder he didn't want to be around her when she made no effort? He couldn't help but compare her to Shelby. That woman really took care of her body and had a real pride in her appearance. She took care of *his* body as well. His mind drifted back to last night in her hot tub; he didn't know anybody could hold their breath that long...

'Michael, why have you got that silly grin on your face?'

'Eh, what? It's nothing, I'm off to work now; did you pack my gym bag?'

'No, I was too busy last night. If you noticed, I did a huge pile of ironing. Your stuff will be on the spare bed.' Hannah turned and busied herself with mashing Jack's rusk, which he'd just started having in the mornings. Let him pack his own gym bag, maybe he'd appreciate what she did for him a bit more.

Grumbling that he was going to be late now, she heard him banging around upstairs and cursing when he obviously couldn't find something or other.

He came down, red in the face. 'Well, now I've got to rush. I'll be late tonight, a few early birthday drinks with the lads.'

'Aren't you going to say goodbye to your son?'

'I don't want that mess on my suit, bye Jack.' He was gone.

As soon as Jack had finished his rusk and rewarded Hannah with a gummy smile, she bathed, changed him, talked to and played with him until he was sleepy, then put him down for a nap.

* * *

The next morning, after Michael had gone, she pulled a case down from the top of the wardrobe and packed his clothes for the weekend. Her bag was carefully packed with all the clothes he hadn't seen her in for a long time, including some new ones she'd made. Hidden in the cupboard, which she brought out now, was the dress she was going to wear tonight when she surprised him. It was black and close-fitting, accentuating her best points. She had put a lining of the special 'pink' fabric from Fae, which showed through in certain places where she'd allowed a cut-out, the shape of which also flattered her curves. It was totally different to the things she normally wore and she was pinning her hopes on that and her 'new look' to bowl him over.

At the office, Michael tried to explain about the meal with Hannah's parents and was gob-smacked at Shelby's reaction.

'Well, of course, Michael, you have to do these things, I completely understand, it's not a problem. We'll celebrate tomorrow and I have a special present for you.' She bent down and whispered in his ear. 'I've got a beautiful butterfly vajazzle.'

'A butterfly what?'

She explained.

'I can't wait to see it.' His fingers trailed up the inside of her skirt.

'Down boy,' she smirked. 'I'm not wearing any underwear.'

'Oh Christ,' he groaned. 'You can't make me wait.'

'You don't have to wait. Let everybody go a bit early tonight, it's Friday, they'll be delighted. You'll have time before your meal and I'll give you a private viewing, here on the desk, I'm feeling *very* naughty.'

Hannah arrived for her appointment and Katrina looked at her in amazement.

'That's a fabulous dress, where did you get that?

'I made it, it's my design.' Hannah was pleased that this fashionable youngster liked it.

Jonathan came over to greet her. 'Darling! You look *faaabulous*. Wait until I've finished with you, you won't recognise yourself. Katrina, a glass of wine for Hannah, if you please.'

'Oh, I don't know...'

'Just what you need to relax, no arguments. Now, I'm going to turn the mirror away so you won't see my wonderful creation until the end.'

Hannah gave up and gave herself over to Jonathan. A little uneasy when she saw the long lengths of hair falling to the floor, she shut her eyes and sipped her wine.

'I'm going to colour it before I give it the final cut and shape,' he said. 'It's looking better already.'

While the highlights were setting, one of the girls gave her a hand massage and tidied her nails. Hannah had never felt so pampered. Grace, the beautician, came and studied her face.

'You've got beautiful skin, it only needs enhancing. But your eyes need to be brought out more and I'll just pop on a few lash extensions, not falsies,' she said, seeing Hannah's doubtful look. 'You won't even know you're wearing these.' She smiled. 'Just trust me.'

Hannah was taken back to the chair, hair snipped again and blow-dried with a lot of mousse and wax at the end of it all. Then Grace took over.

Finally, they stood around, all staring at her. Everybody else had left the salon.

'What's wrong?' Hannah was alarmed. Had this all been a terrible mistake?

'It is even better than I thought,' Jonathan was beaming. 'I have excelled myself, you look 10 years younger. I could almost fancy you myself.' He turned the mirror around with a flourish.

Michael's staff were absolutely delighted to get an early pass. He told them he had drinks with some friends for his birthday and it was *his* present to them. Shelby looked busy at her desk, as if she was finishing off some paperwork. They all knew, of course, it was obvious, and as they left, were gossiping to each other about 'the affair' and taking bets on what his birthday present from her would be.

Shelby was watching the clock; this had to be timed just right. Going to the fridge, she poured two glasses of wine.

'You'd better lock the front door, we don't want to be disturbed. I'll pull the blinds down.' She was careful to make sure there was a light on, which would show through, and also checked that the back door was unbolted.

'Here's a glass of wine, birthday boy. Now, let me show you your present.'

Hannah looked at her reflection in total disbelief. She was silent for so long, the others became nervous.

'You... do like it, don't you?' asked Jonathan.

She found her voice. 'Like it? I *love* it. You were right, I don't recognise myself; this is someone else, not me.'

'I can assure you that *is* you. You were always there; you needed somebody like *me* to find you.' Jonathan was ecstatic. He had performed one of his best transformations.

Hannah was still staring. Her hair was gone and in its place, a totally new style, which lifted her features instead of dragging them down. It was young, spiky and fun. Jonathan was explaining how she would style it herself and she just nodded assent to all the products he suggested. Her eyes looked enormous, sultry and smoky, but not too heavy looking. Her skin had a glow and a faint blush, and her lips looked moist and inviting. He guided her to the full-length mirror and removed the cape from her shoulders. With her new image and the dress, she felt like a different person, a wicked woman about to seduce her lover. Michael would make her feel like the Dukes did with their women, she just knew it.

'I can't thank you enough; I didn't believe you could make me into this.'

Even the painted doll looked suspiciously as if she had a tear in her eye.

Jonathan presented her with the bill, 'And a few complimentary products. Now, go and get him, darling.'

The cases were in the car, which was parked outside. She got in, admiring herself again in the mirror.

Pulling up outside the office, she was surprised to see the blinds down, but there was a light on. He must have sent them home early and stayed. He *did* work hard, she thought, a little guiltily; she never really asked him about it. Well, that would change.

Going to the back door, as she wanted to really surprise him, she tried the code, which was still the same, and was pleased that he hadn't put the bolt over.

A shadow was visible in his office, which looked as if he was standing, hopefully packing up, and then she heard a laugh and a shriek.

Suddenly, feeling very cold, she put her hand on the door handle.

The sight that greeted her would haunt her for years. A pair of long, slim legs were wrapped around his body and she could see his buttocks moving and thrusting into a girl, a naked girl, who had her head thrown back and was shouting his name.

Shelby peeped through her eyelashes. *Wow, she looks gorgeous, and what a fantastic dress.* 'Michael, give it to me, darling.' She'd timed it perfectly. Opening her eyes, she rounded them in shock and she screamed. 'Oh, my God, Michael, stop!'

'Stop, are you crazy?' He finished with a roar and then saw her face. Turning, his blood ran cold. There was Hannah. She looked amazing, what had she done to herself?

Hannah was as white as a sheet and shaking with rage and shock.

Michael was awkwardly trying to pull up and zip his trousers, Shelby just sat, making sure her magnificent body was being shown to its best advantage.

'Michael, who is this?' she asked in all innocence.

'Hannah!'

Hannah had turned and run.

'My wife... she saw us, oh God, oh *God*.'

She saw us alright. 'Michael, calm down. I know it's a shock but at least she knows.'

Michael was the one now shaking. Hannah marched back in with a suitcase and threw it across the room.

'That was what I'd packed for our surprise trip. Take it and stay with ... with *her*. Don't come near me or Jack.' She ran again.

Michael stood with his life, and his trousers, falling down.

Chapter Sixteen

SPLIT BACKSTITCH

Poke the needle through to the back of the
fabric, splitting the stitch as you do

Hannah sat outside the house, hands frozen on the steering wheel. The drive back had been a complete blur. *I shouldn't have driven, I could have hurt somebody, or worse.* The reality hit her and she realised how cold she was. Letting herself into the house, she collapsed on the sofa and then the tears came.

Back in the office, Michael was also in shock. 'She should never have found out that way, it must have been horrible for her. I ought to go home and talk about it.'

That was the last thing Shelby wanted. Dressed now, she feigned concern and worry for Hannah. 'Listen, she's had a terrible shock and needs to sort her head out on her own. Come back to mine tonight, you're in no state to talk now. Both of you should sleep on it and maybe go over later tomorrow when it's sunk in and she's a bit calmer.'

'Do you really think that's the best thing?' He was such a coward, he didn't want to face her at all, but it would have to be done. 'It didn't look like her; she's done herself up, big-time.'

'Has she? Oh dear, it's a bit late now, isn't it? You'd better not lie to her; you'll have to come clean. She may want to talk to me and find out how long this has been going on.'

That fact hit him hard. He really didn't want to hurt her but he knew he had, badly. Would she forgive him? Probably, if he wanted her to, but then he couldn't be with Shelby, and he wasn't prepared to give *her* up. He wasn't happy at home, so what was the point? She had looked good, from what he'd seen. Why hadn't she bothered before?

'Okay, I'll leave it till tomorrow, I'm sure you know best.'

Hannah cried till no more tears came. The pictures in her head wouldn't go away, that girl with her legs wrapped around Michael. Who was she? It must be that assistant manager he'd taken on and never said very much about; the reason was obvious now. She wondered how long it had been going on. Surely, this wasn't a one-off, but then, perhaps it was. They'd been working late together, maybe had a couple of drinks. Who was she kidding, Hannah thought furiously.

Would she forgive him, *could* she forgive him? What was she going to say if he came back tonight? It got later and later, with no sign of him. *Please come back and explain.* If he came back tonight, there may be hope.

Eventually, she tore the dress off and stuffed it in the bin. Scrubbing the make-up off, she looked at her tear-stained, blotchy face. *Look what you've made me turn into.* How could she ever compare to that thin, beautiful girl with legs that went on forever? She lay in bed, crying again, and hoping against hope that she would hear his key in the door.

'I don't know if I'm doing the right thing, Shelby. Maybe I should go back and talk to her tonight. I owe her that, surely?'

For God's sake. 'It's very late now; it won't do either of you any good. Wait until tomorrow, you're not thinking clearly at the moment. You need to get your thoughts together and plan what you're going to say and how you're going to sort it out.'

Michael was nursing a large glass of brandy that Shelby had forced on him. *Sort it out? What a nightmare.*

'It wouldn't be so bad if it was just the two of us, but I have a son...'

'Of course,' she soothed, 'and I would *never* expect you to try and take him away. Children belong with their mothers. You'll be able to go and visit him whenever you want, I'm sure. He'll have to be provided for while he's a child, but she can work in some capacity, can't she?' *I don't want anything to do with it.*

'She works from home now, it's just... where are they going to live? I can't kick them out.'

'It's your house, isn't it? Why don't you suggest she goes back to her parents, make it seem like she can look after them *and* she'll have help with the baby.'

'Well, yes, I suppose so. I'll leave it till tomorrow, you're right. Come here, I need to take my mind off things.'

Shelby didn't need asking twice.

***

Michael wasn't coming back. Hannah's thoughts of forgiveness, maybe trying to get past this situation, were gone. Sleep completely eluded her and she went over and over it all until the dawn light was peeping through the curtains. Jack was now the most important person in her life. Michael would always be his father, she wouldn't deny him that, although he hadn't been much of one so far.

Her parents, they would have to know. As far as they were aware, she and Michael would now be in London, celebrating his birthday. She wouldn't go and see them until later, although part of her just wanted to let her mother make it all better, but that wasn't going to happen. This couldn't be made better and it was her problem to deal with.

She sent Michael a text: *'We need to talk.'* He was going to do right by his son; she would make sure of that, if nothing else. She didn't care about herself and didn't want to stay in this house, of that, she was certain.

In the bathroom, she was shocked again by her new look. Her hair was a complete birds' nest so she dragged a brush through it and pressed a cold flannel on her face until some of the puffiness had gone. She pulled on some old clothes; why should she bother for his benefit now?

There was a text on her phone. *'I'll be over after lunch. Sorry.'*

Sorry, was that it? And how could he think about lunch? The thought of food made Hannah feel sick so she just made a cup of tea. They should have been having breakfast in the hotel she'd booked. *Don't think about it, I don't want to start crying again.*

Michael hovered on the doorstep, wondering whether to just go in or ring the bell. *Damn, it's my house.* 'Hannah?' He walked into the front room and eyed her warily. 'I'm sorry you saw what you did, I didn't want you to find out that way.'

'I guess you didn't want me to find out at all, did you? How long did you think you could carry on with a double life, or maybe you just didn't think?'

'I was going to tell you,' he said feebly, 'I was waiting for the right time.'

'The right time,' she repeated the words slowly. 'Just when would that be, I wonder? On Jack's first birthday, when he starts school, or... no, I've got it, when he grows up and you don't have to be responsible for him.'

'That's not fair; it was going to be soon. You have to admit, we haven't been happy for some time.'

'That was one of the reasons I booked us a weekend away, what a fool I was.'

He looked very uncomfortable; he'd expected her to be in floods of tears. 'I do feel bad about that and... you did look good yesterday.'

'How dare you! You have no right to say that to me. Who is she, by the way, your new assistant manager, I take it?' Her eyes were shining and she was fighting against breaking down in front of him. If he'd taken her in his arms and told her how sorry he was, she may still have melted.

'Yes, but that doesn't matter. Look, I'm sorry, really I am, but I want to be with her.'

That was it, he'd said it, there was no going back.

'So, the last six years and Jack, it all means nothing to you?'

'Of course it means something but people change, Hannah, I've changed. I want more from life. I am really sorry that I've hurt you but,' he suddenly felt very noble, 'I'd hurt you more if I stayed.'

'I see; you're doing me a favour?'

'I get it, you're angry, but there's no need to be sarcastic.'

'No, that isn't me, is it? Meek as a mouse Hannah, well, you said it, Michael, people change. So, what happens now?'

He was rather taken aback; this wasn't going at all as he'd expected. 'Um, well, I thought maybe you'd like to go back and live at your parents' house. They could help with Jack and you know how much your mum loves him,' he added quickly.

'This is our home.' Hannah wasn't going to let him off that easily. 'You have to provide for your son. Don't worry,' she said coldly, 'I don't want a penny of your stinking money for myself, I'll take what's mine, and the car, if that's alright with you.'

Christ, she's like a block of ice. 'I'll provide for Jack and, yes, take anything you want from here. I... you'll still let me see him?'

'You're his father, you can see him as much as you want, although that hasn't been a lot lately.'

'No,' he mumbled, shame-faced. 'You're being very good about this.'

'I'm not staying where I'm not wanted. We'll get a divorce as soon as possible. There's no way back, is there?' *Is this really what I want, if you just give me a sign, maybe...*

'Right, okay, thank you, I guess. I am sorry it ended like this. We're just not right for each other.'

'I don't want people to know, *she* won't come into it. I don't want Jack to find out later that there was someone else, so we'll just split and that's the end of it. What you do after is your business.'

'What about your parents, you'll tell them?'

'I'll have to but they won't say anything. You'd better keep out of their sight for a while.'

Michael thought he'd get out while the going was good. 'I'll pick up some of my stuff and keep away until you've moved out. If I need anything, I'll, er, make sure I come over when you're not here.'

'You'd better let me have your new address in case of an emergency.' Hannah felt as if she was going to choke. *Go, please go before I cry.*

He scribbled it on a piece of paper and she stared at it with blurred eyes. 'Well, I can't compete with that either, can I?'

'It's not about that; I'll go and get some of my things.' Upstairs, he packed two cases with clothes and personal belongings. A flash of guilt went through him when he found all his gym gear clean and ironed, in the cupboard, along with his shirts hanging neatly in the wardrobe. He wouldn't be looked after in that department by Shelby, his laundry bills were going to cost him. For a split second, he hesitated. Why couldn't Hannah just be a bit more… a bit more what, he asked himself. Shelby's body came into his mind and he swallowed his guilt.

Hannah waited downstairs with her fingernails digging into her palms and her teeth biting the inside of her cheeks. *I won't break down in front of him. I must have some pride.* Cold and feeling faint, she knew it was because she'd had nothing to eat and she still had her parents to see, who would be devastated, as was she.

'When will you see Jack?' she asked as he came down the stairs.

'Maybe not this weekend, things are too raw. Next Sunday, if that's alright?'

A week, a whole week before she saw or spoke to him again. 'I'll text you.' That's what their life had come down to, texts.

* * *

At Ivy Cottage, Fae sat quietly in her kitchen. The butterflies picking up on her mood settled quietly, but every so often, one would flutter its wings and a small cloud of golden dust rose.

'I feel so sad for her, the poor girl. I can't do anything; just wait until she comes to me.' There was a gentle waving of wings as if in agreement with her. 'She *will* get past this, of course, although that's difficult for her to imagine now. Unfortunately, there is more to come and she'll feel as if she has nothing. At least there is that lovely boy, and he will keep her focussed.' The gold dust swirled around her.

'What's that? Put myself in her path? Yes, I may be able to do that, but you know I have to be careful. I can't break the rules. It's very difficult when you become fond of somebody.' Fae sighed, she always had this problem, becoming too attached to her charges, and had been in trouble before for 'interfering'. 'I can help when the time comes but it has to be seen as *her* idea, maybe I can drop a small hint.'

The wings fluttered furiously.

'Thank you, my friends, I will tread softly.'

* * *

'Mum, it's me.' Hannah unlocked the door to her parents' house and Mrs Worth came through to the passage.

'Hannah, what on earth…?'

'Oh Mum.' She fell into her mother's arms.

Margaret Worth took one look at her daughter and forced her to have a plate of stew before she said a word.

'Jack's fast asleep and he's been a little angel, so don't worry about him,' she said firmly. 'I like your hair, by the way, but you eat up and then tell me everything. Your father's gone to the farmers' market; you know how he likes to compare his vegetables.' She prattled on, talking about anything to stop Hannah speaking until she'd eaten something. The girl looked terrible. Something awful had happened and it was obviously to do with Michael and the surprise trip. Surely, he hadn't turned it down?

Hannah finished the plateful that had been forced on her and she did feel better. 'I'll just pop up and have a look at Jack, I won't wake him.'

Staring down at her son, she wept softly. 'Not a brilliant start in life for you, Jack, but don't you worry. I'll make sure you and I have the best life we can and you'll never be short of love.'

* * *

'So how did it go?' Shelby demanded, but noticed with pleasure the suitcases.

'Not as bad as I thought. I could see she'd been crying and she looked dreadful, but she was very... cold towards me.' He was still rather shocked by her attitude and felt quite uncomfortable.

'Well, that's good, and is she going to move out of the house?' Shelby had made sure she looked her absolute best for his return, subtle, but sexy. If he was going to be here permanently, there would have to be rules, but one step at a time.

'Yes, she seems happy to go to her parents, and fairly soon I think.'

Thank God. 'What about the boy?'

'I can see him whenever I want. I sort of made an arrangement for next Sunday; perhaps we could take him out for the day?'

Not bloody likely. 'Next Sunday? Oh dear, I said I'd go and see my mother. It may be a bit confusing for him to see too many new people for a while It's best you spend some quality time with him.'

'What shall I do with him all day?' Michael started panicking.

'You don't have to have him *all* day, just a few hours. He's only a baby; you can't even talk to him yet. The gym has a crèche, he'd be happy there.'

'I never thought of that.' *I don't need to tell Hannah, I'll still be having him as far as she knows.* 'That's a brilliant idea and it'll be good for him to interact with other babies. Do they do that at his age?'

'How would I know? That's settled then. Let's sort your stuff out and when we've relaxed a bit, we'll work out how *we're* going to do things.'

* * *

Hannah's father was back and instead of regaling his wife with stories of puny-looking marrows, he was sitting white-faced with her, listening to his daughter telling the story of what had happened last night.

'You had absolutely *no* idea any of this was going on?' Mrs Worth was furious. Never having had the highest opinion of Michael, this was the last straw. There was no way she wanted to see a reconciliation, he would only let her down again, but it had to be Hannah's decision.

'Things weren't good, and he was out so much, but I never suspected that. Maybe I didn't want to see it,' she said sadly. 'I didn't try hard enough.'

'You were far too good for him, the man's a complete arse,' her father said gruffly. 'In the mess, we'd give him a good horsewhipping.'

'Oh Ronald, don't be so ridiculous, you're not in the army now and that went out in the last century. If you'd been in the navy, you'd want to keelhaul him,' his wife snapped.

Even in her depressed state, Hannah gave a snort of laughter. 'Trust you, Dad, I did tell him he'd better stay out of your sight.'

'Hmmph, so what's to do now then?' He stood and rattled the small change in his pocket, as he always did when agitated.

'Would it be difficult if I came back here, with Jack as well, of course?'

'Of course you can come here, but what about your home?' Her mother thought Michael was getting the lion's share.

'As long as he supports his son, it's Michael's house; I don't want anything to do with it. I shall take all the stuff from Jack's room. I'm not leaving those lovely curtains and all the cushions and things I've made.'

'I'm sure Eric will help with his van if there's any large stuff to move. Sooner the better.' Her father was getting very red in the face.

'Calm down Dad. If you get all worked up, Mum will too and that's not good for her.'

'Quite right, sorry.' He gave his wife an anxious look. 'You *are* alright, aren't you, m'dear?'

'I'm fine, let's make a list and get you and Jack settled in.'

'You want me to sell the house and buy part of this flat? But it was a present to you, wasn't it?'

'That's got nothing to do with it, I'm sure you wouldn't expect to live here for free, or perhaps you'd like to pay rent?'

Michael was a bit shocked. Things were moving very fast. He was no longer in control of his life. Shelby had managed to make sure he had an afternoon to remember, but they had to be practical now, she'd said.

'My house wouldn't cover half of this,' he said weakly.

'You'll own a percentage; my father's solicitor will sort it out. You *do* want to live here with me, don't you? Just say if it's Hannah you prefer.'

'No, no it's you I want. It's just everything's closing in on me at the moment, I can't think.'

'I'll do the thinking, you arrange to get the rest of your things and we'll market your house. It's a very good time to sell at the moment; you'll get a tidy sum.'

'I... I should put something aside for Jack, for his future.'

'Yes, we'll sort that out,' she waved a dismissive hand. 'That's a long time in the future, it's only maintenance for him she wants now, isn't it?'

'Yes, that's what she said.'

'Right, make her an offer of monthly payments before she changes her mind. Come and help me now, we're having vegetable curry for tea, you like curry, the vegetables need chopping.'

Yes, he liked curry, preferably one with meat in it. Chop the vegetables? Was *he* expected to do that?

'I buy everything organic,' she said, 'but at least it's all cleaned. I don't want it to look like it's just come out of the ground. It's delivered weekly and good stuff, not cheap. Get started on it and put it all in this pan.'

He looked at what seemed to be an old cigar on the board. 'Err, what is this?'

'Scorzonera, it's a root vegetable. Give it a scrub and chop it up. We'll have it with wild rice.'

Egg-fried rice would be nice.

She put her hands around him and slipped them down the front of his trousers, 'There will be a reward as well.'

He started chopping.

Chapter Seventeen

SINGLE KNOTTED STITCH

A counted thread stitch, which gives the
effect of a fringe

After checking with Hannah to see if she would be at home, Michael received a reply that read, *'House is yours, free anytime'*. A little puzzled, he called around and found it very quiet. Some things were missing in the front room, plants and cushions, they had gone. Looking in the dining room, her sewing machine and all the boxes also had disappeared. Upstairs, the wardrobe and drawers had been cleaned out and Jack's room was stripped bare, not a toy to be seen. In the bathroom, on the soap dish, were her engagement and wedding rings.

Three days, that's all it had taken to wipe herself out of his life. Deep down, he was quite hurt, although he knew he had no right to be. In the kitchen was a note: 'Freezer emptied and defrosted, don't suppose you're eating here.' The house had been cleaned, dusted and tidied right through. It wasn't a home anymore; it was just a house, one like the hundreds he had shown people around.

Over the last three days, Michael had realised his life was going to be very different. Shelby was no housekeeper. She had Vanya in to do the cleaning three times a week and all the laundry was collected and delivered pressed and ready to wear. His could be included, she told him, and quoted a price that made his head spin. How could she afford all this? He then found out that although she was trying to prove herself in business to her father, she was still accepting a generous allowance from him. At least he had the house to sell now and he didn't have to share that with Hannah, but he would have to come to some arrangement about Jack.

Shelby's father had called around to meet him and was all smiles, showing off his expensive whitened teeth. As soon as Shelby visited the bathroom, John Patterson's smile changed to a snarl.

'Michael,' a low growl accompanied his name, 'for some extraordinary reason, Shelby is besotted with you. You'd better step up to the mark, young man. If you mess my daughter around like you did to your wife, I'll have your balls on a plate. Do we understand each other?'

'Y... yes, of course... sir.' Michael was fuming. How dare this big 'I am' tell him how to behave. 'Shelby means everything to me and I'll do right by her.'

'If you mean that, we'll get on fine. Ah, Shelby, I was just saying to Michael here that I'm sure we'll get along just fine.' He slapped Michael on the back in what was supposed to pass as a friendly gesture.

What a bastard, I'll show him. Michael was still fuming later when her father left and Shelby was singing his praises.

Michael took a last look around. He'd packed the rest of his clothes and some photographs, and the remainder could go in a house clearance. He was already thinking he could use the money to buy three flats with a small mortgage on each and rent them out. The rent would cover the mortgages, give him more income and would be his first step to becoming a big cog in the property market. John Patterson could go to hell, once he'd been able to use the man to his advantage, of course. He would have to sweet talk Shelby into letting him get a foot in somewhere and allow him to buy into *her* flat a bit later; he was sure she'd understand.

There was another note on the inside of the front door: 'Don't come to my house, I'll arrange to meet you here or wherever on Sunday so you can have Jack. By the way, I have contacted a solicitor regarding a divorce.' She didn't let the grass grow, he thought moodily. *Solicitors*, what was that going to cost? Surely, they could have sorted it out.

Mrs Figgins was in her garden as he left. 'I saw stuff being taken away. Moving, are you? Where is it you're going, in case anybody asks?'

Nosy, old bag, 'We've split up, so now you know and you can gossip about it to your heart's content.'

Michael slammed his car door and roared off down the road.

'Good riddance,' muttered Mrs Figgins. 'She's better off without you.'

* * *

Hannah certainly didn't feel that way at the moment. She was angry and knew there was no going back, but she *had* contacted a solicitor, as she'd told him in her terse note. Explaining why she didn't want anybody else named, Mr Anderson, of Anderson and Briddlescombe, suggested she do it on grounds of his unreasonable behaviour.

Unreasonable? That was one way of putting it. She did miss him, even so, and tried to remember the good times. There actually hadn't been that many of them, when she realised she could only think of a few occasions. He'd taken her for granted; she'd been a doormat, which was partly her own fault. If they'd had their own place from the start, maybe things would have been different, but she couldn't fight Michael's mother as well. Doreen was hugely to blame for the way he was, but nothing could be done about that now.

Hannah tried not to think about *her*, Shelby Young, that was her name. Watching from her parked car, she had seen Shelby going in and out of the office, stylishly dressed, slim and very pretty. Her mother had told her not to go and look, but Hannah had to, just once. She needed to see what had driven Michael away. It was a huge mistake. Her confidence went to rock bottom and it left her feeling empty, just a shell.

Jack was happy where he was; only being young he didn't really know any different and Hannah had made his room as similar to the old one as she could. His grandparents adored him but they were concerned about their daughter. She didn't eat much and they often heard her crying softly at night. Mrs Worth tried to be as upbeat as possible during the day and kept Hannah busy with a list of jobs she said she 'could do with a hand'.

* * *

One day, Hannah was clearing out the pantry and re-lining the shelves when the phone rang. Her mother picked it up.

'Oh hello, yes, it's er, Mrs Grim, isn't it? How are you?' Pause. 'Actually, she's here, you can speak to her yourself. Hannah, it's that lady from the shop for you.'

Hannah wiped her hands and took the phone. 'Fae, how nice to hear from you, what can I do for you?'

Fae's voice sounded strange on the phone, there was background noise like tiny bells or a tinkling laughter. 'Hannah, dear, how are you?'

'Not good actually, things have happened. I don't feel like sewing at the moment if you wanted anything made.'

'No dear, I was going to ask if you could help me though, maybe you could pop to the cottage? And bring that wonderful little boy of yours, perhaps tomorrow?'

'Yes, I could do that, what sort of help?'

'I'll tell you tomorrow, nothing for you to worry about and, whatever's happened, if you don't want to talk about it, that's fine, but remember what I said before.'

'I will tell you, Fae, see you tomorrow then.'

Hannah told her mother what Fae had said.

'Don't go taking on too much, you have a lot on your mind at the moment.' Mrs Worth was relieved that there might be something else for Hannah to think about, but she was worried about her daughter's frame of mind. 'Do you want your father to drive you over?'

'No Mum,' Hannah smiled, 'I know I'm upset but life goes on, as they say. I have to think about me and Jack and where we're going. If I can do Fae a favour, it may help me focus.'

* * *

The next day, it was lashing with rain. *What a shame, the garden is so lovely.* Hannah bundled Jack up in his waterproof covers until he was safely in the car. She'd tried to do something with her hair, not having bothered with it much up till now; her mother helped her mousse and blow-dry it.

'I wasn't sure, but I think it really suits you,' she said, giving it a light spray. 'Don't let yourself go; it's so easy when things aren't good and he's not worth it. I know it's difficult to see now, but you *will* be happy again, you may even meet somebody else in the future.'

'I don't think so,' Hannah said firmly. 'I shall concentrate on giving Jack the best I can and that's all there is to it.'

Her mother just smiled. *We'll see.*

After driving through terrible rain, as Hannah pulled up outside Ivy Cottage, it miraculously stopped and the sun came out. The only evidence of it was raindrops on the leaves and flowers and a small puddle on the path.

'How is my lovely little boy?' Fae was slightly shocked by the way Hannah looked, but not surprised. She made a big fuss of Jack, who gurgled and smiled at her, and let Hannah relax. 'Kettle's on. I must say, that hairstyle suits you, you look a lot younger.'

'A fat lot of difference it's made to my life now. I'm sorry, Fae, I'm not in the best place at the moment.'

A cup of tea was pressed into her hand. 'If you want to, tell me when you're ready.'

Hannah told the story from the hair salon up to the moment she saw them together, drank some tea and then told the rest, bringing Fae up to date.

'I'm so very sorry, dear, it must have been a terrible shock for you, how are you feeling now?'

'Numb, to tell you the truth. I keep expecting to wake up and find it was a bad dream. But actually, I haven't told my mother this, in some ways, it's a relief. Am I bad to feel that?'

'I think you're entitled to feel any way you please. In what way relieved?'

'Well, I always put him first, thinking what he'd like to eat and doing his laundry the way he liked it. I hardly saw him in the last few months and he seemed to give us his time very begrudgingly. Apart from the upset, I am more relaxed now.'

'Things will settle down, you'll see. Will you have some ginger cake?'

'Ginger cake always makes things better, doesn't it?' Hannah smiled weakly. 'Now, what is it you wanted my help with?'

'First of all, I must tell you, I don't have the haberdashery shop anymore.'

'Oh no, that lovely shop, why?'

'A development or some such, I don't know. Anyway, I was thinking, there's not so much call for that sort of thing now, with the way people can buy from *computers*,' Fae said the word as if it was something nasty. 'You are a designer, Hannah, and I would like to set up a studio for you to work from. I know you have the baby, but you could choose your hours and increase them later when he goes to school. Maybe you could even do dressmaking classes or something like that. What do you think?'

'I don't know what to say, would you be there as well?'

'Oh no, I'm getting too old for all this. Why don't you meet me in town tomorrow and I'll show you where I have in mind? As I said, it would be a base for you, not a shop as such, and you could open to suit yourself.'

Hannah's mind whirled. It would be a wonderful opportunity to build up something for her and Jack's future. 'I don't quite understand how it would work, would I rent it from you?'

'We can sort that out later. Do you remember that I asked you to look upon me as your honorary Godmother? Everybody needs one, a *special* Godmother at times in their life. I would like to give you the opportunity of setting yourself up and you can pay me back once you're up and running.'

'Fae, you don't owe me anything and you're being extraordinarily kind to me. I can't accept an offer like that.'

'Would you feel better if I had a legal document drawn up?'

'I suppose so, I'm still not sure...'

'Come and have a look at the premises with me tomorrow and see what you think. You have a gift and it shouldn't be wasted. It's something you'd like to do, isn't it?'

The butterflies that had been resting quietly began fluttering, disturbing the golden dust. One took flight and flew past Hannah with the sound of a faint laugh, ignoring Fae's glare.

'It's one of those butterflies I saw before, they're much bigger than the ones I normally see in our garden.' The butterfly turned slightly as it went past. 'It... it looked like it had a little face,' cried Hannah. 'I've never seen anything like that.'

'Have some cake, dear, and another cup of tea; a face? It might look like that, the pansies in the garden, they look like they have faces as well, I always think.' Distracting Hannah with a cake plate, she moved over to the corner and shooed the others out of the door with a stern look. 'Please come and have a look before you make your mind up, dear, I think you may be persuaded when you see it.'

'Well I suppose that wouldn't hurt, alright then, but only if you let me buy you tea and cakes in the nice, little café we have in town.'

Fae smiled. 'I'm sure I would enjoy that.'

'It certainly sounds interesting, but why would she do all this with some sort of vague pay me later?' Hannah's mother wondered if there was something dodgy about this arrangement.

'She said it would be all legal, there's no harm in having a look, is there? It is something I'd love to do and with us both living here now, there isn't as much room for all my stuff, especially being able to lay out large pieces of material. As Jack gets older and starts toddling, I couldn't risk an accident with someone's fabric.'

Mrs Worth was delighted that Hannah had something positive to focus on but she did think it was all a bit odd. Perhaps she was being over suspicious, maybe there *were* genuine people around who helped others, and this Fae was elderly and from a more gentle and kinder age.

Hannah also thought it was a bit strange and didn't quite understand what Fae was getting out of it. Rent or a share of the profits, yes, but not immediately, it would seem. When she read her book that night in bed, the Duke's intended was visiting the modiste and being shown taffeta and silks. Hannah slept, dreaming of Regency dress designs and beautiful fabrics.

* * *

'Michael, I don't mean to nag but can you pick up your clothes and sort them? I hate clutter and mess.'

He sighed. Hannah had always picked up after him, as had his mother before, and he'd never realised it until now. He was beginning to appreciate what an easy life he'd had; this one, he had to work at a bit more. The rewards were plentiful – in bed, Shelby was fantastic – but he was finding out she was a bit obsessive about tidiness and order. All the packets and tins in her food cupboard were lined up in a particular order. Her CDs were filed alphabetically and her clothes were hung in precise order and colour. She went loopy one day when she found the toothpaste squeezed from the middle and laying by the sink, looking as if it had been run over by a bicycle. That's how she described it anyway.

In her quieter moments, she did admit she was very fussy, but it stemmed from a time when she and her mother hadn't lived so well and it was her way of coping. Michael promised to be more considerate and she said she would try to relax, then came the shout about his clothes. He had to accept that Shelby was a different animal to Hannah, one that he had chosen and would have to adjust to. He was certainly paying the price with his laundry, he thought ruefully.

He'd asked about bringing Jack back to the flat on Sunday and he thought she was going to have a meltdown.

'This is *not* a place for a child!' she shouted. 'I don't want it here. Can't you take it for a burger or something, that's what fathers do, isn't it?'

'Maybe when he's a bit older. He's not eating that sort of thing yet.' She had no idea about babies; he didn't know much, but he did realise that at least. Apparently, at the gym crèche, they had staff who would feed the children so he could just stay there longer and have a drink or something. The crèche cost a mint as well; these days out with Jack were going to be expensive. Where else could he go if not here? Walk around the park for hours? Maybe when he was on better terms with Hannah, he could spend time with Jack at hers, running the gauntlet of her parents' disapproval as well.

Shelby sidled up to him, dressed in only a very small towel. 'Sorry for going on at you, I'm having a shower, care to join me?'

All his misgivings were forgotten... again.

Hannah waited in the town square, as Fae suggested. Thankfully, they were nowhere near the estate agency.

'Hannah, dear, sorry if I'm a bit late.' Fae was dressed rather strangely, Hannah thought, wearing a cape with a sort of tartan design and a small, pointed hat with a feather on it. Oh well, Fae was unique in her way, so why not in her dress as well?

'It's just down here,' Fae went on to say. 'I have the key.'

On the corner, next to the post office, was a small shop window covered with newspaper. Fae unlocked the door beside it and they stepped into a most wonderful space.

'It's much bigger than I thought from the outside,' said Hannah. 'What was it before? I don't remember.'

'I think it was a watchmaker's shop,' Fae replied, 'He lived upstairs; it comes with a flat as well. Now, look, you could display in this area and curtain off the back space as a workroom and dressing rooms. Have a look upstairs as well.'

As they reached the upper floor, Hannah was even more amazed. There were two bedrooms, a sitting room, already furnished, a reasonably sized kitchen and a bathroom, all modernised.

'There's usable roof space as well for storage or a... playroom,' Fae said innocently.

'I can't believe it, it's enormous.' Hannah opened a door in the kitchen to a pretty balcony with side gate to outside steps.

'I understand it incorporated upper space from the shops below. Quite a little hidden gem, isn't it?'

'This must cost a bomb, in the centre of town like this.'

'I was owed a favour,' said Fae in her vague manner. 'I got it quite reasonably.'

'You've *already* bought it? I thought you were just thinking about it.'

'Couldn't risk somebody else snapping it up, not when it's so perfect for what I've got in mind. I'm sure you could be happy working here and because it's all furnished, you'd just need a cot and you could live here some of the time if you wanted to, especially if you were only doing limited hours to start with, or opening by appointment.'

'But Fae, how could I pay you what this is worth? It wouldn't be fair.'

'Tch, don't talk about fair, it's an investment for the future. I don't need money now, I have what I require in life. I would like to see you making a success of this business. As long as you cover the running costs, we'll see about other things later on.'

Hannah started to cry.

Fae was alarmed. 'Whatever's the matter, dear, have I upset you?'

'Oh no, far from it. Nobody apart from my parents has ever been as kind to me as you have, why me?'

Shaking some golden dust off a hanky, Fae passed it to her. 'You deserve it, my dear. Just pay me back by saying you'll take it on. I have all the fabric and sewing accessories you'll need from the shop to get you going. I'm sure you'll know what to do. Pictures and photos of your designs, some ready-wear made up, that sort of thing.'

Hannah, already in her mind's eye, could see some comfortable chairs, a large, ornate mirror and sample books for people to look through. A modiste, that's what she would be. A smile crossed her face.

'Fae, I can't tell you what this means to me, but yes, thank you, thank you so very much. I would love to take it on and make you proud.'

'I *will* be proud of you.'

Soft tinkles of laughter could be heard as they looked around once more before leaving.

Chapter Eighteen

BARRIER STITCH

When the slanting stitches are from bottom
right to top left, it is known as barrier or
fence stitch

1 YEAR LATER

Hannah turned her sign to 'closed', breathing a sigh of relief. Saturdays were usually busy and this one had been particularly so. A bridal dress with three bridesmaids' outfits had been ordered, and the mother and aunt of the bride were both considering some designs. It had been an interesting afternoon, with a real 'bridezilla' and the mother and aunt both putting their opinions forward, along with sarcastic remarks about each other's choices.

She could smell roast chicken cooking upstairs, courtesy of *her* mother, who came to help with Jack on a Saturday, always cooking enough for tea and Sunday's meal. Hannah was open four afternoons a week and all day Saturday. Sometimes, she had to turn custom away as she was so busy, and had recently been considering taking on outworkers to do all the basics for her.

Hard to believe she'd been there for a year; it hadn't been so easy at the start. The first few weeks saw only one or two people coming through the door, resulting in just a repair. A newspaper advert brought a few more in and then Hannah's mother passed some flyers around at her reading group. When Beatrice Congdon appeared within a fortnight, wearing a smart jacket with trousers that Hannah had made, Mrs Worth could have kissed her and even invited her around for a cup of tea, suffering another lecture on the latest book read. When some of the other ladies saw Beatrice, they came to the shop en masse, and after coffee and cakes were offered, all put in an order, saying what wonderful service was offered.

Hannah still had some of her older customers, who kept her ticking over until the business picked up. Also, she still had alterations from the main bridal shop, who were slightly put out by her set up. Hannah was keen to get some younger people in, but fashion was ever changing and cheap, which was what they wanted, but she did also put some handmade toys, including her teddies and rag dolls, in the window, which people started to buy.

At the start, she had just used the flat at weekends but was now there most of the time. Jack always stayed one night a week with his grandparents, when Hannah cleaned the flat from top to bottom and had an hour or two to herself. She had found a young girl, the daughter of the shop owner next door, who wanted to earn some extra money. She came in after school and watched Jack for two hours. He still had a nap after lunch and would then come down to sit in his playpen in the shop. It was going to be a bit more difficult when he was walking, which wouldn't be long now.

Mrs Worth seemed in good health but Hannah wouldn't risk putting her under pressure so didn't want to rely too much on her. One night a week and Saturdays were enough.

Michael came most Sundays and took Jack for a few hours. The first time, after Hannah had told him about the shop, he was shocked. She'd only just moved out of the house.

'I'm pleased for you, of course, but can you afford it?' He was even more shocked when he'd actually seen it. He knew what that sort of space would bring in with rent.

'It's a business arrangement with a client.' Hannah was very matter-of-fact about it. 'It's not really any of your business, is it?'

Since the divorce was soon to be final, he had to agree, but was puzzled as to what sort of 'arrangement' it was. Finding out it had been sold, he discovered it had been bought through a solicitor for an unnamed client. Suspicious at first and wondering if Hannah had won the lottery and not told him, he had to discount that. He knew she didn't have a dishonest bone in her body and however angry she was with him, she would never do that.

After a few months, he had tentatively asked if he could spend an hour or two with Jack there. 'All his toys are here and it's difficult to... to find places to take him.'

Hannah stared at him. 'You mean *Shelby* doesn't want him at the flat? How supportive of her. Will you never have him to stay over then, not even when he gets a bit older?'

'Maybe then,' he said defensively. 'Shelby's not used to babies or young children.' He couldn't see her ever giving way on that subject. She was adamant that no child was welcome and he was finding it a strain with Jack on Sundays. He missed a Sunday roast as well, and one day when he picked Jack up and saw a plate with a roast beef dinner waiting to be warmed, he felt cheated.

'You're having that for lunch?'

'Any objections?'

'No, it's... it looks very nice,'

'It will be, see you later.' It was at times like that that it would have been so easy to weaken. There had many such occasions when a wistful look or remark almost made her feel sorry for him. Then, she would harden her heart and remember why they were in this situation.

Hannah's world had crumbled, like falling bricks, so she had built her own wall, a barrier between her and the outside world. Many times, she had been approached by men who realised she was on her own. Always polite, she made it clear that she was not in the market for a relationship. She had such low self-esteem, she couldn't accept anyone would be interested anyway.

* * *

A few months after she'd moved into the shop, the divorce had been finalised and Michael paid an amount every month for Jack. Her solicitor had tried again to persuade her to fight for more, but she refused.

Her life centred around Jack and her business. She saw Fae once a month, either going to the cottage for tea or, sometimes, Fae came to the shop. She always brought fabric, cottons and trimmings, the like of which Hannah had never seen. 'Picked up on her travels' was the answer, whenever she was asked where they came from. She always took a great interest in any designs and was delighted that Hannah was so busy. Waving away the offer of some payment, she'd said to let the business get off the ground first. A present was always brought for Jack as well. The last time it was a toy drum, which made Hannah's heart sink, but strangely, it was quite melodic, and the gentle, rhythmic sounds were almost pleasurable.

She read to Jack every night and scoured the charity shops for children's books he would enjoy. She also bought his clothes there as he was growing so fast, and it seemed pointless spending money on new things he may only wear a few times. At her mother's insistence, she did go to the hairdresser, keeping her short style, but once, overhearing Shelby's name mentioned, was careful to make appointments at times she assumed they wouldn't run into each other. Apart from that, she spent nothing on herself and just had two or three smarter outfits that she had designed and made for work, making them appear different with accessories. Because her time was limited, not so much baking was done, and she was keeping her trimmer figure without even realising or caring.

* * *

Shelby was quietly pleased with how things were going. Michael had explained his plans for letting flats so she'd agreed to his paying his share at her flat and giving him a year to get established. Knowing her father was not over impressed with her choice, she was determined to show him they could be a successful partnership, and she and Michael were now joint owners of the new agency. Also, she was a manager in her own right as they had opened another estate agency in the next town.

Not seeing each other every day at work had created more spark between them but she kept a close eye on him, and any new (female) staff were carefully vetted. The only negative point was the child. Shelby hated the fact that he had that tie with Hannah and wanted nothing to do with it. He'd asked a few more times about having the boy over and she still refused. Having no inclination whatsoever to have a child of her own, she certainly wasn't going to be saddled with someone else's.

She would always ask casually about his collection and drop-off arrangements and where he'd been, always referring to Jack as 'the boy' and not using his name, which made him seem not so real in her mind. She knew that Michael had to talk to Hannah about *him* but made sure it was the minimum of conversation. When he'd once mentioned how nice Hannah had made the flat and the success she was making of her business, they had their first serious row.

'I don't care what she's doing and neither should you, *I'm* the only one you should be paying attention to and caring about.'

'I don't care about her, I was just saying…' He realised what a mistake he'd made.

'Well *don't* say, I don't want to hear it. Jolly good luck to her, let her get on with it; it's none of your business now.'

'It is my business how Jack is being looked after. I have to pay towards his care.'

'I'm very well aware of that, didn't I let you pay a lesser rate here because of it? I just don't want to hear about *Saint* Hannah. If she was so wonderful, why did you want me?'

'For God's sake, you know why I wanted you. No other woman comes anywhere near in my mind.'

'Easy to say, if I had… if she hadn't seen us together that time,' Shelby corrected herself quickly, 'you could still be having your cosy life with her and stringing me along with promises.'

'No, never.' He grabbed hold of her. 'You know what you do to me. How could I ever want anything or anybody else?'

She'd won. 'Hmm, well I can feel it, that's for sure.' She smiled, rubbing up against him. 'Shame to let that go to waste, show me how sorry you are.'

* * *

Michael was remembering that conversation as he wheeled Jack around the park for the eighth time. It would get easier as Jack got older; at least they could kick a ball around. He couldn't put him in the gym crèche *every* Sunday, Jack would be a stranger to him, and even though Michael didn't have a lot of time for his son, he didn't want that. After the row with Shelby, he couldn't risk asking Hannah again about spending some time there. If Shelby got wind of that, he dreaded to think what would happen. He saw another man with a small child and as they passed, he gave Michael a sympathetic look as if to say 'we're in the same boat, mate'. *Is it that obvious?* He decided to take Jack to the coffee shop. At least he could sit down and hopefully, the bottle of juice would keep his son happy while he relaxed for a bit.

It was not to be.

As soon as Michael sat down with his latte and toasted sandwich (another secret to be kept from Shelby), Jack let out a piercing scream and threw his bottle on the floor. The women looked sympathetic, the men sighed and tutted, and the group of teenagers laughed.

Michael swore inwardly. 'Come on, Jack, be a good boy, here's some nice juice.' He put the bottle in place. Another scream and the bottle went flying again. The screams went on and Jack's face got redder, as did Michael's. Gulping his too hot coffee down, he grabbed his sandwich and beat a hasty retreat. The sighs of relief could be heard halfway down the street, and the worst thing was, as soon as Jack was on the move, he was quiet and even dropped off to sleep.

This is ridiculous; I can't go on like this every Sunday. What else could he do? He had to find somewhere else he could take Jack or cut his visits down until Jack was a bit older. That made more sense. He could make it up to his son later.

'Am I hearing you right, you want to stop seeing Jack?' Hannah was incredulous and angry.

'Not stop exactly, you don't know how difficult it is,' he whined. 'Just cut the visits down a bit at the moment. He's not very settled with me.'

'Well it's hardly surprising, is it?' She lifted Jack up. 'He's soaking wet, can't you change a nappy? There's plenty of places that have changing rooms for babies. What's the point? He's probably better off not seeing you. Why don't you just go and get back to *her*?'

Hannah tried to slow her beating heart as Michael left, furious that he still made her feel that way. Her eyes filled with tears as she looked at their son. How could he be so unfeeling? She could hardly bear to leave him for the afternoon, let alone a week and now, it would be even longer. Jack was of the age that brought something different every day; his father would miss so much. *Well, that's his own fault, why should I care?*

She did care, deep down, she cared very much. For Jack's sake, she told herself, not for hers. She and Michael were over, that was non-negotiable, but she missed being part of a couple, having someone to help make decisions. He hadn't been part of that process for a long time but it didn't stop her wanting it, and she was sad at the thought of not having anyone in her life, but afraid to take the risk again. It would require a leap of faith that she wasn't ready to make. Instead, she lost herself once more in her books and wished she could conjure up a Regency Duke.

Jack, fed, bathed and ready for bed, was listening to the story of *The Very Hungry Caterpillar*. Hannah knew he wouldn't understand it but he smiled and laughed at the voices and faces she pulled. *How can your dad not be proud of you? He's a fool and he'll never get this time with you back again.*

That night, she looked at herself properly for the first time in ages. The hair did look good and maybe she should make a bit more of herself. There was nothing wrong with taking a bit more pride in her appearance; she was doing it for herself, not for any man. *I could start wearing a bit of make-up and I'll pick some material to make prettier summer dresses.*

Earlier that afternoon, several miles away in the cemetery, Christopher and his daughter, Arianne, were laying freesias on Claire's grave. It would have been her 28th birthday, and already more than a year since she'd died. Christopher still felt angry and railed against the unfairness of taking somebody so young.

Arianne was now seven and because of all the photographs and the fact that her father talked about Claire, it made the memories of her mother still very vivid in her mind.

'These were her favourites, weren't they, Daddy?' she asked as she carefully placed the freesias in the little pot.

'Yes, she liked those. That's why we planted some seeds in the garden. They should come up this summer.' He stared at the grave, remembering the awful sight of her coffin being lowered and his lovely, beautiful wife being consigned to the dark, cold earth. He shuddered. *I must stop thinking about it.*

Arianne patted the ground and chattered to her mother, telling her about some of the things she'd been doing at school. Christopher, although with his own thoughts, listened to make sure he knew as well. She always told him about her day, every night before bed, but because he'd made a promise to himself to be all she needed, he wanted to be fully conversant with everything in her life.

Claire's mother, Francine, was an important part of their lives. Still wanting to retain some private life for herself, she declined Christopher's offer to move in and had moved to her own flat close by. She picked Arianne up from school when needed, looking after her until Christopher got home. Able to work from home for two days a week, he was always there on Mondays and Fridays. They did chores together on the weekends. Any washing that Francine hadn't done they sorted between them, where Christopher always made a point of reading the washing labels and making Arianne giggle when he pretended not to understand them. They dusted and vacuumed and although meals had usually been prepared for them, they always had a 'cook in' night, where Arianne would choose something from the recipe books. They would shop for the ingredients then attempt to make it, with varying degrees of success.

He would not fall into the trap of using the TV as a babysitter but would let her watch her favourite programmes, and then they would play board games or he'd listen to her read. Francine said he was doing a wonderful job but he needed now to have some life of his own. When the first year had passed, she had suggested quietly to him that he try to get out a bit more and meet people.

'Women, you mean. Thank you, Francine, I know you mean well, but there's no room in my life for anybody.

Arianne is my priority. There will be no one but Claire for me.'

'You loved her, Christopher, as she did you, but in the future…'

'Please,' he said firmly, 'I don't want it mentioned again.'

Arianne looked up. 'I've told Mummy everything. Can we go and get a hot chocolate?'

'Yes, my angel, let's go.'

The coffee shop was busy but they found a table in the corner. He got his favourite espresso and a chocolate for Arianne. Just as they sat down, a harassed-looking man struggled in with a pushchair. Leaving the boy sitting in it by a table, Christopher watched him buy a coffee and sandwich. Just as he took a sip of his espresso, he nearly choked as the boy screamed and a bottle of juice flew past him, crashing onto the floor. The red-faced man went to retrieve it and Christopher was aware of the reactions of people around him.

His mind went back to a few years ago, when the angelic-looking child opposite him had thrown a mighty tantrum in the supermarket and his face had been even redder than that poor man's. When he heard the second scream, he was about to turn and commiserate when he realised the pushchair was being manoeuvred out again.

'Thank Christ for that,' said one man, very loudly. 'Children shouldn't be allowed in places like this.'

'I'm a child,' whispered Arianne. 'He's not very nice.'

'No, he's a very rude man, Arianne, drink up and we'll leave, you're not wanted here.' Christopher was equally loud.

'I say, there's no need for that, I wasn't talking about your child, you know.'

'Be quiet, Harry,' said a large woman at his table, 'you're embarrassing us all.' She gave an apologetic smile.

'She's got a coffee cream moustache,' whispered Arianne, a little too loudly, and the tables around erupted.

'Now we *will* go.' Christopher was trying not to laugh as he saw the woman dabbing her face frantically with a serviette.

'What was I saying about children?' Harry's voice bellowed as they left.

'Daddy, you're laughing, you don't laugh very much.'

He stopped, shocked. 'Arianne, you're right.' He picked her up and gave her a hug. 'I promise, from now on, I'll try to laugh a bit more.'

Claire, I will always think of you, but I'll try and remember the fun times.

Chapter Nineteen

LOCK STITCH

A stitch firmly linking together two threads
or stitches

4 YEARS LATER

'Happy birthday, Jack.' Hannah woke her son on the morning of his 5th birthday. 'Time to open a couple of presents and then get ready for school.'

'Mummy,' he jumped up for a cuddle, 'can I take my present to show?' On a Friday, the children were encouraged to take something of interest to show the rest of the class.

'I don't think presents count, Jack,' laughed Hannah. 'It's best to leave them at home. You were going to take the piece of honeycomb, weren't you? And explain about the bees you saw.'

'Oh yes, the bee comb.'

'Honeycomb, but bee comb is a good name for it. Come on, open this one, then have breakfast.'

He squealed in delight at the new Lego toy he'd been hoping for. Hannah knew that they'd spend the weekend adding to 'Lego city', which took up a large part of the upper floor. Fae had been right when she said it would make a good playroom.

'Don't open all the packets of small bricks now,' she warned him. 'We don't want to lose any.'

'I'll take the fireman to watch me have my Weetybix,' he said, running to the kitchen with the figure in his hand.

Hannah glanced with trepidation at the instruction sheet for the fire station. After several of these builds, it didn't get any easier. Michael should be doing this sort of thing with him, she thought sadly, but after one attempt, he had given up. Over the last few years, his visits had begun to increase again, but they were short, stilted affairs. Hannah had relented and let him spend time with Jack in the playroom upstairs, especially when it was cold or wet outside. What he told Shelby she neither knew nor cared, but got the impression that the woman didn't like his being there.

As she followed Jack into the kitchen to stop him pouring cereal everywhere, he beamed at her again.

'Will Daddy come with a present?'

Looking at his eager, trusting, little face, Hannah's heart suffered another wrench. 'I think he'll see you tonight, Jack, he did say he'd be popping in with your present.' *He bloody well better or I'll swing for him this time.* Several times in the past, he had reneged on a promised visit, leaving the little boy in tears. As furious as Hannah was, she always tried to make excuses and never criticised him. Even she didn't think Michael would let him down tonight, not after 'forgetting' the much looked forward to cinema trip a few weeks back. In all the years that he'd known her, he had never seen her so angry when she'd marched into the estate agent's office the next morning and given him a real dressing-down in front of his staff. It left him feeling like a piece of dirt and he was in a foul mood for the rest of the day.

Breakfast was eaten, and with the fireman carefully replaced in the box, she helped him dress for school. It was the basic uniform of supermarket trousers and sweatshirt, which was cheap and reasonably hard-wearing. The stick-down-tab shoes were a godsend, although she was trying to teach him to do laces.

The honeycomb was in a plastic box, which he carried proudly on the walk to the school. That had been collected on their last visit to Fae's, when she had taken him down to the hives and told him all about the bees. Hannah was very worried that he might get stung, and when she saw a bee on his hand, she was frantic. He ran back, telling her all about the bee house and the queen who lived in there.

Jack called her 'Aunty Fae' and always enjoyed his visits to the cottage. Ever since he could toddle about, he was fascinated by the 'butterflies' in the garden and would run after them, shrieking with laughter when they dipped and swayed their way down the paths, or hid behind plants and jumped out in front of him. Hannah could never quite see what was keeping him so amused and would run after him. Eventually, realising the garden was very safe and he *never* fell down or hurt himself, she and Fae would sit chatting and let him explore. She tried hard not to be an overprotective mother but always had one ear or eye listening or watchful of what he was up to.

Hannah saw Jack into the school playground and chatted with some of the mothers who were also there. In the time that Jack had been going to pre-school groups and since he'd started full-time, she had made some friends. When the school realised she ran the dress-making shop, they'd asked if she would like to come in once a week as a volunteer, to help with a small craft group of seven-year-olds. She was delighted and helped mostly girls, but one or two boys as well, in the basics of knitting and sewing simple running stitches. Also, which was Fae's idea, she took in some wooden dolls with four nails in the tops of their heads and taught them French knitting. Coils of multi-coloured, narrow tubes of wool were produced and much enjoyed. This proved so popular, it became a playtime craze, and more of the peg dolls had to be made, which Mr Worth did in his workshop.

The headteacher was thrilled with the surge of interest. 'It's so nice to see some of these older skills being taken up again and not to see them so obsessed with electronic pets and whatever,' she said. 'It's a shame you can't come in more often. We could run at least three more of these little groups.'

'I'd love to, but the shop is so busy,' Hannah replied. She *would* have liked to come in more. 'I *am* thinking I may need an assistant soon, so if that happens, perhaps I could do one more morning. I do enjoy it.'

'So do the children,' beamed the head. 'I even caught the bug myself a bit and got one of my old cross-stitches out that I'd never finished.'

'I've got some of those as well,' laughed Hannah. As she walked away from the school, some of the children waved and shouted 'hello' to Ms Rawlings. Although she would have preferred to go back to her maiden name, because her son was Jack Rawlings, she felt it was less confusing, so settled for the rather obscure 'Ms'.

Her designs were done under the name of 'Hannah Worth', and people were now coming from some distances to have a unique outfit tailored to suit them. She was also, after much persuasion, paying Fae a monthly standing order. What she didn't know was that Fae was putting that straight into a trust fund for Jack.

* * *

Shelby's period was two weeks late. *I can't be, I bloody well can't be.* Distraught at the thought, she'd pick up a test during the day and wanted complete privacy at home. She phoned Michael's office.

'Listen, Mikey darling. I was thinking about tonight.'

Oh no. 'It's Jack's birthday, I did say I wanted to drop a present in…'

'Of *course*, you must drop a present in.' *How old is the brat? 5, didn't he say?* 'Five is a special birthday, isn't it? I think, if *Hannah* doesn't mind, you should spend some time there. Why don't you phone her and see if it's okay, maybe take a cake or something?'

Michael was dumbstruck and stared at the phone as if it had dropped out of space.

'Michael? Are you there?'

'Er, yes. Are you sure, Shelby? I'll just pop in and see him to give him his present, if you'd rather I came home.'

'No, no, don't do that. I really mean it, please, spend some time with him. Maybe… I've been a bit selfish. He's growing up now and should know his father. I'll have a girlie film night and paint my nails. Don't rush.' *For God's sake, don't rush.*

'Well, thanks, sweetheart. I'll, er… see you later then.'

He texted Hannah. Even now, after this length of time, he felt awkward on the phone. A message came back fairly quickly, saying a cake was already organised, but she was sure Jack would be delighted if he could spare some time. Her parents would be there, but she would make sure it was a nice tea for Jack's sake.

That's all I need, Ma and Pa there glowering at me. He wondered what on earth had happened to Shelby to cause some sort of personality transplant. Jack never reached one per cent of her interest or even conversation, so why the sudden concern? Did she want him out of the way for some reason tonight? No, surely not, things were very good between them. He'd recently sold one of the flats, cleared the mortgage and banked a tidy profit, which meant he could put a bigger deposit down on two more flats. Their little empire was growing.

Lately, he'd started thinking about the future. It seemed quite obvious that Shelby wouldn't entertain the thought of having children, so that just left Jack as his son and heir. Michael hoped that he would be around for a long time and Jack would be a grown man before taking over the reins of the business. However, having attended his old boss, Robin's, funeral last month, it had made him think. Robin had been involved in a car accident, which had killed him, leaving his wife and two children in their 20s. That wasn't *so* bad, but an accident could happen to anyone at any time. What if something happened to him, where would that leave Jack? Their rental business was held in joint names; could he trust Shelby to allow Jack into the business when he came of age? Would there still be a business? He had to give this some serious thought.

Hannah had a fairly quiet day, for which she was grateful, and closed early. Most of her customers now came on an appointment system, but she put an apologetic note on the door in case of the unexpected visitor. Her mother and father were picking Jack up from school so she could sort the balloons and decorate the table for tea. Wondering whether to host a proper party for him, she decided against it this year, but hopefully, by the time he was six, he'd have a group of friends she could do something special for. Fae had been invited but declined, saying it was family time. She had delivered a present for him to open at tea and also asked if she could make his cake, which she'd dropped off yesterday.

Taking it out of its hiding place downstairs, where Jack knew he wasn't allowed to poke around, she stared at it in wonder again. When it had been unveiled, Hannah was speechless. Fae had looked around the toy room and Jack had shown her some of his favourites, which was basically his Lego city. The cake looked like the police station, with figures and a police car alongside. The icing was so perfect, it looked like real bricks all clicked together in place. Jack would absolutely love it and Hannah suspected he would be upset at the thought of cutting it up.

The balloons were blown up and the table laid for tea. She was a little apprehensive at the thought of Michael being here, with her parents, but pleased for Jack's sake. In a phone call, earlier, she'd warned her Mother and asked her not to let Dad say anything to upset the party. The few occasions in the past when their paths had crossed had been frosty, to say the least, but they were careful not to say anything in Jack's hearing and it was his day, that was most important.

* * *

The staff wondered why Shelby was in such a mood today and why she announced she had to leave early. They didn't really care, none of them felt particularly close to her, and even though she was the manager, a little friendliness wouldn't hurt on the odd occasion.

She'd insisted on doing a viewing earlier and that was because it was for a very upmarket apartment in a new complex, built by her father, near the river. The lady, a well-known local author, Alison Carrick, was known for being a little eccentric, but always paid for the best. The sale had been agreed, so they were puzzled as to why she came back with a face like thunder. They didn't know that Shelby had admired the striking outfit that Alison had worn, only to be told that it was a 'Hannah Worth' and that Shelby 'simply *must* go and check it out'.

Under any other circumstances, Shelby would have gone straight there, as she had seen other designs by Hannah that she loved, and to wear something unique very much appealed to her. Also, having had to stop on the way back to pick up the pregnancy-testing kit soured her mood.

When she got home, she ran a bath and poured a large glass of chilled white wine, intending to relax fully before doing any damn test. Vanya had been and the flat was its usual pristine and tidy self. Michael's magazines that he liked to buy were in a neat stack in the rack, but they still annoyed her. A couple of tasteful coffee-table books complimented the look of the room, but the magazines that she liked were flicked through then either taken to the office or given to Vanya.

Vanya thought five pounds was an obscene price for a magazine full of ridiculous clothes that would only fit someone resembling a washing line pole. She dumped them and stopped in the paper shop on her way home for 'Have a Break' to do all the competitions and read the handy hints.

Shelby had drunk the best part of the bottle on a day when she was normally alcohol-free. Staring at the test kit box, she nearly threw it out of the window, but she had to know. Feeling a little light-headed, she read the instructions, did the first part of the test, *gross*, and waited.

* * *

Jack came running up the stairs, dropping his lunch box and school bag in the hall. 'Hello Mummy, Granny and Grandad are with me, can I open my presents now?'

'Well, Daddy is coming soon, would you like to wait so that he can see as well?'

Ronald Worth looked grim but kept quiet.

'Daddy?' Hannah's heart jumped at the way his little face lit up. 'Has he got a present too?'

'Yes, he has, and he won't be long. Why don't you change out of your school clothes first?'

'Come on, Jack,' said Mrs Worth, 'I'll help you.'

Hannah smiled at her father. 'Thanks Dad, for being here tonight, I know it's not easy for you.'

'Hmmph, not easy for you either, I should imagine. Don't worry, I've been told to behave m'self.'

'How's Mum been, any more headaches?'

'Nothing too serious, a few small turns, but not getting any worse.'

They were both mindful of her condition and that was one of the reasons Hannah had been careful over the last five years, to strike a balance between letting her mother enjoy being a *grand*mother and looking after Jack without burdening her, even when it would have made her own life a lot easier.

That was another of the reasons she was still resentful towards Michael. He should have been a help and support to her over the years and not the distant, remote figure he had become. At that moment, the doorbell rang.

Hannah had wisely had an intercom fitted when Jack started toddling and she had to put a safety gate at the top of the stairs. She could see it was Michael through the fish-eye lens camera and pressed the button to let him in.

'Daddy!' Jack threw himself into his father's arms. Michael felt a sudden surge of fatherly love and pride as he noticed his ex-in-laws watching with beady eyes.

'Hello Michael,' Hannah said quietly, 'would you like a cup of tea?' That was always the first thing he'd wanted when he got in from work.

'Oh... yes please, if it's no trouble.' Shelby never offered, but then they were both working, as she'd pointed out to him many times. He couldn't stomach the herbal brews that she made at times, so had bought in his own supply of tea and told her he couldn't function without 'proper' tea and coffee.

'Still two sugars?'

'Er, yes thanks,' he replied, a little embarrassed.

Mr Worth cleared his throat. 'So... Michael, how are things, work alright?'

Michael thought if the old fart could meet him halfway, he'd do the same, so they chatted for a short time about the property market, while he had the best cup of tea he'd drunk in ages. He looked down as he felt his sleeve being pulled.

'Have you got my present?' asked Jack, wondering where Daddy was hiding it.

'Jack, you mustn't ask, you should wait,' Hannah said.

'It's okay, Hannah, here Jack.' He pulled out a large envelope. 'I wasn't sure exactly what you wanted, so it's a voucher for the toyshop. You can buy what you want.' Michael announced proudly, and wondered why the other three were looking cross and Jack, a bit perplexed.

Hannah jumped in quickly. 'It's a special card, instead of money, Jack. You know how you save in your piggy bank for things?' He nodded. 'Well, this is like your piggy bank full up, so you can go and get the next Lego you want.' *Why couldn't Michael just ask me?*

'Can we go now?'

'It won't be open now, Jack, but it would be nice if Daddy took you so he can see what you buy.' She wouldn't let him get off scot-free, he could put himself out. 'Maybe you could go tomorrow afternoon?' She looked pointedly at Michael.

'Oh... oh yes, of course, Jack, I'll sort it out with Mummy.' *Damn. I'll tell Shelby it'll only be an hour or two.*

'Good, do you want to open Aunty Fae's present?'

The voucher forgotten, he grabbed at the parcel, tearing off the exquisite wrapping as quickly as possible. 'I can be a fireman.' A shiny fireman's helmet and miniature uniform with a toy hosepipe lay alongside a fire truck with lights and a siren, which was soon being pushed around the room.

'She always seems to know what he likes,' Mrs Worth said pointedly.

'You'll get through batteries with that alright,' Michael answered defensively.

'It's strange, when she's given Jack things before with batteries, they last such a long time. They don't look special, I can never understand it,' Hannah said.

Jack was pushing the truck around with the siren blowing, which happily wasn't deafening, but still loud enough to mask his comment, 'My magic batteries.'

When he could be persuaded to leave the truck, he then insisted on changing into his fireman's outfit before tea. Even though Michael was beginning to get a bit bored, he had to admit his son looked cute when he came back in, and he took a photo on his phone. He tucked into the sandwiches and cakes, things he didn't get to eat so much of now.

The cake was much admired, and eventually, when Jack *did* allow it to be cut, it melted in the mouth with a taste that was indescribably delicious.

The downstairs phone rang. 'That's work, they can leave a message.' Hannah was serving up some more cake.

'It's alright, I'll get it.' Mrs Worth thought it might be important for someone to ring now. They could hear a mumbled conversation and then she came back up looking rather excited.

'That was Lady Thornbury,' she said, a little breathlessly. 'You've been recommended to her and she was wondering if you could call around to The Grange with some samples? She needs a special outfit for the Queen's garden party. Here's her number, I said you'd give her a call in the morning.'

'Okay.' Hannah seemed totally unfazed. 'She's quite a large lady, isn't she? I remember seeing her at the church fair last Christmas.'

Lady Thornbury. Was Hannah going to The Grange? Damn, he'd love to have a snoop around there. Michael was envious. He didn't think John Patterson moved in Lady Thornbury's circle and it would be one up on him if he met her. Lord Thornbury spent most of his time in London, as he had a seat in the House, and tended to come back at weekends. Lady Thornbury was a pillar of the community and much respected.

'That would be a good advertisement for you if you had one of your designs at a Royal occasion.' He tried to be friendly and sound interested.

'I wouldn't dream of mentioning it unless *she* suggested it, and I haven't got the order yet.' Hannah dismissed it like it meant nothing, but she *was* secretly excited. Dressing the larger lady always gave her satisfaction. As she had learnt, when she was a bigger size, how to disguise it, she was well versed in flattering their figures and they always came back with another order.

Tea was cleared and Michael, rather relieved, was able to say goodbye. Hannah reminded him about the next day and he grudgingly agreed to pick Jack up at lunchtime and take him for a burger. At least it would give him chance to have one. As it was still quite early, he stopped off for a pint before going home.

* * *

Shelby looked unbelievingly at the blue line on her test stick. She had expected it, but still hoped it wouldn't be the case. Well, there was no way she was having a baby. It would be sorted as soon as possible. It wouldn't even be discussed with Michael; he'd have no say. She knocked back the last of her wine and decided there and then to get herself sterilised so it could never happen again.

Chapter Twenty

WEB STITCH

*The finished effect has the appearance of
diagonal weaving*

When Michael got home, the flat was quiet and he found a note from Shelby saying she had a headache, had taken a tablet and gone to bed, would he be a love and sleep in the spare bedroom? That pissed him off a bit; did she think he would bother her if she had a headache? He noticed a large, empty wine bottle down by the kitchen bin. That wasn't like her, to drink so much, no wonder she had a headache. After a moment's doubt, he did see only one wine glass on the draining board. Perhaps she'd had a bad day at work and he hadn't been there to listen, or maybe she was more upset by him being with Jack and, of course, Hannah. It had been her suggestion though and he wasn't *that* late. He peeped in to see if she was awake.

Shelby heard him and tried to make her breathing even, keeping very still. She was lying across the centre of the bed, another reason for him not to disturb her. She just wanted to be on her own and couldn't stop thinking about the unwanted *growth* inside her. That's how she perceived it, nothing more, an invader, a mistake, to be removed quickly and without fuss.

'Shelby?' Michael whispered, and then, when there was no reply, he closed the door and went to the other room. She would need some pampering in the morning.

And then he remembered, he was supposed to be taking Jack out. *Oh damn.* Hannah would be much better at that; she would have far more idea of what he wanted. He could make it up to his son another time; Shelby would make his life hell if he wasn't available.

***

The next morning, Hannah had just got off the phone after arranging to visit Lady Thornbury later when she saw the text from Michael. *Emergency my ass!* She was so angry, she almost cried. Immediately calling lady Thornbury again, she explained that her son's sitter had let her down.

'Bring him along,' the woman said immediately. 'I have grandchildren visiting all the time, plenty of things to amuse him here, and my housekeeper, Mrs Owen, will be happy to look after him for an hour.'

'If you're sure, I'm ...'

'These things happen, don't worry about it. I'm looking forward to our meeting, Ms Rawlings.'

Hannah then had to put another note on the door, explaining that the shop would be closing at lunchtime, *damn Michael*, and go and explain to Jack.

His sobs broke her heart, *again*.

'Listen, Jack, Daddy's sorry but something happened that he has to do, it's very important. He's asked me to take you instead and we can still have a burger.'

He sniffed, 'With chips?'

'Of course, but Mummy has to do something first and you have to be a very good boy.'

Hannah pulled up outside The Grange, a rather imposing-looking building, covered with Virginia creeper. She could imagine driving up here in a carriage, and pictured the handsome Duke who would come down the steps to greet her.

'Mummy, are we getting out?'

'Oh yes, sorry Jack. Could you be a big help to Mummy and carry this box for me?'

Jack felt very important as they went to the big front door and he watched Mummy ring the bell. A lady with the reddest cheeks he had ever seen opened the door.

'Hello there, Hannah, is it? And you must be Jack. Lady Thornbury is expecting you, come this way please.'

Jack was fascinated by the house. 'Mummy, there's a suit of armour and funny pictures of people,' he whispered loudly.

'Shush Jack.'

'That's alright, they are funny pictures. I'll show you the armour in a minute, Jack,' said Mrs Owen as she opened doors to a large sitting room.

Jack looked up at Hannah. 'Can I, Mummy?'

'Let me say hello to him first,' said a voice, and a very large lady walked towards them.

Hannah was praying. *Please don't say anything about her bust.* Jack had a fixation about the size of women's chests at the moment, especially if they were very large and wobbly. His remarks were made in all innocence but could still be embarrassing.

'Hello Jack,' she boomed.

'Hello, your bosoms wobble.'

Hannah wanted the floor to open up and swallow her. There was silence for a moment and then Lady Thornbury gave a great snort of laughter.

'Out of the mouths of babes, eh? They do wobble, don't they? I'm hoping your mummy can help me with that. Now, you go with Mrs Owen while we grown-ups talk, there're lots of toys and some guinea pigs outside.'

249

Jack didn't need telling again and took Mrs Owen's hand, leaving without a backwards glance.

'I'm so sorry…'

Hannah's apology was waved away. 'That's children for you. I hope you can design something for me that will stop my bust wobbling when I meet the Queen.' She winked at Hannah. Within a short period of time, they were calling each other Irene and Hannah, while some sketches had been done, showing how the cut of the outfits would flatter and shape.

'Well, I think that's marvellous, you are a miracle worker, Hannah, and I can't wait to see them. Now I've picked my fabrics, let's go and find your boy. If I know Mrs Owen, she'll be feeding him in the kitchen.'

Sure enough, Jack was tucking into chocolate cake and lemonade.

'I hope this is alright, Ms Rawlings, he seemed hungry.'

'He'll always eat. I hope you said thank you, Jack.'

'Mummy, there are baby guinea pigs, can I have one?'

'Oh dear, that was my fault,' said Mrs Owen. 'I said we needed homes for them in a couple of weeks.'

Hannah had had guinea pigs, hamsters and a puppy when she was young and would have loved for Jack to have a pet. 'We don't have anywhere for them, Jack; guinea pigs normally live outside. We only have the balcony, it wouldn't be fair to them.'

'Could they live at Granny and Grandad's house?' he pleaded.

'We'll have to talk about it, Jack, they can't look after pets now, it wouldn't be fair to *them* either.'

His face fell. 'Pleeeez Mummy.'

Lady Thornbury jumped in quickly. 'We will look after them here, Jack, until you and Mummy can sort something out, how's that? Now, here's a shiny 50 pence, if you're allowed to spend that in the sweet shop.'

After another look at the guinea pigs, which brought fond memories back for Hannah, they collected all her samples with the order details, said goodbye and set off for the toyshop.

* * *

Shelby was subdued in the morning. 'I'm sorry, I had a pig of a day and just drank too much.'

'How do you feel now? Is there anything you need?'

'Just a large glass of orange juice. Listen, I need to talk to you, I want a week off as soon as possible.'

'You can have a week off. What do you want it for? Do you want me to take time off as well?' he asked

'No! I mean, no, not this time. I thought it was time I treated my mother and I'm going to take her away to a health spa for a week.'

'That'll be nice for you both, whereabouts?'

'I'm looking a few up. It's going to be a proper retreat, no internet or phones or anything, so I'll be out of circulation for that time. I'll let you know that we've arrived, of course.'

'Oh right.' A bit disgruntled at first, he then thought he could enjoy a few takeaways and proper food while she was away, to say nothing of lounging in front of the TV, watching football, which she hated.

'Vanya will still be coming in,' she said quickly.

'So?'

'She'll give me grief if the place is a mess.' *And let me know if you've been up to anything.*

'It won't be a mess, I can look after this place and myself for a week, you know.'

'Yeah, okay, I'll let you know the dates as soon as possible.'

One Lego pirate ship much later, Hannah's nerves were frazzled by the time they left the toy store. Full of screaming, tantrum-throwing children and clowns (a pet hate of hers), she was so relieved when Jack finally picked what he wanted. The voucher more than covered it, so she bought some books and a lovely children's atlas to put away until a bit later.

'Can we do the Lego now?' Jack was jumping up and down with excitement.

'We can start it tonight, but we're going for a burger first.' *And I shall have a double whatever one for myself.*

The burger shop was heaving, as she knew it would be on a Saturday, but Jack wanted to eat in and colour his placemat, so they found a space and she sat him down while she went to get the order. There were three girls in front of her waiting, about 12 years old, she guessed. They were chattering about a film they'd been to see. One of the girls turned to the menu board and Hannah was struck by the contrast of her pale skin and very straight, black hair. The girl seemed aware that she was being watched and gave Hannah a shy smile, then turned back to her friends.

'How long have we got, Ari, is your dad picking you up?' one of them asked.

The girl answered quietly, 'Yeah, you know what he's like. It took me ages to get him to start letting me go into town on a Saturday, it's only 'cause I'm with the two of you. I think he realised now I've started at my last school, he's got to let go a bit.'

'He's still on his own then?' asked the other girl.

'Yep, I keep trying to persuade him to get out and meet people. I think he's weakening a little bit now.'

'It's so romantic,' the first girl said in a dreamy voice. 'He can't get over his lost love...'

'Yes, girls, what's it to be?' The young man at the counter broke into their conversation and they moved forward.

Hannah wondered what that was all about. Obviously, the girl's father was single, divorced probably. Like me, she thought glumly. His lost love, surely the mother hadn't gone off? The girl must live with him, by the sound of it. Her thoughts were then interrupted by *her* call to the counter and getting back to Jack, she forgot about the overheard conversation.

* * *

Shelby had to get her mother on board so that she wouldn't accidentally put her foot in it if she spoke to Michael. Telling him she wanted to tell her mother about the surprise in person, she went to see her.

'Well, this is an honour, to what do I owe this pleasure?' her mother said sarcastically as she let Shelby in.

'I was here a few weeks ago, there's no need to be like that.' Shelby had always blamed her mother for not being able to keep John by her side when she found out she was pregnant. Even though he had more than made up for it, she still felt she'd missed out as a child. Since they had met up, she had been cooler towards her mother. 'I need your help, but I'll make it worth your while.'

'I don't need your money and it'll only come from your father anyway.' Monica Young waved a bottle of wine in Shelby's direction. 'Drink?'

'You look like you've had enough already. For God's sake, pull yourself together. You've got this lovely house now and your own money. My father's looked after you.'

'Oh yes, *now* he has, when there's something he wants. You obviously want something too. The apple didn't fall far from the tree in his case, what is it?'

'I'm pregnant, it was a mistake and I don't want it.' She went on to tell her mother what her plan was.

'So, Michael doesn't know about any of this?' Monica was aghast.

'No and he's not going to, so you need to keep quiet about it. I'll pay for you to go to a spa; a detox would do you the world of good.'

'I never for one minute considered getting rid of you, even when your father washed his hands of me. What you're doing in your life is a great disappointment to me, but even if I had my time over, I would make the same decision. You could live to regret this, Shelby, you need to think about it seriously.'

'I have thought about it! I don't want a child, I never have and never will. It's my body and my choice. Are you going to support me or not?'

Her mother sighed. 'Of course, you're my daughter, I'll always support you. I take it your father knows nothing.'

'No, and as you've said many times, he didn't want to know me, did he?'

'It would be his grandchild; he hasn't got anyone else.'

'Well, Michael's got a son. Maybe when he's a bit older, he'll be tolerable. I'll be his stepmother.' She shuddered. 'That's good enough.'

'So, you do see yourself... staying with Michael then, being a proper family?'

A momentary shadow of doubt flitted across Shelby's face and then was gone. 'Yes, why not? We rub along okay and we both want the same things out of life.'

'And does your father like him?' Monica asked slyly.

Another fleeting shadow. 'Yes, he does, so that's the end of it. Now, I'll let you know when I'm going to book you in, alright?'

'Yes, fine.'

Monica Young poured herself a large glass of wine when Shelby left and wondered, not for the first time, what had happened to the sweet, little girl her daughter had been. Believing that John Patterson was the love of her life had destroyed her, when he'd turned his back after she admitted the pregnancy.

'Get rid of it,' he'd snarled. 'I'm not being saddled with a wife and kid now. I've got all my life ahead of me.' She never had or would tell Shelby what he'd said at the time.

When he'd come back into their lives, because of Shelby's age, he'd had to make the approach via Monica. He showed no shame or remorse, just announcing that he wanted to get to know his daughter. She gained some small satisfaction finding out that he had no other children by then, but even though she hated him, she wouldn't deprive Shelby of the chance to meet him. That had changed everything between mother and daughter.

Shelby idolised John and, realising what he could give her, became greedy and selfish, drifting away from her mother and creating a rift between them that was now difficult to bridge.

One day, she may need me again, Monica thought sadly. John still had no other children and Shelby was his only link to the future. It would serve him right, she thought, if his grandchild was never born. If he'd had his way, he would have had no daughter either. *What would he do if he found out?* Maybe it would destroy the relationship. Monica was sorely tempted, but was that fair? Was it her own revenge she was taking? She worried about what sort of person Shelby was turning into, especially when she'd heard about the relationship with Michael. A married man with a small baby? That wasn't right and she felt very sorry for the ex-wife, even though she seemed to be successful now.

However, one never knew what went on in a marriage, and maybe *they* were never happy together. Shelby *appeared* to love Michael, which made this abortion decision even more strange. Why wouldn't she talk to him about it? She poured another glass of wine. Things always seemed better after she'd had a drink.

* * *

The next morning, Hannah and Jack finished the fire station and she flatly refused to even look at the pirate ship for a few days.

'Play with that one first Jack. Anyway, we're going to see Aunty Fae this afternoon so you can thank her for the present.'

'Can I dress up?'

'Yes, I'm sure she'd like to see it.' Hannah sighed with relief. Anything to take his mind off building yet another extension of the city.

Fae was waiting at Ivy Cottage, worrying about what she was going to say to them. Events that were destined would happen now, with or without her, and she was needed in other places soon. But she'd become very fond of Hannah and of Jack, who was a lovely little boy. She would miss this cottage as well, although she knew who would appreciate it.

It was always her failing, that she became too involved with her charges, this particular one having taken quite a long human time to sort out. The 'butterflies' were somewhat subdued as well. Her little helpers and messengers, they would also miss this place.

Subconsciously, she'd been twisting thread while thinking and now, looking down, she saw a beautiful multi-coloured pattern like a spider's web, stretched between her fingers. Carefully, she unhooked it and attached it to one of the bushes. *Oh well, I'd better see to the ginger cake, I won't be making it many more times.*

An hour later, an excited little fireman ran up the path to the cottage. 'Aunty Fae, look at me.'

'Well, don't you look very smart, young man? I won't worry about any fires while you're here.'

'Thank you very much and for my fire truck, it makes a great noise.'

'I'm so pleased. Hannah dear, how nice to see you, come in.'

'Thank you, Fae, you're looking well as usual.' *And never a day older, how does she do it?*

Over the usual tea and cake, Jack chattered about his presents and then ran around the garden making siren noises.

Hannah told her about the party and the visit to Lady Thornbury. 'She's ordered two outfits and one for the garden party.'

'I knew you'd make a success of that business, dear. Now, listen, I may have to leave this place and move away.'

'Oh no, Fae, I shall miss you so much and this lovely cottage. Why are you leaving?'

'I have a... sister, further up the country, who isn't very well, and she needs looking after. I'm sorry to have to leave. I'll miss you and Jack.' Fae was grateful that the butterflies were outside, keeping an eye on Jack, she didn't need their fluttering distraction as well.

Hannah said nothing as she didn't want to appear rude, but she thought Fae was a little old to be looking after somebody else, although she could never quite work out how old Fae was.

'I was going to ask a favour,' Fae went on. 'I don't intend to sell the cottage at this time, so I was wondering if you would keep an eye on it for me?'

'Certainly, so... do you think you might come back?'

'Who knows. Best to leave the option open, isn't it? That's a weight off my mind. Now another weight off my mind would be to see you settle down with a nice man.'

'I can't be thinking about that. Jack takes too much of my time anyway.'

'He won't always and you deserve some personal happiness. All I'm saying is don't write it out of your life. You should be getting out occasionally and meeting people.'

'That's what my mother keeps saying,' said Hannah crossly. Secretly, she wanted someone to share her life with, but after what had happened with Michael, she was scared.

'You mustn't be scared,' Fae said softly, making her jump. 'There is a perfect man out there somewhere, just waiting for you to come into his life. Come and see this.' She led Hannah out into the garden and showed her the threaded web on the bush.

'That's so beautiful and delicate,' said Hannah.

'That just came about by accident, I didn't even realise I was doing it. That's how you will meet somebody, not by drawing him into your web,' Fae added quickly, and smiled, 'but you won't even realise at first and then you will weave your lives together, *like* a web. First, though, you need to get your confidence back, so get yourself out and about and *meet* people.'

'Maybe,' Hannah said doubtfully. 'But back to you first, when will you be going?'

'In a month or two, I think. Don't worry, everything to do with the shop will be sorted by my solicitor and all correspondence will be through him. My sister is what you might call a traveller, so I will never know exactly where I'll be.'

'But if she's not very well…'

'She's a law unto herself. Now let's have another cup of tea and talk about more pleasant things while we have the chance.'

Chapter Twenty-One

FORBIDDEN KNOT

*A loop is made and tightened after the needle
has entered the fabric, before it is pulled
through completely*

Three months later, Hannah sat in Fae's solicitor's office, listening in disbelief to what he was saying.

'To put it simply, Hannah, I may call you Hannah? Mrs Grim has signed the cottage and the shop over to you in its entirety. The funds that you would have paid her are to go into an account that is held in trust for young Jack, to mature at various stages of his life. There is provision, should you have any further children.'

'I don't understand, she only asked me to keep an eye on it for her, there must be a mistake. She can't possibly mean to give me all that. I'm not her family or anything.'

'She was quite specific.' The solicitor peered over his glasses, which were balanced precariously on the end of his nose. 'It's perfectly legal, all signed and witnessed, and I can assure you, she was of sound mind when it was done.'

'I didn't mean to imply that she wasn't,' Hannah protested, 'but it's just too much.'

'She did leave a personal letter for you to read in your own time.' He passed over an envelope, which shimmered in the light and showered golden dust over her skirt as she held it.

'How can I get in touch with her? I need to talk to her about this.'

'I believe everything you need to know is in the letter, there's nothing else I can tell you. If you could just sign here… and here for me, please.'

In a daze, Hannah signed and, taking her letter, walked to the park and found a shady, quiet spot to open it.

My dearest Hannah,

I know this will be a tremendous shock to you, but I hope, with time, you will come to look upon it as the gift that I intended it to be. You came into my life at a time when you needed a friend; I would like to think that is what I became.

I have seen you go through the greatest happiness with the birth of Jack and also, the greatest sadness over the break-up of your marriage.

Time, as they say, is a great healer and you have healed well.

There is an emptiness in your life that is still to be filled, and I hope you will believe me when I tell you that will happen.

I have to move on now and I do not think our paths will cross again, but trust me when I say, I will always be watching over you and I wait for the day when you find happiness again.

**Treasure what I have given you and use it well,
in whatever way you see fit.**

Your friend and honorary Godmother

Fae Dorothy Grim

My God, she's dying. That was Hannah's immediate thought when she read the letter. There was no sister, Fae had told her that and gone away somewhere. How could she do that?

'I have to move on now' – that's what she must have meant. Hannah was angry and very sad. Not realising she was actually crying, she was startled by a quiet voice.

'Excuse me, are you alright?'

Looking up, Hannah saw a pale-faced, young girl with straight, black hair. She looked concerned but also wary.

She looks familiar, do I know her from somewhere? 'Thank you, yes, I'm fine. I just had some bad news about an old friend.'

'I'm sorry, has she died? Oh, it's not my business, I shouldn't ask.'

'She hasn't died, but I'm afraid she might, soon. She's gone away and I don't know where she is.'

'My mother died was I was young. I try to remember her but it's difficult sometimes. Were you and this person friends for a long time?'

'Quite a time, yes, I'm sorry about your mother. Do… do we know each other, have we met before?'

'Don't think so,' replied the girl. 'Anyway, if you're alright, I'd better get on.'

'Thank you for being kind.' Hannah smiled at her.

'People were kind to me and my dad when Mum was sick. He says we should give kindness back.' She gave a wave and ran on down the path.

A voice seemed to come from nowhere. *I really have had to go away. The child will be the key.*

'Fae?' *I'm dreaming, what did that mean, what child?*

It must mean Jack, Hannah thought, as she walked home. Did he need a father figure, was that what Fae was trying to tell her? Michael wasn't much of a father, but it would mean her having to enter into another relationship and she didn't know if she had the courage to do that.

* * *

There was definitely something wrong with Shelby. She had not been herself for over two months. The spa should have rejuvenated her but she returned from her week away pale and listless. Explaining it away by saying she'd had an upset stomach, she then seemed to have the longest 'monthly' ever and made him move into the other room until she'd recovered.

He went to the vegetarian takeaway that she favoured and tempted her with some of her favourite dishes, which were picked at half-heartedly. In addition, she was not ready to go back to work and Michael had to take on her job, with the help of a temporarily upgraded member of her team, as well as his own.

At least he was back in the marital bed, so to speak, but the spark was definitely missing. Maybe that was the problem, it *wasn't* the marital bed. Should he propose? They were as good as married anyway. She'd expect a ring, and one from a catalogue wouldn't do this time. He persuaded her to let him take her out for a romantic meal when she was feeling up to it and, as she realised it was time to pick herself up, she agreed.

What's the matter with me, she thought crossly, I made the right decision so I could get on with my life.

The next day she was back at work, her usual efficient and impersonal self. There was a tap on the door.

'Miss Young, Katie has popped in with her new baby.'

'Katie?'

'Katie, who worked here. She left two months ago and she's come to see us. I thought you might like to say hello.'

Katie, she remembered now. The girl who looked like she'd swallowed a watermelon just before she left.

'Well, it's not exactly convenient, but I suppose I could spare a couple of minutes, what was it we bought her?'

'We gave her a voucher for the baby store.' She didn't add that everybody else had given her individual presents with thought put behind them.

Shelby made a point of looking at her watch before stalking out to the main office. The cluster of staff parted like the Red Sea and she was faced with the biggest pair of blue eyes she'd ever seen. A sprouting of blonde curls and the prettiest little pink dress with matching baby bonnet.

Her heart fell to the floor.

'A girl. You had a little girl.' *A little girl, a little mini-me, I never thought it could be like that.*

'Yes, she's called Ella, Ella Louise. Would... would you like to hold her?'

'I...' The baby was offered and she instinctively took it into her arms. Ella stared up at her and waved little hands in the air. Shelby brushed her finger against the tiny fist whose fingers clasped around hers. Looking at that bond broke her.

'Take her back please, I need to get back to my office.' *They mustn't see, please let me get in there before they see.*

Inside, with the door locked, she almost collapsed. *What have I done? I killed a beautiful little girl.* In Shelby's mind, it would have been a girl for definite. Visions of gorgeous little dresses and other designer outfits flashed through her mind. She could have had a nanny; her father would have helped, she felt sure. Celebrities had babies, they managed. Tears poured down her face. *I murdered my daughter, why didn't somebody stop me?* Ignoring the memory of the clinic's psychologist, who tried to make sure she was happy with her decision and what her mother had said to her, she railed against the world. *Everybody is against me.*

Eventually, she composed herself, pressed an ice pack against her red eyes, and got back to work after remembering to unlock the door.

The staff avoided her for the rest of the day, not knowing what was wrong. They could see something had upset her and when she was upset, her temper would quickly rain down on the nearest victim.

Shelby screeched into the parking area of the apartments without a second look at the gateman, who was quite used to it. Stepping out of the lifts, which were exclusively for the penthouses, she saw her Arabian neighbour. The odd times she'd seen him over the years, Michael had always been with her when they met and she didn't want to force an introduction. A polite nod or the odd smouldering look when Michael's back was turned was enough for her to realise he was still interested. This was the first time she was on her own, and she saw the flash of lust that crossed his face.

'Shelby,' he gave a slight bow. 'How nice to see you again, I hope you are well?'

He was always so polite. Knowing she didn't look her best, she smiled. 'Kharim, it's nice to see you too, are you here on a business trip?'

'Yes, but alas, just a three-day stopover. May I invite you in for some chilled pomegranate juice, or… something stronger?'

Michael was going to the gym and wouldn't be back for at least two hours. What harm could it do?

'I just need to shower and that would be wonderful, thank you.'

He stood to one side, pushing his door open and looking at her with his big, soulful, brown eyes. *Like Dr Zhivago*. Her mother had been a huge fan of the film and its star, Omar Sharif. Shelby could see the attraction when she looked back into Kharim's eyes, they made her melt.

'Why don't you use mine and I will prepare you a drink and a plate with nuts and fruit? You look like you need to… relax,' he said with a slow, lazy smile.

God, yes, that's what I need. She slipped through the door, feeling his hand brush down her back, lingering on her bottom.

***

Hannah returned to the flat to see a couple of messages on the phone. One was from Lady Thornbury, saying how many compliments she had received at the garden party, and although Her Majesty hadn't said anything, a look of approval had been detected. Some winter outfits would be much appreciated, at Hannah's convenience. A slightly more strained note came when she mentioned two guinea pigs still in a spare hutch and did Jack still want them.

The other message was from Furze House. Hannah paid a dutiful visit every few weeks, although Doreen was completely in a world of her own now. Recently, she had been suffering from a bad chest infection, and the message was to tell Hannah that she was beginning to slip away and wasn't expected to last the week. When she phoned them back, she was told Michael had also been informed. They stressed that a visit was not necessary and also unwise, with the risk of germs being taken back to a small child in her house. Hannah asked to be told, whatever time it was, and she would come then, to pay her last respects.

* * *

The call came two days later, early one morning. After dropping Jack at school, she went straight to the home. Doreen seemed at peace for the first time in years and although they hadn't been exactly close, Hannah still felt saddened. As she was leaving, Michael drove into the car park.

'I'm sorry about Doreen, Michael, whatever she had become, she was still your mother. Please let me know when the funeral will be.'

Michael realised he'd have to deal with all of that. Hannah would have done it without even being asked, but as Shelby didn't even know her, he couldn't expect her to be involved. 'Where do you think...'

'She hadn't been to church for years, is it in her will?'

'I don't know, I'll check. Thanks for coming to see her. Is... Jack alright?'

'If you mean about his grandmother, he didn't really know her, but if you mean about his father, I'm sure he'd appreciate a visit. I'll see you at the funeral then.'

Hannah drove away, leaving Michael with a sour taste in his mouth.

Why do I feel sorry for him, why? She was furious with herself. It was *his* job to arrange everything, let him get on with it. She would certainly attend, feeling she owed Doreen that much, but that was as far as it went.

Driving straight to Lady Thornbury's house, she was welcomed by Mrs Owen, who opened the door with a smile.

'Hello, I'm afraid she's not in at the moment.'

'It's okay, I'm here to collect the guinea pigs, I'm so sorry you've been left with them.'

'Oh, don't be upset about the phone message, their noise gets on her nerves at times. Would you like the hutch?'

'If it's going spare, yes please.' Hannah had had a brainwave. The school had a few animals, including an ancient guinea pig, so hopefully these could be added and Jack could then see them every day.

Before going to the school, she drove to Ivy Cottage, accompanied by the squeaking of the guinea pigs in their hutch on the back seat. It was the first time since finding out it now belonged to her. Previously, she'd seen herself as a caretaker, always hoping that Fae would come back; now, she knew that wasn't going to happen. It looked as it always did, with a faint smell of beeswax and the ever-lingering scent of ginger cake. A few of the golden dust motes still danced in the sunbeams, but it was the silence that Hannah noticed. No welcoming call, no sound of tinkling laughter.

Mine, this is mine now. Slowly, she climbed the stairs, only having ever taken a quick look up there before, it was unfamiliar. One large bedroom with wardrobes and a neatly-made double bed looked over the garden. A room led off it, which had a large skylight and table, perfect for a workroom.

The bathroom was modern and functional, with a bath and separate shower. A large, fluffy white towel lay invitingly over the rail. Again, another room led off from it, which was a large walk-in airing cupboard. It never seems this big from the outside, she thought.

A further bedroom with box room attached was already decorated in a pale blue with curtains and a quilt covered in motifs of small animals. The roof was exposed in this room of... Jack's? It also had a staircase going up to a mezzanine floor, where there was plenty of room for toys.

It's just lovely she thought, could we live here? It wasn't that far from the town, half an hour at the very most. He could stay at the same school and they could still use the flat over the shop as well. Would it make more sense to rent one of the places out? The thought of somebody else in this cottage didn't seem right at all. *I won't make a hasty decision about the flat, we'll see how it goes.* Deciding to bring Jack to see it without 'Aunty Fae' being here would be the decider.

The school were delighted with the new pets.

'Old Bertie's not long for this world, I fear,' said the head. 'These two will soften the blow.' Jack was summoned and was very excited that 'his' guinea pigs were joining the school. Hannah was very relieved.

* * *

The funeral for Mrs Rawlings was a week later. As Michael thought, Shelby had no intention of attending.

'I've never even met the woman and Hannah will be there, I suppose?'

'Well yes, she feels some duty to what was her mother-in-law.'

'I suppose so.'

He was amazed she hadn't made a bigger fuss, but she had been a little distracted over the last few days. He'd come home one night and was bemused to see her watching 'Babies do the Funniest Things'. When she realised he was there, she'd acted all surprised, changed the channel quickly, saying something about 'not even realising what was on', and made a big show of shuffling her magazines about. He was hoping to arrange their 'special' meal within the next week or so, and had hidden a box from the jewellers in his briefcase.

* * *

It was raining on the day of the service. Jack wasn't there, Hannah said he was far too young, and she'd told her parents not to come out in the bad weather either.

A couple of staff from Furze House came, also Mrs Figgins, who made a point of talking to Hannah and ignoring Michael. No one from Michael's family bothered to turn up so it was a small group at the cemetery afterwards. Words were said and earth was thrown, then people began to disperse. Michael made a half-hearted attempt to invite everyone to the pub, but no one seemed keen. As they walked out, Hannah glanced at one grave that had the most beautiful bunch of freesias adorning it. The rain hadn't spoilt them yet, so they must have been put there only that morning.

'Thank you for coming, Hannah, I mean, for my mother's sake.' Michael stood awkwardly by his car.

'I always knew this day wasn't far off, of course, I would be here. There weren't very many people, were there?'

'None of the family ever visited her once she went into the home,' he said.

Not voicing her thoughts aloud about *his* lack of visits, she smiled gently. 'Her memories drift away on the wind. Somebody said that to me once.'

'Nonsense,' he said. 'Anyway, thanks again.'

* * *

Christopher made Arianne's favourite night-time chocolate and tapped on her bedroom door.

'Come in Dad, I'm just finishing my homework.'

He put the chocolate down and sat on the end of the bed. 'Thanks for leaving early with me this morning to do the flowers, for your mother.'

'It's a shame about the rain, they'll spoil quicker, but I'd never miss her birthday.'

He glanced at her sketchbook on the bed, open and covered with drawings of ladies' clothes. 'Still designing?' he chuckled.

'Yes, I have so many ideas. I think I'd like to do something in fashion later. I like art and English anyway, and I could do textiles in school later.'

'You're going to be the next Coco Chanel, are you?'

'Who?'

'You'd better read up on her if you want to study fashion,' he laughed.

She sipped her chocolate. 'Dad?'

He looked wary. 'What is it?'

'Please don't bite my head off but I wish you would go out with some ladies.'

271

'Arianne, not this again.'

'Yes, this again,' she said firmly. 'I'm almost fourteen and I need to talk about lady things, it would be nice for me to have a friend.' She slipped off her chair and sat next to him. 'Grandma's too old now; it's not fair on her. I want you to have someone in your life. You've been a wonderful dad to me, but now it's time for you. I *know* Mum wouldn't have wanted you to be on your own forever.'

'I'm not on my own, I've got you.'

'You won't always have me, not here all the time, I mean. Please Dad, just give it a try, for my sake?'

'For you? I'll give it a try, but I'm not promising anything. If it makes you happy, I'll go on a few dates,' he sighed. 'How on earth do I go about meeting someone now? I'm too old to go clubbing.'

Arianne laughed. 'You'd better not. Let's have a look on the internet, on the dating sites.'

'What do you know about dating sites?'

'Oh Dad, everybody knows about them. Come on, let's just see what's out there.'

In a slight state of panic, he watched as she scrolled through pictures and information about women in the area.

On the chest of drawers sat Mr Bear, gently beginning to shimmer once again.

Chapter Twenty-Two

SATIN STITCH

Flat stitches that are used to completely cover a
section of the background

*'Remove your shift.' As Cassandra did as he bid, Gregory,
Duke of Fellswold, stared in admiration at the perfect
body before him. Rich, deep-chestnut hair tumbled in
waves down her shoulders, teasing the small, pert, pink
nipples...*

Hannah gave a sigh and put down the book. She still
devoured her Dukes and there were always so many new
ones appearing in the 'historical fiction' section of the
bookshop. *So many books and so little time. Oh well,
perhaps a few more pages before I go to sleep.*

Two months had passed since Doreen's funeral. Hannah
and Jack had moved into Ivy Cottage, which he adored,
and they stayed at the flat on Tuesday and Thursday
nights, when he had some after school activities.

The first time Michael had to come to collect him
for a Sunday outing, he was most put out to find her
established there.

'*Gave* it to you, why would she do that? She's only
some old woman you barely know.'

'She became a very good friend, actually, not that you were around to notice.' *He might as well know.* 'I own the shop and the flat as well now.'

'What?' He couldn't believe his ears. A prime piece of real estate in town, what a waste. 'Are you renting the flat? I have tenants…'

'Not at the moment, it's handy some nights when we don't want to be late home.'

'Isn't it a bit isolated out here, is it safe for Jack? And you, of course,' he added.

'Your concern is very touching, but we're perfectly alright here. Nobody ever calls unless I'm expecting them.'

This was very true. Beatrice Congdon, an avid rambler as well as a reader, had complained to Hannah's mother after she had been walking in the area. Upon hearing that Mrs Worth's daughter had moved out there, she thought she could cadge a cup of tea and a nose around. But, she moaned, the cottage was nowhere to be seen, and she had scoured the area.

Mrs Worth had said how strange that was; they themselves had been out several times and it was easy to find. Wanting to spare Hannah the 'pleasure' of a visit from Beatrice, she explained that they were not often at home anyway as her daughter and grandson liked to get out and about.

Michael had seethed. The large plot of land that she owned would have been plenty of room for a dozen or so flats with a communal garden. That old biddy must have been soft in the head, giving away all that. He was slightly mollified when she suggested he take Jack out on the bike along the old railway track and then, if he liked, he could come back for a pasty, as she was making a batch.

274

If he liked? Of course, he liked. He could never take a pasty home to eat, Shelby said they smelt disgusting. At least now they worked in separate offices, he grasped the opportunity for lunchtime favourites and often nipped to the pub for steak and kidney or sausage bake. It made the veggie options more palatable in the evenings.

Surprisingly, he'd enjoyed the walk, and seeing Jack without the stabilisers made him swell with pride. Being a father wasn't so bad now his son could talk and didn't need changing all the time. He enjoyed the pasty immensely, along with two cups of strongly-brewed tea. He rather regretted having to leave so soon, when it was pleasant sitting in the garden, having a civilised conversation about their son's schooling.

* * *

Shelby was pregnant again; she'd been given her second chance. Not a word was going to be said to anyone until she was certain it was a girl, that's what she wanted. Not exactly sure who the father was caused a little concern. She herself didn't care, but Michael had to believe it was his. Brown eyes were not a problem, but she hoped the baby wouldn't be too dark-skinned. Kharim wasn't, so hopefully, she'd get away with it. Her scan was booked, then she would know the sex.

She'd never realised how much baby designer stuff was available. Not only clothes but furniture, wallpaper, accessories, everything. Researching the minor celebrities around the area, she discovered where the best nannies came from and where they all shopped. Having met a couple of 'B' list people through her father's connections, she realised she needed to get into their circle. One couldn't have a proper baby shower party without celebrities.

The nanny would need to live in; that would mean moving to a large house, and she had just the one in mind. In the larger town where she now worked was a row of four-storey Georgian townhouses. Not quite as splendid as The Crescent, in Bath, but a fair substitute. A lot of them were inhabited by different solicitors' offices and one or two private consultants. There were still some, however, that were privately owned, and one was for sale on their books at just over £1.4 million. She had put herself in charge of viewings, and a muttered remark here and there had put potential buyers off. The whole of the top floor was suitable as a nursery, with accommodation for a nanny. The ground floor comprised a large entrance hall with kitchen and utility areas at the back and a useful lower-ground floor, housing a vast boiler, along with plenty of room for laundry and even a wine cellar.

Vanya would be replaced with a housekeeper-cum-cook, while Shelby could be involved in property at a more managerial level, her father would like that. It was a house for entertaining and she could still enjoy her daughter without any of the hard work. Why hadn't she realised before? Her father would probably prefer the baby to be a son of her own rather than just a stepson but maybe, later, once she knew the responsibility of caring for him would rest with other people, she'd think about it.

Her flat would take care of almost half the cost and she hoped to persuade her father to see it as a family home. Michael had money now, he would put some in, but she would ensure it was still *her* house. He'd been badgering her to go out for 'a romantic meal' for weeks and she'd put it off for various reasons, but finally, had agreed on tonight. The least she could do if she was fobbing another man's child off was to be more appreciative towards him.

* * *

Christopher was not looking forward to his evening at all. To placate his daughter and show her he *was* making an effort, he'd signed up to one of the dating agencies. Having been paired with a divorced lady from 20 miles away, they'd agreed on a meeting at a pub around the halfway mark. There was nothing wrong with the lady herself, she looked very nice, he just wasn't enthusiastic. The texts to each other were polite but friendly, and neither of them seemed to be expecting more than a meal and getting to know each other.

Her name was Stephanie and the message said she'd be wearing a blue dress. Christopher took flowers, not freesias, but a small bouquet, so as not to look over-keen. It might be nice, he thought for a change, to talk to someone who hadn't known about Claire and what had happened.

At the pub, a quick glance around showed no sign of a woman fitting the description, so he ordered a soft drink and sat where he could keep an eye out. Eventually, a lady came through the door in the promised outfit.

Good grief, she's a midget, was his first thought. She wasn't actually a midget, but she was very small, and unfortunately, Christopher was nearly six foot, so when he went over to meet her, they did look an odd couple. On a level, her eyes were somewhere in the middle of his tie.

'Stephanie? I'm Christopher, it's very nice to meet you. I, er… these flowers are for you.'

'Thank you, you are very tall, aren't you? I did say in my application that I was petite and didn't want too tall a man.'

Although rather taken aback, Christopher smiled politely. 'Well, maybe they realised we had other interests in common. Shall we sit? Then the difference won't be so obvious.'

'Yes, I didn't mean to be rude, it's just that I might get a crick in my neck talking to you.' Then she laughed.

A few people glanced around, smirking. Christopher thought for one second that there was a horse looking through the window and whinnying. *I've never heard anyone laugh like that.*

She ordered what seemed a very large meal for her tiny frame and then sat back. 'You'd better tell me a bit more about yourself. Single, you said?'

'Widowed actually…'

'Oh, was that recent? I hope you haven't decided to find somebody else too quickly.'

'Er, no, it was…'

'The last man I dated had only just got divorced and said he wanted to put himself back on the market right away.' She stopped for a breath and to take a sip of her drink.

Christopher jumped in quickly. 'I lost my wife five years ago, I have a daughter of thirteen."

'A daughter? You didn't mention that in your messages. Thirteen, you say? That's a difficult age.'

'Is it?'

'Oh yes, *boys*, you know.' She gave him a knowing look.

'I don't think she's interested yet…'

'Mark my words, you'll have trouble soon.' *And I don't want to take that on, thanks very much.*

The meals arrived and they ate in relative silence. While waiting for dessert, Christopher tried again. 'What about you, Stephanie, what are your interests?'

'I like to get out and about, see different places.' Christopher brightened. She continued. 'My bingo club goes out at least once a week to visit other clubs and we have a meal out.'

Bingo? No thanks. 'Do you get time to actually visit the places you go to?'

'Not really, by the time we get there, we just want to get a good seat. I'm quite lucky, you know, only last night, I got £10 for a line.'

'Really?' Christopher sounded bemused. *What's a line?*

'Yes, and I get a full house once a month usually.'

The desserts were coming. *Thank God.* 'A full house, that's good, is it?'

'It's not bad. The amount I play, I should get more. I tell you, Mabel Cleethorpe got two houses in one night. If that's not a fiddle, I'd be surprised.'

Christopher ate his dessert and thankfully, she declined coffee. He hoped she wasn't expecting to be invited back for one. He insisted on paying the bill and walked her to her car, where she hovered expectantly.

'Stephanie, it's been a pleasure meeting you, but I think maybe I'm too tall for you. I hope you meet somebody else, at the bingo club maybe?'

'Oh, well, yes, maybe, thank you for the meal. Remember what I said about *boys*, you need someone to have a talk with that daughter of yours.'

He watched her drive away, feeling a great weight lifting from his shoulders. Arianne would want to hear all about it tomorrow. Realising he'd have to give it another try as one experience couldn't count, at least he could put it off for a while now.

Shelby wondered whatever was the matter with Michael. He'd been fidgety throughout the meal and was playing nervously with his spoon, not having eaten much of the dessert.

'Is something wrong? You're wriggling on your seat like a schoolboy.'

'I, er… want to ask you something.'

'Well ask then, what is it?'

'We've been together a long time now…'

Michael's voice faded as realisation dawned. Shelby knew what was coming. She wasn't against marriage, but her mother had hit the nail on the head when she'd asked if he was the one for keeps. To be honest, if she wasn't pregnant, she'd fob him off with an excuse. As nice as he was, she hadn't envisaged them growing old together. *Growing old! What a terrible thought.* If she was keeping this baby, however, he *would* be a suitable father and it was advantageous at times to be attached. But, if she didn't keep it?

'Shelby, you're in a dream, what do you say?' Michael was looking terribly pleased with himself, as if she had been rendered speechless by his request. She focussed on a small box lying open on his hand with a ring. A *tiny* diamond, but a diamond all the same.

'Michael, I don't know what to say, I never saw this coming.' She slipped the ring on. It was very pretty and had obviously cost him a lot of money. She had to be sure of the baby first. 'You know the correct response from me is "please let me think about it"?'

'What's there to think about? We've lived together long enough, I told you, I love you, Shelby, you're the woman for me, and I'd like to think I'm the man for you.'

'I know how you feel, but please, let me do this the proper way. I'll give you my answer in a couple of weeks. I just need to get used to the idea.' Her eyelashes fluttered as she looked down demurely at her plate.

He took her hand. 'If that's what you want, I'll wait. I'm sure you won't disappoint me.'

* * *

On Tuesday, Hannah popped up into the town at lunchtime to post some letters. Walking past one of the bars, she saw a sign saying 'Singles night. Come and make friends. Meet people. Meet somebody special.'

Was it time? Should she make an effort? *I don't look too bad*, she thought, as she caught her reflection in the window. As she was so busy these days, her baking had cut back considerably, and she tried to encourage Jack with healthy eating. The short hairstyle still suited her and she knew her clothes made her look good. *I could give it a try, I don't have to stay.* It was one of the nights they stayed in the flat and it didn't start until eight, so she would have time to collect Jack from his after-school club and drop him at her parents for the night. Her mother would be delighted that she was getting out. Treating herself to some new make-up, she began to feel quite excited.

Entering the pub at just after eight and feeling nervous, she was glad to see it was very busy and she could lose herself in the crush. It was not to be.

'A single, are you?' A girl who looked like she was hardly out of school put a sticker on the front of Hannah's dress and waved a felt pen. 'Wassurname?'

'Er, Hannah.' Her name was written in wobbly letters and spelt wrong so that it looked like 'Manna'. *That's a great start, I better get a drink.*

As she eventually got a diet cola, she turned from the bar and saw a straw-coloured head peering at her chest. Just about to say something, she realised he was trying to read her name.

'Manna?'

'It's Hannah actually.' Her heart sank. He was about 70, good head of hair, which had deceived her until he stood up. Still, he might be nice to talk to.

'Good, old-fashioned name, are you a good, old-fashioned girl?'

Oh God, he's only got about four teeth. 'I'm not quite sure what you mean?'

'Man, master of the house and that sort of thing.' He lurched towards her. 'Discipline, that's the key to a good relationship.' He winked and, reaching around, patted her bottom.

You disgusting, old letch. 'Excuse me, I think I see someone I know over there.' *This is hopeless.*

She turned and stepped on the toe of a striking-looking woman. 'Oh, I'm so sorry, are you alright?'

The woman smiled. 'I'm fine, darling, Manna?'

'Hannah, the girl couldn't spell, you are...?' She hadn't noticed until she looked but the woman's bust was almost completely exposed in a very low-cut top and this was causing quite a stir amongst the men standing around her.

'Maxine,' she said. 'There wasn't much room for the label. It's quite a crush, isn't it? Shall we move over there?' She indicated a quieter area. 'So, Hannah, what do you do then and what brings you here?'

'I'm a designer and dressmaker. Why am I here? Same as you, I suppose. To meet somebody.'

Maxine rested her hand on Hannah's arm, giving it a gentle squeeze. 'I've been to these a few times, but I'm glad I've met you.' She was staring rather intently and her squeeze had turned into more of a caress.

Oh crap, she fancies me. 'Umm, Maxine, I was... I meant, I came to meet a man.'

'Don't fancy the alternative? Maybe I could change your mind. You're just my type, and you know what they say, don't knock it till you've tried it.'

'I'm very flattered, Maxine, but really, it's not for me. I hope you meet somebody.'

'Oh well, if you change your mind, come and find me, I'll be here for a while yet.' She released Hannah's arm regretfully.

Hannah made good her escape and as she slunk back towards the door, a quite nice-looking man stopped her.

'Manna?'

She tore off the badge. 'It's Hannah,' she said firmly and looked at his badge,' and you're Richard?'

'Yes, are you alright for a drink?'

Thank goodness, somebody sensible. 'I just got one. Have you been to these things before?'

'Once or twice. At our, sorry, *my* age, it's difficult to meet people socially unless your friends set you up, and I've had a few disasters that way.'

He's actually rather nice, maybe this isn't such a bad idea. 'Have you, er, always been single?'

'Nope, divorced. Usual thing, got married too young, a couple of kids. They live with the mother, thank God. I mean, they're alright, but too much at times. I like my freedom. What about you?'

Hannah's enthusiasm had dimmed considerably. 'Divorced as well, yes, with a son. Actually, I rather miss him, so I'll be off. Good luck with your hunting.'

She left with a spring in her step and a weight off her shoulders. She'd given it a try. Maybe in a while, she'd try again, no rush.

✳ ✳ ✳

Shelby was having her scan. *God, this is so undignified. It would be even worse if I wasn't a private patient.* 'Can you see what it is?'

'Not yet, but it's a nice, strong heartbeat. There's the head, do you see?'

'Yes, I see the head. Are there any dangly bits?'

'Dangly bits? Oh,' the woman laughed, 'hoping for a boy, are you?'

Shelby gritted her teeth. *I must say the right things.* 'I really don't mind, as long as it's healthy and all that. I would like to know the sex. I don't like surprises.'

'Well I can see now and I can tell you...'

Shelby held her breath.

'It's a girl.'

Thank you, thank you. Shelby had got her wish.

That night she poured a glass of wine for Michael and a mineral water for herself.

'I can give you my answer now.'

'Oh Shelby.'

'Please don't get all gushy on me. The answer's yes, I will marry you, but I have something else to say. We either get married right away or we wait at least a year.'

'Why a year?'

She looked smug. 'So that I can get my figure back after our daughter is born.'

Michael thought he was hearing things. 'Y... you're pregnant?'

'Yes, it does happen, you know, especially when people are at it all the time.'

'But you don't like babies.'

'I've changed my mind. I have big plans; this is how we're going to do it...'

Chapter Twenty-Three

KNOTTED LOOP STITCH

Can be worked in lines, used singly or scattered

Shelby was getting her wish. She had begged and pleaded for a C-section but even she couldn't sway the doctor. Now the baby seemed in some distress and they were going to do it anyway.

'If anything happens to this baby, I'll sue you all,' she screamed. The C-section she had wanted was to save her from messing up 'down there', but now it was happening, all she could think about was the little girl she wanted so desperately.

The house had been acquired with her father's help and a top designer brought in to decorate a nursery fit for a baby princess. The walls had been done in pale pink, washed silk, and the most elaborate swan bed was waiting as soon as she would be out of the top-priced cot. Sitting next to that was a handmade, traditional rocking horse. The wardrobes were already full of designer outfits and the nanny established and under strict orders from Shelby.

Michael had foolishly remarked that it seemed a bit over the top, and then wished he'd never opened his mouth. Even then, he didn't feel as bad as when he'd told Hannah that he was going to be a father again. She had gone very pale, quietly congratulated him, and asked him to explain to Jack that he was going to get a baby sister or brother.

'Umm, sister actually, we already know. I'm sorry, Hannah, I know it must hurt.'

'Do you, do you really? I don't think you have any concept of how I feel. I sincerely hope that you'll be a better father this time around.'

He had left feeling like a worm but determined, as she'd said, to do a better job this time. Shelby's attitude to motherhood worried him. The nanny, the nursery and her planned schedule seemed not to leave much time for her and her daughter to be together. It was as if the baby would be a special doll, to be picked up, dressed up and shown off at her own convenience.

Now, he sat at the private hospital, awaiting the birth.

Shelby had been given an epidural and was aware of what was happening. A name was already in her head, an Arabic name, Lina, meaning little palm tree. It didn't sound too Arabic, and even if Michael was the father, she still liked it. Although she couldn't see what was going on, or actually feel anything, she had the sensation of something being pulled and then heard a cry.

'I want to see her!'

'Just a few minutes, we need to do checks and we'll wipe her clean for you.'

Yuck, maybe that's best. The promised few minutes later and there she was. A light café-au-lait-coloured skin, with dark curls plastered to her head. Eyes tightly squeezed shut but definitely Kharim's aquiline nose. Then the eyes opened, pools of melting chocolate stared at her. Kharim was the father, of that there was no doubt. *My little Arabian princess.*

'We could let the father in now for a quick look, we just need to take her away for a while to make sure she's okay, but she looks fine.'

'Kh... the father? Oh Michael, er, yes.' She was feeling very sleepy now.

Michael was ushered in to see Lina. Dutifully, he gave Shelby a kiss first. A daughter! Every man wanted a son but there was something special about a daughter. She had his brown eyes he thought with pride. Her skin was... a little darker than he'd thought it would be, but not unattractive.

'Shelby, she's gorgeous... Shelby?'

She was asleep.

* * *

Michael had invited Jack to his daughter's first birthday this weekend and Hannah had made something for the little girl. It was his half-sister, after all. She had been to Jack's school for harvest festival and was pleased to see him settling well in the junior section. She now had a competent assistant, a retired dressmaker who came in three mornings and one full day a week, so Hannah could get out to see more clients and have some time to herself. She was quite a wealthy woman now and the only sadness she had was that Fae was not around to see it. She had so much to thank her for and even after badgering the solicitor, she had no idea where Fae was, or even if she was still alive.

There was her favourite bookshop. Perhaps this was a good time to see what new titles may have been put on show. Making a bee-line for historical romance, she scanned the shelves. *Oh, there's a whole set*. Six books, all with a picture of a chisel-featured, handsome man with a swooning beauty in his arms adorning the covers. All six were paid for and stuffed into a carrier bag.

'I thought of you when they came in,' beamed the assistant. 'I knew you'd be in soon, you're one of our regulars, and I said to myself, "That lady will have these", I said.'

Oh, dear am I that predictable? 'Umm. Yes, they do look good, thanks.' She walked quickly out of the shop. Straight into a tall, chisel-featured, *very* good-looking man. The carrier bag slipped from her grasp and the books tumbled out onto the pavement.

'I'm terribly sorry,' she gasped and went to grab them quickly.

'My fault, I wasn't looking. Let me help you.'

Oh no, 'I've got them, really…' *What a voice.* Hannah had never truly believed that such a thing could make a woman go weak at the knees, but that had now been totally proved true.

Christopher had picked up two of the books and was looking at the covers. 'The Devil Dukes?' He arched an eyebrow.

He arched an eyebrow! Oh, my God. 'M… my mother, she loves these… umm… types, thank you so much,' she mumbled, reaching for them.

He was still looking. 'The Duke's Pact with the Wanton?' he grinned. 'Sounds much better than some I've read lately.'

'I… I wouldn't know, my mother you know… I said.'

'Yes, you did say.' *She's rather nice looking, and they're definitely for her. Her mother indeed.* He passed over the other two. 'Are you sure you're alright? You look a bit flushed; do you need to sit down?'

If he spoke many more words to her, Hannah thought she'd end up swooning in his arms like one of the women on the covers. Funny thing was he did look a bit familiar. 'I'm fine, really, I was just in a hurry. Thank you again and… sorry.'

No wedding ring, 'That's alright, maybe we...' But Hannah had already turned and hurried away.

He was gorgeous and I'm sure I've seen him before. Surely, she would remember. She wished she could have met *him* at one of her singles' nights. After the first disaster, she'd waited several months and then tried a couple in the bigger town so as hopefully not to meet anyone she'd already rejected as a dead loss. One or two had been promising and even a couple of further dates had been arranged, but they fizzled out when Hannah felt there was no 'spark' there. In the last few weeks, she'd more or less decided to give up. Somebody like him wouldn't be available anyway, she thought miserably.

Christopher was disappointed that he'd missed the chance of having a proper chat with her. She probably wasn't available, an attractive lady like that. Just because she wasn't wearing a ring, didn't mean anything. He chuckled over her discomfort about the reading material. A bit of escapism, why not? With luck, their paths might cross again one day soon.

* * *

Lina was one year old and the house was full of balloons and presents. Shelby had invited a few select guests, upmarket mothers she had met in the circuit of designer shops and expensive baby pampering salons. One First Division footballer's wife was now her 'best friend'. The only benefit to Michael was the fact they got tickets to the matches. He was never going to be Premier League material, Michael thought, but that was okay. His daughter was treated like a princess and spoilt to the hilt by her grandfather. He had slapped Michael on the back when he'd come to the hospital, and made it clear that he'd expect Michael to produce a son next. What was Jack, thought Michael, a little peeved, chopped liver? Okay, he wasn't related, but he didn't have to be ignored as he usually was.

Jack was actually at the party, on Michael's insistence, introduced as 'the boy from the previous'. Michael was very proud of his son. He'd grown into a well-mannered child, and had bought a present with his own pocket money. As Hannah wanted a good relationship between the children, she'd sent a beautiful dress of her own design with matching bootees and hat.

The 'WAG', whose real name was Caroline, now Charleene, enthused over it and said she simply *must* get an outfit for the end of season party. Shelby, seething, agreed, but the dress was exceptional and she looked forward to seeing Lina wearing it.

A few guests wondered quietly to themselves about Lina's skin colour. She wasn't dark, but both Shelby and Michael were very fair-skinned, while she had a glow, reminiscent of a holiday tan. Shelby could see Kharim in her daughter every day. As they had moved from the flats, she had no worries about them ever seeing each other. Kharim would know, the second he saw her, of that, Shelby was sure. Whether he would acknowledge her was another matter. A boy, maybe, probably not a girl.

The nanny, always quietly in the background, was sure Michael wasn't the father. She thought it was ridiculous, the way the child was treated, but did she care? Her salary was good, and as long as she kept Shelby happy, she had a good life. The occasional screaming tantrum, from the mother, not the child, was a small price to pay.

Shelby's mother, Monica, was also there. It was under the condition that she didn't drink. Monica sipped her mineral water, making small talk and watching John Patterson lording it over everybody. She hadn't had a drink for several months, not that Shelby needed to know. John had nodded to her as if she were a nobody. *The pompous prat.* She had only been to the house once or twice and had to admit that Shelby had it all now. The only fly in the ointment was that baby. If Michael was the father, she was a Dutchman. The way Shelby had changed her mind about a child was quite extraordinary, but Monica was pleased she had, and her granddaughter was a dear little thing.

'Shelby, I hope you don't mind, but I asked somebody if they could pop over here with a contract I need to sign. It's a hotel, big conversion job.' John Patterson had caught Shelby and Michael on their own for a minute. 'It is very important it's signed today.'

'Of course I don't mind,' Shelby slipped her arm through her father's. 'Who is it?'

'You probably remember him, Kharim Alhahabi, who rents the other penthouse where you used to live.'

Shelby's glass of champagne fell and shattered on the marble floor as the doorbell rang.

The hired member of staff who was hovering nearby automatically opened it and standing there, looking just as handsome as before, was Kharim.

'Ah, Kharim, good of you to come over, you remember Shelby, of course.' Her father's voice boomed, from what seemed a long way away. Everything was a blur. Where is Lina, she thought in a panic. *Please, please don't let him see her.* Her mouth opened but all that came out was a squeak.

'Shelby.' The voice was so polite. 'It is a great pleasure to see you again, and what a very lovely house you live in.'

'Th... thank you, would you please excuse me a moment.' *Oh no, no, no, noooo.*

The nanny was bringing Lina towards them.

'Ah, excellent. Kharim, meet my lovely granddaughter. As I mentioned to you, it's her first birthday today.' John Patterson's voice echoed around the room.

Two pairs of identical brown eyes stared at each other. Kharim felt as if he'd been hit by a thunderbolt and he glared accusingly at Shelby, who was as white as a sheet. Not so with Lina; her golden skin shone like a beacon in the hallway.

'How delightful,' Kharim said slowly. 'May I?' He held his arms out and the nanny obligingly passed the child over. 'One year old, you say?' Holding the girl close to him, he turned so that they were both facing the large hall mirror.

Michael looked and then stared. A few people who had been milling around also stared and there were gasps. A ripple of conversation swept through the ground floor like a tsunami, and before anybody could say anything, there was a crowd, all staring at this handsome Arab, holding a miniature version of himself.

'What the devil...' John Patterson looked like he was going to have a heart attack. Monica reached for a glass of champagne from the many trays and felt a guilty twinge of satisfaction.

Charleene started tittering and a few nervous laughs accompanied her.

'You bitch,' was the retort from Michael, who grabbed Jack and walked out of the front door, slamming it behind him.

'Out!' shouted John. 'Everybody, get out, NOW!'

* * *

Hannah had enjoyed her Saturday afternoon off. Heather, the lady who assisted her, had just closed up and gone. As she wasn't expecting Jack for another two hours or so, she sat with a large mug of tea and her book. The one that the gorgeous man had remarked on. *Sounded better than some he'd read lately.* That's what he'd said as he passed it back to her. She imagined him as the Duke on every page.

The doorbell to the upper flat was ringing incessantly. *Damn, who's that?* With surprise, through the camera, she saw it was Michael and Jack. They were early. Jack came running up the stairs first. 'I didn't get any cake,' he said furiously, 'or a party bag.'

'Michael?' He looked terrible, she thought. 'What's the matter?'

'Not in front of...'

'Jack,' Hannah said soothingly, 'I think there was a mix-up, but I have some of your favourite ice cream. Why don't you go and put the TV on and you can eat it while you watch?'

She listened in disbelief to the story. 'At the party, in front of everybody? That must have been so embarrassing. I'm very sorry, that was a terrible shock to find out she wasn't your child. What are you going to do?'

'I don't know, it's the betrayal, it's terrible.'

Hannah stared at him. 'Yes, it is, believe me.'

Realising what he'd said, he had the grace to be ashamed. 'Oh God, Hannah, I... I'm so sorry. I never realised and I never appreciated you. Look, I know it's a cheek to ask, but I can't go back there tonight. Could I possibly... just for one night?'

'You are joking.'

'Sorry, I shouldn't have asked, I'll go to a B&B.'

He looked so miserable and Hannah knew she should harden her heart. 'You can stay for one night, and I mean one.'

'Oh Hannah, thank you...'

'Jack and I will go to the cottage. We'll come back at teatime tomorrow and then you leave, if you haven't already. I suggest you go and spend half an hour with Jack now and try to explain why he didn't get his party bag.'

Hannah didn't allow herself any feeling of satisfaction. If anything, she felt sorry for him, but it was his business, not hers. He was Jack's father and if she could help him out for a night, she would do so, but that was the limit. He would have to sort it out.

The house was eerily quiet, Lina had been taken upstairs by the nanny. The staff, hired for the day, had made themselves scarce, after being given a wad of notes by Shelby's father. In the formal dining room sat a grim-faced Kharim, an ashen-faced Shelby, her mother, a little red-faced from the champagne she wasn't used to, and John, also red-faced, but with anger and embarrassment.

'It was just that one night, Kharim, I... I wasn't sure,' Shelby began nervously.

'Don't insult my intelligence or your own,' he said coldly. 'It is patently obvious who the father is. You even called her Lina, which means little palm tree,' in a slightly softer voice.

'I didn't think you'd even acknowledge her...'

'You didn't give me the chance!' He banged his fist on the table. 'If you had told me, we could have come to some arrangement, but now,' he stretched back in his chair, his eyes narrowing, 'I will make life very difficult for you.'

'Now hang on a minute,' her father started blustering.

'What is it to do with you?' Kharim asked. 'I assume from your reaction, you had no idea, so this is between me and your daughter. By the way, you can forget the hotel contract. What is the expression you use? Ah, yes, you can swivel.'

John went even redder. 'Kharim, my friend, we can sort this out.'

'I am *not* your friend. Where is the poor man who believed *he* was the father of this girl? He has been greatly dishonoured.'

'He won't answer his phone or any of my messages,' Shelby said miserably. 'He's angry, of course, he'll come back.'

'Are you sure of that?' asked her father. 'That man worshipped the ground you walked on and I warned him never to mess you around. Now, you do something like this.'

'Kharim caught me at a bad time, I was depressed.'

'How dare you!' shouted Kharim. 'Women do not come to me because they are *depressed*, they let me bed them because I am magnificent.'

Monica choked on the champagne she was sipping, Shelby didn't know where to look and John suddenly looked 20 years older. He deflated in his chair and muttering, 'I don't feel well,' collapsed on the floor.

***

Hannah and Jack had gone. Michael sat, alone and lonely. How could she have done that? *Why* did she do it? She made him believe that Lina was his. Checking his phone again, he noted the list of many missed calls and unread messages. For the want of something to do, he started to listen. Panicky, tearful calls, begging him to come back and talk to her. Angry ones, demanding to know where he was and then, one last one from half an hour ago.

He listened in horror. Shelby, quiet, subdued, and pleading. Please would he come to the hospital, her father had suffered a massive heart attack, it was all her fault. She needed him.

'Even if you can't forgive me, I need you so much now, please, darling Michael, please come.'

He picked up his car keys and left the flat.

Chapter Twenty-Four

UNPICKING AND RE-ATTACHING

Joining the fabric will ensure strength and ensure one part does not fall away

John Patterson's heart attack was not fatal but left him a shadow of the man he had been, constantly living in fear of another striking at any time, despite constant reassurances from the medical staff. Shelby, distraught, still managed to lay the blame squarely at Kharim's feet and not, for one minute, at her own. Her father could no longer run his company. He wouldn't hear of her being involved and handed the reins to the chief executive, with major decisions still being referred to him.

Michael had gone to the hospital and, seeing Shelby so contrite and upset, said he would come home. But he was not happy. The wedding was not mentioned again. Shelby knew she had pushed her luck and tried making it up to him. Her calls to Charleene went unanswered, apart from one message left, which said 'she was sooo terribly busy, maybe another time.' Shelby had been ostracised. Remarks and looks in the designer shops that she had frequented left her in no doubt that she was the topic of juicy gossip.

Kharim, through his solicitor, demanded a DNA test, which confirmed what they had all known. The entry in the birth register had to be changed, with a court order, to show the new father's name. Kharim, of course, paid maintenance, but expected to see Lina on every visit, and Shelby was terrified that he would smuggle her out of the country. Kharim knew this and although he had no intention of doing such a thing, as he had many daughters, it pleased him that it worried her so much.

John was curt and cold towards his daughter, making it clear she had a lot more to prove to him now. At least he let her keep the house, but extra money was not forthcoming and Michael refused to pay for a nanny when it wasn't his child. Michael also did not want to lose the lifestyle he'd got used to and John was a little more sympathetic towards him. So, after six months of separate bedrooms, he allowed himself to forgive her and even agreed to them trying for another child. Kharim's money at least paid for a child minder, so Shelby went back to work on the understanding that she looked after Lina properly on the days when she was at home. He would be as much as a father to Lina as he always had been, but insisted, as soon as she was old enough to understand, the situation would be explained to her.

Around about the time that they resumed the sharing of a bedroom, Shelby asked if they could move Monica in with them. Whereas before, Michael would just have been informed it was happening, he was now asked. Using the excuse that they could keep an eye on her mother's drinking, it was a chance for some unpaid childcare, and when Shelby suggested a holiday to help them bond again, Michael wasn't so against the idea.

So, they settled back into a relationship and although very different for both of them, an uneasy truce was formed.

Hannah kept her own counsel about what Michael should and shouldn't do, it was up to him. A huge box of chocolates arrived with a short 'thank you' two days after he'd left. She put them immediately in the shop, where customers sat looking at her portfolios, so she wouldn't be tempted. Having kept her trimmer figure for some time, she had no intention of spoiling it. She only had to look at Lady Thornbury to see how easy it would be to slide.

When Michael came to collect Jack two weeks after the disastrous birthday party, she enquired as to how things were going. Tersely, he replied that he was back at the house and they were working things through. One interesting change was that Jack would now have a room there and could stay over perhaps once a week. Saturdays, Michael suggested, would be best, and although it meant Hannah was alone at the cottage, she didn't mind, she felt so at home there.

* * *

After several months, Hannah was approached by the head of the secondary school to ask if she would go and talk to the year that were taking specialist subjects for GCSEs. There were several interested in fashion and design, and would it be possible to show them some of her work, explaining how she came to be where she was. Hannah protested, saying that she was self-taught and had never studied the subject or gone to college, but the head pooh-poohed that, saying it was the end results they would like to see and get an idea of how it got from sketchbook to coat hanger.

So, a few weeks later, armed with portfolios, fabrics and some of her outfits, including her wedding dress, she set off for the school. Looking at the dress again brought a lump to her throat. What dreams and expectations had filled her mind when she wore this. It still shimmered and glowed as it came out of its protective wrapping. It wouldn't fit me now, she thought, she had lost a lot of weight back then, but she was happy with the way she looked now.

Checking in with the school secretary, two boys were asked to help carry the bags and boxes to the room where Hannah was expected. There were about a dozen girls and three boys; Hannah was pleased to see that. Fashion design was most certainly not exclusively a female pursuit and she would stress that many of the most successful designers were male.

The teacher introduced her as 'Mrs Worth', which Hannah did not bother to correct. She spoke to them for about half an hour, saying how she had always been interested in sewing and how she had started to make her own clothes when she was their age. Noticing one chubbier girl, she carefully mentioned how she had made her designs flattering to her curves, as she was a bit larger than most of the cheaper fashion shops catered for, and was pleased to notice the girl sit up a bit straighter and listen more intently.

During a break, the pupils flicked through her portfolio and handled some of the clothes, examining and chattering amongst themselves.

'Thank you so much for doing this, it's really piqued their interest,' the teacher remarked.

'I'm enjoying it,' Hannah replied, realising that she really was.

Watching the girls together, she thought she recognised one of them. *I'm sure that's the girl who was in the park. I won't acknowledge her though; she may be embarrassed.*

After a short break, she spoke to them a little longer and was then invited to look at some of their work while they all scuttled off to the canteen for 20 minutes. The teacher came back with a cup of tea for Hannah while she was looking at a sketchbook.

'These are rather good and quite unusual,' Hannah said, studying a careful drawing of what looked like an evening dress, done from several different angles, with notes on fabric and colours.

The teacher glanced over. 'That's Ari's, she's always designing, has a real flair for it, I think.'

'That wouldn't be the small girl with the long, dark hair, would it?'

'Why yes, do you know her?'

'Not exactly, just come across her before, but no, I don't know her.' *But it's strange, I feel I do somehow.*

When the youngsters came back, there were questions and answers, and general discussion about fashion.

'We have a fashion show in GCSE year,' the teacher said. 'Perhaps, Mrs Worth, you might consider being one of our judges?'

'I'd absolutely love to, and that will be... when?'

'About six months' time. I'm sure they would love to show you what they're working on for that.'

Hannah spent the rest of the time examining some of the work and quietly watching Ari. It was definitely the girl from the park, and when she had seen her there, the girl seemed familiar in some way.

She picked up a sketch. 'What is this?'

Ari stepped forward. 'It's my idea for my prom dress next year. We've all decided it's going to be a black and white theme, and I'd love to have a go at making it myself, but it's quite complicated.'

'It's a lovely design and maybe...' Hannah pulled out one of her business cards. 'Why don't you pop into the shop sometime and we'll have a chat about it. Perhaps I could help you with it.'

'I... well, I mean, are you sure?'

'Of course, I wouldn't have said it otherwise.'

At that, the teacher realised the time. 'They have other classes now, Mrs Worth, but I'm sure they're very grateful to you for coming in.'

'My pleasure,' said Hannah, and was pleased to see a shy smile from Ari as she left the room with the others.

* * *

Monica Young poured herself a glass of vodka and pushed the bottle behind the wine in the cupboard. Despite her best intentions, she'd started drinking again. Moving into Shelby's house had not been such a good idea. It was okay at first, but she was being leant on now. Michael had laid the law down, to begin with, but Shelby was gradually turning the tables on him again and the poor sod couldn't see it.

Lina was playing on the floor with her toys. She was such a lovely child and Monica did love her, but she was going to turn into a Shelby if nothing was done. They'd come back from their holiday, all loved up again, and Monica was becoming an unpaid childminder.

She heard the front door and quickly downed her vodka, putting the glass in the dishwasher. *Damn, how many have I had?* As Michael came into the kitchen, she turned and stumbled. 'Oops,' she giggled.

'Monica, have you been drinking? We told you, it has to stop, especially when you're looking after Lina.'

'Oh well, I'd never get a drink at all then, would I? I don't do much else *but* look after her these days.'

Michael frowned. He had noticed Shelby was going out a bit more without her daughter. 'I'll have a word.'

'You can try, my son, much good may it do you.'

'That's not fair, Shelby's tried to make up for her mistake. Maybe she's entitled to a little fun.'

Monica snorted. 'Fun, is that what you call it? Look what happened the last time.'

'That was a mistake and we don't talk about it anymore. I'm very disappointed that Lina's not mine and I never thought she wanted children anyway, but it seems she does and maybe there'll be another one.'

'Shame the one before Lina never got a chance, that one was yours.'

You could hear a pin drop.

Monica suddenly realised what she'd said and went white, sobering up rather quickly.

Michael had also gone white. 'What exactly do you mean by that?'

'Nothing, I don't know, I was talking rubbish, forget I said anything.'

Michael crossed the room quickly, grabbing Monica by the shoulders and shaking her. 'Tell me the truth. Don't leave anything out.'

His world collapsed for the second time as he heard how his baby had been callously aborted without his knowledge or any discussion about it.

'She was adamant about it,' Monica was saying in a shaky voice. 'No children under any circumstances. I don't know what changed her mind.'

'Ali Baba changed her mind.' Michael was furious. There was no going back from this. Picking Lina up, he

303

gave her a kiss. *Goodbye Lina, I'm sorry I couldn't be a father to you.*

Upstairs, he packed all his things and collected the paperwork for their joint ventures. From the safe, he took half the cash; he wasn't going to let her swizzle him out of anything.

Downstairs, he looked coldly at Monica. 'You can explain why I've gone, tell her no pleading texts or calls will work. I have nothing to say to her, I'm finished with her.' Picking his bags up, he loaded the car and drove away. Not to Hannah's, he couldn't do that. He'd have to go to a hotel and talk to Hannah later. What a complete and utter fool he'd been. The perfect wife had been right under his nose and he threw her away. She was very well set up these days. *Maybe, we could start over. There's Jack, she's a forgiving sort deep down.* These thoughts made him feel happier.

***

Christopher had walked around the town several times over the last few months, hoping that he might see the lady with the books again, but had no luck. Maybe she was just passing through, he thought glumly. She had looked rather nice and he'd been amused by her embarrassment over her reading material. He was about to give up and resort to the internet dating site again when he found himself outside the bookshop. *I could do with some more books anyway.*

Christopher enjoyed biographies and was tucked away, perusing that section, when Hannah came in and made for her favourite, historical fiction. Having picked two, he was at the till paying and Hannah was just making her way there when she suddenly thought she'd just have a look at the hobbies and see if there were any new sewing or handicraft books, and turned away as he turned towards the door.

Halfway down the street, Christopher realised he'd left his wallet on the counter. Cursing, expecting it to have gone, he returned to the shop, just in time to see that book woman at the counter.

It must be fate, he thought.

'Oh, there's a wallet here.' Hannah suddenly noticed it as she took her change.

'I think that's mine,' came a deep, deep voice from behind her. Turning, she saw the man she had bumped into outside this very shop.

The lady behind the till had obviously clocked him as well. 'Yes sir, I remember you, just a minute ago.'

'Thank you so very much, please allow me,' he said, as he took her carrier bag of purchases. 'We wouldn't want you bumping into anybody on your way out.'

Hannah felt herself flush. *He is so gorgeous.* Stepping out onto the pavement, he turned to her. '*I* was hoping to bump into you again and I promise that's the last time I'll refer to it. Could I... would you like to have a drink with me?'

'What? Sorry, I mean, yes... please. Are you sure?' *Am I dreaming?*

'Of course I'm sure, shall we go in here?' He indicated the wine bar that Hannah had never been in but always thought looked rather nice.

Christopher led the way to a table and let Hannah sit first. 'Before I get us a drink, I think we should have some rules.'

Gulp. *Does he have some sort of fetish?* 'Rules, what do you mean?'

'You've been a mystery to me since I first b... met you, so I'd like you to stay a mystery for a while, book lady. I suggest we just tell each other our Christian names and not talk about what's gone before, or our personal circumstances. I don't want to know what you do or where you live. Just get to know each other as two single people, with no history. That can come later.'

Later. There's going to be a later? With that voice, Hannah would have been happy to sit and listen to him reading the wine list, let alone have a conversation. 'Well, it's a bit unusual but it sounds like fun.'

'I'll get a bottle of wine. You're not in a rush or anything, are you?'

'No, not at all, I've got all day,' she said dreamily.

Over the wine, they talked about their favourite books, films, music and food.

'Food!' Christopher said suddenly. 'I'm starving, shall we have their lunch special?'

'Why not, but only if you let me contribute.'

'I won't hear of it; you can do it next time.'

Next time, oh yes, yeeeees.

Over lunch, they exchanged telephone numbers and Christopher asked her if she would like to go to a concert next week.

'What sort of concert?'

'It's classical, but it's outdoors and we could take a picnic. Shall I provide wine and soft drinks, along with cheeses and fruit?'

'Sounds lovely, I'll make up some things for mains. Er, where shall we meet?'

'Hmm. Without giving it away, do you live far from here?'

'Not too far,' she smiled, thinking of the shop, less than five minutes' walk away.'

'Okay then. I'll text you the meeting time. I've really enjoyed talking to you and I'm glad I found you again.' Remembering her reading material, as they left and said goodbye, he took her hand, and with a sweeping bow, kissed it, much to the amusement of the passers-by.

Hannah was on cloud nine and felt sure she'd seen him before, but then he looked like the heroes on the covers of her books, so maybe her ideal man was already in her head and he just happened to match up to it. She enjoyed the mystery. Who was Christopher really, where was he from, and what was his story? It was very exciting and she was glad he'd come up with the idea. Planning what she would make for her picnic hamper, she realised it was nearly time to collect Jack.

Michael had bought flowers, a bottle of wine and some handmade chocolates. Hannah could never resist chocolate. Feeling very confident, he was strolling through the town when he saw her. About to call her name, he saw her turn and smile at a man who followed her out. She was simpering like a damn schoolgirl! What was up with her? And no man had the right to be that good looking. Whatever was he doing with Hannah?

He then *bowed* and kissed her hand, what was he playing at? They looked very at ease with each other, he thought grimly. Well, he'd soon make sure Mr Poncey Manners was put in his place. Following Hannah back to the shop, he waited while she went upstairs and then, putting on his most charming face, rang the bell.

Hannah had just pressed a cold flannel to her flushed skin. Flushed by the wine or Christopher? Who cared? She was feeling very happy with how their meeting had gone when her bell went. Heather was down in the shop so it must be for her. To her annoyance, she saw it was Michael. Jack wasn't here, she'd be leaving to fetch him shortly, so what did he want?

Pressing the button to let him in, she waited as he came up the stairs.

'Hannah, ah, I was hoping we could talk. These are for you.'

'That's very nice of you, but why, what's it for?' *More chocolates, I can't let myself start on those.*

'I've finished with Shelby, I realised what a terrible mistake I made and I was hoping that you could see your way to forgiving me and maybe, we could try again? I'd like to take you out for dinner.' He looked very pleased with himself but she could detect an undercurrent of panic.

'I... see. You've jumped out of her bed and want to jump back into mine, have I got that right?'

Like the time he saw her after he'd been caught out, this wasn't going as he'd planned. 'No, of course not. I realise I'll have to "woo" you for a while, but we were good as a couple. Jack would love to have Mum and Dad back together.'

'How dare you. You have *another* disagreement with Shelby and come crawling back. Take your flowers and chocolates. Oh, and you can take the wine as well, I've just had some with a very nice man that I'm seeing. I wouldn't take you back if you were the last man on earth. Please leave. I'm going to collect *our* son from school.'

'Hannah... please, give me a chance. I'll make it up to you.'

She gave him a withering look. 'Out, now, and please don't bother me again.' Following him down the stairs, she noticed he'd left the flowers, so going back and collecting them, she stuffed them into the dustbin in front of his shocked face. 'Only fit for the bin, as are your promises. Goodbye Michael.'

Chapter Twenty-Five

CLEAN FINISHING

Turning under and stitching ensures that all the
threads of the fabric are caught in the
seam finish

On Saturday, Hannah was pleased to see Ari come into
the shop.

'Hello,' she said. 'Have you got time to see me today?'

'Certainly, sit down and let's have a look at what
you've brought along.'

Ari took out her sketchbook. 'I've done a few more
drawings and made some notes. Can I ask, the wedding
dress you brought in for us to see, was that your own?'
As she saw Hannah hesitate for a second, she apologised.
'I'm sorry, I shouldn't have asked.'

'No, it's fine. Yes, it was mine, a long time ago, it
seems now.'

Ari glanced at Hannah's ring finger. 'You're not
married anymore, are you a widow?'

'No, we got divorced, but he's my son's father, so I see
him occasionally.'

'My father's a widower, my mum died when I was
young.'

'You *are* the girl from the park, do you remember,
you asked me if I was alright?'

Realisation dawned on Ari's face. 'I *thought* I'd seen you before. Was everything okay… with your friend?'

'I hope so; we just seem to have lost touch. Anyway, that's enough of that, before we start, I bet you could drink a hot chocolate, and would you like a flapjack?'

Her face lit up. 'Oh, yes please.'

'Heather's here today, so we'll pop upstairs for it.'

Over 'elevenses' Hannah quizzed Ari about school and what exactly she wanted to do.

'Well, A levels, of course, and then I'd like to go to art college and specialise in textiles and design. I'll see what happens after that and what openings there are. You said you were divorced, umm, I'm trying to get my dad fixed up with somebody. I'm sure he'd like you.'

Hannah laughed. 'Well, that's a kind thought, but actually, I've just met a very nice man and I'm seeing him again next week.'

'Oh, shame. Although Dad has made an effort and I know he's going out next week, but he's been a bit secretive about it. Some of his dates before haven't come too much, he probably doesn't want to disappoint me. These flapjacks are gorgeous; did you bake them, would you teach me?'

Ari's conversation flitted backwards and forwards, making it hard for Hannah to keep up at times, and so she tried to get the conversation back on track. 'Your prom dress, you said it was a black and white theme?'

'Yes, why?'

'I hope you don't mind me giving advice but you are quite pale, white may wash you out a bit. Would a cream colour be allowed?'

Ari looked surprised but hopeful. 'You won't believe this, but I was actually thinking that myself. My white school shirts make me look quite anaemic. I can't wait for the sixth form when we can wear what we like. The wedding dress, sorry to mention it again, but it's the perfect colour and just the material that I want. Do you have any or can you get some?'

'I'm afraid my... supplier for that is no longer in business. It's quite an unusual material, I'm sure we could find something like it.'

Ari's face fell. 'I really had my heart set on it and I have for quite a while.'

Hannah felt sure that material was unique. 'But you hadn't seen it until I took it into school, had you?'

'Oh yes, it must be available. Look, I have some. I brought it to show you that it was like yours.'

Out of her bag came a bear, not just any bear, but the 'bear to watch over somebody'.

'Where... did you get that?' Hannah felt breathless.

'When I was six, I was at the hospital with my grandmother. We were in the garden and a kind lady gave it to me when I told her my mother wasn't going to be around anymore.'

Hannah felt such a connection with this child she couldn't believe it. 'Ari, Arianne... isn't it?'

'Yes, how did you know?'

'I remember it very well, that lady was me. I made that bear.'

Ari looked at her in shock and then wonder. 'I felt sure when I saw you in the park, I'd seen you before. Really? That was you? Oh, I'm so pleased.' Without thinking, she gave Hannah a hug, then pulled away, embarrassed. 'S... sorry.'

'Don't be sorry, it's lovely to see the bear again and I'm glad you liked him. He's obviously been in a good home since I gave him to you.'

'He sits on my dressing table; he's called Mr Bear.'

Hannah looked at the bear and could almost have sworn it winked at her. 'That's a splendid name for him.' Hannah was thinking, this girl was special in some way. 'Listen, I told you I was divorced. On the day of my marriage, that dress was special, it still is, but not in the same way. Looking at your sketch, I think it could be used for your dress.'

Ari went even paler than she normally was, with shock. 'I couldn't, we couldn't, not your wedding dress, that's not fair. It's very kind of you but I can't let you do that.'

'You most certainly can,' said Hannah firmly. 'I've made my mind up. Now the first thing to do is get a rough pattern made up and cut it out in muslin. When we know how it's going to fit, we'll work out the best way to use the dress. Do you want any black with it?'

Ari was almost speechless. 'I thought maybe a wide sash, like a belt?'

'Perfect,' said Hannah, 'I'll hang the dress up in the back room so that we can get inspiration.'

'Umm. Can you tell me how much this is going to cost? Dad did say he'd pay for my prom dress, but this is going to be too expensive.' Ari was biting her lip and trying not to look too upset.

Hannah knew there would have to be some charge for the girl's pride. 'Well, let me think. The material was given to me as a gift, so I tell you what we'll do. You pay me what you would have paid for a normal dress and you unpick all the stitches in the wedding dress for me because that's a pig of a job. How's that?'

'Really, is that all? I'll do it. Can I take it home and do some in the evenings because I can only come here on Saturdays, and maybe Thursdays after school?'

'That would be alright, now let's go down and start on your pattern. You might as well learn pattern cutting now.'

Later that night, Christopher saw Arianne cover the dining table with a rather fancy-looking dress and start fiddling with a small pair of scissors.

'What on earth is that and what are you doing?'

Ari explained all that had happened and the kind offer she'd been given.

'Her wedding dress, is she quite sure about that? I'm not sure she should do that,' Christopher frowned.

'Well, she is divorced, I suppose it's not a good reminder. She's a really nice lady, Dad, I would have liked to set you up, but she's seeing someone, she said, quite recently. My timing was bad.'

Christopher laughed. 'You've done quite enough already, getting me on internet dating. Well, as it happens, Miss Fix-It, *I've* met somebody and we're going out next week. I did mention it to you.'

'Who is it? Tell me.'

'Oh no, I've told you before and it's come to nothing. Allow me to keep this one secret for a while longer.'

She looked glum. 'Okay. But you'll have to come and meet Mrs Worth when my dress is ready for a try on; I want you to see it.'

'Pay for it, you mean.'

She grinned, 'Well, that too.'

✳ ✳ ✳

Jack was eating his tea. 'Mum?' he asked in a careful voice.

'What is it, Jack?'

'Dad told me he and Shelby aren't together anymore, so I won't be staying at the house. Dad's in one of his flats now, but I can stay there, he said.' Jack pushed his chips around the plate. 'He...'

'He what?'

'He said he'd made a mistake and it would be nice to be a family again.'

Hannah said nothing for a moment. *How dare he, how dare he use Jack as a pawn like that.* 'What do you think about it, Jack?' she asked carefully.

He looked up at her. 'It would be nice to have my mum and dad together again, but not if it makes you unhappy. Maybe you could just stay friends.'

'Come here.' She gave her son a hug. 'He'll always be your dad and I don't hate him,' *not anymore*, 'but I wouldn't want to live with him again. What about if... if I ever met somebody else one day?'

'Oh, you mean like a stepfather? William in my class has got one of those, he says he's alright. I s'pose it would be okay, if you liked him.'

'Well, that's nice to know, Jack,' Hannah smiled.

***

Three days later, Hannah delivered Jack to his grandparents for the night after telling them she had a special date.

'She's going out with my new stepdad,' Jack announced loudly.

'What?' spluttered her father. 'First we've heard of it.'

'Hannah?' her mother enquired.

'It's only a date, the second one, for goodness sake. It's just something Jack and I had a discussion about, that's all.'

Her parents nodded and a knowing look passed between them. Hannah sighed in exasperation and left them to it.

A text had come from Christopher the day before, checking she was still on for the evening, and then after receiving her confirmation, he said he would collect her from their meeting place at seven.

She had been busy for the last couple of days. Not wanting to go overboard, she concentrated on producing some tasty, quality items. If it was a picnic, nothing fiddly was best, she thought. There were pork and apple sausage rolls, some mini pasties, chicken drumsticks with a barbeque glaze, celery sticks with dips, and homemade potato crisps. That should do it.

Deciding what to wear was difficult. She guessed they'd be sitting on a rug, so comfortable, but flattering was the choice. She decided on a pair of cut-off jeans, a recent purchase, something she'd never owned before, and a loose blouse, reminiscent of the gypsy style she'd had when she was younger. Packing a pashmina, in case it got chilly later, she did her hair and spent a little time getting her make-up right, just accentuating her eyes, which she copied from a magazine. Looking in the mirror, she was quietly pleased with the result.

Waiting outside the wine bar with her picnic basket, she felt very self-conscious, but shortly, a shiny black 4x4 pulled up and Christopher jumped out. Hannah was pleased to see he looked casual, but smart, in chinos and an open-necked shirt with the sleeves rolled up. He gave her a peck on the cheek as he took the basket, stowing it in the boot next to a large cool box. The obligatory tartan rug was also there.

'Okay Hannah? Looks like it's going to be a nice evening and not too windy, should be perfect. I hope you like Beethoven, the *Pastoral Symphony* is one of the main parts.'

'Oh, I loved that sequence in the *Fantasia* film...' Then she stopped, feeling a little silly.

'Me too, and the hippos were great, weren't they?'

Hannah fell a little bit in love with him at that moment. Any man who liked a Disney film was okay in her book.

The concert was in the grounds of a stately home a few miles away, and any shyness Hannah felt soon disappeared with Christopher's easy and relaxed conversation. Parking up, they found a nice spot and spread out the rug. Then he produced two glasses and a chilled bottle of sparkling wine.

'Just the one for me as I'm driving, but you enjoy,' he said, filling her glass. 'Cheers, here's to getting to know each other better.'

'Cheers.' *I'll drink to that.*

It was a wonderful evening. All the pieces of music played were popular and well known, and during the break, they tucked into the picnic.

'God, these are wonderful, the pastry just melts,' said Christopher, after his third sausage roll. 'You made all this?'

'Except for the celery,' she laughed. 'I like cooking; it's nice to have the chance to do something different.'

'I'm afraid my dessert is bought, but it did look tempting, hazelnut and raspberry meringue with cream.'

Hannah declared it to be delicious, after allowing herself a small second helping.

Christopher leant forward with a napkin. 'You have a blob of cream...' and gently wiped the side of her mouth. His lips were awfully close and her heart started to race, imagining what it would be like to feel them on hers. He was looking quite intently at her but then the tannoy announced the second half and the spell was broken.

I would have liked to lick that cream off, he thought wickedly.

I wonder if he will kiss me tonight, she thought.

As they neared the town on the way home, Christopher pulled over. 'Look,' he said, 'I know we're keeping our lives a little private at the moment but I really feel I should drop you at your door, I need to know you're home safely.'

'Well, my car is actually at my parents' house. My father dropped me home when I left my... something for them to look after tonight.'

He started to laugh. 'This is ridiculous, are they babysitting?'

'Yes, my nine-year-old son.' *Is he going to run a mile now?*

'Ah well, if its confession time, I have a daughter. Shall we leave it at that for tonight? I'll drop you at their house and you text me when you're back home, okay?'

She directed him and they pulled up outside. Immediately, he jumped out and opened her door.

'Thank you, I had the most wonderful evening.'

'So did I,' he said softly, and then he *did* kiss her. Tentatively at first and then, when he sensed no resistance, more firmly.

It's just like in my books, she thought, and melted into him.

'Goodnight Hannah,' he said gently. 'Don't forget to text me; I would like to see you again in a few days.'

* * *

For the next six weeks, Hannah and Christopher saw each other once or twice a week. They still kept their personal details fairly secret, but agreed to explain their circumstances the next time they met. Christopher said he had a business trip for four days and then he had to have a day with his daughter, as she wanted him free for something important. Perhaps they could meet on Sunday and talk over lunch?

Hannah said that was fine, she was busy on Saturday anyway, and Sunday would be lovely.

Saturday was the day that Ari would be trying on the dress. They had both worked hard on it, keeping it as true to the girl's design as possible. Ari had loved the jagged hem that Hannah had done, so that was incorporated, and the beaded bodice was turned into a small clutch bag. A black sash had been made to go around her waist and Hannah had even helped her cover a cheap pair of ballerina pumps in the same fabric, which had almost come to life as it was re-designed, shimmering and glowing as it was sewn.

The Thursday before, Ari came after school to do the last bits and pieces.

'I think it's just about finished,' Hannah had said, 'apart from a few little tweaks. I'm sure your father will be very impressed.'

'I told him to come about 3p.m. on Saturday, is that okay?'

'No problem, I'll steam and hang it all ready for you.'

Ari gave Hannah another hug, but this time, did not pull away. 'You've been so kind to me and helped me with everything. I don't know how to thank you.'

Hannah felt quite choked. 'It's been a pleasure; I've really enjoyed it. Now come upstairs, I've made a carrot cake.'

'Hi Ari,' said Jack as they came up. He'd met her a few times over the last few weeks. She was 'okay', for a girl, although he would never speak to her if he ever saw her when he was with his friends.

'Hi Jack, everything alright?'

'Yep.'

That was about the sum total of their conversations and they were both happy with that.

※ ※ ※

On Saturday, the dress looked beautiful on its hanger, and even though Ari had tried it on several times, today, with all the accessories, it would be special.

She arrived after lunch with some flowers and a basket of soaps and shower gels for Hannah.

'Oh Ari, you shouldn't have, there was no need, but thank you, it's a lovely thought.'

'I was going to get you something anyway, but Dad suggested it as well. He's looking forward to seeing it. Can I put it on just before he gets here?'

'We'll have you all ready.'

At 3p.m., Christopher parked nearby and made his way to the shop Arianne had given him the address of. He saw dresses in the window and took no notice of the shop name, realising this must be the place. A bell rang as he opened the door and a muffled voice called from behind the pulled curtains in the corner.

'Be with you in a moment.'

'I'll stay here,' Hannah whispered to Ari. 'You go out first and let him see you.' Holding the curtain aside, she let Ari slip through.

'What do you think, Dad?' There was silence and Hannah imagined her doing a twirl. The silence continued and then she heard him blowing his nose.

'Dad, are you crying?'

Hannah thought she had better go out.

There, in front of her, looking at his daughter with such love and pride was Christopher.

'Oh Dad, this is Mrs Worth.'

Christopher looked up and saw the reflection of his own shock in Hannah's eyes. 'H... Hannah... you're Mrs Worth?'

'You're Ari's father?'

Ari stood dumbfounded 'You two *know* each other?'

Then, they all started laughing and talking at once, Christopher trying to explain that 'Mrs Worth' was his mystery woman, Hannah, saying that it all made sense now, and Ari, excited, piped up, 'I knew you two would be perfect for each other.'

Jack came downstairs. 'What's all the noise?' When it was explained, it didn't seem like such a big deal to him, but eyeing Christopher up, he reckoned he *might* be okay as a stepdad.

'I need to pay for this dress now,' Christopher said as it all calmed down. Hannah opened her mouth and he stopped her quickly. 'Whatever you're going to say, don't. I *will* be paying for it. Do you take cards?'

'Of course.' Hannah told him the amount and took the card. A quick glance at the name and then, another look.

'Duke. Christopher *Duke*?'

'Is that a problem?' He was grinning, remembering her reading material. 'I know you're not a wanton, but I'm sure we could make some sort of pact.'

Hannah went bright red.

'Whatever are you going on about, Dad? Mrs Worth, *is* there a problem?'

'Oh Ari, please call me Hannah and, no, there's absolutely no problem at all.'

Epilogue

ALL SEWN UP

To mend completely

SIX MONTHS LATER

Hannah, Christopher, Jack and Arianne were all in the garden at Ivy Cottage. They usually spent Sundays there and Hannah would cook lunch. Christopher and the two children did the washing-up and then sometimes, they'd all go for a walk, or as today, just enjoy the sunshine. Jack was down at the bottom of the garden somewhere, building his den, and Arianne was collecting flowers to press.

Christopher tangled his fingers with Hannah's. 'I wanted to ask you something and I waited till we were here again because it's such a magical place.'

'It is a bit special, isn't it? I've always felt that when I've been here. What did you want to ask me?'

He pulled out a small box and opened it to reveal a beautiful ring with a cluster of diamonds.

Suddenly, a mass of butterflies appeared and the faint sound of tinkling laughter echoed around the garden. The two of them seemed to be in a little bubble, oblivious to everything else.

'I never thought I'd be happy again after Claire died, but you've brought the light back into my life, Arianne adores you and I've grown very fond of Jack. That's not important, of course, it's how *you* feel, but I know how *I* feel and I hope you feel the same. Would you make me very, very happy and be my wife? I can't make you a duchess, but I can make you Mrs Duke.'

Hannah thought her heart would burst with happiness. 'Oh yes, yes, Christopher.'

Jack was coming up the garden path and saw Arianne watching the two of them.

'Yuck,' said Jack, 'they're snogging.'

'Yes, isn't it wonderful? You're going to be my brother now,' she smirked.

'Great'.

Before they left the cottage, Hannah went to collect something from upstairs. On the dressing table was an envelope with her name on. Guessing it was a note from Christopher, she opened it.

My dearest Hannah,
I am so pleased you have found happiness.
I always knew you would find your real-life Duke.
He was there, waiting for you.
Your loving friend,

Fae Dorothy Grim

Hannah was mesmerised, how was this possible? The letters danced in front of her face until she felt giddy. They seemed to be re-arranging themselves.

Fae Dorothy Grim was disappearing and settling into two new words...

Fairy Godmother

The End

Carmella lives in Plymouth, Devon and, along with her sister Alison, has been writing for a few years.

30 years as a presenter on local radio made her want to interact face-to-face with people, rather than just through a microphone.

She became a registrar and is still marrying Plymouth couples in venues that vary from the register office, to the top of Smeaton's Tower on Plymouth Hoe.

Now, almost retired, she has taken up writing to expound the ideas which have hibernated in her head for years.

Haberdashery is the first book to be published and you can find out more about Carmella below:

Follow Carmella on Facebook
www.facebook.com/carmellamckenzieauthor/

Or visit her website
www.mckenziesisters.com

Carmella would love to hear from you if you have enjoyed this story. Please also leave her a review on Amazon.

NOCTU...
& FIVE TALES of
LOVE & DEATH

Gabriele D'Annunzio

NOCTURNE
& FIVE TALES of
LOVE & DEATH

Translated and with a Preface
by Raymond Rosenthal

The Marlboro Press
Marlboro, Vermont

The publication of the present volume is made possible by a grant from the National Endowment for the Arts.

Manufactured in the United States of America

Library of Congress Catalog Card Number 88-60729

Clothbound edition: ISBN 0-910395-40-3
Paperbound edition: ISBN 0-910395-41-1

THE MARLBORO PRESS

MARLBORO, VERMONT

Contents

Preface	1
The Virgin Orsola	9
The Vigil	65
The Sea-Going Surgeon	77
Giovanni Episcopo	91
Leda Without Swan	155
Nocturne	217

Preface

GABRIELE D'ANNUNZIO was born in 1863 in the seaport town of Pescara in the Abruzzo region of Italy, and died in 1938 in his grandiose but rather gaudy villa on Lake Garda. The dates are important because they measure not only the span of an unusually fertile and exuberant artistic life (as one critic has said, only two other writers can boast of the same long, unfailingly brilliant and evocative production: Goethe and Victor Hugo) but they also show that he came into life with the birth of the modern age in art and departed from it just after it had passed its apogee. In 1874 Nietzsche had published his great essay *The Birth of Tragedy*, and the same year Rimbaud's "Drunken Boat," *Illuminations* and *A Season in Hell* appeared together with the first large show of Impressionist painters, while Mallarmé provided the Symbolists with a manifesto with his poem "Afternoon of a Faun" in 1876. In Italy, always a little behind in the European artistic scramble, Verga published his masterpiece, *The House by the Medlar Tree*, in 1881 and Italo Svevo his second important novel, *As a Man Grows Older*, in 1898. In other words, D'Annunzio's career straddled an era of violent transition, and this innate romantic, who tried vainly over the years to become a Naturalist, a Symbolist, a Decadent, even an avant-garde modernist, never settled comfortably into any of these assumed artistic roles.

Yet he was undoubtedly a prodigy, a prodigy in the gorgeous use of words, publishing his first book of poems to critical acclaim at the age of sixteen. He had what many regarded as a dangerous facility; but, as Yeats put it, "Words alone are certain good," a good that makes up for many a failing, even for a lack of artistic maturity and of that deliberate development of a vision and a style that characterizes the greatest of writers. "I have my language," D'Annunzio declared, "as one of my most powerful instincts." The sentence is perhaps a key to his entire work because the comparison of his expressive gift to the natural, the indwelling in him—his instincts—is beautifully appropriate to the rhythms and substance of D'Annunzio's writing, whether good, bad, or indifferent. It is in fact D'Annunzio's life-long, often inspired concern with the body's sensuous life that assures him a place in serious literature. There is no writer in the late nineteenth century and the beginning of the twentieth who explored this area of experience with more subtlety, more delicacy, more power and more intensity. As the German critic Adorno rightly said, the true subterranean history of recent European consciousness is its degradation and humiliation of the body, and in this context D'Annunzio, whatever his political opinions, is unquestionably the body's least inhibited and most imaginative celebrator, the forerunner of D. H. Lawrence and Henry Miller.

Indeed, around the turn of the century nobody connected with the art of writing would have found it odd or unusual if one were to call D'Annunzio a great writer and poet. The young James Joyce thought that D'Annunzio was the only European writer after Flaubert to carry the novel into new territory, and, later on, he classed him with Kipling and Tolstoy as the three "most naturally talented writers" to appear in the nineteenth century. Henry James, whose long essay on D'Annunzio's novels is certainly the best in English, considered him a supremely gifted writer ("a rare imagination, a poetic, an artistic intelligence of extraordinary range and fineness" are some of the laudatory things he has to say about him) whose predominantly esthetic view of life seemed to James a kind of test case for this particular artistic position. In fact, in the final reckoning James felt that the esthetic stance was terribly inadequate and in some of its dealings, especially in the presentation of love affairs, even vulgar, due to the blindness it affected as regards the full complexity of human relations. And Joyce also had his critical reservations, pointing out that D'Annunzio, Tolstoy and Kipling had all been seriously compromised as writers by "their semi-fanatic ideas about religion or about patriotism." "Patriotism" was Joyce's nice way of alluding to D'Annunzio's wavering from right to left in politics throughout his life.

In any event, this praise and the strictures that accompanied it are worth recording because the worst thing that can happen to a writer has happened to D'Annunzio: if he is at all famous today—and this is certainly true of his fame outside Italy—it is not for what he wrote but for what he did. He is a gossip-star, a perennial favorite of the fashion magazines, since many of the etiolated, often perverse aristocratic or bohemian ladies he had affairs with were advance models of the prototypical "model" that graces their pages. (Fashion is a dream-world and its prime images and fantasies have changed very little since D'Annunzio's scandalous days in turn of the century Rome.) He was also an adventurer in politics and on the battlefield, a hero in combat during the First World War, a fiery orator, and the commander of a band of freebooters who seized the city of Fiume in an attempt to annex it for Italy in defiance of the agreements being made at Versailles. The expedition failed but the precedents it set in illegal activity helped Mussolini greatly in his drive to Fascist power. The fact is that Mussolini was afraid of D'Annunzio, afraid in the way a hack would naturally fear a genius, and took care to lock him away under guard in

3

his gimcrack palace, the Vittoriale. But all this, though interesting, even entertaining, is precisely what this anthology has been fashioned to overcome, that is, to ignore the gossip-star and return to the artist, confining its selections to his best and most representative writings in prose. Of course D'Annunzio was first of all a poet, but each of the writings included in this book illustrates and underscores a stage in D'Annunzio's creative journey that will certainly enhance an eventual reading of his poetry.

The first three stories are taken from the volume titled *Tales of Pescara* [*Le novelle della Pescara*, 1884-86]. D'Annunzio was an eager conduit in Italy for all the latest European literary movements, and in these stories one can see an obvious transposition of Zola's Naturalism to Italian soil, particularly in the story "The Virgin Orsola" [*La vergine Orsola*]. The incredible description of the pathological ravages of typhus is precise and powerful, but D'Annunzio's particular talents go far beyond the Naturalistic formula. Above all he is adept at catching the movements of the spirit as they are reflected in the flesh. His marvelous account of Orsola's convalescence, the upsurge of sexual impulse that accompanies it, sharpened by the overt carnality and suggestive drama of a relígious ceremony—all this is presented with a richness of nuance and implication that one hardly associates even with the most refined products of Naturalism. The sardonically romantic D'Annunzio appears again in the next two stories. "The Vigil" [*La veglia funebre*], which combines the mystery and boredom of a wake, the invasive sexuality of a languorous summer night—the very landscape seems to swell with sexual yearning—and the brutality of pure lust, is by some magic both tender and cruel; while "The Sea-Going Surgeon" [*Il cirusico di mare*] also exploits the surrounding seascape, first in a lulling calm and then a fierce storm, both depicted as the inscrutable "moods" of an indifferent nature, mirroring the impassive and indifferent cruelty of the men aboard the brig.

The long novella "Giovanni Episcopo," which was published in 1891, is another example of D'Annunzio's cultural and literary omniverousness. Dostoevsky's novels had just been issued in France and D'Annunzio, who was going through one of his periodic crises, turned in desperation to the Russian master's confessional mode in an effort to overcome his creative stasis. More sentimental than psychologically penetrating, it recreates the atmosphere of clerkly life in Rome—which had just become the nation's capital and was filling up with immigrants from all over the country—giving us an unforgettable picture of these crowds of raffish young men, living in squalid boarding houses, eating miserable meals, scrounging along on meager wages, trying pathetically to snatch some moments of pleasure. The chief characters are stock figures, the low-life "fatal woman," the inevitable bully and his inevitable butt, yet D'Annunzio's skill confers an intensity and sincerity upon what in other hands would have been absurd melodrama.

The last two selections show D'Annunzio at the height of his powers. The long story "Leda Without Swan" [*La Leda senza cigno*] was written in France in 1913 but published in Italy in 1916. Its action takes place in the Landes region of France, that sandy country of pitch pine forest along the Atlantic Coast between Médoc and Adour, bordered by great dunes which enclose the many inland ponds. "Leda Without Swan" is, among other things, a kind of summation and repudiation by D'Annunzio of the chief Decadent themes which played so great a part in both his poetry and his novels. And it is perhaps the first time that his prodigious facility has found an art form that is entirely his own and fully expresses his spirit. The "fatal woman," who gathers into herself all the world's sensuality, is shown as beautiful but miserable, more her own victim than the victimizer of others, and the usual trio of death, voluptuousness, and love as a sadistic perversity seems to have been viewed at last as squalid makeshifts that do not penetrate to the core of reality. D'Annunzio is sad about these repudiations but his sadness is more authentic and moving than many of his exultant moments and gives birth to his loveliest and most incisive prose.

"Nocturne" [*Notturno*] was written in 1916 but D'Annunzio waited until 1921 before he published it. Printed here are excerpts whose combined length amounts to about a quarter of the Italian volume. The peculiar circumstances of its creation demanded that D'Annunzio have a period of relative calm to interpret and re-order the "more than ten thousand strips of paper" on which he had inscribed his lyrical thoughts and reveries. On January 16, 1916, while on a combat flight during the First World War, D'Annunzio's plane, on which he was an observer, was forced to make an emergency landing and D'Annunzio was flung against the machine gun mounted in front of him and as a result of the blow lost the sight of his right eye. The doctors insisted that he go to bed and lie perfectly immobile, declaring that if he did not he might lose the sight of his other eye as well. So from February 23 to the end of April, in a handwriting that was nearly illegible, D'Annunzio set down this "commentary on the shadows," a succession of memories and dreams that rose spontaneously from his unconscious as he lay supine, or during the long nights of insomnia. "I had inside my wounded eye a forge of dreams which my will could neither direct nor interrupt. The optic nerve drew on all the strata of my culture and my previous life, projecting on my vision innumerable figures with a rapidity of transition far beyond the most daring lyricism." This is of course D'Annunzio with at least one foot in the camp of modernism. From then on he confined his writing to just this sort of autobiographical musing, the perfect form for an impenitent egocentric.

RAYMOND ROSENTHAL

THE VIRGIN ORSOLA

The Virgin Orsola

I

THE VIATICUM appeared under the portal of the church at noon. The season's first delicate snow lay on the streets, on the houses, everywhere snow. But on high, among the snowy clouds, large blue islands opened, dilating over Brina Palace and slowly filling with light toward the Bandiera quarter. And in the white air over the white town the miracle of the sun was suddenly revealed.

The viaticum started on its way to Orsola dell'Arca's house. The people along the streets paused to watch the priest go by, solemn and grave, striding with his bare head and purple stole under the broad scarlet umbrella, between the burning lanterns carried by the altar boys. The small handbell rang out limpidly, accompanying the psalms whispered by the priest. In the narrow lanes stray dogs scampered out of the way as the procession passed. At the corner of the piazza, Mazzanti stopped shoveling snow and bowed, uncovering his bald skull. And just then, from Flaiano's bakery, the warm, hearty smell of fresh bread spread through the air.

The people gathered at the sick woman's house heard the peals of the bell; they heard the visitors' steps mounting the stairs. Supine on her bed lay the virgin Orsola in the grip of a feverish stupor, of an inert somnolence, her rapid breathing broken by sharp, rattling gasps. On the pillow rested her head almost completely stripped of hair and her face of an almost bluish color in which the lids half-hid her viscous eyeballs and the nostrils seemed to be smeared with soot. With her fleshless hands she made small, uncertain gestures, vague attempts to seize something from the void, weird, startling signs which gave those around her a feeling almost of terror; her pale arms were shot through by muscular contractions, twitchings of the tendons; and now and then an unintelligible babble came from her lips, as if the words were caught in the soot on her tongue, the clinging mucus on her gums.

That tragic stillness which always precedes supreme events began to fill the room: a stillness in which the sick woman's breathing, her groping gestures, the raucous explosions of her cough, made the expectation of death more dreadful. Through the open windows poured the pure air, and out of them drifted the miasmas exhaled by the disease. A vivid white glare was reflected by the snow on the cornices and Corinthian capitals of the Arch of Fortanuova; at the level of the room icicles glittered like crystal flowers. Inside, on the walls, hung large, holy medallions of brass—the images of saints. Under a glass bell, her face, her breast, her arms completely black, like a barbaric idol, a Madonna of Loreto glimmered in her robe adorned with golden crescent moons. In one corner, on a small, immaculate altar, between two blue Castelli jars full of aromatic herbs, stood an old crucifix made of mother-of-pearl.

At the bedside, deathly pale, Camilla, the sister, the only relative, with a linen cloth soaked in vinegar wiped the sick woman's black lips, her encrusted teeth. The doctor, Don Vincenzo Bucci, sat staring at the silver knob of his handsome cane, at the beautiful carved cornelians set in the rings on his fingers, and waited. Teodora La Iece, a weaver who lived next door, stood erect, silent, intent on giving a sorrowful expression to her sallow, freckled face, her steely eyes, her cruel mouth.

"*Pax huic domui,*" the priest said as he entered. In the doorway, tall and emaciated on his enormous feet, with the undulating movements of a caterpillar, Don Gennaro Tierno appeared. Behind him came Rosa Catena, a woman who in her green years had made a public trade of lewdness and was now redeeming her soul by attending to the dying, bathing corpses, dressing and composing them in their coffins without taking any recompense.

Everyone in Orsola's room was kneeling, all heads were bowed. The sick woman heard nothing; a profound stupor continued to obliterate her senses. The aspersorium rose above her, flashed through the air, sprinkling the bed.

"*Asperges me, Domine, hyssopo, et mundabor . . .*"

But Orsola did not feel the purifying wave which made her whiter than the snow in the eyes of her Lord.

With frail fingers she stroked the counterpane over her chest, a tremulous movement quivered on her lips, in her throat gurgled the sound of the word she was unable to pronounce.

"*Exaudi nos, Domine sancte . . .*"

Then a loud wail echoed through the Latin words, and Camilla hid her tear-stained face against the side of the bed. The doctor had approached and encircled Orsola's wrist with his bejeweled fingers. He wanted to rouse her, prepare her to receive the sacrament from the hands of Christ's minister, get her to hold out her tongue for the Host.

Orsola mumbled, her hands again fluttered vaguely as she was being propped up against the pillows. Only a tingling sensation struck the distempered nerves in her ears—now it was a shriek, now music. As they lifted her up the bluish flush on her face immediately became a cadaverous pallor; the pouch filled with ice slipped from her head onto the sheet.

"*Misereatur . . .*"

At last she offered her trembling tongue covered by a patina of mucus mingled with dark blood, and there the virgin Host rested.

11

"Ecce agnus Dei, ecce qui tollit peccata mundi . . ."

But she was completely unconscious and so did not withdraw her tongue at that contact: the light of the Eucharist did not break through her stupor. Camilla, her reddened, swollen eyes filled with terror and grief, stared at that ashen face from which, little by little, all sign of life was fading; at the gaping mouth which looked like that of someone strangled. With the solemnity of his office, the priest slowly continued to recite the Latin prayers. All the others remained on their knees under the diffused auroral light which the noon-hour drew from the snow outside. The smell of warm bread rose with the wind and the nostrils of the altar boys quivered.

"Oremus! . . ."

Urged by the doctor, Orsola closed her mouth again. They laid her flat on her back as the priest intoned the first part of the sacrament of Extreme Unction. Softly, the kneeling boys recited the antiphony to the seven penitential Psalms.

"Ne reminiscaris . . ."

From time to time Teodora La Iece, at the foot of the bed, her face hidden in her hands, emitted a stifled sob. At her side, a yellowish secretion continually oozing from one half-closed eye, the other staring blind and white because of a cataract, Rosa Catena stood upright, fingered her rosary and muttered. And while the Psalms rose from the floor in a whisper, the sacred formula pronounced by the priest soared above the confused murmur as, making the sign of the cross, he annointed the inert woman's eyes, ears, mouth and hands.

". . . indulgeat tibi Dominus quidquid per gressum deliquisti. Amen."

It was Camilla who uncovered her sister's feet: from between the sheets two feet appeared, yellow, scaly, with bluish nails, and at their touch she was filled with the disgust dead limbs inspire. And her tears fell on the dry skin, mingling with the oil of Extreme Unction.

"*Kyrie eleison, Christe eleison. Kyrie eleison. Pater noster . . .*"

The Lord's anointed now lay immobile, breathing, her eyes closed to the light, her knees drawn up and her hands squeezed between her thighs in the position typical of those stricken by typhoid fever. And after pressing the crucifix once more against her lips, and having made the sign of the cross from the center of the room with a broad gesture of his large hands, the priest went out, followed by the boys. The wan odor of incense and wax that clerical vestments give off still lingered in the room. Outside, beneath the windows, Matteo Pariello hammered away at his resoled shoes, singing to himself.

II

THE ILLNESS'S symptoms slowly lost their virulence, the fourth seven-day cycle of the disease began, and now stupefied inertness was followed by the natural quiet of sleep, a lasting calmness during which, little by little, the perturbations that had obscured her consciousness subsided, her senses' faculties grew less clouded, her respiration less rapid and agitated. But now and again a harsh fit of coughing burst from the sick woman's chest, shaking her backbone, while a painful deterioration of the skin and soft tissues at the elbows, knees, and lower back progressed day after day. When Camilla leaned over her bed calling "Orsola!" she tried to open her eyes, turn toward that voice. But her weakness weighed her down; and again lethargic apathy overwhelmed her senses.

She was hungry, hungry. A bestial longing for food tortured her empty bowels, communicating to her mouth the vague movement of jaws demanding something to chew on, sending through the pitiful bones of her hands the prehensile contractions which move the fingers of a gluttonous monkey at the

13

sight of an apple. She was racked by the ravening hunger that accompanies the convalescence from typhus, the dreadful craving for vital nourishment clamoring from every cell of a body exhausted by long illness. Only a feeble wave of blood still circulated through the tissues; in the weakly irrigated brain all activity stagnated as in a machine deprived of the fuel's propelling energy. Only fitful vibrations stirred in her body and prompted reactions that had been habitual in her former life, nor was the convalescent woman at all aware of this muted mechanical process. Mostly she recited the litanies aloud; or painstakingly divided the senseless words into syllables; or she would threaten her pupils with severe punishments, or sing the quinary rhymes of a hymn glorifying Jesus. Almost incessantly, the index finger of her left hand ran swiftly along the cuff of the counterpane with a pointing motion, as if by that gesture she were guiding a pupil's eyes along the lines of a book. Then, at times, her voice rose, took on an almost menacing solemnity, pronouncing the admonishments of the *seven trumpets* or confusedly repeating the words of Fra Bartolomeo da Saluzzo, and perhaps before her marvelling eyes she had a vision of those old woodcuts that swarm with deformed, trumpeting angels and vanquished demons. But there was never an intelligent gaze in her eyes. The drooping eyelids half-covered her irises, those discolored irises floating contourless in the sclera which seemed covered by a film of yellow mucilage. She lay stretched out upon her bed, flat and stiff, her head supported by two pillows. She had lost almost all her hair during the illness; a dusty pallor—the kind of pallor under which it seemed impossible there should be any life left—covered her face, the hollows in her face; and beyond it was visible the skull, and through the brittle dryness of the rest of her skin transpired the skeleton, and all around that rigging jumble of bones, in the places where pressure was exerted on the bed, the connective tissue was decaying. Yet, an immense, ravenous hunger animated that ruin and tor-

tured the intestines where the typhus ulcerations were slowly
healing.

Outside, the Christmas Novena, the lovely festivity of
young and old, had begun. The early evenings were luminous
and freezing cold and in their light the entire town of Pescara
swarmed with sailors and rang with the sound of bagpipes.
The pungent odor of fish stews spread in the air from the open
doors of taverns. One by one the lamps lit up at the windows,
in the doorways, the streets. The sun lingered roseate on the
stone balconies of Farina's house, on the chimney-pots of
Menna's house, on San Giacomo's belltower. Like beacons,
the shining pinnacles overlooked the town invaded by dusk.
Then, all of a sudden, night began to stud the vaulting sky
with stars, a sickle moon looked out from behind the bastions
above the houses of Sant'Agostino, between the red lantern
and the telegraph, and grew larger night after night.

All that bustle of life rose to Orsola's room with the confused buzz of an awakening bee-hive.

The bagpipers' carols approached from house to house,
from door to door. Those sounds which the shepherds of
Atina drew from their sheepskin bags and their bundles of
perforated reeds rang with a devout and familiar festiveness.
The convalescent woman heard, and rose in her bed; for that
sensation aroused in her the ghosts of other, past sensations,
and her eyes filled with sacred visions of radiant holy cribs
and white flights of angels soaring through immaculate blues.
And she began to sing praises, holding out her arms. Often,
suddenly breathless, she sat there, her mouth agape as her
voice faltered in her throat; she praised Jesus in a transport of
sweet and ardent love, enraptured by the sound of the approaching carols, hallucinated by the holy images hanging on
the walls. She ascended to heaven amid the music of cheru-
bim, the fumes of incense and myrrh.

"*Hosanna!*"

Her voice failed her. She held out her arms. Camilla, at her side, tried to make her lie down again; Camilla felt almost subjugated by those blind outbursts of faith; her hands, her lips trembled. Orsola fell back, her head abandoned on her pillow, her throat and breast bared, her eyes showing only their whites in the dreadful pallor of her face, smiling at some invisible thing, in the attitude of a virgin martyr. The bagpipes passed; later came and passed the drunken songs of sailors brawling through the night on their way back to the boats on Pescara's river.

III

THE INSTINCTIVE craving for food became keener as her senses cleared. When the warm smell of bread rose in the air from Flaiano's oven, Orsola begged; she begged and pleaded, whimpering like a starved beggar, holding out her hand to her sister. She devoured her food rapidly, overwhelmed by a brutish pleasure of all her being, looked around suspiciously lest someone try to snatch the food from her hands.

The convalescence was long and slow but a mild feeling of well-being was already beginning to spread through her limbs and clear her mind. The healthy diet of proteins and lean meat began to produce fresh blood; her lungs, now fully dilated by air, vivified the blood laden with nourishing substances; and the tissues irrigated by the swift, warm wave, took on color and formed anew, grew back over the bedsores, which were gradually covered with epidermis; and stimulated by that even flow the brain began to function secure and steady; and the ramifications of the nerves in her sensory organs, no longer distempered and disrupted, limpidly transmitted all sensations; and under her scalp the bulbs of her hair thrived strong and dense; and from that newly re-established order of the mechanical laws of life, that surge of energies that before had been submerged by the illness, from the intense desire to live and feel alive that had seized the convalescent, from everything around her, slowly, as through a second birth, arose a more perfect being.

It was the beginning of February.

From her bed Orsola could see the top of the Arch of Portanuova, the reddish bricks among which grew tufts of greenery, the crumbling capitals where the swallows would soon build their hanging nests. The violets of St. Anna in the cracks of the frieze had yet to blossom. The sky above opened up with beatific serenity; and, at intervals, the call of bugles traveled through the air from the Arsenal.

It was during those days that, almost with a sense of astonishment, she thought about her past existence. It seemed as if that past did not belong to her, were not hers; an immeasurable distance separated her from those memories; a dreamlike distance. She no longer had a clear sense of time; in order to remember she had to look at the objects that surrounded her, to make a great mental effort, to concentrate at length. With the tips of her fingers she touched her temples where the hair was growing back soft and fine, and a vague, abstracted smile fluttered on her lips, flashed through her eyes.

"Ah!" she whispered and, gently, her fingers returned to her temples.

It had been a melancholy and monotonous life there in those three rooms, among all those small, deformed statues of saints, all those Madonnas, all those children repeating aloud and in unison, for five hours a day, day after day, always the same words chalked on the blackboard. Like the glorious martyrs of the legend, like St. Tecla of Lycaonia and St. Euphemia of Calcedonia, the two sisters had consecrated their virginity to the heavenly Spouse, to the nuptials with Jesus. They had mortified the flesh by dint of abstinences and prayers, breathing the air of the church, incense and the smell of burning tapers, living only on vegetables—beans and lentils.

They had stupefied their spirits in that long and arid spelling drill, the cold distilling of words, the mechanical to and fro of thread and needle over eternally identical white linens odorous of lavender and sanctity. Never did their hands reach out for the soft feel of their pupils' hair, the sweet warmth of those fair, angelic heads; never did their lips touch the children's brow in a sudden effusion of tenderness. They taught elementary catechism, the first religious chants. Upon those playful heads they brought down the admonitions of Lent; in grave voices they spoke of the horrors of sin, of eternal damnation, and the children's large eyes filled with wonder, their small pink mouths opened in astonishment. In the children's vivid imaginations, all around them, the sacred objects came alive: the waxen profiles of mysterious saints leaped from the background of old pictures, and the Nazarene, crowned with thorns and blood-red drops, stared from all sides with agonized, haunting eyes; and beneath the hood of the hearth each puff of smoke twisted into an atrocious shape. And this is how they instilled faith in those ingenuous souls.

Now the memory of that sterility turbidly reawakened in Orsola's mind. She thought back, back to the earliest years; compelled by an instinctive impulse of her spirit, she sought refuge at the source; and a sudden flood of jubilation bathed her as though in a single moment her entire childhood had streamed back into her heart.

"Camilla!" she called. "Camilla, where are you?"

But her sister did not answer from the next room, she was not there. She had gone out, perhaps: to church, for Vespers. Then Orsola was seized by the temptation to feel the ground with her feet, to try to take a few steps on the floor, there and then, all alone.

She laughed to herself like a shy little girl who hesitates as she is about to undertake a difficult task; she closed her eyes, lingering to enjoy the sudden delight of her thought; with her fingers she felt her knees, her frail calves, as if to gauge her strength; and she laughed and laughed because that laughter penetrated her with a sweet languor, a subtle, vibrant elation.

A dart of sunlight grazed the windowsill and lanced the water of a basin in the corner; its moving, restless reflection shimmered on the wall, like a delicate mesh of gold. A flight of doves flashed through the air and alighted on the Arch; it seemed an omen. Slowly she moved the covers aside, then she hesitated again: sitting on the edge of the bed, groping with the point of her thin, yellow foot for her woollen slipper. She found it, found its mate; but now a sudden, melting tenderness assailed her, her eyes filled with tears and everything before her wavered in a hazy, milky light, as if the objects around her were losing their substance and vanishing. Tears streaked her cheeks, gathered at her mouth, warm and salty; she drank them, savored their taste. Outside, one by one, in pairs, the doves rose again, fluttering. With a movement of her jaws Orsola forced back the surge of tears; then she leaned against the edge of the bed and pushed, and finally stood on her feet; she smiled through her tears, looking at herself. She hadn't realized how weak she was, that her legs would not support her; she felt a strange prickling sensation in her shins, a twitching in her muscles, almost the sensation of someone who, having broken a bone, gets up before it is well mended. She tried to take a step, she put one foot in front of her, timidly; she became frightened and sat down again on the edge of the bed, looking around as if to make sure no one was watching her. Then she sought a goal—the window; and she started again, carefully, her eyes fixed on the foot in front of her, balancing herself, clutching her green shawl to her chest, invaded by a slight chill. When she had gone halfway, a sudden fear froze her: she staggered, thrashed her hands, turned back toward the bed, took three or four precipitous steps, falling back onto the edge of the bed. She remained there for a short while, panting; she crawled back under the covers where she still found some warmth, bundled herself up tightly, and huddled there shivering.

"Oh Lord, how weak I am!"

And she looked curiously at the spot on the floor where she had taken those few steps, almost expecting to see her footprints.

IV

SHE DID NOT TELL her sister about that first attempt. When she heard Camilla come back home, she closed her eyes and lay motionless as if she were asleep, feeling, deep inside her, a strange pleasure at the deception, straining to hold back the laughter which tickled in her throat and tried to rise to her lips. She was delighted with her small secret; day after day she waited anxiously for the moment when Camilla would descend the stairs and leave; she would sit up and remain still, listening, until the sound of slowly descending footsteps faded; then she would get out of bed, stifling bursts of laughter, leaning against the walls for support, against the furniture, uttering startled little cries whenever her knees threatened to give way, whenever she was about to lose her balance.

Almost always, around that hour, the smell of bread rose from Flaiano's bakery to tease her. She went to the window trying to sniff the breeze; inhaling that hearty aroma, she experienced both torture and a voluptuous pleasure, her tongue swam in her watering mouth and her eyes shone with greed. Then she was seized by a frenzy to search and rummage everywhere, dragging herself fitfully through the rooms; and afterward she made vain and angry attempts to force the locks whose keys Camilla had taken with her. One time, in the hidden corner of a small table-drawer, she found an apple and sank her teeth into it with relish. For a long time, on her strict convalescent's diet, she had not tasted the flavor of fruit. This had a fresh scent of roses, the scent which gathers in certain pale and withered apples. She returned to the drawer and searched again, hoping; but she only found a kind of greenish pod which, probably, contained a cluster of seeds; she took it and examined it with curiosity, and hid it under her pillow.

Thus she spent that hour, in secrecy, with the acrid pleasure that convalescent children extract from forbidden things, small thefts, infractions of the doctor's orders. Her only witness was a cat, speckled like the skin of a snake. Sometimes he followed her around with his familiar meowing or, if the doves fluttered their wings on the Arch outside, he halted in his tracks, poised for an impossible leap. Little by little, Orsola was growing fond of that discreet companion. She welcomed him into the warmth of her bed and whispered nonsense to him, or watched him fixedly as he licked his paw with his pink tongue or offered his lizard-like throat to her endearments, a yellowish throat which throbbed with a husky and tender sound similar to the cooing of turtle-doves among the trees. Owing perhaps to a natural recrudescence of her previous mysticism, she loved the sudden fires that smoldered in the creature's eyes in the dimly lit room, the phosphorescent sparks emanating from that mysterious and silent shape crouching in the darkness.

Camilla observed her sister's strange foibles with a certain diffidence, perhaps even with rankling resentment, but she held her tongue. And slowly, almost imperceptibly, their souls drew apart, mutually repulsed.

They had lived, before, in a constant communion of habits and feelings because all the conflicting traits of their temperaments, all rebellious impulses had been equalized and placated by their shared faith, the unshakable cult of Christ's deity, the contemplative worship that had become the sole purpose of their lives. But as they were completely absorbed in this cult, the ties of their consanguinity had on the contrary gradually been covered and overwhelmed by those of their common religiosity; therefore no tender effusions, no intimate exchange of hopes or memories had ever drawn them together as sisters. They belonged to the same Church, they both were members of Christ's great family, lost on the earth and yearning for Heaven.

So that when, due to the change wrought in her first by the illness and then by her recovery, Orsola began to reveal certain unexpected tendencies, certain unusual attitudes, rejection followed immediate and inevitable, and the slumbering voice of their common blood did not rise to oppose it.

V

THE PUPILS came back—for the first time on a morning in early March. Orsola had got up; she sat on the edge of her bed with the warmth of the sun bathing the nape of her neck and shoulders. In the room hung the pungent smell of the vinegar that Camilla had poured into the dusty inkwells and, through the open windows, from time to time, the wind bore the scent of the violets that now blossomed on the Arch.

A premonition of the children's presence breathed in the room like a gust of that light March air. At first, in the doorway, a tumultuous bustle of small heads straining, one above the other, to get a glimpse inside; then hesitation, shyness, a kind of naive astonishment at the sight of their teacher, so pale and thin that they could barely recognize her.

But the virgin Orsola smiled, overwhelmed by the sudden turmoil of her blood; she called them to her, confusing their names in her excitement; she held out her hands. First singly, then in twos, threes, the children approached; they wanted to catch her hands and touch them with their lips, they recited the get-well wishes they had learned by heart at home, swallowing the words in their haste.

"No, no, no—enough!" Orsola cried, overcome as they pressed around her, but she relinquished her hands to their soft, warm mouths. She felt she was going to faint.

"Camilla, stop them, stop them!"

Each child had brought a gift: there were flowers, fruit. The violets had at once filled the air with their perfume and in that perfume, in that light, the children's faces, flushed with their healthy, plebeian blood, smiled at her.

Then, in the next room, the lesson began. The first grade chanted vowels and diphthongs, the second grade spelled out words; and above the silvery chorus, now and then, rose Camilla's admonishing voice.

"*La, le, li, lo, lu . . .*"

When there was a moment's pause, Orsola heard Matteo Pariello hammering at his shoe-leather or the clacking of La Iece's loom.

"*Va, ve, vi, vo, vu . . .*"

She grew restless. The monotony of those sounds and voices filled her head with a disagreeable heaviness, it made her drowsy. Whereas she wanted to stay awake, still sensing all around her the children's vitality, the joyous emanation of all those lives.

"*Bal, bel, bil, bol, bul . . .*"

She took the flowers and put them in a glass of water to keep them fresh. Then she smelled them, her nostrils buried for a long time in their freshness, wholly absorbed in that olfactory sin.

"*Gra, gre, gri, gro, gru . . .*"

A big white cloud veiled the sun. Orsola went to the window, leaned against the windowsill and looked down into the piazza. Across the way Donna Fermina Memma stood on her balcony wearing a pink dress, amid pots spilling out carnations; and a group of officers passed below her, laughing and striking the pavement with their ringing sabres. Farther ahead, in the park, the lilac bushes were ready to bloom, the crown of the huge pine-tree swayed in the wind. From Lucitino's tavern came Vedura, the eternal drunkard, staggering and vociferous.

Orsola withdrew. This was the first time, after so long, that she had looked out into the piazza. It was as if she were looking down from a tremendous height; she felt slightly dizzy.

"*Nar, ner, nir, nor, nur . . .*"

The chant inside still continued, on and on and on.

"*Pla, ple, pli, plo, plu . . .*"

She began to choke, her head began to reel under the torture: her poor frayed nerves were giving way. The chant continued relentlessly, following the beat of Camilla's pointer rapping on the desk.

"*Ram, rem, rim, rom, rum . . .*"

"*Sat, set, sit, soit, sut . . .*"

And a sudden fit of sobbing assailed her, flung her onto the bed. And she lay there, prone, her arms outflung, weeping, pressing her face into the pillows, racked by sobs, unable to stop.

"*Tal, tel, til, tol, tul . . .*"

VI

HER HAIR had all grown back, tightly curled and chestnut colored as before. She was anxious to look at herself in the mirror; for, with one of those mawkish exclamations that still revealed the old trollop she had been, Rosa Catena had passed a hand over her body and said: "What a beauty!"

So again she waited for Camilla to leave the house. Then she climbed out of bed and took down from the wall one of those gold-framed rococo mirrors antiqued with misty green stains; with a corner of the blanket she removed the dust and looked at herself in the glass, smiling. Her throat was bare and covered with bluish, almost protruding veins, and there was something goatlike about her small, long, oval head: the thin lips, the sharp chin, her eyes—the color of chestnuts like her hair, but lighter, almost yellow. Her translucent pallor and her smile gave her twenty-seven years a new charm, a new youthfulness.

She examined herself for a long time; and she played, holding the mirror off at a distance, drawing it closer, delighted to see her image vanish in its sea-green light as if under a veil of water and then slowly emerge again. She was conquered, dominated by vanity. She began to see many small details she had never noticed before: a beauty-mark, for instance, like a small lentil on the skin over her left temple, and a fine scar across the arch of one of her eyebrows. Then, in a transport of sudden joy, she looked around for some other pleasure.

The pod she had found hidden in the drawer had opened its valves like a sea-shell, exposing a dense bunch of blackish seeds. Each seed seemed to be attached to a strand of fine filaments with a silvery sheen, and the cluster hung together, compact. But when the virgin Orsola breathed upon it, a cloud of minute white plumes instantly rose into the air and scattered glittering in all directions: they were what people called "spies." The seeds seemed to have wings, they looked like fragile, evanescent insects which dissolved at the touch of the sun, or like swansdown, barely visible; they floated, began to descend, became entangled in Orsola's hair, grazed her face, covered her whole body. She tried to ward off the assault, to chase away that fuzz which tickled her skin and clung to her hands, but she kept laughing and could not blow it away.

At last she lay down, stretched out, and let that soft snowfall slowly drift down upon her. She kept her eyes half-closed to prolong its melting sweetness; and as a heavy drowsiness invaded her limbs she had the sensation of sinking into a deep bed of feathers. The room was filled with the pale, steady light of a March afternoon when the sun shines shyly, fading into the wide opalescent sky like a premonition of dawn.

When Camilla returned she found her sister still asleep with the mirror next to her and "spies" in her hair.

"Oh Jesus! Oh Lord Jesus!" she whispered through clenched teeth, joining her palms in a gesture of bitter compassion.

The good woman was just coming from church where she had sung the litanies for the Annunciation and listened to a sermon on the Archangel's message to the Virgin Mary. *Ecce ancilla Domini.* The preaching friar's thundering eloquence had intoxicated her; some of his admonitory words still rang in her ears.

Just then Orsola woke up with a voluptuous yawn, stretching her limbs.

"Oh, is that you, Camilla?" she asked, bewildered for a moment by that presence.

"Yes, it's me, it's me! You will lose your soul, you wretch, perdition is awaiting you!" the pious woman shouted, pointing at the mirror on the bed. "You are playing with the devil's tools."

And excited by her first outburst, she went on, raising her voice, spewing out the scorching words of the sermon, slashing the air with her hands, lashing out with threats of eternal damnation—she spoke not only to her sister, she rose to chastise a world of sinners.

"*Memento! Memento!*"

Orsola had stopped hearing, stunned by that screaming, vociferous onslaught.

Suddenly, at the corner of the piazza, the military band struck up with a crash, the clarion call of twenty trumpets.

VII

THE LAST ROOM in the rear of the house was low-ceilinged
and narrow, the overhead beams blackened by smoke, reek-
ing with odors of onions and dishwater and doused charcoal.
The copper pots hung in an orderly row upon the walls,
lusterless; the Castelli plates with their gay motifs of flowers
and birds and laughing faces were lined up on a shelf; old-
fashioned brass oil-lamps, empty bottles, scraps of withering
vegetables were strewn about on the tables; and over all this,
protectively, reigned St. Vincent, portrayed with the great
book in one hand and a red flame bursting from his skull.

In that room, long ago, surrounded by the steam of boiling
water and the fumes of vegetarian meals, Orsola had often
heard, hurtling down upon her head from a tiny window high
in the wall, couplets of bawdy songs followed by coarse howls
of laughter. On summer evenings the singing and the laughter
grew louder, amid the strumming of guitars and the stomping
on the ground of dancing feet. At certain hours all the sounds
of the life of the most wretched scum rose all the way to their
window and made those poor brides of Christ, humbly bent
over their earthenware pots filled with the ascetic innocence
of beans and vegetables, tremble with horror. But now, with
the coming of a new and merry spring, one day, at the sound
of those voices, a strong longing to look outside stung Orsola's soul.

Camilla was not at home; it was the fifth Sunday after
Lazarus. After the brief rains, the imminence of April stirred
in the air with a sweeter, milder breath; and in that air the
maiden sensed her re-birth more clearly and fully. And as she
wandered through the rooms in idleness, she was inevitably
overcome by curiosity, captivated by the morbid spell that
obscene spectacles exert even upon the purest souls.

She climbed onto a chair to reach the opening, but before
lifting her eyes to peer outside, she was seized by anxious

tremors and, quivering, still standing on the chair, she looked to all sides, afraid lest someone surprise her in that position.

Everything around her was quiet; on and off a drop of water fell into a basin, with a pattering sound. Outside the voices rose and enticed.

Reassured, the virgin Orsola looked out. The filth in the alleyway had fermented under the rain like yeast; a black mire covered the flagstones where fruit peels, scraps of vegetables, rags, rotten slippers, hat-brims, all the decomposed rubbish that poverty flings into the streets, blended together. Facing that sewer from which the sun drew insects and putrid exhalations, a row of tiny houses seemed to pant, leaning against the barracks for support. Yet from every window, every crack, streamed carnations spilling from their pots; and the large pink and red flowers dangled in the sunshine, splendidly open, magnificent, in full bloom. And among those flowers appeared the flabby, painted faces of the whores; obscene songs, hoarse laughter trooped by; and down below, on the pavement, beneath the barracks' grilled windows, other trollops reached out to the soldiers, speaking in loud voices, taunting. And the soldiers whose blood called out those evil flowers of Aphrodite, stretched their arms between the iron bars to snatch whatever they could, like starved beasts slavering at the sight of those women long worn out by the lechery of countless drunken crews and sodden stevedores.

Orsola could not move, stunned by that spectacle of corruption which mounted all the way to her window, fermenting beneath the benign sun of Lent. She still did not turn away; but, lifting her eyes, at a dormer-window on the barracks' roof she saw a blond man looking at her and smiling. She got down from the chair in a flurry, paler than ever, for she thought she had heard Camilla's voice. She ran to her room and threw herself on her bed, dismayed, breathless, as if someone were pursuing her, threatening her.

VIII

FROM THAT DAY ON, every hour, every minute that Camilla was not at home, a diabolical temptation drew her to that spectacle. She tried at first to resist, in vain—weakly she gave in. She went to the window eager and wary like someone going to meet a lover; she lingered there for a long time, hiding behind the decrepit shutter while the miasma from the brothel aroused and corrupted her.

She observed everything, straining her eyes, trying to catch a glimpse of what went on beyond the carnations that screened the windows. The sun was hot and heavy; swarms of insects milled in the air. From time to time, when a man turned into the alleyway, the women would call out from the windows; half-naked women with bare breasts rushed into the street to offer themselves. Then the man and the one he had chosen would disappear through one of those dark doorways. The women who had been passed up would follow the couple with mocking insults and bursts of laughter, and then would go back to lying in wait behind their carnations.

And so lust began to smolder inside the virgin Orsola. The need for love, latent before, now rose from all of her being, became a torture, an incessant, ruthless torment against which she was helpless.

A warm wave of healthy energy filled her; sudden joyful feelings stirred her blood, aroused in her breast a fluttering like that of wings, filled her mouth with songs. At times a breath, one of those faint tremors in the air which spread in the sunshine, the song of a beggar, a smell, a nothing was enough to fill her with vague bewilderment, moments of abandon when it seemed to her she felt all over her limbs something like the caressing touch of the velvet of a ripe fruit. Thus she hovered weightless and lost over unknown depths of delight. The irritation of abstinence, the unaccustomed copiousness of lymph, the continued tensing of her nerves under stimuli, all this kept her in a sort of daze akin to the first stage of intoxication. The past vanished, drowsed at the bottom of her memory, no longer sprang to life. And at every moment, everywhere, desire laid its traps for her: the saints on the walls, the Madonnas, the naked crucified Christs, the small misshapen figures of wax statuettes, all the things surrounding her, for her took on impure appearances. From all objects impurity emanated and touched her body, burningly.

"Now, now I'll go down into the street," she said to herself, unable to resist.

Then her hands trembled on the door as she opened it. The strident sound made by the bolt pulled through its iron rings dismayed her. She turned back, threw herself on the bed almost in a swoon, deathly pale, beneath the shadow of a man.

IX

ON PALM SUNDAY, after all those months, she left the house for the first time; and Camilla wanted to accompany her to give thanks to the Lord for her recovery. When the bells began to ring festively, Orsola looked out of her window. The entire town radiated the joy of Easter under the April sun. The entire community swarmed in the streets, carrying the peacful symbol of the olive branch.

She must now put on her holiday best; the people in the streets were going to see her when she went by. A frenzy of vanity seized her; she locked herself in her room, looked for the brightest dresses at the bottom of the chest. A sharp odor of camphor rose from those old clothes stored away in there for years; they were large skirts of flowery silk, green and violet and iridescent, a crinoline which, full and rich, had perhaps once swelled around the hips of a young bride; they were long bodices with full sleeves, light beige pelerines trimmed with white laces, veils meshed with silver threads, collars of fine, hand-embroidered linen; a heap of things impossible to use, uncouth, covered with mould-stains.

As if guided by a new instinct, Orsola picked up and discarded, perfuming her hands with camphor as she searched. All that useless silk and those veils irritated her. She found nothing that fit her! She slammed the chest shut angrily and shoved it back under the bed with a thrust of her foot. The church bells rang out for the third time. Then, with Camilla looking on, she hastily slipped on her usual drab, ash-gray dress, biting her lips to keep back the tears.

The bells called. Along the streets the sheaves of palm leaves emitted a mobile, silvery glitter; from every knot of country folk rose a hedge of branches; and the pure clemency of the Christian benediction filled the air from those branches, as if the Galilean were approaching, the poor, sweet king sitting on the she-ass amid the mob of his disciples, to meet the hosannas of the redeemed people. *Benedictus qui venit in nomine Domini. Hosanna in excelsis!*

Inside the church the crowd was immense beneath the grove of palms. Because of one of those currents that form irresistibly in a mass of people, Orsola was separated from Camilla; she found herself left alone in that surge, amid all those contacts, all that shoving and breathing. She tried to open a path for herself: her hands touched a man's back, there were other warm hands whose touch disturbed her. She felt her face grazed by an olive leaf, her step impeded by a knee, an elbow nudging her hip, her breasts, her shoulders offended by anonymous pressures. With that odor of incense, under the sacred palms, in the mystical dusk, in all that crush of Christian men and women jostling together little erotic sparks were set off and spread; secret loves found each other again and were carnally united. Past Orsola streamed young peasant girls with palm sprigs on their breasts, fleeting laughter in the flashing whites of eyes turned toward admirers who pursued them temptingly: and so, feeling love stream by all around her, she placed her body between those bodies straining to reach each other, became an obstacle to those hands trying to touch each other, separated those grasping hands, the tangle of those arms. But something of those interrupted caresses penetrated her blood. At a certain point she stood face to face with a blond soldier; she almost rested her head on his tunic, for a throng of people was pressing at her back. She lifted her eyes; the young man smiled at her as he had once smiled from the attic window of the barracks. Behind her the pressure continued; the fumes of the incense spread more densely, and from the depths of the church rose the voice of the deacon chanting:

"*Procedamus in pace.*"

And the choir answered:

"*In nomine Christi. Amen.*"

It was the introduction to the procession, which caused a tremendous commotion among the faithful. Instinctively, without thinking, Orsola clung to the man, as if she already belonged to him; she almost let herself be lifted by those arms which seized her hips, in her hair she felt that virile breath with its slight scent of tobacco. And that's how she walked, weakened, exhausted, crushed by the voluptuousness which had suddenly overcome her, seeing nothing but a confused dazzle before her.

Then from the main altar moved the thurifer, scattering clouds of sweet bluish smoke over the congregation; and a white procession uncoiled in the center of the church. The celebrants carried olive branches in their hands and sang.

X

THE ENTIRE HOLY WEEK protected virgin Orsola's love with its darkling complicity. The churches looked immensely vast in the crepuscular light of Christ's Passion, the crucifixes on the altars were covered with heavy purplish cloths; the sepulchres of the Nazarene were surrounded by tall white plants grown in cellars; a perfume of flowers and of benzoin hung heavy in the air.

There, upon her knees, Orsola waited, until a light step behind her made her start. She could not turn because Camilla watched her; but she felt completely embraced by the gaze of that man, as if by a subtle flame, and a turbid tenderness welled through her flesh. Then she stared at the triangle of tapers on a wooden frame near the altar. The priests chanted in front of a large book; and one by one the tapers were put out. There remained only five, there remained only two; darkness issued from the depths of the side chapels over the people absorbed in their prayers. The last small flame finally disappeared: all the benches resounded under the lashes of the reeds. Orsola in the darkness, as soon as she felt herself touched by two groping hands, rose from the marble floor with a jerk, dismayed. Then, when she left the church, the thought of having desecrated the holy place filled her with repentance; sudden and crushing, the fear of punishment reappeared. She then sank into a kind of dream where the livid figure of the dead Christ and the crash of flagellations and the thrills of her stimulated flesh and the heavy, redolent odor of the flowers and the breath of that blond man all mingled together in an ambiguous sensation of sorrow and pleasure.

XI

BUT WHEN JESUS triumphantly re-ascended to His heavenly glory, the aromatic effluvia of Easter no longer comforted the love of the virgin Orsola. For its setting her love now had the domain of alley cats and tame pigeons. The tender gestures traveled from the barracks' attic to the kitchen window; in between lay the brothel, like a slimy ditch along whose edges grew the flowers fed by putrefaction. The pigeons flew aloft, flashing the green and gray shimmer of their feathers.

Her lover had a beautiful, ancient name—he was called Marcello and wore beautiful red and silver insignia on the sleeves of his uniform. He wrote letters brimming with eternal fire, replete with impetuous sentences which made the enamored woman nearly faint from tenderness and tremble from ill-contained voluptuousness. Orsola read those pages in secrecy, night and day kept them hidden in her bosom; because of the warmth of her flesh, the purple handwriting was imprinted upon her skin, and it was like a gentle tattoo of love, which delighted her. Her replies were endless: all the grammatical knowledge of a schoolmistress, the entire thesaurus of a devout believer's psalmistic apostrophes, all the flowing sentimentality of an over-ripe maiden poured onto the paper of the blue-lined school notebooks. She wrote and forgot herself, carried away by a wave of sonorous verbosity. It almost seemed that a newly born ability were expressing itself within her, unexpectedly taking on maniacal aspects. That great sediment of mystical lyricism accumulated through the reading of the prayer books over so many years of faithfulness to the Heavenly Spouse, now, stirred by earthly love, rose confusedly and assumed unsuspected flavors of profanity. Thus the tearful implorings addressed to Jesus became hopeful sighs of yearning for the delights of much less ethereal embraces; the offers of the flowers of the soul to the Supreme Good were transformed into tender surrenders of the flesh to the desire for the blond lover; and the aphrodisiac light of the moon was crowned with all the epithets by which the Holy Ghost is rendered radiant. Nor did the soft breezes of spring fail to waft away the heavenly scents of the festive banquets of Paradise.

XII

THEIR MESSENGER was one of those men who seem to sprout, like mushrooms, from the moistness of the tainted street and to bear upon their bodies almost a native tint of mud; one of those gray-invisible men, who burrow in everywhere, who are always there whenever a cent is to be earned, a bit of fat is to be lapped up, a rag is to be snatched—today junk-dealers and tomorrow procurers of maids or loose women, today fake mercantile middlemen and tomorrow catchers of stray mongrel dogs.

This man had an operatic name—he was called Lindoro; from the Ospedale quarter to the bastions of Sant'Agostino a great notoriety had sprung up around this name. He was born from the mating of a vagrant clarinet player with a market woman who hawked vegetables, and he had inherited his father's nomadic instincts and his mother's natural greed. He had at first dragged himself over the garbage piles of every household with broom and basket; then he had washed glasses and dishes in a tavern, where soldiers and sailors threw in his face the dregs of their cups and the bones of the badly fried fish. After the tavern he had landed in a bakery, where he pushed the loaves toward the fire on a long shovel, all night long, sweating, blinded. From the bakery he had gone on to the position of lighter of the public street lamps, wearing out his shoulder under the weight of the ladder he carried. Dismissed from that position because he stole kerosene from the large white zinc drums, he began to roam the streets, buying and re-selling old clothes, doing the most miserable kind of odd jobs throughout the workers' and artisans' neighborhoods, offering his services as a pimp and ruffian to soldiers and newcomers, striving in this way for his daily bread.

On his body and in his soul each trade had carved a mark, left behind an habitual gesture, the development of certain muscles, the debilitation of a particular organ, a callous, a cadence, an accent of the voice, a phrase of the jargon. He was small in stature, thin, with an enormous, almost bald head, patches of sparse bristles on his cheeks and boils among the bristles. His clothes were hybrid, varied, unpredictable; all manner of styles alternately covered his body, were superimposed with a jarring contrast: aristocratic, greenish morning coats over trousers once puce-colored and now patched everywhere, maroon felt hats and servants' slippers, shiny metal buttons, disks of white bone, military braids, laces—that potpourri of decayed opulence and ignoble penury which clutters the store of any Jewish junk-dealer.

XIII

NOW THIS MAN was the go-between. He delivered Marcello's epistles together with jugs of Pescara river water at Orsola's house and left with his jugs empty and her answering letters. When she heard him come up the stairs, Orsola went pale, racked her brain for pretexts to get rid of Camilla, to remain alone with this bearer of water and of joy. Then there were rapid, surreptitious, clandestine contacts; there were exchanged between her and her go-between those sidelong glances of complicity, those fleeting contractions of the facial muscles, those whispered monosyllables which are the instruments of human guile and which as time goes by form tenacious bonds between deceivers. Little by little Orsola's love was suffused by something of Lindoro's vileness; a kind of familiarity gradually established itself between the woman in love and the messenger. If he arrived during Camilla's absence, she plied him with questions, her head so close to his he could feel her breath, inadvertently placing a hand on his shoulder at times. Lindoro gave rein to his loquaciousness, interspersing bits of jargon, lewd silences, sly revelatory smiles, equivocal gestures, smackings of his tongue and lips.

He played the go-between with artistry, adroitly insinuated corruption into Orsola's spirit, cleverly lured the prey little by little into Marcello's trap. And the virgin listened to him intently and thoughtfully while a flame grew deep in her eyes and lewd excitement dried her mouth; she listened and did not interrupt him. Lindoro could tell at once that he had awakened lust in the woman; and faced by that body that was wholly tensed, completely ravaged by passion, the male in him was suddenly aroused and he was struck by the temptation to pluck the prize he was preparing for another man's pleasure. But fear rising from the depths of his cowardice restrained him and froze his ardor.

Then, finally, Orsola agreed to a meeting with Marcello. The assignation would take place in a remote house on the outskirts of town, tucked away in a deserted alleyway, where nobody would be able to see them, on a Sunday in June when Camilla stayed longer in church and Lindoro could be on the look-out.

During the days preceding the great event, Orsola was gripped by bitter excitement, a kind of fever which at times made her teeth chatter, brought a hot flush to her face and shivers to her scalp and the nape of her neck. She was unable to keep still, couldn't remain seated, because a frenzy of restlessness filled her limbs. During school, surrounded by the even, monotonous murmur of her pupils, surrounded by that unremitting drone of scanned syllables, a dazzling surge of rebellion would suddenly blind her, and she would have liked to pounce on the children, tousle their hair, overturn the blackboard, the charts, the benches, burst out screaming, smash something, stun herself. Under Camilla's cold and inquisitive eyes she came close to fainting, such was her agitation, her rage, her immense inner effort at dissimulation.

Then, when Camilla went out, she would flounce through all the rooms, move chairs from here to there, nibble at a flower, drain a large glass of water in one gulp, stare at herself in the mirror, look out the window, fling herself down across the bed, give vent in a thousand ways to her restlessness, the exuberance of her sensual vitality. Her entire body, in the belated, seething ebullience of virginhood, had become richer and fuller. Her head was not beautiful, it lacked the vigorous bold structure, the olive-tinted splendor of certain races of the Abruzzo, those pure lines of nose and chin drawn with Grecian definition upon the ample planes of the Latin face. But, though unaware of it, concealed by the clumsiness of her drab clothes, beneath their drooping, haphazard pleats and folds, she possessed a lovely, delicate body.

Those were the first days of June: the summer arose out of the spring as an aloe out of a grassy field. Between sea and river, the entire town of Pescara rejoiced in the salty breeze and in the river's cool air, as if it were reaching out its arms toward those natural boundaries of salt and sweet water. Then during those days the blandishments of the season rose to Orsola's room; lustrous insects knocked against her window panes and bounced back, like the grains of a golden hail.

The virgin, when she was alone, felt a need to stretch her limbs, to throw off her long dresses, lie down, and absorb through her skin that mysterious beguilement that hung in the atmosphere.

She began slowly to undress with lazy movements, her fingers lingering upon the laces and hooks, making faint, half-hearted efforts at pulling her arms out of sleeves, halting listlessly in the process and letting her head with its short crinkly hair fall back, that head which was so much like the head of an adolescent boy. Gradually, under her laboring, caressing hands, from out of the shapelessness of the garments, like a statue disinterred from the dross of time, the naked body appeared. A heap of coarse wool and linen cloth lay at the feet of the thus purified maiden, and from that heap as from a pedestal she rose in the light, crowning her head with her arms, while at the touch of the air a barely visible quiver rippled over her skin. In that momentary attitude all the lines of the torso softly stretched and rose towards the encircled head; the slight roundness of the abdomen, not yet disfigured by conception, flattened out; and the outline of the rounded thighs took on full relief. Then, if an insect got into the room, the hum of its wings circling around her and threatening to touch that nakedness—that hum distressed Orsola; and she tried to ward off the dreaded sting, making serpentine movements, her muscles twitching beneath her skin, her arms and legs forming frightened knots, her ankles twisting feebly, not powerful enough to accomplish anything.

Then, excited in this way by her movements and feeling warm, she was overcome by new yearnings. She opened her door, cautious and wary; and stuck out her head, peering into the adjacent room. There was a musty odor, that lifeless squalor which fills a classroom when the children are gone. On the square charts the large block letters of the alphabet and the groups of diphthongs and syllables loomed, the room's silent sovereigns. Orsola advanced, her bare feet avoiding the cracks in the irregular floor, experiencing the titubation of someone who walks barefoot for the first time over an uneven surface and the confusion of a woman who no longer feels her step impeded by the skirts she is used to wearing. She went like this all the way to the third room, where they kept the water. She plunged her hands into it, sprinkled it all over her body, bravely, shivering when a heavier drop ran down her skin. She left the room, all glittering with dew and walked to the mirror of an old chest of drawers.

On that dresser fragments of inlay still remained here and there. The mirror, which concealed a cabinet on top of the dresser, had a frame decorated with gilded and colored fretwork and at the top floated two decapitated cupids. Lured by an irresistible desire to see herself naked, Orsola strained on tiptoe before the mirror. Her entire body, still covered by fresh, cool drops of water, rose in the mist of the mirror as though in the green-blue depths of the sea. She gazed at herself, smiling. Her smile, each movement of her muscles, seemed to impart a quivering light to every contour of her nakedness, caught by the mirror as if they were those of an image seen in a reflection in the water. Then she began a kind of vain mimicry, watching all her gestures reproduce themselves in the glass, parting her lips to show her teeth, lifting her arms to show her armpits, offering her arched back and forcing her head to turn as far back as possible; until, at the sight of that view of herself, a mad burst of hilarity shook her whole body. Far, far off, in the distant background, behind the woman, the alphabet chart was reflected from the opposite wall.

XIV

NOW, DURING ONE of those moments, Lindoro, who had come up the stairs with his jars, knocked at the entrance door. Orsola cried to him: "Wait!"

And she hastily gathered her clothes up from the floor, hastily put them on, and went to open.

It was six o'clock in the evening; the white gleam from Brina Palace filled the room; all Pescara, a great asylum of swallows, was singing.

The two of them stood in the center of the room, discussing the imminent meeting. Lindoro with his loquacity was trying to dispel the girl's last hesitations; for he had already received part of his reward and was anxious to lay his hands on the rest. The game of deceitful persuasion gave a lively sparkle to his words, his eyes, his gestures. His breath smelled heavily of wine and, because of a razor's recent scraping, his face, his cheeks were studded with small pinkish and purplish spots.

As he spoke he revealed the row of his regular and healthy teeth, one of those strong sets of teeth that often grow fiercely in plebeian mouths; and this singularity stood out strikingly in the man's general look of turpitude.

Orsola resisted, expressing misgivings, fears, interrupting him; but the procurer's shameless arguments having been expressed with increasing heat thanks to his wine-induced excitement, she already became uneasy. Little by little she backed up to the wall, leaning against it for support. Glimpses of linen showed through her clothing here and there, telling of the haste in which she had dressed. Her throat was completely bare, and on her stockingless feet everything could be seen save for the toes inside her slippers.

But at a certain point, involuntarily, because of that blind instinct which warns a woman that she is faced by an aroused man, she swiftly moved her hand to fasten the hooks over her throat, her breasts. That movement by which Orsola acknowledged the man in the go-between, that unexpected gesture provoked in Lindoro's abjectness an uprush of masculine pride. Ah, he had made a woman respond to him! —And he came closer; and then, since the wine gave him courage, this time no cowardly restraint held the brute in check.

XV

ORSOLA LAY THERE inert, stretched out on the brick floor, her clothes, her entire body expressing the dishevelment of an outraged woman.

But when she heard Camilla's steps on the stairs, she rose on her elbow from the depths of her exhausted languor; rapidly ran her hands over her disordered clothing, was able to summon up speech and tell her sister that a sudden weakness had caused her to collapse in the middle of the room.

Outside night was falling. Over the town unfolded the vast,

glaucous coolness of a June evening, coming in from the Adriatic. Voices and laughter filled the piazza; all through the building rang the Sabbatical joy of its relieved tenants. From the second floor landing Teodora Lo Iece cried: "Neighbor Camilla, neighbor Camilla, are you coming?"

Orsola followed her sister—without speaking, without thinking. She had made an effort to remember: a sort of lethargy still imprisoned her memory. Teodora filled their ears with her vicious, petulant chatter.

"Have you heard, neighbor, that the daughter of Rosa Catena is getting married?"

"Oh."

"Have you heard, she's taking Giovanni Speranza, that red-headed fellow who runs a tavern at the Pesceria and has Saint Donato's sickness, God preserve us."

"Oh."

"Have you heard, neighbor, Checchina Madrigale has run off again to Francavilla. You know her, she's that fat woman who lives at Gloria's house, dark, with a beaked nose—that one."

Teodora had fallen into step with Orsola. Camilla followed a little behind, her head bowed, not paying any attention to the sin of slander the weaver's tongue was committing against her neighbor. Along the streets everyone was out enjoying the cool air; knots of women passed in cotton dresses, their arms bare to the elbow.

"Neighbor, just look at Graziella Potavigna, at the flounce she's wearing! Look at Rosa Zazzetta, with one sergeant in front and one behind . . . Oh, you didn't know?"

And here followed a tale of intrigues full of salacious indiscretions, whispered into the ear. To forget, Orsola let herself become completely absorbed by the gossip, with a kind of convulsed frenzy not giving herself the time to think, asking questions, inciting Teodora to go on wagging her tongue, fearful of pauses, filling them with bursts of laughter. She almost found a bitter pleasure in hearing other people being reviled.

"Oh, there's Don Paolo."

Walking towards them with his enviable placidity came Don Paolo Seccia, an octogenarian still as pungent and green as a juniper.

"Do come with us, Don Paolo; we can walk together."

All the butcher shops along the street, on both sides, displayed their freshly slaughtered heifers, strung up across the doorway; the odor of the raw meat spread from the gaping bellies and attacked one's nostrils. Farther on, long rows of macaroni were spread out under the light of the moon, which looked down on them from above a flagpole set on the barracks roof. Groups of shouting soldiers crowded round the fruit peddlers.

"Let's go to the Bandiera," said Teodora, stepping aside to let Don Paolo and Camilla walk ahead.

Orsola moved dazedly through all those sounds, those pungent odors. By now a vague despair was beginning to move deep inside her, twisting her lips when she laughed, paralyzing her tongue when she spoke. Certain little physical pains also molested her and called her back to reality. She could no longer run away from herself; her voice died under her teeth, anguish clenched her throat, the specter of her tremendous, irreparable sin rose before her. She now felt she would die from the effort she had to make to stay on her feet, to keep on walking—she was pounded by the ruthless bustle of life in the street which belongs to everyone.

"So, as I was saying, that one-eyed husband of hers, without knowing a thing . . ." said Teodora, picking up the thread of her momentarily interrupted back-biting.

They walked through the Bandiera quarter. To the left the bridge of barges straddled the river. On the opposite bank the stern and gloomy bulk of the bastion was outlined against the pallid sky. The old iron cannons, their muzzles solidly dug into the ground, stood in a long row with the thick hemp mooring ropes slung around them; huge iron anchors cluttered the pier. On the decks of the boats, along the embankments, sailors ate and smoked under their canvas tents; the lit-up tents with their blood-red glow clashed with the cold whiteness of the moon. Around the prows broad patches, as of putrifying matter, floated lazily.

". . . sent for Don Nereo Memma, just imagine!" Teodora continued inexorably.

"Did someone just mention Doctor Dulcamara?" broke in Don Paolo, who had heard the name, laughing, his frank mouth still spiked with shining ivory.

Orsola no longer heard anything; she was as pale as the face of the moon. At first all that profound, luminous peacefulness pouring down from the sky upon the river and all those long currents of marine odors mingling with the cool night had soothed her; for in that soft and tender scenery the phantom images of love deep within her revived, and the extreme aspirations of her feelings shone resplendent in the lunar night. Then, immediately after, there was a confused tumult in which all she heard was the throbbing of her arteries, a deafening murmur that seemed to expand and in a moment clog the whole atmosphere. The ground gave way under her feet. As dizziness seized her, the river's shore became blurred, the river invaded the street; waves—waves—waves surged all around her. Then suddenly a glitter of dazzling sparks lit up in her eyes, a glowing flicker of tiny flaming will-o'-the-wisps which exploded, intertwined, moved away, melted and vanished like writhing snakes in the darkness. In that glimmer Marcello's image rapidly appeared and disappeared, changing as in a dream. The dizziness ceased. Orsola recognized the streams of moonlight mirrored by the placid river; she continued to walk, stupefied, exhausted, almost about to faint.

"You're tired, eh? You're not used to it, of course. Lean on me, hold on," said Teodora. "Donna Mentina Ussoria's daughter, the youngest one, she's pock-marked, was standing right in front of the store, you know—on the small piazza . . ."

They reached the Coast Guard barracks. Large piles of carob pods gave off an odor as strong as tanned hides; and the road strewn with broken oyster shells crunched under their feet. Favored by the moon, two fishermen were silently pulling in eels with nets close to the shore. But the resounding sea filled the silence with its immensity. The rolling salt patches which again and again appeared shining above the veil of sweet water announced the river's mouth.

"Let's go back, my pretty ones," said Don Paolo, picking up a carob pod from the pile nearby.

Orsola let herself be led. She found it difficult to conceal her frantic gasps; for now her condition, with overwhelming dreadfulness, appeared before her and crushed all the amorous emotions, all the yearnings and excitements evoked by the voluptuous moonlit night. The inexorable fixed idea in her mind set before her the image of the living Lindoro; once again she felt herself seized and mauled by those harsh, coarse hands, suffocated by that breath inflamed with wine and lust, felt herself again being violated on the room's brick floor. But at that moment, she thought, she hadn't resisted, she hadn't screamed, she hadn't made the slightest attempt to fight him off; she had surrendered, all her strength drained, no longer able to distinguish anything, feeling only an immense joy mingled with the pain flooding through her body. Then revulsion and languor alternately seized her flesh, freezing her, inflaming her, like ice, like fire. Mindless, she stared straight ahead, pale, her eyes enlarged and darker.

"Listen to the wine singing!" said Don Paolo, pausing for a moment.

Aboard the boats the sailors lay stretched out between the coils of rope, surrounded by the smoke of their Dalmatian tobacco, and they sang about beautiful women, loudly, in chorus.

XVI

CAMILLA, on the *prie-dieu*, her bowed head against it, her hands clasped, prayed for a long time in a low voice; then for the night she lit the votive lamp before the Virgin Mary; and finally she surrendered to sleep, holding the sweeet heart of Jesus between the withered flowers of her breasts. Her devoutness was so great that even as she slept her breathing seemed to caress the sacred host lying there on its sacred paten. On the vaulted ceiling the shadows followed the flickering of the tiny flame fed by the oil in the lamp. The sounds of wood that swells and of wood-worms that gnaw, the mysterious voices of old furniture in the nocturnal quiet, broke the silence.

Orsola lay in the same bed at Camilla's side, stretched out motionless, open-eyed, for a great sleepless weariness weighed upon her limbs and the unrelenting vigilance of anguish tortured her wretched soul. She listened to the silence; she examined herself with fretful curiosity, as if to find out what change had been wrought in her being.

Of a sudden, Camilla began to mumble confused words in her sleep, fragments of incomprehensible words, barely moving her lips, and heaving deep sighs. Her head, gaunt, sharp, rigidly carved by penance and fasting, yellow in the light of the lamp, rested on the whiteness of the pillow like a poorly gilded effigy of a saint on a monstrance. Small, purplish shadows marked the inside of the nostrils, the furrows of the tense, stringy neck, the hollows of the cheeks, the deep sockets from which bulged eyeballs concealed by the lids' slack skin. Thus she seemed the corpse of a martyr, into which the spirit of God was descending.

Although this was not the first of Camilla's nocturnal soliloquies, Orsola felt her scalp turn to ice: a sudden terror gripped and oppressed her. She instinctively huddled up, tried to move away from her sister's body, retreating to the very edge of the bed; she remained still, holding her breath during the intervals of silence, her eyes fixed on the lips of the sleeping woman, feeling shaken by a dark ominous pang deep in her chest whenever those lips moved to pronounce more words. She did not understand them; but something remotely profound and solemn was contained in that uninterrupted murmur, a supernatural mystery emanated from that inert, unconscious body that spoke without hearing its own voice. The room was touched by the breath of the grave; for in the sleepless woman's distraught imagination the oscillating shadows took on the terrifying, threatening shapes of phantoms; the air seemed to be furrowed by mysterious sounds. All the objects toward which the hallucinated woman's eyes turned for refuge, all those objects changed form, became alive and advanced towards her. Then once again the thought of punishment and eternal damnation rose to haunt her conscience. She lay stricken under the incubus of her sin, crossing her arms over her breasts to protect herself from the threats of the demons, trying to pray, her tongue paralyzed by terror, with an ultimate, devout impulse clinging to the anchor of repentance, the last salvation. She felt damned, from the depths of her heart she begged for mercy from the divine Spouse she had betrayed, from kind and generous Jesus, from Him who forgives.

Camilla's voice petered out in sighs, turning into a confused and tremulous gurgle, fading away in a slow, even respiration, as the exhilaration of the mystical dream slowly abated. The shadows continued to flicker. But the Crucified did not yet descend from the wall to gather in His arms the lamb returning to the fold.

XVII

"THE LORD hath said by the mouth of his prophet Joel, son of Pethuel: 'It will come to pass that I shall pour my Spirit

over all flesh, and your children will make prophecies; your
elders will dream, your young people will see visions.'

"This spirit of which the Apostles gathered the first fruits
and beatitudes was for them and for us a Spirit of truth, a
Spirit of sanctity, a Spirit of strength . . . Oh divine love, oh
holy bond uniting the Father and the Son, omnipotent Spirit,
faithful consolation of the wretched, penetrate into the deep
abysses of our hearts and fill them with your great light!"

So preached Don Gennaro Tierno at Pentecost, from the
main altar, addressing the listening populace. Over him, high
above, the third person of the Holy Trinity spread the radiant
arc of its golden wings, and in the church the burning tapers
diffused a reddish glow like that of a great conflagration. The
huge stone columns supporting the two naves, covered with
barbaric Christian sculptures, moved in heavy strides toward
the altar; on the walls scintillated the remains of mosaics: here
and there the head of an Apostle, the rigid arm of a Saint, the
wing of an angel still emerged from the obliteration, the
crumbling wrought by the centuries. Between the mosaics
were hung small votive boats offered to the temple by the
survivors of shipwrecks. And amid rough stones and the misty
crusts of plaster gracefully lifted a group of rose-colored spi-
raled columns supporting the marble pulpit, which was gar-
landed with acanthus leaves and animated by bas-reliefs.

"Spread your sweet dew over this barren earth, so that its
long aridity may cease. Send the celestial rays of your love to
the sanctuary of our soul, so that in penetrating us they kindle
flames to consume our weaknesses, our omissions, our de-
spondency!" the priest continued, his eloquence and vocal
power reaching their greatest heights.

Orsola, nearby, listened, absorbed in meditation. She had
sought refuge in the house of the Lord, she had returned to his
chamber; she wanted the Lord to purify her and welcome her
once more into the benignity of his all-embracing arms. That
sudden bright blaze of faith blinded her, made her forget

almost every previous error. It seemed to her that the stains upon her soul were instantly erased, and that from her flesh the dregs of worldly impurity fell away. Never before had she approached the altar of God with a more profound tremor of hope; never had she listened to the word of God with greater exaltation.

From the instant in which the horror of damnation rose in her consciousness, she had gathered herself in a kind of dark, meditative concentration, standing guard over herself, over her actions, her thoughts, her slightest impulses, for fear lest that vehemence of repentance be dispersed, and with it an anxious desire to preserve intact within herself that flower of faith that had suddenly germinated. It was a kind of elevation toward Jesus, together with the repudiation of every human tie. She fed her exaltation by reading inspirational books; she plunged into the contemplation of the holy images and mysteries; she struggled against the craven frailties of the flesh, the sensuous heat of the day, the insidious snares of the night, the fragrant odors carried to her by the wind, the gusts that rose from her impure memories, the voices that seemed to caress her ears and whisper to her of secret pleasures never thought of before.

After that week of solitary torments she now laid her sacrificial offerings at the foot of the altar, drank in the soothing potion of God's word, her gaze fixed aloft on the radiant dove and feeling herself sink little by little in the sea of ecstasy.

"So descend, descend unto us, oh tender comforter of all afflicted souls, refuge in time of danger, guardian in time of despair. Oh, descend unto us, for you cleanse all souls of every stain and heal their wounds. Come, strength of the weak, support of those who have fallen. Come, star of seafarers, hope of the poor, salvation of the dying!" Don Gennaro Tierno rushed on, standing tall in his silver chasuble, his face flushed purplish red, his eyes bulging from their sockets, with gestures that seemed to reach the very heavens.

Throughout the church a dense sultriness hung over the faithful. The naves seemed to crush the columns; in a stained glass window the head of St. Luke the Evangelist sparkled, struck by the sun, and his broad mantle carved a zone of cool green dusk in the penumbra. The marble pulpit rose like a miraculous mystical flower in that vaporous cloud of light.

"Come, oh Holy Ghost, descend unto us and have mercy on us!"

Orsola kept her eyes fixed on high: on the wave of all those invocations she ascended toward the nimbus, penetrated by the ineffable bliss which draws the soul toward the scent of spiritual essences. For an instant she thought she saw the golden dove send her a lightning flash of assent, and her heart leaped jubilant in her breast, as St. John had leaped in the womb of Elizabeth at the sight of the Virgin Mary.

"For our Lord Jesus Christ. Amen."

The priest, all silver, turned toward the monstrance, reciting the Credo in a low voice. Two white-robed incense bearers flanking the altar began to swing their smoking, aromatic thurifers. A cloud of incense enveloped the violated virgin who knelt close by; and instantly an irresistible gush of nausea from the depths of her pregnancy rose to her throat and twisted her mouth.

XVIII

WAS THERE NO WAY out, then? For a good many days she had still wavered doubtfully, waiting for the final proof. Her head spun in the morning when she got up, when her feet touched the floor; confused spells of exhaustion overwhelmed her toward evening, a general listlessness in which her mind, her will, her memories seemed to blur, to fluctuate drowsily as in the early morning hours. She did everything mechanically, with the movements of a somnambulist, wearily. In the classroom, if the wind brought her a whiff of bread fresh from the oven, she felt all her strength desert her, her entrails leap suddenly into her mouth; a pungent taste of soap and ashes spread on her tongue. One day, while one of the children was sucking a cherry, a violent desire for that fruit made her squirm on her chair, turn pale and sweat. Then, after her meal, bitter with nausea, she stretched out on her bed, surrendered to a dazed inertia: the heat was heavy, the flies buzzed, the cries of a peddler selling eyeglasses passed below her window, hoarse in the silence.

Without hope, she no longer turned for help to the church; even its incense repelled her.

She stopped thinking about Marcello; she no longer saw him, of him she preserved only an uncertain memory, as of a remote dream. Her present anguish entirely possessed her.

Lindoro came to bring water, as before. He arrived upstairs, flushed and dripping sweat; he set down his jars, glancing at his victim surreptitiously out of the corner of his eye. Orsola fled to the other room or bent over her work, clenching her teeth with repressed rage. Lindoro left, like a beaten dog; but the thought of having possessed that woman stirred his blood; he would now have liked to force her to go off with him, have her for himself, own her like a piece of merchandise he could use and sell. In him sensual lust and desire for gain joined hands.

One evening he waited near the street door for Camilla to leave the house; then he rushed upstairs to catch Orsola by surprise, to find her alone at home. When he knocked at the door and Orsola recognized him, she was shaken to the core.

"What do you want from me? What?" she demanded in a muffled voice, without opening.

"Listen to me for a moment, listen! Don't be afraid; I won't hurt you . . ."

"Go away, you dog, coward, murderer . . ." the woman cried with shrill vehemence, giving vent to all her accumulated hatred of him. "Go away, go away!"

And, exhausted, she retired to her room, buried her head in the pillows, biting them and weeping.

XIX

THERE WAS NO WAY out. The daughter of Maria Camastra had drunk vitriol and had died, a three-months-old baby in her belly. The daughter of Clemenza Iorio had flung herself from the bridge and had died in the mud of the Pescarina. So she too must die.

When this thought flashed through Orsola's mind, the afternoon was ending. All the church bells were ringing out festively for the vigil of Corpus Domini; large tribes of swallows shrieked and twirled over Brina Palace and assembled in chattering groups on the Arch. A red cloud hovered over the town, similar perhaps to the cloud from which burning pitch poured down upon the godlessness of Sodom.

At the flare of this thought Orsola felt lost, frightened. Then gradually, as her feeling of shame convinced her of the necessity of that step, in her depths a dark rebellion of vitality began to seethe, her entrails quivered. She felt a sudden warmth as a rush of blood brought blotches of color to her forehead, her cheeks. She rose from her chair, twisting her arms as she struggled with herself. And at last, propelled by a nervous impulse, she left the room, went into the kitchen, looked for a glass on the tables and a box of matches. The strong odor of the charcoal turned her stomach; dizziness filled her head. She had everything she wanted: put matches in the water to dissolve, returned to her room and hid the lethal glass in a corner, underneath a chest of drawers.

"Help me, oh God, help me!"

She was now afraid to be there, alone, facing her decision. In her imagination she suddenly saw again the dead body of Christina Iorio which she had glimpsed that day as it was being carried on a stretcher to her mother's house: a body swollen like a barrel, with slime in its hair, in the eye-sockets, in the mouth, between the toes of the purple feet . . .

"God, I must die—oh God!"

And she gave a start, as if her head had been touched by a stiff, cold hand; a chill passed through her limbs, lingered for a moment on her scalp, making her feel as if a blade were cutting into it to detach the skin.

"No, no, no!" she cried in an altered voice, as though she wanted to keep something horrible from touching her. And she went to the window, leaned out, looking for some sort of refuge.

She remained there, nailed to the floor, stunned by that vision of Biblical conflagration and that horde of black birds. Turning part way around, she saw a strange gleam in the darkness of the room: the shimmer of the golden crescents on the robe of the Madonna of Loreto and the glitter of the medallions. She grew even more frightened; she flattened against the windowsill, leaned farther out; and stayed there without daring to move. Then, in that immobility, the exhaustion that came on every evening began to invade her; she clutched her heavy head between her hands, shut her eyes.

"Oh!"

Suddenly a passage opened up in her soul. —Yes, yes, how could she have forgotten! Spacone, the witch doctor, that old man with the long beard, the one who performed miracles and had a medicine for every illness . . . He'd come to town several times riding a small white mule, with two golden triangles hanging from his ear-lobes and down his front a row of buttons that looked like the bowls of silver spoons. So many women had come out on their doorsteps, had greeted and blessed him. He had cured every sort of malady with certain herbs and certain potions and certain signs he made with his thumb and certain magic words. He certainly must have a remedy for that trouble, too . . . Yes, yes, he certainly did!

And in Orsola a flicker of hope revived, while the dizziness got worse and worse. Before her eyes, objects drowned in the twilight; the crimson day, extinguished by the ashes of encroaching night, swooned away in a slow discoloration, without contrasts. A swallow, like a bat, swooped past and grazed her head. The sudden breath of summer blew into her face, strummed every vein in her body, shook the innermost roots of her life.

With an involuntary, unconscious gesture, she placed her hands on her lap and held them there for a moment. The indefinable feeling of motherhood flooded her soul. And from deep inside her, mysteriously, a memory of her distant convalescence awoke. —Oh, it was March . . . a vast laughing whiteness . . . and above her the "spies," the soft fuzzy seeds poured down on her.

XX

AND SO IT WAS that she left the house the following morning, surreptitiously; and, the town behind her, set out alone on the new road leading to Chieti.

Spacone lived in the vicinity of San Rocco. Below the majesty of a druidic oak, he performed his miracles and formulated his oracles. The entire populace for twenty miles around turned to him for help, as to an Apostle of Providence. During epidemics among the local cattle, herds of oxen and horses gathered around the oak to receive the talisman that would protect them from the disease; equine and bovine hooves traced a circle of enchantments in the plain grass that covered the ground.

When Orsola set out, the landscape surrounding Pescara was enlivened by a great play of lights and shadows. Through that Arabian sky of the month of June the wandering clouds were migrating from the seashore to the mountains, like caravans with copious provisions of water. At intervals vast tracts of land sank deep in shadow, while others emerged shining brightly; and, since the shadow was blue and flowing freely, the countryside looked like a floating archipelago luxuriant with trees and wheat. The songs of the birds praised the ripeness of the oats.

At first that sight gave Orsola a feeling of unaccustomed relief; for the freedom of the countryside, the happiness of the light on the greenery, the cordial smells in the air, by suddenly enveloping her body, revivified her blood, and with the opening up of the horizon the new hope inside her was fortified and exalted. She cast off all her anxieties and lived only for two emotions—for the hope of her physical salvation and the desire to reach her goal. Far away, at that goal, in her imagination she saw the beneficent old man rise up and become mystically illuminated. Because of her innate susperstitious propensity, she transformed that figure, endowed it with enormous powers and garbed it with Christian kindness, surrounding it with a halo. Then all the stories repeated among the populace came back to her and cast sprays of miraculous light on Spacone's brow. Then she remembered that on a distant day of her illness Rosa Catena had spoken about the Old Man with reverence, mentioning certain miracles: a blind man from Torre de' Passeri had gone to San Rocco and returned after three days with eyes that saw and a blue cabalistic sign on his temple. A woman from Spoltore, possessed by evil spirits, had returned as meek as a lamb, after she had drunk two sips of water from a small dry gourd.

Thus, gradually as she walked along the road, the coming together of so many scattered elements formed a kind of legend in Orsola's mind. And little by little, for men can do nothing without the aid of God, there also arose the conviction that the Old Man was an envoy of Heaven, a redeemer of souls from subjugation to the flesh, a dispenser of heavenly grace on earth to those who had succumbed. —Had not the extreme hope descended upon the sinner suddenly, almost by divine influence, amid signs burning in the sky? And during Pentecost, had not the dove sent down from on high, before the praying woman's eyes, a lightning flash of hopeful promise?

The promise was now being fulfilled on the holy day of Corpus Domini. So, burning with faith and exultation, Orsola went forward in the dust of the new road, indifferent to the effort that every step cost her. On both sides of the road the shrubs shone white as though covered by the droppings of birds. Clumps of rustling poplars stood along the borders; and the silvery trunks reverberated with variations of light. The peasant women of the Villa del Fuoco, dwarfs with flat, Hamitic noses and broad lips, fair-skinned Berber women, came from the opposite direction in twos and threes. The life of the clouds occupied the immense stage of the countryside.

Orsola passed the Mill, then the Villa. A nervous energy animated her step. She felt the wind blowing upon her neck and at intervals heard the poplars rustle overhead. But the wavering of shadows and the dust was beginning to affect slightly her vision; the warmth of her exertion rose to her head; her will was completely concentrated on the unaccustomed physical effort of walking. Thus she advanced in an increasing daze which was turning into a sensation of discomfort; then, overcome by fatigue and the heat, she yielded to the temptation to rest in the shade of an olive grove standing on a slope to the left of the road.

Four or five half-naked gypsies, the color of bronze, with shining amulets on their chests, went riding past, straddling reddish donkeys. One of them was whistling, striking the belly of his beast with his heels. They all held switches in their hands and leather saddle bags lay on their thighs. They looked at the woman resting among the olive trees and murmured something in a low voice, laughing.

Orsola was frightened by those eyes whose whites glistened as they looked, and she remained tense with fear until they disappeared in the distance. Discouragement was beginning to seize her; her loneliness was beginning to fill her with dread, for through the countryside ran prolonged shivers announcing rain and an almost lugubrious silence descended through the air from the gathered clouds. She was leaning against a tree trunk; intermittent cool gusts tore at her body and chilled the sweat on her skin, gusts that fell upon her with the rustling sound of a furtive animal in the grass, while all around the shimmer of sunlight seemed the glitter of remote waters. Pale flowers, yellow as sulphur, wavered at the feet of the olive trees.

A memory then descended from the good trees into the woman's soul. —That day the church was crowded with consecrated olive branches and scents; and she walked through the throng in a state of agitation, sustained by Marcello's arms ... But as she lingered on this thought, her memory wandered; everything eluded her grasp with a dreamlike uncertainty. Yet dark throbs battered her heart; gasps of anguish quickened her breathing. She now had the blunt sensation of a torpor that seemed to crash down on her brain with the weight of a sledgehammer. A last trace of vigilant determination helped to rouse her weakly, and she stepped down onto the road.

The clouds gathered in the direction of the Maiella had taken on the diaphanous gray color of a suspended mass of water. Large waterspouts approached from the sea with heavier loads; and yet here and there a broad patch of blue fanned out high in the sky. A smell of humidity was already rising from the dust, from the entire countryside gasping heavily with expectation. Immobile, the trees seemed to absorb the light, rose black in the misty air, populated the distance with blurred, uncertain shapes.

Orsola walked on with an immense weariness, feeling that

all her strength would soon leave her. "Yes," she thought, "I'll just be able to reach that tree and then I'll fall." But she did not fall. The houses of San Rocco came into view on the right. A peasant was coming from the opposite direction at a run.

"Good man, is that San Rocco?"

"Yes, yes, you turn off at the first path."

Heavy, pattering drops were beginning to fall; then suddenly the increasing rain cut through the air with long white darts, long whips which cracked as they lashed down. A monstrous tumult now agitated the clouds: beams of light broke through here and there. All the hills, far off, beyond the sheets of rain, lit up for an instant and turned dark again. A frail, silvery brightness rose over the Maiella, seemed to sharpen like a thin sword.

Orsola tried to run toward the oak which stood about a hundred yards away. The raindrops struck the nape of her neck, coursed down her back between her shoulderblades, hit her in the face; her clothes were already wet through. Her feet slipped on the wet ground. She fell and got up again, twice. Then, half-crazed, she began to shriek in the direction of the house.

"Help me! Help me!"

A woman came through the door and ran to assist her, followed by two barking dogs.

Pale as death, her features distorted, Orsola let herself be led, no longer able to utter a word through her clenched teeth. Only after a while did she collect herself, brought round by the questions the woman addressed to her. And then, on hearing the name Spacone, she at once remembered everything.

"Where is Spacone?" she demanded.

"He went to Popoli, my saintly woman; they sent for him."

Orsola couldn't contain herself any longer; she began to sob and tear at her hair.

"What do you want, saintly woman? What is it? I am his wife, I'm here . . . " whimpered the witch, clutching her wrists, urging her to speak.

Orsola hesitated for a moment; then she told her everything, precipitously, sobbing, hiding her face.

"Hold on. There is a remedy. But it costs fifty soldi, my saintly woman," said the witch in her soft, vowel-filled idiom, chanting that beautiful interjection.

Orsola untied a knot in her handkerchief and held out five small silver coins. Then she waited, calmer.

The room was low-ceilinged but spacious. The wall, where saltpeter blossomed here and there, was flaked and greenish. Crude Christian idols made of pottery populated the back wall of that lair; strangely shaped tools and instruments cluttered the tables. It was like a rustic sanctuary guarded by a herbalist monk.

Standing in front of the hearth Spacone's wife was brewing her philter in silence. She was a tall, bony woman with an extremely pale face, a rotting nose as purple as a fig, straight red hair over her temples, an albino's tiny eyes, and with tattooes on her chin, forehead and the backs of her hands.

"Here, saintly woman! Take heart."

Orsola swallowed the liquid in one gulp; but immediately afterward she felt an atrocious bitterness claw at her palate and entrails. She remained motionless as if paralyzed, her mouth agape, pressing her belly with her hands, rapidly stamping her feet against the ground, in the spasm of the first uterine contraction.

"Be brave, saintly woman, be brave!" the witch repeated, staring at her with her milky eyes, massaging her loins. "You have just enough time to get back to Pescara . . . Go! Go!"

Orsola could not answer; only screams rose to her mouth. Cramps gripped her stomach, blocked her diaphragm, made her want to vomit. Her eyeballs turned back, as though she were showing symptoms of an epileptic attack. All through her feeble body the excessive power of the potion was now producing unexpected effects. The miscarriage took place almost immediately, with one of those terrible hemorrhages with which the forces of life quietly, imperceptibly flow away.

"Oh Jesus, Jesus, Jesus," mumbled the witch, fretfully, seized by sudden fear at the sight of that poor fallen body. "Oh Jesus, help me."

Under her proddings, Orsola regained consciousness. And since after a while the flow of blood seemed to wane, the wretched creature managed to get to her feet: went outside, pushed by the woman; reached the road, staggering, pale, as if drained of her last drop of blood, but kept alive by the hope that the greatest danger was past.

Now the fields were all fresh and luminous after the rain. A line of carts loaded with gypsum rolled past, and the big carters from Letto Manoppello, full of wine, lay sprawled on the sacks, smoking. As Orsola began to walk at the end of the line, one of them, the nearest to her, yelled: "Hey, do you want to ride up here with me, pretty girl?"

Half-unconscious, Orsola let herself be hoisted up by the man's strong arms and sat there on the sacks. She did not hear the lewd laughter and the obscene jokes that spread from one cart to the next.

With instinctive energy she held her knees tight together to stem the flow of blood. She felt a gradual dullness invade her senses, so that the frequent jolts of the wheels on the gravel caused her only a numb pain and she barely noticed the stench of the men's pipes. Then a remote murmur reached her ears, a quivering brightness became visible to her eyes. Several times she would have fallen if she hadn't been held up by the hands of the carter, who, encouraged by her docile silence, attempted a few rough caresses.

At the end of the road, silhouetted against the sun, appeared the town of Pescara, whose sounds came forth to greet them, borne upon the wind.

"The procession is out," one of the men said. All the others whipped their beasts; and the road rang with the sound of heavy hooves, the jangling of collar bells, the cracking of whips.

That violence of jolts and crashing noises recalled Orsola for a moment to a sense of the surrounding reality. But when the man put one arm around her waist and blew his wine-sodden breath on her cheek, out of blind impulse she started to scream and thrash about as if she had suddenly become delirious. And before her darkened eyes Lindoro's phantom image suddenly rose with clarity enough to awaken the revulsion of horror in her almost insensible mind. As soon as the cart halted she got down, slipping from the sacks to the ground; she began to walk, with the frenzied anxiety of someone trying to reach a safe place before collapsing.

From the opposite direction young maidens were advancing down the road, covered by their immaculate white veils, holding colored tapers in their hands, and singing. Following this angelic swarm, a great fluttering of banners and baldaquins crowded the air soothed by the recent rain. And they sang:

> *Tantum ergo sacramentum*
> *Veneremur cernui . . .*

Orsola, half blinded, turned into an alleyway; reached the house of Rosa Catena, entered it; overcome by vertigo, she fell on the floor. And, as the copious bleeding started once again, paralysis gripped the lower half of her body, and all capacity for voluntary movement left her.

Rosa was not at home; that day everyone in town had joined the procession. In a corner of the room, Mua', her father, a monster of human decrepitude, a blind man nailed for years to the wood of a chair by crippling arthritis, made vague attempts to probe the brick floor around him with the tip of his cane in order to discover the reason for the unexpected noise; and a slobbering mumble dribbled out of his toothless mouth.

Then, at the feet of that horrendous monster, soaked in the blood of sin, her thumbs clenched in her fists, without a cry, the violated bride of the Lord squirmed for a few moments in the throes of death.

"Out, out of here! Go! Go away!"

Thinking the butcher's mastiff had come into the house, and seeking to chase the beast away, the old man waved his cane about; and it struck the dying woman.

THE VIGIL

The Vigil

MAYOR BIAGIO MILA'S corpse, already completely dressed, a cloth drenched in vinegar and water spread over its face, was laid out on the bed, almost at the center of the room, surrounded by four lighted tapers, one at each corner. The dead man's wife and brother were keeping vigil, facing each other across the room.

Rosa Mila was about twenty-five years old. She was a woman in full bloom. Her complexion was fair, her forehead rather low, her eyebrows were traced in a long arc, her eyes gray with irises as variegated as agates. She had a luxuriant mass of hair, and, generally, unruly strands hid her eyes and the nape of her neck. Her entire person shone with the luster of health, and her fresh skin gave off the perfume of rare, delicate fruit.

Emidio Mila, the cleric, was more or less the same age. His body was thin and had the bronzelike color peculiar to people who live in the countryside exposed to the sun's full power. A soft reddish fuzz covered his cheeks; his strong white teeth lent a virile beauty to his smile, and, at moments, his yellowish eyes gleamed like new gold coins.

Both were silent; she, letting the glass beads of a rosary glide between her fingers; he, watching the rosary glide. Both were full of the indifference with which our country folk confront the mystery of death.

With a long sigh, Emidio said, "It's hot tonight."

Rosa raised her eyes, agreeing.

In the low-ceilinged room the light wavered in accordance with the restless flames of the tapers. The shadows gathered now in a corner, now on a wall, changing in shape and intensity.

The windows were open, but the shutters were closed. The white muslin curtains stirred, almost seemed to breathe. On the stark whiteness of the bed, Biagio's body seemed to be asleep.

Emidio's words sank into the silence. The woman again lowered her head, and again let the rosary glide slowly through her fingers. Beads of sweat studded her brow, and her breathing was heavy.

After a while Emidio asked, "When are they coming to take him away, tomorrow?"

"At ten, with the Congregation of the Sacrament."

Then they were silent again. From the fields came the frogs' persistent croaking and, at intervals, the scent of grass in that perfect quiet. Rosa heard a hoarse gurgle coming from the corpse and with a horrified gesture rose from her chair, as if to run away.

"Don't be afraid, Rosa. It's just liquids," her brother-in-law said, reaching out with his hand to reassure her.

She grasped the hand instinctively and held it, still on her feet. The gurgle inside the dead man's belly continued and seemed to make its way to his mouth.

"It's nothing, Rosa. Calm yourself," he added, making a gesture for her to sit down on a hope chest covered by a flowered bright cushion.

Still holding his hand, she sat down beside him. The chest was not very large, and as they sat their elbows touched.

Silence returned. The song of the peasants who were threshing rose in the distance.

66

"They are threshing at night, in the moonlight," she said, speaking to conquer her weariness and fear.

Emidio said nothing. And the woman withdrew her hand because the contact had begun to give her a vague feeling of uneasiness.

Both were now filled with the same thought which, all of a sudden, had risen in their minds: both were captured by an identical memory, a memory of rustic ardor at the time of their puberty.

They lived at that time in a cluster of houses called the Caldore, on a sun-drenched hill where the roads crossed. There, at the far edge of a wheat field, rose a high wall built of stones and clayey mud. On the side facing the south, which belonged to Rosa's relatives, where the sun's warmth was denser and sweeter, a family of fruit-bearing trees throve and multiplied. With the coming of spring the trees blossomed in festive communion; and the silvery or rose-colored cupolas, curving gently against the sky, crowned the wall, rocked to and fro as if to lift themselves up into the air and, all together, hummed with the drowsy sound of mellifluous bees.

Behind that wall, on the trees' side, in those days Rosa used to sing. Her voice, clear and fresh, rose and fell like a fountain beneath the flowering crowns.

Through a long season of convalescence, Emidio had listened to her voice. He was weak and famished. To escape the diet imposed on him he would often leave his house furtively, hiding a large chunk of bread inside his jacket, and follow the wall, walking along the last wheat-furrow until he reached his place of bliss.

There he sat down with his shoulders against the warm stones and began to eat. He bit into the bread and plucked a tender ear of wheat: each small grain enclosed a minute drop of juice like milk and with the fresh flavor of flour. After his long illness the sensual pleasure of tasting and hearing almost blended into a single, infinitely delectable sensation. And so, in that idlness, in that heat, among those fragrances which gave the air the hearty substance of a wine, the woman's voice also became for him a natural, strengthening nourishment, a physical food, which melted into his bloodstream.

So Rosa's voice was a cause for recovery, and even when his recovery was complete Rosa's voice continued to affect his senses.

After that period, the two families having become quite intimate, Emidio was seized by one of those silent, shy and solitary loves which devour all the strength of adolescence.

In September, just before Emidio's departure for the seminary, one afternoon the two families went together on a picnic in the woods along the river.

The day was listless, and the three carts drawn by oxen made their way along the canebrakes in bloom.

In the woods they picnicked on the grass in a circular clearing circumscribed by the trunks of giant poplars. The grass was short and crowded with tiny purple flowers which gave off a subtle perfume; here and there, through the thick leafage, large swaths of sunlight poured inside the secluded shelter.

After the picnic some of them went roaming along the river banks, while others remained there, stretched out on their backs.

Rosa and Emidio found themselves together; they linked arms and started down a path marked through the brush.

She leaned against him with abandon; she laughed and tore leaves from the branches as they passed, nibbled at the bitter stems, and flung her head back to follow the flight of the scattering jays. And with that movement, the tortoiseshell comb slipped from her hair, which suddenly slipped down over her shoulders in all its stupendous richness.

Emidio bent down with her to pick up the comb. As they straightened up, their heads bumped together lightly. Clutching her forehead with both hands, Rosa cried amid peals of laughter, "Oh God, oh God!"

The young man looked at her, feeling his body quiver through and through, feeling his face turn pale, fearing that he might give himself away. Using her fingernails, she pried a long tendril of ivy from a tree trunk, wound it round her hair with a quick twist and put an end to the rebellion by affixing the teeth of her comb at the nape of her neck. The green leaves of the ivy, some with a reddish tinge, were loosely bound and burst free at random. She asked, "Do you like me like this?"

Emidio did not say a word; he did not know what to reply.

"Oh, this is no way to behave! Are you deaf and dumb, perhaps?"

He wanted to fall down on his knees. And, since Rosa's laughter sounded disappointed, he could almost feel tears rise to his eyes from the frustration of being unable to think of some simple words to say.

They continued walking. At a certain point an uprooted sapling blocked the path. With both hands Emidio lifted the trunk, and Rosa slipped past beneath the bright green leaves which, for a second, wreathed her head like a crown.

Farther on, they found a well at both sides of which stood two rectangular stone basins that were set around and above the well. The dense trees formed a cloister of greenery. The shadow there was deep, almost damp. The verdant cupola was perfectly reflected by the water which reached halfway up the brick parapet.

Flinging out her arms, Rosa said, "How wonderful it feels here!"

Then she scooped up some water in the cup of her palm with an alluring gesture and drank. Drops of water slipped through her fingers and clung like pearls to her skirt.

When her thirst was quenched, with both palms she scooped up more water and offered it enticingly to her companion: "Drink!"

"I'm not thirsty," Emidio stammered, in a daze.

She threw the water in his face, making an almost contemptuous grimace with her lower lip. Then she lay down in one of the dry troughs as if in a cradle, letting her feet hang over the rim and shaking them impatiently. Suddenly she jumped up, giving Emidio a strange look.

"Well? Let's go."

They started back to the clearing to rejoin the others, in complete silence. The blackbirds whistled above their heads; horizontal sheaves of sun cut across their steps, and the scent of the woods grew more intense around them.

A few days later Emidio would leave.

A few months later Emidio's brother would take Rosa for his wife.

During his first years at the seminary, the cleric thought about his new sister-in-law quite often. In class, as the priests explained the *Epitome historiæ sacræ*, he daydreamed about her. In study hall, while his classmates, hiding behind their lecterns, paired off for obscene practices, he hid his face in his hands and gave himself up to impure fantasies. In chapel, as the Virgin's litanies rang out after the invocation to the Mystical Rose, he fled into distant realms.

And then, after he had learned corruption from his fellow students, the scene in the woods had appeared to him in a new light, and the suspicion of having failed to understand, the regret at having failed to pluck the fruit which was being offered to him, would then strangely torment him.

Did it mean this? Did it mean that Rosa had once loved him? Did it mean that he had unknowingly passed by a great joy?

And every day this doubt became more acute, more insistent, more goading, more anguished. And every day he fed on it with greater intensity of suffering until, in the long monotony of his seminary life, this doubt became for him a kind of incurable illness, and, confronted by the event's irremediability, he was overcome by an immense feeling of futility, an unending melancholy.

Yes, he had failed to understand.

In the room now drops of wax were falling from the tapers. Between the slats of the closed shutters entered stronger gusts of wind which made the curtains rear up.

Slowly pervaded with drowsiness, Rosa's eyelids lowered now and then; but whenever her head fell upon her chest, she would open her eyes with a start.

"Are you tired?" the cleric asked in a gentle voice.

"Not me," the woman answered, rallying her energies and straightening up on her hips.

But in the silence her senses were again overcome by drowsiness. Her head rested against the wall; now her hair covered her whole neck; through her parted lips came slow, regular breathing. She was very beautiful like that; and nothing in her was more voluptuous than the rise and fall of her breasts and the shape of her knees discernible beneath the thin cloth of her skirt. A sharp gust drew a moan from the curtains and extinguished the two tapers closest to the window.

And what if I kissed her? thought Emidio, prompted by a sudden fleshly urge as he gazed at the dozing woman.

The singing voices again cascaded through the June night with the solemnity of liturgical cadences; and from different points, always farther removed, rose the answers in varying tones, unaccompanied by instruments. The full moon must have been high in the sky because the dim light inside did not subdue the cool white light which poured copiously over the shutters and seeped through the slats.

Emidio turned to face the death bed. His eyes gliding over the rigid black outline of the corpse involuntarily halted at the hand, a swollen, yellowish hand, with nails that looked somewhat like claws, its back crossed by livid webs; and his eyes quickly shrank away from this sight. Little by little, in the unconsciousness of sleep, Rosa's head, almost tracing a semi-circle on the wall, bent towards the perturbed cleric. The slow reclining of that beautiful feminine head inspired a melting tenderness; and, since the movement somewhat altered the woman's sleep, between her ever so slightly parted lids the rims of the iris appeared and immediately disappeared in the white cornea, like the petal of a violet floating in milk.

Emidio remained immobile, letting her weight rest against his shoulder. He held his breath for fear of waking the woman from her sleep, and a tremendous anguish was cast upon him by the throbbing of his heart, his wrists, his temples, which seemed to echo through the entire room. But, since Rosa went on sleeping, little by little he felt drained and drifted into an invincible listlessness, looking at that feminine throat marked with voluptuousness by Venus' necklaces, breathing in her warm breath and the smell of her hair.

A fresh breeze laden with nocturnal fragrance bent the flickering flame and blew it out.

Then, no longer thinking, no longer timorous, yielding fully to temptation, the keeper of the funeral vigil kissed the woman full on the mouth.

At that contact she awoke with a start, fixed her wide, astonished eyes on her brother-in-law's face and went very pale.

Then she slowly gathered together the hair on her neck; and then just sat there, holding herself erect, tensely guarded, staring straight in front of her at the shifting shadows.

"Who put out the tapers?"

"The wind."

Nothing else was said. They both remained on the wedding chest as before, sitting side by side, grazing each other with their elbows, in a painful uncertainty, by a mental artifice not letting their conscience judge the event and condemn it. Spontaneously, they both turned their attention to external things, injecting into this act a fictitious intensity, even helping it along by the position of their bodies. Gradually a kind of intoxication was taking possession of them.

The singing voices in the night continued, lingered in the air, and from call to call grew alluringly softer. The male and female voices wove an amorous composition. At times one single voice emerged sharp and high above all the others, striking a single note around which the harmonies swelled like waves drawn to the central current of a river. Now, at intervals, at the beginning of each stanza, rose the metallic vibration of a guitar tuned in diapente, and between one round and the next came the measured thuds of the threshing flails against the ground.

Both listened.

Perhaps because of a change in the wind, the smells were no longer the same as before. From Orlando hill, most likely, came the powerful perfume of orange and lemon groves; from the Scalia gardens, perhaps, came the perfume of roses, so thick that the air had the flavor of wedding candies; and perhaps from the swamps of Farina the damp fragrance of irises which, once inhaled, was as delightfully refreshing as a draft of cold water.

They still kept silent, sitting motionless on the chest, oppressed by the voluptuousness of the moonlit night. In front of them the last flame flickered rapidly and, bending, made tears of wax fall from the almost consumed taper. Again and again it seemed about to die. They did not move. Tense and hesitant, their eyes fixed and dilated, they watched the tremulous, moribund flame. Suddenly the inebriating wind blew it out. Then, unafraid of the darkness, with the very same avidity, at the very same instant, the man and the woman drew close, clutched, searched for the other's mouth, lost, blindly, without speaking, smothering each other with caresses.

THE SEA-GOING SURGEON

The Sea-Going Surgeon

ALONG ABOUT EVENING the brigantine *Trinità*, carrying a cargo of wheat, sailed for Dalmatia. She made her way down the calm river between Ortona's fishing boats lying at anchor in two rows, while on shore fires lit up one by one and the men just back from sea were singing. Then, gliding smoothly through the narrow mouth of the inlet, the boat rode out into the sea.

The weather was fair. In the October sky, almost skimming the water, the full moon hung like a soft, rose-colored lamp. The mountains and hills being left behind were shaped like reclining women. Up in the sky wild geese swept by without honking and vanished.

At first the six men and the cabin boy all worked in unison to set the sails to catch the wind. Then, when the sails, all red and adorned with crude images, swelled aloft, the six men sat down and began smoking quietly. The cabin boy straddled the bow and hummed a nostalgic song.

The elder Talamonte flashed a long streak of saliva into the water and, sticking his well-worn pipe back into his mouth, said, "The good weather won't hold."

At this prophecy they all looked out to the open sea and did not speak. They were tough sailors, inured to the vicissitudes of the sea. They had sailed before to the Dalmatian islands and Zara, and to Trieste and Split; they knew the way. Some of them even harbored a pleasant memory of the wine of Dignano, which has the perfume of roses, and also of the fruits of those islands.

Ferrante La Selvi commanded the brig. The two Talamonte brothers, Cirù, Massacese and Gialluca made up the crew— all of them came from Pescara. Nazareno was the cabin boy.

Since the moon was full, they lingered on the deck. The sea was strewn with fishing boats at work.

From time to time two trawlers running together passed alongside the brig and the men called out to each other with familiarity. The catch seemed to be good. When the fishing boats were left behind and the sea was once more deserted, Ferrante and the two Talamontes went below to sleep. After they had finished smoking, Massacese and Gialluca followed them. Cirù remained on watch.

Before they went below, Gialluca, pointing to his neck, said to his companion, "Look, what do I have here?"

Massacese looked and said, "It's nothing. Don't worry about it."

There was a red blotch, similar to that produced by the bite of an insect, and at the center of the blotch a small protuberance.

Gialluca added, "It hurts."

During the night the wind changed and the sea began to swell. The brig started to labor through the waves and was pulled eastward, losing headway. As they tacked and Gialluca helped trim the sails, he gave a small cry of pain now and then, for at every abrupt movement of his head he felt a dart of pain.

Ferrante La Selvi asked him, "What is it?"

In the light of dawn Gialluca showed him what hurt him. On the skin the red blotch had spread and a small pointed abscess rose at its center.

Ferrante, after examining it, also said,. "It's nothing. Don't worry about it."

Gialluca got a handkerchief and bandaged his neck. Then he began to smoke.

The brig, battered by the waves and buffeted by the head wind, still fled eastward. The clamor of the sea drowned the men's voices. At intervals a wave broke on deck with a deep, hollow sound.

Towards evening the storm abated and the moon emerged like a cupola of fire. But since the wind fell, the brig floated almost motionless in the lull; the sails fell slack. From time to time a short-lived breeze sprang up.

Gialluca complained about the pain. Being at leisure, his companions began to take an interest in his ailment. Each man suggested a different remedy. Cirù, who was the oldest, spoke up and suggested a cataplasm of flour and apples. He possessed a few vague medical notions, because back home on land his wife practiced medicine together with the arts of magic, healing illnesses with nostrums and spells. But they had neither apples nor flour. Sea biscuits would not serve the purpose.

Then Cirù went to get an onion and a handful of wheat; he pounded the wheat, chopped up the onion and prepared the cataplasm. At the touch of that poultice, Gialluca's pain got worse. After about an hour, seized by a fury of irritation, he ripped the dressing from his neck and threw the whole business over the gunwale.

To master his discomfort, he went to the stern and held the tiller for a long period. The wind had risen and the sails shivered gaily. In the bright night a small island, which had to be Pelagosa, loomed in the distance like a board resting on the water.

In the morning Cirù, who had by now taken charge of Gialluca's trouble, examined the abscess. The swelling had dilated, spreading over a great part of the neck, and had taken on a different shape and darker color, which at the apex had turned purple.

"What's happening here?" he exclaimed, perplexed, in a voice that made his patient flinch. And he summoned Ferrante, both Talamontes, and all the others.

Opinions varied. Ferrante's imagination produced the vision of a horrifying disease that could end up by strangling Gialluca. His eyes extraordinarily dilated, quite pale, Gialluca listened to the prognostications. The sky was shrouded with mist, the sea looked gloomy, flocks of gulls flashed shrieking towards land— and so a kind of terror descended upon his soul.

In the end the younger Talamonte proclaimed, "It's a malignant boil."

The others agreed: "Yes, could be."

And indeed the next day the cuticle covering the abscess was forced up by a blood-colored serum and split open. And the entire area took on the appearance of a wasp's nest from which a flow of purulent matter oozed profusely. The inflammation and the suppuration went deeper and spread very rapidly.

Gialluca, terrified, invoked Saint Rocco, the healer of sores. He promised him ten, twenty pounds of candle wax. He knelt in the center of the deck, raised his arms to the sky, made vows with solemn gestures, called out the names of his father, mother, wife and children. All around him his companions blessed themselves gravely at each invocation.

Ferrante La Selvi, feeling the approach of a powerful gust of wind, shouted a command in his hoarse voice through the roar of the sea. The brig heeled completely over on one side. Massacese, the two Talamontes, and Cirù all scrambled back to their positions on deck for the maneuver. Nazareno slid along one of the masts. The sails were dropped in a flash; only the two jibs remained in place. And the brig, listing sheerly from side to side, was broached to and began to run precipitously along the waves' crests.

"Saint Rocco! Saint Rocco!" screamed Gialluca with mounting fervor, also excited by the surrounding tumult, doubled over on his hands and knees to withstand the ship's roll.

Again and again a bigger wave than the others broke over the bow and swept the deck from end to end.

"Go below!" Ferrante yelled to Gialluca.

Gialluca, drenched, climbed down into the hold. He was plagued all over his skin by a bothersome heat and a feverish dryness, and the fear inspired by his sickness gripped his stomach. Down below in the dim light the shapes of things assumed singular aspects. He could hear the deep, resounding blows of the sea against the sides of the vessel and the creaking of the whole structure.

After half an hour Gialluca reappeared on deck completely ashen, as if rising from a grave. He preferred to be out in the open, to expose himself to the waves, see the men, breathe the wind.

Ferrante, shocked by his pallor, asked, "What's wrong now?"

The other men, remaining at their posts, began to discuss remedies, raising their voices, almost shouting so as to be heard above the roar of the storm. They became excited. Each had a treatment of his own. They argued with the assurance of full-fledged physicians. In the dispute, they forgot all danger. Two years before, Massacese had seen a real doctor operate on Giovanni Margadonna's side in a similar case. The doctor had cut, then had rubbed the wound with two pieces of wood steeped in a steaming liquid and had burnt it. With a kind of spoon he had scooped out the scorched flesh, which looked like coffee grounds. And Margadonna had been saved.

Massacese, almost in a frenzy, repeated, like a ruthless surgeon, "We've got to cut! We've got to cut!"

And with his hand he made the gesture of cutting in the direction of the sick man.

Cirù shared Massacese's opinion. Both Talamontes also agreed. Ferrante La Selvi shook his head.

Then Cirù put it to Gialluca. Gialluca refused.

With a brutal impulse that he was unable to restrain, Cirù yelled, "Then die!"

Gialluca grew even paler and stared at his companions with huge, horror-stricken eyes.

Night was falling. In the darkness the roar of the sea seemed even louder. The waves glittered, rolling beneath the gleam cast by the bow lamp. Land was far away. The men clung to a line to stand up under the waves. Ferrante was at the helm, shouting from time to time into the storm, "Go below, Gialluca!"

Because of a strange aversion to being alone, Gialluca would not go below, even though he was in great discomfort. He too hung on to the line, clenching his teeth from the pain. Whenever a wave beat down on them, the men ducked their heads and in unison gave a shout, the sort they used to accompany a common effort at work.

The moon came out from behind a cloud, reducing the feeling of horror. But the sea continued rough all through the night. In the morning, Gialluca, dazed, said to his shipmates: "Cut it." They discussed it seriously, holding a kind of final consultation; and then they examined the swelling abscess, which was now the size of a man's fist. All the craters, which before had lent it the appearance of a wasp's nest or sieve, had now become a single crater.

Massacese said, "Don't be afraid! Let's get started." He was going to be the surgeon. He tested the edge of various blades on his fingernail. Finally he chose the elder Talamonte's knife, which had been sharpened recently.

"All right. Let's go!"

Almost a shiver of expectation shook him and all the others.

The sick man now seemed to be seized by a dark stupor. He kept his eyes fixed on the knife without saying anything, his mouth half open, his hands dangling at his sides, like a halfwit.

Cirù got him to sit down, took off the bandage, while with his lips he made the instinctive sounds that express utter revulsion. For a moment they all bent down over the sore in order to look at it.

Massacese said, "This way and this way," indicating the direction of the intended cuts with the point of his knife.

Then, suddenly, Gialluca burst into·a wild fit of tears. His entire body shook from the sobs.

"Don't be afraid! Don't be afraid!" the men kept repeating, grabbing his arms.

Massacese set to work. At the first touch of the blade Gialluca let out a scream; then, gritting his teeth, he breathed out a muffled moan.

Massacese cut gingerly but with determination, sticking out the tip of his tongue as he was in the habit of doing when he concentrated on anything. Since the brigantine often lurched and staggered, the cut was not the same all the way; the knife went in deeper at one place than another. The sudden blow of a wave made the blade dig down into the healthy flesh. Gialluca howled again, struggling, blood all over him, like a steer in the butcher's hands. He didn't want to submit quietly to it any longer.

"No, no, no!"

"Come here! Come here!" Massacese yelled at him, jumping up to follow him, wanting to finish the job because he was afraid that the interrupted cut could be more dangerous.

The sea, still running heavily, roared all around them, ceaselessly. Clouds shaped like upended funnels rose at the horizon and embraced the whole sky, which the birds had deserted. Now, in the midst of that tumult, beneath that light, a singular excitement seized those men. Involuntarily, while struggling with the wounded man to hold him still, they became enraged.

"Come here!"

Massacese made another four or five cuts, rapidly and at random. Blood mixed with whitish matter bubbled up from the wounds. All the men were smeared with blood, except for Nazareno, who was at the prow, trembling, overwhelmed by the atrocity of the event.

Ferrante La Selvi, who suddenly saw the boat tilt perilously to one side, shouted a command at the top of his lungs: "Take down the mainsail! Hold the tiller due north!"

The two Talamontes, Massacese and Cirù sprang to carry out the order, trimming the sails. The brig continued to scud ahead, pitching up and down. They could see Lissa in the distance. Long zones of sunlight flooded the water, the light pouring down from among the clouds; and the zones varied in accordance with the clouds in the sky.

Ferrante remained at the tiller. The other members of the crew returned to Gialluca. They had to even out the cuts, cauterize it with fire, and cover the wound with a dressing of frayed hemp.

Now the wounded man was in a state of profound prostration. It seemed that he could no longer understand anything. He stared at his comrades with deadened, bleary eyes, already murky like the eyes of animals when they are about to die. He kept repeating at intervals, as if to himself, "I'm dead! I'm dead!"

Cirù tried to clean him up with some raw hemp; but he had a rough touch and irritated the wound. Massacese, wanting to follow the example set by Margadonna's surgeon to the bitter end, was carefully sharpening some strips of fir. The two Talamontes were busy with the tar, since boiling tar had been chosen to cauterize the wound. But it was impossible to light the fire on the deck, which at every moment was being flooded by waves. The two Talamontes went below.

Massacese yelled to Cirù, "Wash him with sea water!"

Cirù followed the advice. His teeth chattering, Gialluca submitted to everything, whimpering all the time. His neck had swollen enormously, was completely red and in some places almost purple. Around the cuts a few dark brown patches began to appear. The sick man was finding it hard to breathe or swallow, and he was tormented by thirst.

"Put your soul in Saint Rocco's hands," Massacese told him. He had just finished sharpening the pegs of wood and was waiting for the tar.

Propelled by the wind, the brigantine was now off course, going up toward Sebenico, losing sight of the island. But, although the waves were still high, the storm gave signs of abating. The sun stood in the center of the sky surrounded by rust-colored clouds.

The two Talamontes came up with a terra-cotta jar full of boiling tar.

Gialluca knelt to pray again to the saint. They all made the sign of the cross.

"Oh, Saint Rocco, save me! I promise you a silver lamp and enough oil for years and thirty pounds of candles! Oh, Saint Rocco, save me! I have a wife and children . . . Have pity on me! Have mercy, my dear Saint Rocco!"

Gialluca kept his hands clasped; he spoke in a voice that no longer seemed his. Then he sat down again, saying simply, "Go ahead!"

Massacese twisted some hemp around the pieces of wood, and as he proceeded he dipped the prepared swab into the boiling tar and with this rubbed the wound. To make the cauterization deeper and more effective, he also poured some water into the cuts. Gialluca did not cry out at all. The men watching shivered in dismay at seeing that terrible pain.

Ferrrante La Selvi, from his place at the tiller, shook his head and said, "You've murdered him!"

The other men carried Gialluca below and laid him on a pallet. Nazareno stayed with him to watch over the sick man. He could hear Ferrante's guttural cries as he ordered the crew to trim the sails, and then the sailors' rapid steps on deck. The

Trinità swerved sharply, creaking in every joint. Suddenly Nazareno noticed a hole which was letting in water; he yelled. The sailors came down in a tumult, excited, all shouting at the same time, trying hastily to stop the leak. It looked as though the boat was going to sink.

Although completely drained of strength and spirit, Gialluca sat up on the pallet, thinking that the boat was about to go down; and he clutched one of the Talamontes with desperate hands. He was begging like a woman, "Don't leave me! Don't leave me!"

They reassured him and stretched him out again. He was frightened. He blurted out meaningless sentences. He cried. He didn't want to die. Since the growing inflammation filled his whole neck and cervix and had also spread little by little down his chest, the swelling had become even more monstrous. He felt that he was being strangled. Every so often he would open his mouth wide to gulp some air.

"Take me on deck! I can't breathe down here. I'm dying down here . . ."

Ferrante called the crew on deck. The brigantine was now tacking, trying to gain headway. The maneuver called for a lot of work with the sails. Ferrante would watch the wind and then give the appropriate command from his place at the tiller. As evening approached, the waves grew calmer.

After some time Nazareno rushed up on deck, completely distraught, crying, "Gialluca's dying! Gialluca's dying!"

The sailors ran to him; they found their shipmate already dead on the pallet, his body lying in a twisted position, his eyes wide open and his face swollen like a man who has been strangled.

The older Talamonte said, "And now?"

The other men stood there silently, bewildered at the sight of the corpse.

They went back on deck, silently. Talamonte repeated, "And now?"

The light slowly retreated from the surface of the water. Calm filled the air. Once again the sails hung slackly and the ship did not move. They caught sight of the island of Solta.

The sailors, all assembled at the stern, discussed what had happened. All of them were gripped by a sharp feeling of anxiety. Massacese was pale and pensive. He said, "What if they say we killed him? What if we get into trouble?"

This fear already tormented the minds of these superstitious, distrustful men. They replied, "That's the truth."

Massacese went on, "Well? What should we do?"

The older Talamonte said simply, "Is he dead? Let's throw him in the sea. We'll pretend that we lost him overboard during the storm . . . It's sure to work."

The other men agreed. They called Nazareno.

"Listen, you . . . mum as a fish, you hear." And they sealed the secret in his soul with a menacing gesture.

Then they went below to bring up the corpse. Already the flesh on the neck gave off a noxious smell; at every jostle the pus in the suppuration dripped out.

Massacese said, "Let's put him in a sack."

They got a sack; but only half of the corpse could fit in it. They then tied the sack at the height of the knees, and the legs stuck out. As they were working on the corpse they looked around them, instinctively. They couldn't see any sails; after the storm, long, slow, ample, rolling waves covered the sea; the island of Solta looked all blue over there on the horizon.

Massacese said, "Let's put in a rock, too."

They got a rock from the ballast and tied it to Gialluca's feet.

Massacese cried, "Let's go!"

They lifted the corpse over the side and let it slide into the sea. Gurgling, the water closed over it; at first the body descended with a slow oscillating motion; then it quickly disappeared.

The crew went back to the stern and waited for the wind.

They smoked and didn't talk. Now and then Massacese made an involuntary gesture, as men who are brooding will sometimes make.

The wind rose. After fluttering for an instant, the sails filled out. The *Trinità* began sailing in the direction of Solta. After two hours of good sailing, they passed through the inlet.

The moon lit up the shore. The sea had the tranquil look of a lake. From the port of Spalato came two ships which sailed out to meet the *Trinità*. Their crews were singing.

Hearing the song, Cirù cried, "Say! They're from Pescara."

Seeing the marks and numbers on the sails, Ferrante said, "Those are Raimondo Callare's brigs." And he shouted to them.

The sailors from their home port answered with loud shouts. One of the boats was carrying a cargo of dried figs, the other young donkeys.

When the second boat passed about ten meters from the *Trinità*, they exchanged greetings. One voice shouted, "Hey, Gialluca! Where's Gialluca?"

Massacese answered, "We lost him at sea during the storm. Tell his mother."

Then some loud cries and exclamations rose from the brig carrying the donkeys; and then cries of farewell.

"So long! So long! See you at Pescara."

And as they sailed off, the crews began singing again under the light of the moon.

GIOVANNI EPISCOPO

Giovanni Episcopo

Ego autem sum vermis, et non homo;
opprobrium hominum, et abjecto plebis.
Omnes videntes me, diriserunt me . . .
Psalm XXI, 7,8.

Judica me secundum justitiam tuam.
Psalm XXXIV, 24.

SO, YOU want to know . . . What do you want to know, my
dear sir? What should I tell you? —Oh, *everything!* —So you
want me to tell it all, from the very beginning.

All, from the beginning! How can I? I no longer know
anything; I no longer remember anything, truly. How can I do
it, sir? How?

Ah, my God! Well, here it is . . . —But wait, please, wait. Be
patient. The truth is I don't know how to talk. Even if I could
remember anything, I wouldn't be able to tell it. When I lived
among men, I kept silent. I was silent, even after I'd been
drinking: always silent.

Well, not always. I used to talk with *him*; only with him.
On certain summer evenings, outside the city's gates, or in the
piazzas, or the public parks . . . He would link his arm in
mine, that poor, emaciated arm, so frail that you could barely
feel it. And we would walk together, discussing this and that.

Eleven years old—think of that, sir—he was eleven; and he
conversed like a grown man, he was sad like a grown man. It
seemed that he already knew everything about life, that he
had borne all of its sufferings. His mouth already knew the
bitter words, the words that hurt so much and can't be forgotten!

But who ever forgets anything? Who?

I told you that I no longer know anything, I no longer remember anything . . . But it wasn't true.

I remember everything, everything, everything. Do you understand? I remember his words, his gestures, the way he looked at you, his tears, his sighs, his cries, every act of his existence from the time he was born until the time he died.

He's dead. It's already sixteen days since he died. And I'm still alive! But I must die; I must die as soon as possible. My little son wants me to leave. Every night he comes, sits, watches me. He's barefoot, poor little Ciro! I have to strain my ears to hear his footsteps. All the time, continually, from the moment it gets dark, I sit there listening; continually. When he sets his foot on the threshold, it's as though he put it on my heart; but gently, gently, without hurting me—oh, so lightly . . . Poor soul!

He's barefoot now, every night. But, take my word for it, never, never in his life did he go without a pair of shoes. I swear it: never.

I will tell you something. Now listen carefully. If someone dear to you should die, be sure that he doesn't lack for anything in his coffin. Dress him yourself; if you possibly can, do it with your own hands. Dress him completely, minutely, as though he were to live again, get up, walk out onto the street. Nothing must be missing for someone who leaves this world, nothing. Remember what I tell you.

Here, look at these shoes. —Do you have children? —No. Well, you can't know, you can't realize what these two worn-out shoes which contained *his* feet, which have preserved the form of *his* feet, mean to me. I could never tell you, no father could ever tell you; no one.

At that moment, when they entered the room and came to take me away, weren't all of *his* clothes there, on the chair next to the bed? Why didn't I look for anything but the shoes, anxiously, under the bed, feeling my heart burst at the thought of not finding them, and didn't I hide them, as if in them a little of *his* life were left? Ah, you can't understand.

On certain cold winter mornings, when the time came to go to school . . . He suffered from chillblains, poor child! During the winter, his feet were covered with sores, bleeding. I used to help him put on his stockings, his shoes. *I knew how to do it* very well. Then, when I laced them up, stooping over I could feel his hands resting on my shoulders tremble already from the cold. And I would try to procrastinate . . . No, you can't understand.

Then, when he died, this was the only pair; this pair I'm showing you. And I took them off him. And so of course that's how he was buried, like a poor little waif. Who loved him, except for his father?

Now, every evening, I take these two little shoes and put them one next to the other on the threshold for him. Do you think he sees them as he walks by? Perhaps he sees them, but he doesn't touch them. He knows perhaps that I would go crazy if I couldn't find them there in the morning, in their place, one next to the other . . .

Do you think I am crazy? Oh, no? I think I can read in your eyes . . . No, sir; I'm not crazy yet. What I'm telling you is true. *Everything is true.* The dead come back.

That *other one* also comes back, sometimes. Horrible! Oh, it's horrible!

You see: I have trembled like this for whole nights, my teeth have chattered and I couldn't stop them; I thought that the terror would shake my bones loose at the joints; I felt the hairs over my forehead stiffen like needles until morning—hard, rigid. Isn't my hair all white? Tell me: isn't it white?

Oh, thank you, sir. You see: I'm not shaking anymore. I'm sick, very sick. How many days of life would you still give me, judging from the way I look? You know: I must die, as soon as possible.

But yes, yes, there, I'm calm, perfectly calm. I'll tell you the whole story from the beginning, as you wish. Everything, in the proper order. I still haven't lost my wits. Believe me.

So, here it is. It was in the house in the new section of Rome; a kind of private *pensione*, about twelve or thirteen years ago. There were about twenty clerks living there, both old and young. We would go there to dine in the evening, all together, at the same hour and at the same table. We all knew each other, more or less, although we didn't all work in the same office. That's where I met Giulio Wanzer, twelve or thirteen years ago.

Did you see . . . his corpse? Don't you think there was something extraordinary about that face, those eyes? Ah, but the eyes were closed . . . Not both eyes, though; not both of them, I know. I must die, at least to remove from my fingers the feel of those eyelids that resisted me . . . I feel it, I feel it here, always; as though a little of that skin had stuck to them—here. Look. Isn't this a hand that has already begun to die? Look at it.

Yes; it's true. One shouldn't think of it. Forgive me. Now I'll go straight on to the end. Where were we? I'd begun so well and immediately went astray! It must be due to not eating; nothing else, surely, nothing else. For almost two days now I haven't eaten a thing.

At first, I remember, when my stomach was empty, I experienced a slight delirium, very strange. I felt my mind was wandering; I saw things . . .

Oh, of course, that's right. I remember now. You're right. I was saying that that's where I met Wanzer.

He lorded it over everyone there; he bullied them; he couldn't bear to be contradicted. He always raised his voice; sometimes, his hands. Not an evening passed that he didn't get into a quarrel. He was hated and feared there, like a tyrant. Everyone spoke badly of him, they murmured against him, plotted; but as soon as he appeared, even the angriest of them fell silent. The timid ones would smile at him, flatter him. What did that man have?

I don't know. At table he sat almost directly opposite me. I tried not to, but somehow I kept looking at him, continually. I had a strange feeling, which I can't quite express: a mixture of revulsion and attraction, indefinable. It was like an evil fascination, very evil, which that robust, sanguine, violent man exerted over me, so weak then, sickly and irresolute; and, to tell the truth, something of a coward.

One evening, as we were finishing the meal, a dispute started between Wanzer and a certain Ingletti who sat next to me. As usual, Wanzer began to shout and got furious. Ingletti, emboldened by the wine, refused to back down. I sat there stiffly, my eyes fixed on my plate, not daring to raise them; and my stomach all knotted up, horribly. Some insulting words were exchanged. Suddenly Wanzer picked up a wine-glass and threw it at his adversary. He missed him; and the glass smashed on my forehead, here, where you can see a scar.

As I felt the blood running down my face, I fainted. When I came to, my head was already bandaged. Wanzer was there, looking sorry; he muttered some excuse. Together with a doctor he took me home; he watched as I received the second medication; he wanted to stay in my room late into the night. He returned the next morning. He visited me often. And that started my slavery.

The only attitude I could have toward him was that of a frightened dog. When he walked into my room, he was the master. He would pull open my drawers, comb himself with my comb, wash his hands in my basin, smoke my pipe, rifle through my papers, read my letters, carry away with him any object he happened to fancy. Day by day his domination became more relentless, and day by day my spirit became more groveling, more feeble. I had lost my will. I no longer had a will. I submitted to him completely, without the least protest. He robbed me of all sense of human dignity, just like that, suddenly, with the same facility with which he would have tweaked out a hair.

And I wasn't in a daze. I was aware of everything I did, I was conscious of everything: of my weakness, my abjection and, especially, *of the absolute impossibility* of escaping from that man's power.

I can't explain to you, for example, the profound, obscure emotion that that scar inspired in me. And I can't explain the enormous perturbation that swept over me one day when my executioner took my head between his hands to look at this scar which was still tender and completely red. He passed his finger over it a number of times and then said:

"It's healed perfectly. In a month you'll no longer see a thing. You can thank the Lord."

Instead it seemed to me from that moment on I bore on my forehead not a scar but a mark of servitude, a shameful, very visible sign that would remain there for my entire life.

I followed him wherever he wanted to go; I waited for him for hours in the street, in front of a door; I stayed up late into the night recopying papers from his office for him; I would carry his letters from one end of Rome to the other; a hundred times I climbed the stairs of the public pawnshop, rushing panting from money-lender to money-lender to procure him a certain sum of money that was supposed to save him; a hundred times I stood behind his chair in a gambling den until dawn, dying of weariness and nausea, kept awake by his fusillades of profanity, the acrid smoke clawing at my throat; and he would be annoyed by my coughing, would blame his bad luck on me; and then if he had lost, when we left, walking down the deserted alleyways, surrounded by the mist, he dragged me along like a rag, gesticulating and cursing, until a shadow would loom up at a corner and offer to sell us some brandy.

Oh sir, who will be able to unravel this mystery for me before I die? So there are indeed men on earth who, when they meet other men, can do what they wish with them, can make them their slaves? So the will can be taken away from a man just as one takes a blade of straw from between a man's fingers? Can one do this, sir? But why?

Confronted by my executioner, *I no longer had any will.* And yet I was intelligent; and I too had a head full of thoughts; and I'd read many books, knew a great deal, understood a great deal. One thing, one thing above all I understood: that I was *lost*, irremediably lost. I felt continually in my depths a fright, a tremor; and ever since that evening I was cut, I had a fear of blood, a vision of blood. The crime stories in the newspapers upset me, kept me from sleeping. On certain nights when, coming back with Wanzer, we passed through a dark passageway, down a dark stairway, and the matches were hard to light, I felt a shiver down my back and my hair became prickly, sensitive. I had the idea fixed in my head that some night he would murder me.

That didn't happen. Instead what happened was *that which could not happen*. I used to think: to die by those hands one night, atrociously, this surely is my destiny. Instead . . .

But listen to me. If that evening Wanzer had not come to look in Ciro's room; if I had not seen the knife on the table; if *someone* had not entered into me, suddenly, to give me that terrible push; if . . .

Ah, it's true. You're right. We're still at the beginning and here I'm speaking of the end! But you wouldn't be able to understand if first I didn't tell you everything. And yet, I'm tired already; I'm confused already. I have nothing more to say, sir. My head is light, light, like a bladder full of air. I have nothing more to say. Amen, amen.

There, it's passed. That's enough. Thank you. You are very kind; you have pity for me. Nobody has ever pitied me, nobody on this earth.

I feel better; I can continue. I'll tell you about *her*, about Ginevra.

After that business with the wineglass some of our companions left the *pensione*, others declared that they would stay only if Giulio Wanzer was excluded. So Wanzer received a sort of dismissal from the landlady. After cursing and yelling as usual at all of them, he left. And when I was able to go out, he wanted to take me with him; he expected me to follow him.

For a long time we wandered listlessly from trattoria to trattoria. Nothing was sadder for me than what for other working people is a relief and, sometimes, a form of escape. I barely ate, forcing myself, disgust growing in me at the noise my fellow diner's jaws would make: a mastiff's jaws, formidable, that could have crushed steel. And little by little I began to develop that *thirst* which, once it starts, lasts until death.

But one evening Wanzer left me free. And the next day he told me that he had found a very pleasant place, to which he wanted to take me immediately.

"I found it. You'll see. You'll like it."

In fact the new *pensione* was perhaps better than the old one. The terms were to my liking. Some clerks from my office lived there. Also, several others were not completely unknown to me. I stayed. Nor would I have been able—as you know— not to stay.

That first evening, when the soup was brought to the table, two or three men asked with unusual intensity, in unison: "What about Ginevra? Where's Ginevra?"

The answer came that Ginevra was sick. Then they all inquired about her illness, they all showed great concern. They were told that it wasn't serious. In the conversation the absent woman's name was on everybody's lips, spoken amid ambiguous phrases betraying a sensual desire which perturbed all those men, old and young. I tried to catch what they were saying up and down the table. A dissolute young fellow sitting across from me spoke at length about Ginevra's mouth, becoming quite excited; and he looked at me as he talked, because I was listening so attentively. In my imagination, I remember, there then took form a figure of the absent woman that was not very different from the woman I later actually met. I shall always remember Wanzer's expressive gesture and the curl, I would say, almost of voracity his lips took in pronouncing an obscene sentence in dialect. And I remember that when we left I was already infected with the contagion of desire for that woman I had not seen—and also a slight disquietude, and a certain very strange, almost prophetic sense of exaltation.

We left together—I, Wanzer, and a friend of Wanzer's, a certain Doberti, the same man who had talked about her mouth. As we walked the two of them continued to talk coarsely about sex; and they would stop now and then to laugh long and loudly. I stayed a bit behind them. An almost oppressive melancholy, a quantity of obscure, confused thoughts swelled my already humiliated, quaking heart.

Even now, after about twelve years, I can remember that evening. I haven't forgotten a thing; not even the most insignificant detail. I know now, as I sensed then, that on that evening my fate was decided. From whom then did I get the warning?

Is it possible? Is it possible? The mere name of a woman, three ringing syllables, can open before you an inevitable abyss, which you can see, which you know to be inevitable. Is this possible?

Premonition, clairvoyance, inner vision. . . Words! Words! I've read them in books. It's not that way, it's not that way. Have you ever looked inside yourself? Have you ever examined your soul?

You suffer. Does your suffering seem new to you, *never experienced before?* An error, an illusion. Everything has been experienced, everything has taken place. Your soul is composed of thousands, hundreds of thousands of fragments of souls which have lived a whole life, which have produced all phenomena, have seen all phenomena. Do you know where I'm heading? Well, listen to me carefully, because what I am telling you is the truth; the truth discovered by someone who has spent year after year continually looking inside himself, alone among men, alone. Listen to me carefully because this is a truth much more important than the events you want to know about. When . . .

Another time? Tomorrow? Why tomorrow? So you don't want me to explain my idea to you.

Oh, the facts, the facts, always the facts. —The facts are nothing, they don't mean anything. There is something in this world, my dear sir, which matters much more.

Ah well: another mystery. Why did the real Ginevra resemble most faithfully the image which had flashed into my mind? Well, let's leave that aside. —After two or three days' absence, she reappeared in the dining room, carrying a large soup tureen that veiled her face in steam.

Yes, my dear sir, she was a waitress, serving meals at a clerks' *pensione.*

Did you ever see her? Did you know her? Did you ever talk to her? And did she ever talk to you? Well, you too, I'm sure, experienced that sudden, inexplicable perturbation, if she touched you with her hand.

All the men desired her, every one of them wanted her; they still want her. Wanzer is dead; yet she will still have a lover, a hundred lovers, until she grows old, until her teeth fall out of her mouth. When she walked down the street, the prince in his coach turned round, the beggar stopped to look at her. I've caught the same gleam in all eyes, I've read the same thought.

She's changed, changed a lot. At that time she was twenty. I have always tried in vain to *see her again* within myself, just as I saw her that first time. There's the secret. Have you ever noticed this? A man, an animal, a tree, anything whatsoever, presents its true aspect only once, that is, in the fleeting moment of that first perception. It is as though it gave us its virginity. Immediately after, it's no longer the same; it's something else. Your soul, your nerves transform it, falsify it, obscure it. Farewell.

Ah well, I've always envied the man who saw that creature *for the first time*. Do you understand me? Maybe you don't. You think that I'm raving, that I'm getting confused and contradicting myself. It's hopeless. Let it go. Let's get back to the facts.

. . . A room lit by gas lights, overheated, with an arid heat that dries up the skin; and the smell, the steam rising from the food; and a confused noise of voices, and over all those voices Wanzer's harsh voice, which made every word crude and rough. Then, all of a sudden, an interruption, a silence that seemed frightening to me. And a hand brushes past me, picks up my plate, sets down another; it makes me shiver as though it had given me a caress. All of them around the table, one after the other, experienced the same thrill: it was visible. And the heat became suffocating; ears began to turn red, eyes began to glisten. A base, almost bestial expression appears on the faces of those men who have eaten and drunk, who have attained the only goal of their daily lives. The emanation of their impurity wounds me so deeply that I think I'm going to faint. I gather myself together on my chair, draw in my elbows to increase the distance between myself and my neighbors. A voice cries through the hubbub: "Episcopo's got a belly-ache."

Another voice shouts: "No, Episcopo is feeling *sentimental*. Didn't you see the look on his face when Ginevra changed his plate?"

I try to laugh. I raise my eyes and meet Ginevra's fixed on me with an ambiguous expression.

She leaves the room. Then Filippo Doberti makes a clownish proposal.

"My dear friends, there's only one way out. One of us must marry her . . . on behalf of the others."

That isn't exactly what he said; he used the coarse word; he indicated the act, the role of the others.

"Let's vote. Let's vote. We've got to elect a husband."

Wanzer yells: "Episcopo!"

"Episcopo and Associates Incorporated."

The brawl increases. Ginevra returns, perhaps she's heard. She smiles a calm, assured smile, which makes her seem intangible.

Wanzer yells: "Episcopo, ask for her hand."

Two other men, with studied gravity, get up and ask in my name for Ginevra's hand.

With the same smile, she replies: "I'll think it over."

And again I meet her eyes. And I really don't know if it is I they are talking about, if I am the one this is addressed to, if I am that Episcopo they're laughing at. And I can't possibly imagine the expression on my face. . . .

A dream, a dream. That whole period of my life is like a dream. It's impossible for you to understand or imagine the sense I had of my own being and the consciousness I had of the things I was doing. In a dream I re-lived a part of life already lived; I watched the inevitable repetition of a series of events that had taken place already. When? Who knows? You can add that I was not sure of being I, myself. Often it seemed to me that I had mislaid my personality, at times I felt I had an artificial one. What a mystery a man's nerves are!

I'll cut it short. One evening Ginevra quit her job; she said she was leaving that sort of work; she said that she didn't feel well, that she would go to Tivoli, would stay there for a few months at her sister's house. All of them, when they said goodbye to her, clasped her hand. Smiling, she kept saying to them: "We'll see each other."

And then, laughing, to me: "Remember, Signor Episcopo. We are *betrothed*."

That was the first time I touched her; and it was the first

time I looked into her eyes with the intention of trying to penetrate her thoughts. But she remained a secret for me.

The following evening the meal was almost gloomy. They all seemed disappointed. And Wanzer said: "You know, Doberti's idea wasn't bad."

Then some of them turned to me and stupidly prolonged the mockery.

The company of those idiots had become unbearable to me; but I made no attempt to get away. I continued to go to that house where, amid the jesting and laughter, I could feed my dark sweet fantasies. For many weeks, undergoing the worst material difficulties, humiliations, anxieties and terrors of my slavish life, I experienced all the anguish of the most delicate and violent love. At twenty-eight a kind of belated adolescence had suddenly manifested itself in my spirit, with all the languors, all the tender feelings, all the tears of adolescence . . .

Ah, my dear sir, you can imagine this miracle in a creature like myself, already old, withered, parched to the marrow. Picture an unexpected flower that suddenly sprouts on a dry stalk.

Another extraordinary, unexpected event astonished and overwhelmed me. For several days now Wanzer seemed harder, more irascible than usual. He had spent five or six nights in a gambling den. One morning he had come up to my room looking pale as a corpse, had flung himself in a chair; two or three times he had tried to speak; then, suddenly, giving it up, he had left without saying a single word, without answering me, without looking at me.

I didn't see him again all that day. I didn't see him at dinner. I didn't see him the following day.

We were at table when a certain Questori, a colleague of Wanzer's, came in and said: "You haven't heard? Wanzer's run away."

At first I didn't understand it or I didn't believe it; but my heart leapt to my throat.

Some of the men said: "What are you saying? Who's run away?"

"Wanzer, Giulio Wanzer."

I really don't know what I felt; but certainly my first feeling of agitation was in great part composed of joy. I made an effort to contain myself. And then I heard all the resentments, all the rancors, all the repressed hatreds explode against the man who had been my master.

"And what about you?" the most ferocious of the men shouted at me. "Don't you have anything to say? Weren't you Wanzer's servant? Didn't you carry his suitcases to the station?"

Another man said to me: "You've been marked on the brow by a thief. You'll get ahead."

Another man: "Whose lackey will you become now? Will you move on to the police?"

That's how they insulted me, for the sheer pleasure of hurting me, because they knew I was a coward.

I got up and left. I walked down the streets, wandering at random: free, free, free at last!

It was a night in March, serene, almost warm. I climbed the slope of Via Quattro Fontane, turned up toward the Quirinale Palace. I was looking for broad open spaces; I wanted to drink in a single breath an immensity of air, look at the stars, listen to the sound of water, do something poetic, dream of the future. Continually I kept repeating within myself: Free, free; I am a free man. I still couldn't reflect, gather my thoughts, examine my state. I was assailed by childish whims. I would have liked to perform a thousand deeds all at once to prove my freedom to myself, to savor my freedom. Passing by a café, I was washed by a wave of music and it stirred me to the depths. I walked in, my head held high. I felt that I had a proud air. I ordered a cognac; and I made the waiter leave the bottle on the table. I drank two or three glasses.

It was suffocating in that café. The act of taking off my hat reminded me of my scar, reawakened in my memory the cruel sentence: "You've been marked on the brow by a thief." —Since I felt that everyone was looking at my forehead and had noticed the mark, I thought: "What can they think? They most likely think it's a wound received in a duel." —And I, who would never have fought, was pleased by this thought. If someone had come to sit next to me and struck up a conversation, I certainly would have found a way to describe that duel. But nobody came. After some time a gentleman came to take the chair opposite me, on the other side of the table. He didn't look at me, didn't ask my permission; he didn't notice, when he took the chair, whether or not I was resting my feet on it. It was rude of him; don't you agree?

I left, started walking about the streets again, aimlessly. I felt deeply unhappy, without quite knowing why. Gradually a vague disquiet arose from that bewilderment; and as my disquiet grew it suggested a thought to me: "Maybe *he* is still in Rome, hidden? Maybe he's going about the streets in disguise? Maybe he's waiting for me in the dark, on the stairs?" —I was afraid; I turned round two or three times to make sure I wasn't being followed; I went into another café, as one goes into a place of refuge.

When it was late, very late, I finally made up my mind to set out for home. Every appearance, every noise frightened me. A man stretched out on the sidewalk in the dark looked to me like a cadaver. —"Ah, why didn't he kill himself?" I thought. "Why didn't he have the courage to kill himself?" And indeed it was the one thing he should have done—I realized then that rather than news of his flight, only that of his death would have calmed me.

I slept little and it was an anxious sleep. But in the morning, as soon as I opened the shutters, a sense of relief began again to spread through my whole being: a peculiar feeling, which you can't understand because you have never been a slave.

At my office I got a detailed report on Wanzer's flight. It

was due to grave irregularities and a theft of bonds from the Central Treasury, where he had been a clerk for a number of years. An order for his arrest had been issued, but with no result. Some people thought he had already reached some safe place, far from the police.

Then, securely free, I lived only for my love, my secret. I felt that I was convalescing; I had a lighter sense of my body, less troubling; I cried very easily, like a child. The last days of March and the first days of April had for me a sweetness and sadness whose memory alone, now that I am dying, consoles me for having been born.

For that one memory I forgive Ciro's mother, the woman who did us so much harm. You cannot understand, sir, what the revelation of his own hidden goodness, the discovery of a vein of tenderness in the core of his own being is for a man hardened and warped by sufferings and injustice. You can't understand, and perhaps can't even believe what I'm saying. Well, I tell you. At certain moments, may God forgive me, I felt in me something of Jesus. I have been the most miserable and the best of men.

Here, let me cry a little. Do you see how I am able to cry? In all those years of martyrdom I learned to cry like this, without sobs or outward signs, so as not to be heard, so as not to trouble the person who loved me, the person who made me suffer. There are few people in the world who know how to cry as I do. Well, sir, this at least will be marked down in my favor, when you remember me. You'll say, when I'm dead, that poor Giovanni Episcopo at least knew how to cry silently, all his life.

How was it that on that Sunday morning—Palm Sunday— I found myself going to Tivoli on the tram? Actually, I have an uncertain memory of it. Was it a fit of folly? Was it the act of a somnambulist? Truly, I do not know.

I went toward the unknown, I let myself be dragged along

by the unknown. Once again the sense of reality eluded me. It even seemed to me I was surrounded by a peculiar atmosphere that isolated me from the outer world. I don't know how to express it. The Roman countryside, for example, the countryside I was going through, seemed to me indefinitely far away, separated from me by an incalculable space . . .

How can you form a picture of so extraordinary a mental state? What I'm describing must seem to you necessarily absurd, inadmissible, unnatural. Well, just think that I have lived amidst these disorders, these perturbations, these alterations almost continually until today. Paraesthesis, dysaesthesia . . . They've even told me the names of my illnesses. But nobody has been able to cure me. I have lived all my life on the brink of insanity, aware of it, like a man bending over and looking down into an abyss, waiting from one minute to the next for the final spell of dizzyness, the great moment of darkness.

What do you think? Will I lose my reason before I close my eyes? Is there some hint on my face, or in what I say? Do you notice anything? Answer me frankly, dear sir; answer me.

And what if I do not die! If I must survive for a long time in an insane asylum, a lunatic!

No; I must confess that this is not my real fear. You know . . . that *they* might come at night, both of them. Some night, I'm sure of it, Ciro will meet that *other one*: I know it, I foresee it. And . . . then? —The explosion of rage, of furious madness, in the dark . . . Oh, my God, my God! Will this be my way of dying?

Hallucinations, yes; nothing else. You've put it perfectly. Oh, yes, yes, you've put it well: all I need is a lamp to be tranquil, because I sleep deeply; yes, yes, a lamp, simply a lamp. Thank you, my dear sir.

Where were we? —Ah, yes, at Tivoli.

. . . A sharp stench of sulphurous water; and then, everywhere, all around, olive trees, olive trees, groves of olive trees; and in me the strange primitive sensation that one is being dispersed in the wind as our tram speeds ahead. I get off. There are people in the streets; strips of palm leaf glisten in the sun; the church bells toll. I know that *I will meet her.*

"Oh, Signor Episcopo? How did you come? Why are you here?"

It's Ginevra's voice; it's Ginevra, with her hands outstretched, standing right in front of me, who am overwhelmed.

"Why so pale? Have you been sick?"

She looks at me and smiles, waiting for me to manage to speak. Is this the woman who walked around the table in the smoke-filled room, under the gaslight? Is it possible that this is the woman?

Finally I stammer out a few words.

She insists: "But why are you here? What a surprise!"

"I'm here to see you."

"So you remembered that we're *betrothed?*"

She laughs and adds: "Here's my sister. Come with us to church. You'll stay with us today, won't you? We'll act as if we're engaged. Say you will."

She's gay, talkative, full of unexpected ideas, of new seductiveness. She's dressed simply, unpretentiously, but with grace, almost with elegance. She asks news of our friends.

"And that Wanzer!"

She learned it all from a newspaper, by chance.

"You two were great friends. Weren't you?"

I do not reply. A short silence; and she seems pensive. We go into the church bedecked with sacred palms. She kneels alongside her sister and opens a prayer book. I am standing behind them and I stare at her neck; and the discovery of a small brown mark gives me an ineffable thrill. At that very moment she turns around a little and flashes a glance at me out of the corner of her eye.

The memory of the past is abolished, the anxiety for the future is calmed. There is only the present; there is nothing on this earth for me but this woman. Without her the only possibility is to die.

Leaving the church, without speaking she offers me a palm. I look at her, without speaking; and it seems to me that from that look she has understood everything. We walk towards her sister's house. I am invited in. Ginevra says to me, going towards a balcony: "Come, come here for a while, to enjoy the sun."

We are on the balcony, side by side. The sun strikes us with its full force; the roar of the church bells passes over our heads. She says softly, as though talking to herself: "Who ever would have thought it!"

My heart swells with a boundless tenderness. I can barely stand it. I ask her, in a voice become unrecognizable: "So we're betrothed?"

She remains silent for a moment. Then she replies slowly, blushing just a trifle, lowering her eyes: "Do you want it? Well, yes, we are."

They call to us from inside. There's her brother-in-law; some other relatives; the children are there, too. I am really the fiancé! At the table Ginevra and I are placed next to each other. At a certain point we hold hands, under the tablecloth; and I think that I am going to faint, the feeling of voluptuousness is so keen. The brother-in-law, sister, relatives suddenly look at me with mixed curiosity and astonishment.

"But how is it that nobody knew about this?"

"But how is it that you, Ginevra, never told us anything about it?"

We smile, embarrassed, confused, also astonished at what is happening with the ease and absurdity of a dream . . .

Yes, absurd, incredible, ridiculous; above all, ridiculous. But it happened in this world between a man and a woman of this world, between me, Giovanni Episcopo, and the living Ginevra Canale, just like that, just as I have told it to you.

Ah, sir, you may laugh, if you wish to. I won't be offended. A *tragic farce* . . . Where did I read this phrase? —Truly, nothing more ridiculous, nothing more ignoble and nothing more atrocious.

I went to her mother's home in an old house on Via Montanara, up some narrow, damp and slippery stairs, like the steps leading down to a cistern, a dubious, greenish, almost sepulchral light filtering down from a slit overhead: unforgettable. I remember it all! As I went up I paused upon almost every step; because I felt I was losing my balance at every moment, as if I were treading on moving ice. The higher I climbed, the more that staircase, in that light, seemed fantastic to me, full of mystery, of a grim silence, where certain very distant, incomprehensible sounds seemed to come to die. Suddenly I heard a door open violently on the landing above; and an outburst of profanity shrieked by a female voice resounded through the whole stairwell; and then the door closed again with a loud crash that made the house shake from top to bottom. And I shook too, intimidated; and I stayed there, hesitating. A man was gradually coming down, indeed he seemed to slither along the wall like some soft thing. He was grumbling and whimpering beneath the turned-down brim of a whitish hat; but when he bumped into me, he raised his head. And I saw a pair of dark glasses, the kind that are enclosed in a protective mesh, enormous, jutting out from a face red as a piece of raw meat.

The man, thinking he recognized me, called: "Pietro!"

And he grabbed me by the arm, breathing his wine-laden breath into my face. But he realized his mistake and resumed his way down. Then I continued my climb, automatically; and I was sure, I don't know why, that I had met a member *of the family*. I found myself before a door on which I read: "Emilia

Canale, pawnbroker attached to the Public Pawnshop, authorized by the Commissioner of Police, Rome." To end the anguish of hesitation, I made an effort and pulled the bell-rope; but I pulled it much harder than I intended and the bell began ringing furiously. An irate voice answered from within, the same voice that had shrieked the curses; the door opened; and I, seized by a kind of panic, without seeing, without even waiting, gaspingly said, swallowing my words: "I am Episcopo, Giovanni Episcopo, clerk . . . I have come, as you must know . . . for your daughter . . . as you already know . . . Excuse me, excuse me. I pulled it too hard."

· I was standing before Ginevra's mother, a still good-looking, florid woman, dressed à la pawnbroker, wearing a gold necklace, two huge gold ear-rings, and gold rings on all of her fingers. And I was timidly asking for Ginevra's hand in marriage—you remember?—the famous proposal made by Filippo Doberti!

Ah, my dear sir, you may laugh if you wish. You won't offend me.

I must tell you everything, in detail, day by day, hour by hour—isn't that so? You want all the little scenes, all the little events, all my life of those days, so bizarre, so senseless, so comic and miserable, right down to the *great event*? Do you want to laugh? Do you want to cry? I can tell you everything. I read my past as in an open book. This great clarity comes to someone who is near death.

But I am tired, I'm weak. And you, too, you must be a little weary. It's best to cut it short.

I'll do that. I know you'll readily agree.

The pawnbroker seemed already informed as to my job, my pay, my situation. She had a ringing voice, a determined way of gesturing, a malign rapacious look, which at certain moments became caressing, almost lewd, somewhat resembling Ginevra's. When she spoke to me, standing up, she came too close to me, touched me continually; now she gave me a little push, now she pulled at one of my jacket buttons, now she flicked a speck of dust from my shoulder, now she picked off a hair, a thread. I felt deeply upset, all my nerves tense. It was torture, that continual touching on the part of that woman who more than once I saw lift her fists in her husband's face.

And her husband was in fact the man on the stairs, the man with the green eyeglasses, a poor idiot.

He had worked as a typographer, this man. An eye disease now prevented him from working. And he lived on his wife, his children and son-in-law, badly treated by all of them, martyred, like an intruder. He had the vice of drinking wine, the habit of getting drunk on it, the *thirst*, the terrible thirst for it. Nobody at his house gave him a penny for drink; but, in order to earn a little money, he must certainly have earned it on the sly, God knows on what street, God knows in what shop, from what people—plying some ignoble little trade, base, facile, hiring out by the day. When he got the chance he would snatch up some stuff from the house and run off to sell it, so he could drink, so he could abandon himself to his unrestrainable passion; and even the fear of curses and blows didn't stop him. At least once a week his wife threw him out, pitilessly. For two or three days he would not have the courage to return, to knock at the door. Where did he go? Where did he sleep? How did he live?

From that first day, the day I met him, I liked him. While I sat there and bore the chatter of my future mother-in-law, he sat facing me with a smile on his face, a continuous smile that made his lower, somewhat pendant lip tremble, but it did not come from the sort of cage in which his poor sick eyes were enclosed. When I rose to leave, he said in a low voice, with obvious fear: "I'll come too."

We left together. His legs were pretty weak. Going down the stairs and seeing him hesitate and lurch, I said to him: "Do you want to lean on me?"

With me as his support we went down, and out on the street he continued to hold his arm under mine, although I made a movement to free myself. He kept silent for a while; but now and again he turned to me and brought his face so close that he touched me with the brim of his hat. He still smiled, accompanying his smile with a peculiar sound in his throat, to break the silence.

I remember it was almost dusk; a pleasant evening. People were sauntering along the street. Two musicians, a flute and guitar, were playing an aria from *Norma* in front of a café. I remember: a wagon went by, transporting a wounded man sitting between two policemen.

Finally he said, squeezing my arm: "I'm happy; you know? Really happy. What a good fellow you must be! I already like you a lot, you know."

He said all this with a kind of anxious haste, having one fixed idea, one desire, and being shy about expressing it. Then he began to laugh, stupidly. Another pause. Again he said: "I'm happy."

He laughed again, but convulsively. I realized that he was gripped by nervous agitation, and that it made him suffer. When we were in front of a glass window with red curtains which glowed brightly, being lit up from inside, he said suddenly, rapidly: "Shall we have a glass together?"

And he halted and detained me at that door, in the reddish reflection staining the pavement. I could feel he was shaking; and the light helped me to see his poor inflamed eyes behind those lenses.

I replied: "Let's go in."

We entered a tavern. There were a few customers; they were playing cards in a group. We sat down in a corner. Canale ordered: "A liter, of red."

He was seized by a sudden hoarseness. He poured the wine in the glasses, shaking like a paralytic; then drank his down in one gulp; sucking his lips, he poured himself another glass. Then he laughed, setting the bottle on the table; and naively he confessed: "For three days I haven't had a drink.

"Three days?"

"Yes—three whole days. I haven't any money. At home nobody gives me a cent. You understand? You understand? And I can't work anymore, with these eyes . . . Look, my boy."

He lifted his glasses; and so much had the expression of his face changed, it almost seemed to me that he had lifted a mask. His lids were ulcerated, swollen, without lashes, filled with decay, horrible; and in the midst of that redness and that swollenness barely opened two tear-filled pupils, infinitely sad, with that profound and incomprehensible sadness one can see in the eyes of a suffering animal. Faced by that revelation, a mixture of disgust and pity stirred in me. I asked: "Does it hurt you? Does it pain much?"

"Oh, you can imagine, my boy! Needles, needles, jagged edges of wood, splinters of glass, poisonous thorns . . . If they stuck all this in me, it would be nothing in comparison, my boy."

Perhaps he exaggerated his sufferings, because he saw himself being pitied by me, pitied as a human being and who knows after how many years! Who knows how many years had passed since he had heard a pitying voice! He exaggerated perhaps to increase my feeling of compassion, to feel himself consoled once again by a fellow human being.

"Do they hurt you very much?"

"Very much."

Very slowly he passed over his lids a kind of rag which had neither color nor shape. Then he lowered his glasses again; and drained his second glass in one gulp. I drank too. He touched the bottle and said: "There's nothing else in the world, my boy."

I looked at him. Nothing in him, truly nothing reminded one of Ginevra: not a feature, not an intonation, not a gesture, nothing. I thought: "He isn't the father."

He drank again; ordered another liter of wine; then went on talking in a tone of voice which rasped like a falsetto: "I'm happy that you're going to marry Ginevra. And you can be happy too . . . The Canales are an honest family! If we hadn't been honest . . . by now . . ."

Lifting his glass, he wore an equivocal smile that disturbed me. Then he went on: "Eh, Ginevra . . . Ginevra could have been a treasure for us, if we had wanted. You understand? We can say these things to you. Not one, not two, but ten, twenty offers . . . And what offers, my boy!"

I felt I was turning green.

"Prince Altini, for instance . . . All the time he was on my neck! He even wanted me to come to his palace one evening, a few months ago, before Ginevra left for Tivoli. You understand? He wanted to give her three thousand lire right away; and then he would rent a house for her, and so on, and so on. Ah, no, no. Emilia has always said: It doesn't pay, it doesn't pay. We married off the first girl, we'll marry the second. A clerk with a good career, a halfway decent salary . . . We'll find him. You see? You see? You came. You're named Episcopo, isn't that so? What a name! So it's Signora Episcopo; Signora Episcopo . . ."

He had become loquacious. He began to laugh.

"How did you see her? How did you meet her? In Rome, right? At the *pensione*. Tell me, tell me. I'm listening."

At that point a man came in, a man with an ambiguous look, repugnant, something between a waiter and a hairdresser, with a pale face covered with reddish pimples. He greeted Canale.

"To your health, Battista!"

Battista called him over, offered him a glass of wine.

"Teodoro, drink to our health. Here is my future son-in-law, Ginevra's fiancé."

The stranger, surprised, muttered something, looking at me with whitish eyes that made me shiver, as if I had felt a cold, slimy touch on my skin. He murmured: "Oh, so, the gentleman . . ."

"Yes, yes," Battista broke in quickly. "Signor Episcopo."

"Ah, Signor Episcopo. It gives me great pleasure . . . Congratulations . . ."

I didn't say a word. But Battista laughed, his chin on his chest, assuming a sly, nasty look. After a while, the other man stood up to leave.

"Goodbye, Battista. We'll see each other again, Signor Episcopo."

He offered me his hand, and I gave him mine.

When he had left, Battista said to me in a low voice: "You know who he is? Teodoro, the . . . *confidant* of Marchese Aguti, the old one, who has a palace nearby. A year he's been pestering me about Ginevra. You understand? The old man wants her, wants her, wants her; he cries, shrieks, stamps his feet like a child, because he wants her. Marchese Aguti, the man who has them tie him to the iron bars of a bed, has his women whip him until the blood runs . . . We've heard the howls, from our house . . . Then the police intervene . . . Ha, ha, ha, poor Teodoro, how disappointed he looked! Did you see how he looked? He didn't expect that, he didn't expect that, poor Teodoro!"

He went on laughing stupidly, right in front of me, who was dying of anguish. Suddenly he stopped and spat out an imprecation. Beneath the rim of the glasses his cheeks were streaked by two trickles of impure, yellowish tears.

"Oh, these eyes! When I drink, it pains me even more!"

And again he lifted those frightening green eyeglasses; and again I saw that whole deformed face, which seemed almost flensed, red like the behinds of certain monkeys—you know? You can see them in the zoo. And I saw those painful pupils in the middle of those suppurating wounds. I saw him pressing that rag against his lids.

"I must go. It's already late for me," I said.

"Good, let's go. But wait."

And he started to rummage comically through his pockets,

as if to take out some money. I paid; and we got up and walked out. Again he put his arm under mine. It seemed that he didn't want to leave me that evening. Every so often he laughed like an idiot. And I felt that the excitement of just before was returning, the agitation, the inner laughing, as of someone who wants to say something but doesn't dare and is ashamed.

"What a lovely evening!" he said; and he gave the same convulsed laugh as before.

Suddenly, with the same effort a stammerer makes when he gets stuck, his head low, hiding beneath the brim of his hat, he added: "Give me five lire. I'll return them to you."

We stopped. I put five lire in his hand which was shaking a great deal. Immediately he turned and walked away, vanishing in the dusk.

Ah, sir, what a sad business! The man who is devoured by vice, the man who struggles in the grip of vice and feels himself being eaten up and lost and doesn't want to be but who can't save himself . . . What a piteous thing, sir, what a piteous thing! Can you think of anything more profound, more enticing, more obscure? Tell me, tell me: what, among all human matters, is sadder than the tremor that seizes you faced by the object of your desperate passion? What is sadder than hands that shake, knees that buckle, lips that twist, a human being racked in every part by the implacable need of a single sensation? Tell me, tell me: what upon this earth is sadder? What?

And to see this enemy all around you, to see it with prodigious lucidity, to discern all its traces, divine all its corrosions, its *hidden* devastations. To see—you know what I mean?—to see the suffering in each man, to comprehend, always to comprehend, and to have fraternal pity for every strayed soul, for every wretched person, and to feel within oneself in the depths of one's own flesh the voice of this great human fraternity, and not to regard any man on the street as a stranger

. . . You understand? Could you understand this in me, in me whom you regard as pusillanimous, abject, almost idiotic?

No, you cannot understand. And yet, that's how it is. There are men who walk among the people as though among a forest of completely identical, indifferent trees; and there are some men, continually anxious, who search in every face for the silent reply to a silent question. For such men there are no strangers upon this earth.

Alas, his heart is for everyone, no heart is for him.

I know, I know. Who cares about him? Who is concerned about his goodness and his love? Every man harbors a secret dream which is not goodness or love but rather a reckless desire for pleasure and self-aggrandizement. I know. No human creature loves another human creature—man has never been loved by another human creature. I have never dared confess the horrible truth to myself, for fear of dying of it.

Well, sir, from that evening on I felt tied to that wretch, I became his friend. Why? Through what mysterious affinity? Because of what instinctive foresight? Perhaps because his vice was beginning irresistibly to overpower me too? Or because I was attracted by his unhappiness without hope and without possibility of escape which was so much like mine?

After that I saw him almost every evening. He would come looking for me everywhere; he waited for me outside my office; he waited for me at night on the stairs of my house. He would not ask me for anything; nor could he speak with his eyes, since they were covered up. But it was enough for me to look at him to understand. He would smile his usual silly or convulsed smile; and he never asked for anything, just waited. I was unable to resist him, I would not send him away, humiliate him, greet him with a frown, speak to him harshly.

—But did that mean I was being subjected to another tyranny? That Giulio Wanzer had a successor? —Often his presence troubled me acutely; and yet I did nothing to free myself from him. Sometimes he was given to ridiculous or saddening effusions of love for me, which wrenched my heart. Once he said to me, wrinkling up his mouth as children do when they are about to cry: "Why don't you call me papa?"

I knew that he was not the father; I knew that his wife's children were not his. Perhaps he also knew this. And yet I called him papa, when nobody could hear, when we were alone, when he needed to be consoled. Often, to gain my pity, he would show me a bruise, the mark of a beating, with the same gesture with which beggars display their deformities or misfortunes to elicit alms.

I discovered, by chance, that on certain evenings he stationed himself in the shadows, away from the street lamps, and would beg in a low voice, adroitly, without attracting attention, walking for a way alongside the passer-by. One evening, at the corner by the Forum of Trajan, I was approached by a man who was muttering: "I am an unemployed worker. I am nearly blind. I have five children who haven't eaten for twenty-four hours. Give me something to buy a piece of bread for those poor creatures of God . . ."

I recognized his voice immediately. But there in the darkness, barely able to see, he didn't recognize me. Fearful that he might I quickly walked away, I fled.

Even the basest action did not revolt him, provided he could satisfy his atrocious thirst. One time he came to my room; he seemed upset. I had just got back from the office and I was washing up. I had laid my jacket and vest on the bed, and in the pocket of my vest I had left my watch, a small silver watch, a memento of my dead father. I was washing behind a screen. I heard Battista move about the room in an unusual way, as if he were nervous. I asked him: "What are you doing?"

He answered a bit too promptly and in a voice that seemed a trifle different: "Nothing. Why?"

And he immediately came behind the screen, with a bit too much concern.

I dressed. We went out. At the foot of the stairs, I reached into my pocket for my watch to see what time it was. I failed to find it. It wasn't there.

"My goodness! I left my watch up in the room. I must go back up again. Wait for me here. I'll only be a moment."

I went up, lit a candle, looked everywhere for the watch. After a few minutes of futile search, I heard Battista's voice asking: "Well, did you find it?"

He had come up; he stood in the doorway, swaying a little.

"No. It's strange. And yet I think I left it in my vest pocket. Have you seen it?"

"I haven't seen it."

A suspicion had already flashed through my mind. Battista remained in the doorway, standing there, his hands in his pockets. I started searching again, impatiently, almost angrily.

"It's impossible that I mislaid it. I had it before, before I undressed; I know I had it. It must be here; I must find it."

Battista had finally moved. I turned suddenly; and I read the guilt on his face. My heart sank.

He stammered, confused: "It must be here; we'll find it."

And he picked up the candle and bent over to search around the bed; he got down on his knees, lurching a bit; raised the covers, looked underneath the bed. He was upset, troubled, panting; and the candle was dripping on his unsteady hand.

That bit of play-acting irritated me. I shouted at him harshly: "Enough! Get up; and don't make such a fuss. I know where we ought to search . . ."

He put the candle on the floor; and stayed there for a while on his knees, hunched over, trembling like someone about to confess a misdeed. But he didn't confess. He got up with an effort, without speaking. Once again I read the guilt on his face; and I felt a sharp pang. I thought: "Of course, he has the watch in his pocket. I should force him to admit it, to give me back the stolen object, to repent. I should stand here and watch him weep with repentance." But I didn't have the strength. I said: "Let's go."

We left. On the stairs the guilty man followed me slowly, clinging to the railing. How sad it was!

When we reached the street, he asked me in a feeble voice: "So you think I took it?"

"No, no," I replied. "Let's not talk about it any more." After a while, I added: "I'm sorry, because it was a memento of my dead father."

I noticed that he made a slight, quickly repressed movement, as if he had the intention of taking something from his pocket. But it was nothing. We continued to walk.

After another interval he said to me, almost brusquely: "Do you want to search me?"

"No, no. Let's stop talking about it. Goodbye. I'm leaving now because I have some business to attend to this evening."

And I left him, without looking at him. It was so sad!

During the following days I did not see him. On the evening of the fifth day he showed up at my house. I said, gravely: "Oh, it's you?"

And without pausing for a moment, I went back to working on certain office documents. After an interval of silence, he dared to ask me: "Did you find it?"

I pretended to laugh, and went on writing. After another long interval, he added: "I didn't take it."

"Yes, yes, all right; I know. It's still on your mind?"

Seeing that I remained seated at my table, he said, after another pause: "Good night!"

"Good night, good night!"

I let him leave just like that; I didn't stop him. But I was sorry; I wanted to call him back. Too late; he had already left.

He did not come around for another three or four days. As I was entering my house late one evening, just before midnight, he was standing there before me, under a street lamp. It was drizzling.

"Oh, it's you. So late!"

He could barely stand upright; he looked drunk. But, when

I looked more closely, I realized that he was in a miserable state: covered with mud as if he had rolled in a ditch, haggard, distraught, with a face that looked almost purple.

"What's happened to you? Tell me."

He began crying wildly and came close to me as though about to collapse in my arms; and he stood like that, close to me, sobbing and trying to tell his story between sobs that were choking him, through tears that dripped down into his mouth.

Ah, sir, under that street lamp, in that rain, what a terrible thing! What a terrible thing, the sobs of a man who hasn't eaten for three days!

Do you know what it means to go hungry? Have you ever looked at a man half dead from hunger, who sits down at a table and lifts to his mouth a piece of bread, a piece of meat, and chews the first mouthful with poor, weak teeth that wobble loosely in his gums? Have you ever seen that? And wasn't your heart pierced by sadness, by sympathy?

I really didn't want to talk so much about that wretched man. I let myself be carried away; I forgot all the rest—why, I don't know. But the truth is that in my life that wretch has been my only friend and I have been his. I have seen him cry and he has seen me cry, more than once. And I have seen my vice reflected in his, as in a mirror. And we also had in common the same trouble, we have suffered the same injury, we have borne the same shame.

No, he wasn't Ginevra's father; he had not given his blood to the veins of the creature who has done me so much harm.

I've always thought with restless, unsatisfied curiosity about the *real* father, the unknown man, the nameless one. Who indeed was he? Surely not a plebeian. A certain physical fineness, certain naturally elegant features, a certain cruelty and certain complicated perfidies, and, besides, the instinct for sexual pleasure, the facile disgust, that very special way of wounding, crushing a person with a laugh—all these things and others revealed the presence of aristocratic blood. Who was the father then? Perhaps an obscene old man like Marchese Aguti? Or perhaps a priest, one of those gallant cardinals who strewed offspring through all the households of Rome?

I've always thought about it. And sometimes there appeared in my imagination the figure of a man, not vague or shifting but rather well defined, with a particular physiognomy, a special expression, who seemed to live an extraordinarily intense life.

Of course, Ginevra must know or at least *sense* that she had nothing in common with her mother's husband. In fact, I was never able to detect in her eyes, when they were looking at the unfortunate man, any gleam of affection or, at the very least, of pity.

Instead, indifference, often disgust, contempt, aversion, even hatred appeared in her eyes when she looked at the poor man.

Ah, those eyes! They said everything; they said too many things in an instant, too many different things; and they made me forget and bewildered me. When by chance they met mine, they seemed made of steel, gleaming, impenetrable steel. Then, suddenly, they were covered as if by a pallid veil and lost all sharpness. Think, my dear sir, of a blade misted over by a breath . . .

But no, I cannot talk to you about my love; I can't, I can't talk about my love. Nobody will ever know how much I have loved; nobody. She has never known; she does not know now. I know that she has never loved me even for a day, even for an hour, an instant.

I knew it from the start; I knew it even when she gazed at me with those misted-over eyes. I didn't deceive myself. My lips never dared to proffer the tender question, the question all lovers repeat: "Do you love me?" And I remember how, being close to her, feeling myself swept by desire, I would think more than once: "Oh, if I could kiss her on the face and *she did not notice my kisses!*"

No, no, I cannot talk about my love. I will tell you the facts, the petty, ridiculous facts, the small miseries, the little moments of shame.

The marriage was set. Ginevra stayed on in Tivoli for another few weeks, and I would often travel out there on the tram. I would stay for half a day, a couple of hours. I was glad that she was living outside Rome. My constant worry was that some of my office colleagues might discover my secret. I employed no end of precautions, subterfuges, excuses, lies, to hide what I had done, what I was doing, what I was about to do. I didn't go to the usual places; I met all questions with evasive replies; I ducked into a shop, a doorway, a side street when I recognized from far away some of my old acquaintances from the *pensione.*

But one day I could not avoid Filippo Doberti. He overtook me, in fact, to put it more accurately, he sank his claws into me.

"Oh, Episcopo, so long since we've seen each other! What have you been doing? Have you been sick?"

I couldn't control my unreasonable agitation. I answered thoughtlessly, "Yes, I've been sick."

"It's obvious, obvious. It does look like that, you look green. But now what sort of life are you leading? Where do you dine? Where do you spend your evenings?"

I told some more lies and tried to keep from looking at his face.

"We were talking about you the other night," he went on. "Efrati said he saw you on Via Alessandrina, arm in arm with a drunkard."

"With a drunkard?" I cried. "Efrati's been dreaming."

Doberti burst out laughing.

"And you blush, eh? You're always looking for fine company, aren't you . . . A propos, have you heard the news about Wanzer?"

"No, I don't know anything."

"What! Don't you know he's in Buenos Aires?"

"I don't know a thing."

"Ah, poor Episcopo! Goodbye; I leave you. Take care of yourself, take care of yourself, you hear? You look pretty bad to me, pretty bad. Goodbye."

He turned up another street, leaving me in a state of agitation that I couldn't repress. All his words on that far-off evening when he had talked about Ginevra's mouth came back to my memory—precise, vivid. And I remembered other, crueler, more vulgar words. And again I saw that room lit by gas, I saw the long table at which all those men, their bellies now full, excited by the wine, a trifle hazy, were united by the same obscene interest. And again I heard the laughter, the hubbub, my name yelled by Wanzer, acclaimed by the others; and then the atrocious motto: "Episcopo and Associates Incorporated." And I thought that the horrible thing could actually come true . . .

It could come true! It could. —But is such an ignominy possible? Is it possible that a man, apparently not crazy, not moronic, not a half-wit, could let himself be trapped by such ignominy?

Ginevra returned to Rome. The marriage day was set.

Together with the pawnbroker, in a hansom cab, we drove around to find a small apartment, to buy the nuptial linen and other necessary furnishings—in short, to make all the usual preparations. I had withdrawn from the bank a deposit of fifteen thousand lire, my whole fortune as an orphan.

So we went around the city in an open carriage, all over Rome, triumphantly: I crouching on the small front seat, and the two women facing me, our knees touching. Whom did we meet? Who recognized us? Although I kept my head lowered, out of the corner of my eye I more than once saw someone waving at us from the sidewalk. A very elated Ginevra leaned out, turned, saying each time: "Look, it's Questori! Look, it's Micheli! And there's Palumbo, together with Doberti!"

And so the word spread. For my colleagues at the office, for my old *pensione* companions, for all my acquaintanceship, it was an occasion for endless merriment. In all their looks I could read irony, derision, malign hilarity, sometimes even a kind of insulting pity. Nobody spared me his little jab; and I, just to do something, would smile at each joke, producing the same grimace, like an impeccable automaton. What else could I have done? Act insulted? Fly into a rage? Give way to violence? Hand out a few slaps? Fling an inkwell at some of them? Brandish a chair? Fight a duel? —But all these things, wouldn't they too have been ridiculous, my dear sir?

One day at the office two "young wits" staged an interrogation. The dialogue was between a judge and Giovanni Episcopo. To the judge's question: "What profession?" Giovanni Episcopo replied: "A man who has no self-respect."

Another day I overheard these words: "He has no blood in his veins; not a single drop of blood. The little he did have Giulio Wanzer took out of his forehead. That's right, you can see that he hasn't got one drop of blood left . . ."

It was true, it was true.

But how did it happen that I suddenly decided to write a letter to Ginevra to ask her to release me from my promise? Yes, I wrote a letter to Ginevra to call off the marriage—I, I wrote her, with this very hand! And I took it to the post office myself.

It was evening, I recall. I walked past the post office a number of times, excited, like a man who is about to decide to commit suicide. Finally I stopped and slipped the letter into the slot; but it seemed I couldn't detach my fingers from it. Did I remain for a long time like that? I don't know. A guard tapped me on the shoulder, asked me: "What are you doing?"

I opened my fingers; let the letter drop in. And I nearly fainted, right there in the arms of the guard!

"Tell me," I stammered, almost whispering, "what can I do to get that letter back?"

And at night, the anguish I was prey to at night! The next morning, visiting the new apartment, the conjugal apartment already prepared to receive the married couple and suddenly rendered useless . . . turned into a mortuary.

Oh that sun, those beams of almost cutting sunlight on all those new, polished, untouched furnishings, giving off a warehouse smell, an unbearable smell . . .

That afternoon at five, leaving the office, I met Battista on the street and he said to me: "They want you at my house, right away."

We set out for it together. I was trembling, like a captured criminal. At a certain point I asked, in order to prepare myself: "What do they want?"

Battista knew nothing. He shrugged his shoulders. When we got to the street door, he left me. I climbed the stairs slowly, sorry now that I had obeyed the summons, thinking with insane fright of the pawnbroker's hands, those terrible hands. And upon reaching their landing, and raising my eyes and seeing the door open and on the threshold the pawnbroker all ready to pounce on me, I cried immediately: "It was a joke, a joke."

And so a week later the marriage took place. My witnesses were Enrico Efrati and Filippo Doberti. Ginevra and her mother had insisted that as many of my colleagues as possible be invited to the wedding feast, so as to dazzle the poor folk on Via Montanara and in the surrounding neighborhood. All my fellow diners from the *pensione* were present, I think.

I have a confused, vague, fragmented memory of the ceremony, the banquet, the crowd, those voices, that hubbub. I believe that at a certain point there passed over that table something akin to the ardent, impure breath which in the past had passed over that *other table.* Ginevra's face was ablaze and her eyes were amazingly bright. Many other eyes around her glistened; many smiles gleamed.

I remember how a heavy sadness swooped down on me, filled me, blurred my consciousness. And I can still see, down there at the end of the table, all the way down, at an incredible distance, poor Battista, who drank, drank, drank. . . .

At least one week! I don't say a year, a month, but just a week: at least the first week! —No, not at all; without the slightest pity. Not even a single day did she wait; she began immediately on the very night of our marriage to treat me cruelly.

If I were to live one hundred years I could never forget that burst of unexpected laughter that froze me to the core in the darkness of our bedroom and mocked my timidity and my awkwardness. I couldn't see her face in the dark; but for the first time I felt all her nastiness in that bitter, mocking, shameless laughter, which I had never heard before, unrecognizable. I felt that a viper lived at my side. Ah, my dear sir, she had laughter in her teeth, as snakes have poison.

Nothing, nothing served to make her less cruel: not my silent submission, my silent adoration, my pain, my weeping, nothing. I tried everything to touch her heart—to no avail. Sometimes she listened to me with a serious face and grave eyes, as if on the point of comprehending; and then, suddenly, she would begin to laugh, with that frightening laughter, that inhuman laughter which flashed more from her teeth than her eyes. And I stood there, annihilated . . .

No, no, it is impossible. My dear sir, permit me not to talk about it; let me pass over it. I can't speak about her. It's as if you had forced me to chew something bitter, something mortally, unbearably bitter. Can you not see that telling it twists my mouth?

One night—it was about two months after the wedding—

in my presence she had an indisposition, a sort of fainting fit
... You know; the usual scene ... And I who, all aquiver,
was secretly waiting for that revelation, that indication, that
fulfillment of my highest wish, that immense joy in my misfortune, I fell on my knees, as though before a miracle. —Was
it true? Was it true? —Yes, it was; she told me, confirmed it.
She had *another life* growing inside her.

You can't understand. Even if you were a father, you
couldn't understand the extraordinary emotion that then
overwhelmed my soul. Just imagine, sir, imagine a man who
has suffered everything a man can suffer under the sun, a man
on whom all the ferocity of other men has been relentlessly,
ceaselessly vented, a man who has never been loved by anyone
and yet in his depths preserves a great wealth of tenderness
and goodness, a wealth to be lavished, inexhaustibly; think,
sir, of the hopes of this man who looks forward to a creature
of his own blood, a son, a delicate, sweet being—oh infinitely
sweet—whose love he could win ... you understand?—finally to be loved!

It was September, I remember. Those were calm, golden
days, a trifle sad—you know very well—when the summer
dies. Always, always I was dreaming about him, about Ciro.

One Sunday, at the Pincio gardens, we ran into Doberti and
Questori. Both were very glad to see Ginevra; they joined us,
to continue their stroll. Ginevra and Doberti walked ahead, I
and the other man stayed behind. But those two ahead seemed
to trample on my heart at each step. They were talking a lot,
laughing together; and people turned to stare at them. Their
words came to me indistinctly through the waves of music
from the band, even though I strained my ears to catch something of what they were saying. My anguish was so apparent
that Questori called out to them: "Go slow! Don't get so far
away from us. Episcopo's here and he's dying of jealousy."

They joked, made fun of me. Doberti and Ginevra continued
to walk ahead, laughing and talking, amid the crashing music

which most likely exalted and intoxicated them, while I felt so unhappy that, walking along the parapet, I had the crazy idea of taking a sudden leap over the wall to end all that suffering once and for all. Also Questori, at a certain point, fell silent. I noticed that he was looking attentively at Ginevra's figure, and that his desire for her upset him. Other men, walking towards us, turned two or three times to look at her; and they had the very same glitter in their eyes. It was always that way, always, when she was out and there were others around: walking among them, it was as though she produced a furrow of impurity. It seemed to me that all around us the air was contaminated by that impurity; it seemed to me that none of them could get their minds off this woman they desired and thought easy to get, all, it seemed to me, had a single obscene image fixed in their brains. The waves of music spread out through the dense light; all the leaves on the trees glistened; to my ears the wheels of the carriages made a deafening racket. And in that light, that noise, that crowd, surrounded by that confused spectacle, seeing before me that woman who was gradually letting herself be captivated by that man, feeling the impurity all around—I thought with terrible anguish, with a wrench of all of my most delicate fibres, of the tiny creature that was starting to live, the little, unformed being who was perhaps at that very moment suffering the contractions of that womb from which he would start life . . .

Oh my God, my God, how that thought made me suffer! How many times that idea lacerated me before *he* was born! Do you understand? The thought of contamination . . . Do you understand? It was not so much the infidelity, the guilt that afflicted me, but the son who was not yet born. It seemed to me that something of that shame, that ugliness would cling to him, would certainly dirty him. Do you understand my horror?

And one day I had a surge of unusual courage. One day, when my suspicion was most tormenting, I found the courage to speak out.

Ginevra was at the window. I remember: it was All Saints' Day; the church bells were ringing; the sun was pouring down on the windowsill. Truly, the sun is the saddest thing in the universe. Don't you agree? The sun has always made my heart suffer. In all my most painful memories there is a little sunlight, a few yellow sunbeams as though around mortuary drapes. When I was a child they once left me for a few minutes in a room where my sister's corpse was laid out for viewing on a bed, surrounded by wreaths of flowers. I still feel I can see it, that poor white face all carved with purplish shadows, which, during his last moments, Ciro's face so much resembled . . .

Ah, what was I saying? My sister, yes, my sister lying on the bed, amid the flowers. Good; that's what I was saying. But why? Let me think a bit . . . Ah, here it is: I approached the window, dismayed; a small window looking out on the courtyard. The house opposite seemed to be uninhabited; one never heard human voices from it; nothing stirred. But on the roof a huge throng of sparrows kept up a heartbreaking chatter, continuous, endless; and beneath the gutter, on the gray wall, in the gray shadows, a streak of sunlight, a yellow line, straight, very sharp, was gleaming wickedly, with incredible intensity. I no longer dared turn around, and stared fixedly at the yellow line, as if under a spell; but I *felt* behind me—you understand?—while my ears were filled with the din of that immense chattering, I felt within me the frightening silence of the room, that cold silence which congeals around a corpse . . .

Oh, sir, how many times in my life have I seen that tragic streak of sunlight again! How many times!

Very well, what was I saying? So, Ginevra was standing at the window; the church bells were ringing; the sun washed into the room. There was also, on a chair, a wreath of evergreen with a black ribbon which Ginevra and her mother were going to take to the Verano cemetery to put on some relative's grave . . . —What a memory! you must be thinking. Yes, indeed, I now have a terrible memory!

Listen to me. She was eating a piece of fruit with that provocative sensuality she brought to everything she did. She didn't notice me, she wasn't aware that I was looking at her. And never had that profound indifference toward me pained me as it did on that particular day; never had I realized with such clarity that she did not belong to me, that she could belong to everyone, that in fact she would inevitably belong to everyone, and that I would never be able to lay claim to any right of love, even any right based upon force. And I kept looking at her, looking at her.

Has it ever happened to you, when looking for a long time at a woman, to suddenly lose all notion of her humanity, her social condition, the emotional ties which bind you to her, and *to see*, with an obviousness that terrifies you, the bestiality, the sheer femaleness, the blatant brutality of sex?

This is what I *saw* as I looked at her; and I realized that she existed only for the carnal, for an ignoble function. And another terrible truth rose in my mind: human life, all human preoccupations are based on ugliness—a horrible, horrible truth!

Well, what could I do? Nothing. But that woman bore in her womb *another life*, fed with her blood the mysterious creature who was my constant dream and highest hope, my adoration . . .

Yes, yes, even before *he* was born I adored him, I wept tenderly for him, I said unimaginable things to him in my heart. Think, think, my dear sir, of this martyrdom: not to be able to separate an innocent image from an ignominious one; to know that the object of your ideal worship is tied to a being from whom you expect the worst infamies. What would a zealot feel if he were forced to see the Sacrament on his altar covered by a filthy rag? What would he feel if he could not kiss the divine object save through a veil smeared with filth? What would he feel?

I don't know how to put it. Our words, our acts are always

vulgar, stupid, insignificant, whatever may be the grandeur of the emotion from which they spring. I had within me that day an immense confusion of painful, stifled feelings; and it was resolved in a cynical little dialogue, in buffoonery and humiliation. Do you want the facts? Do you want the conversation? Well, here it is.

So she was standing at the window, and I went over to her. I remained there for a bit, in silence. Then, with an enormous effort, I took her by the hand and asked her: "Ginevra, have you already deceived me?"

She looked at me, amazed, and said: "Deceived you? How?"

I asked her: "Do you already have a lover? Doberti . . . perhaps?"

She kept staring at me, for my whole body was trembling horribly.

"But what sort of scene is this? What's eating you now? Are you going off your rocker?"

"Answer me, Ginevra."

"Are you crazy?"

And while I was trying to seize her hand again, she shouted, pulling away from me: "Don't bother me! Enough!"

But I, like a madman, threw myself on my knees, holding her by the hem of her skirt.

"Please, I beg you, Ginevra, I beg you! Have pity on me, a little pity! Wait at least until the poor creature . . . my son . . . is born . . . Mine—isn't that true? Wait until he's born. Afterward, you can do whatever you want; and I'll keep quiet and bear everything. When your lovers come, I'll leave. If you order me to do it, I'll clean their shoes, in the next room . . . I'll be your servant, I'll be their servant; I'll endure it all. But wait, wait! First give me my son! Have pity on me . . ."

Nothing, nothing. In her look there was only a kind of mocking curiosity. She stepped back, repeating: "Are you going crazy?"

Then, since I continued to beg her, she turned her back on me, left and shut the door behind her. She left me there, kneeling on the floor.

There was the sun on the tiles; and that funeral wreath on the chair; and my sobs did not change a thing . . .

What can we change? Do our tears have any effect? —Each man is *just anyone*, to whom just anything can happen. This is the whole story; there is nothing else. Amen.

We are tired, my dear sir; I from telling my story, you from listening. After all, I have wandered a bit, perhaps too much; for—you know very well—this is not the question. The *real point* lies elsewhere. It will take another ten years to get to the *point*; ten years, ten centuries of pain, misery, and shame.

And yet, everything could still have been remedied. Yes, that night when I heard the howls of the woman giving birth, inhuman howls, unrecognizable, the howls of an animal in the slaughterhouse, I thought, with a convulsion of my entire being: "If only she died, oh, if only she would die and leave me the baby alive!" —She was howling so dreadfully that I thought: "Anyone who howls like that cannot die." —I had this thought; well, yes, I had this hope. But she didn't die; she survived in order to be the agent of my and my son's damnation.

He was my son, truly mine, the son of my flesh and blood. On his left shoulder he had the same peculiar mark I have had since birth. May God be blessed for that mark which helped me recognize my son!

Now, should I tell you about our ten years of affliction? Should I tell you everything once again? No, it can't be done. I would never reach the end. And then, perhaps, you wouldn't believe me; because what we suffered is incredible.

Here, in a few words, are *the facts*. My house was turned into a brothel. Sometimes I even met strange men, when I entered my house. I never got so far as to do what I had said—

I never cleaned their shoes in the next room; but in my own house I was nothing but a menial. Battista was less unhappy than I; Battista was less humiliated. No human humiliation could ever be compared to mine. Jesus would have wept all His tears for me; because I, among all men, have touched the bottom, the very depths of humiliation. Battista, believe me, could have pitied my state.

And it was comparatively easy, during the first years, when Ciro did not yet understand. But when I realized that his intelligence was awakening, when I saw that in that weak, frail creature intelligence was developing with prodigious speed, when I heard from his lips the first cruel question—oh, then I saw myself damned forever.

What could I do? How could I hide the truth from him? How could I save myself? I saw that I was truly lost.

His mother did not take care of him; she forgot about him for days on end; sometimes she would even make him go without necessary things; she even beat him now and then. And for long hours I was obliged to be away, far from him; I could not always give him the protection of my sympathy and tenderness; I couldl not make his life sweet, as I had dreamed, as I would have wished. The poor thing spent nearly all his time in the company of a maid in the kitchen.

I put him in school. In the morning I myself would take him there; in the afternoon, at five, I would go and pick him up; and then I didn't leave his side until he went to sleep. In short, he learned how to read, to write, he was well ahead of all his classmates; he made extraordinary progress. You could see the intelligence in his eyes. And when he looked at me with those large dark eyes, which already illuminated his entire face, and were so deep and sad, sometimes I felt within me a kind of dread; and I couldn't bear his look for long. Oh, sometimes in the evening at table, when his mother was there and silence descended upon us three . . . Then all my silent anguish would be reflected in those pure eyes of his.

But the really terrible days were still to come. My shame was too widely known, the scandal was too serious, *Signora Episcopo* was too famous. Besides, I neglected my duties at the office; my paperwork was filled with mistakes; on certain days my hand shook so violently that I wasn't able to write. My colleagues and superiors considered me a dishonored, degraded, brutalized, benumbed, cowardly man. I received two or three warnings; then I was suspended from the job; and finally I was dismissed in the name of outraged morality.

Until that day I had at least represented the value of my salary. From that day on I was not worth as much as a rag, a peel one finds on the street. Nothing can give you an idea of the ferocity, the rage my wife and her mother showed in torturing me. And yet they had taken from me the few thousand lire I had left; and the pawnbroker had opened up a dry goods store at my expense. It was on the basis of that small business that the family still managed to live.

They considered me a hateful parasite; I was put on a par with Battista. On certain nights I too found the door of my house locked; I too went hungry. And I adapted myself to all sorts of trades, all kinds of work, all the lowest, most menial tasks. To get my hands on a few cents, I worked as a messenger boy. I was a prompter in an operetta company. I was doorman at a newspaper, I worked as a clerk in an employment bureau. I did everything I got a chance to do, I crawled before all sorts of people, accepted all sorts of filth, bent my neck to every yoke.

Now, tell me: after all this travail, all these interminable days, did I not deserve some small respite, some little escape? In the evening, when I could, as soon as Ciro had closed his eyes, I would go out. Battista was waiting for me on the street, and we would go together to a wine shop, to drink.

Respite? Escape? Who has ever really known the significance of these words: *to drown one's sorrows in wine?* Ah, sir, I have always drunk because I felt that I was parched by an unquenchable thirst; but wine has never given me an instant of joy. We sat opposite each other, and we did not feel like talking. In fact in there nobody talked. Have you ever gone into one of those very quiet wine shops? The drinkers are all by themselves, their faces are tired, they prop their temple on the palm of a hand; and before them stands the glass. Their eyes stare at the glass but perhaps do not even see it. Is it wine? Is it blood? Yes, my dear sir, it is both.

Battista had become almost blind. One night, as we were walking together, he stopped under a street lamp and, palping his stomach, said to me: "You see how swollen it is?" Then, taking my hand to have me feel the hardness of the swelling, he said to me in a voice altered by fear: "What could it be?"

He had been in that condition for many weeks without revealing that he was sick. Some days later I took him to the hospital to be examined by the doctors. It was a tumor, indeed a group of tumors that were growing rapidly. One could attempt an operation. But Battista didn't want it, though he wasn't resigned to dying.

He dragged his illness about for a few more months; then he was forced to go to bed, and he never got up again.

What a long and atrocious death! The pawnbroker had shut the wretched man up in a kind of closet, a dark, stifling little hole, far away so they wouldn't have to hear his complaints. And every day I would go in there and Ciro wanted to come with me, wanted to help me . . . Oh, if you could have seen him, my poor child! How courageous he was in that work of charity, next to his father.

I would light a bit of candle to see a little more clearly, and Ciro would hold it. And then we saw that great deformed body which moaned, which did not want to die. No, it was not a man invaded by a disease; rather—how should I put it?—it was rather an image of disease, a thing outside nature, a monstrous being, living on its own, to which were attached two miserable, thin human arms, two miserable human legs, and a small, fleshless, reddish, revolting head. Horrible! horrible!—and Ciro would hold the light; and then into that taut flesh which shone like yellowish marble I injected some morphine with a rusty hypodermic syringe.

But that's enough, enough. Peace be with that poor soul. Now I must come to *the point.* I cannot digress any more.

Destiny! —Ten years had passed, ten years of a desperate life, ten years of hell. And one evening, at the table, in Ciro's presence, Ginevra said to me right out of the blue: "Did you know? Wanzer's come back."

Certainly I didn't turn pale: because, you see, my face had long been this color, unchanging, which not even death will change and I will take it with me just like this under the ground. But I remember that I couldn't manage to move my tongue.

She stared at me with her sharp, cutting look, which already filled me with the same apprehension an extremely sharp knife inspires in the pusillanimous. I realized that she was staring at my forehead, at the scar. She wore an irritating, intolerable smile. And she said to me, alluding to the scar, knowing she would hurt me: "You haven't forgotten Wanzer, have you? After all he did leave a fine souvenir on your forehead . . ."

Then Ciro also stared at my scar. And I could read on his face all the questions he wanted to ask me. He wanted to ask me: "How is that? Didn't you once tell me that you fell and cut yourself? Why did you lie? And who is this man that gave you the scar?" But he lowered his eyes again and didn't say a word.

Ginevra went on: "I ran into him this morning. He recognized me immediately. At first I didn't recognize him, because he has let his beard grow. He knew nothing about us. But he told me he'd been looking for you for three or four days. Our friend wants to see you again. He must have made his fortune in America, judging at least from how he looked . . ."

As she talked she continued staring at me and continued smiling inexplicably. From time to time Ciro cast a quick glance at me; and *I felt that he felt I was suffering.*

After a pause, Ginevra added: "He's coming tonight, quite soon."

It was raining heavily outside. And it seemed to me that that steady, monotonous noise did not come from outside but rather from within me, as if I had swallowed a large dose of quinine. And suddenly I lost my sense of reality; and I was surrounded by that *offensive atmosphere* which I've already mentioned once before, and again I had profoundly *the feeling of the repetitiveness of what was happening and was about to happen.* Do you understand me? I thought again that I was again witnessing the inevitable repetition of a series of events which had already taken place. Were Ginevra's words *new?* Was the anxiety of my waiting *new?* Was it *new*, that malaise produced by my son's gaze turned too often, perhaps involuntarily, to my forehead, to this cursed scar? No, *nothing was new.*

All three of us around that table were silent. Ciro's face expressed an unusual anxiety. There was something extraordinary in that silence: a profound, very obscure significance which my mind could not succeed in penetrating.

Suddenly, the doorbell rang.

We looked at each other, I and my son. Ginevra said to me: "It's Wanzer. Go and let him in."

I went. The act was in my person, so to speak, but the will was outside my person.

Wanzer entered.

Must I describe the scene? Must I tell you his words again? There was nothing extraordinary in what he did and said, in what we did and said. Two old friends met again, embraced, exchanged the usual questions and the usual answers: that was the appearance.

He wore a large rainproof cape with a hood, thoroughly

drenched by the rain, glistening. He seemed taller, broader, prouder. He wore three or four rings on his fingers, a pin in his tie, a gold bracelet. He spoke without embarrassment, as a man completely sure of himself. Was this perhaps the thief who had returned to his country after the expiration of the statute of limitations?

Among other things he said to me, looking me over carefully: "You look much older. But Signora Ginevra is even younger looking than before . . ."

He stared at Ginevra from beneath half-closed lids, a sensual smile on his face. He already desired her and was thinking that he would possess her.

"But to tell the truth," he added, "wasn't I the person who arranged this marriage? Of course it was me. Don't you remember? Ha, ha, ha! Remember?"

He began laughing and Ginevra laughed too; and I also tried to laugh. I was really playing Battista's role very well, I believe. That poor Battista—peace to his soul—had bequeathed to me his convulsed, stupid way of laughing. Peace to his soul!

But Ciro kept looking incessantly at me, at his mother, and at the stranger. And his gaze when it rested on Wanzer took on a hard expression I had never seen before.

"He looks a lot like you, this boy," Wanzer continued. "He looks more like you than his mother."

He stretched out a hand to caress his hair. But Ciro jumped, avoided that hand with so proud, so violent a movement of his head that Wanzer was dumbfounded.

"Take this," his mother cried, "you little boor!"

The slap resounded loudly.

"Take him away, take him away immediately," she ordered me, pale with anger.

I got up; I obeyed. Ciro hung his head, but he didn't cry. His teeth were clenched and I could just hear the gritting sound they made.

When we were in our room, I lifted his head as gently as I could; and I saw on his poor emaciated cheek the imprint of her fingers, the red mark left by the slap. My eyes filled with tears.

"Does it hurt? Tell me: does it hurt very much? Ciro, Ciro, answer me. Does it hurt you very much?" I asked him, bending with desperate tenderness over that poor offended cheek which I wanted to cleanse not with my tears but with some miraculous balsam.

"Ciro, Ciro, my son, answer me!"

He didn't answer. He jerked away from me, walked to his bed and began undressing without a word. I started to help him with almost timid, humble gestures, feeling myself die at the thought that he might have a grievance against me. I knelt before him to untie his shoelaces; and I lingered there on the tile floor, bent over his feet, holding my very heart at his feet, a heart that weighed like a ton of lead, that I felt I could never lift up again.

"Papa, Papa," he burst out suddenly, grasping me at the temples.

And he had the dreadful question on the tip of his tongue.

"Speak, go ahead! Speak to me!" I implored him, still at his feet.

He stopped, didn't say another word. He got into bed, drew up the covers, sank his head into the pillow. And, after a bit, his teeth began to chatter, as would happen on certain bitterly cold winter mornings. My caresses didn't calm him, my words did not seem to do him any good.

Ah, sir, anyone who has gone through what I did then deserves to go to heaven.

Did only an hour go by? —At last it seemed that Ciro had become quieter. He closed his eyes as though to fall asleep; gradually his face became more composed; the trembling ceased. I remained next to the bed, immobile.

Outside it continued to rain. From time to time a flail of

rain would shake the windowpanes; and Ciro would open his eyes wide, and then shut them again.

"Sleep, sleep! I am here," I repeated each time. "Sleep, my dear son!"

But I was afraid; I couldn't stifle my fear. Above me, all around me, I felt a terrible menace. And each time I repeated: "Sleep, sleep!"

A sharp, lacerating shriek burst over our heads. And Ciro sat up in bed, grabbed my arm, gasping, dismayed.

"Papa, Papa, did you hear that?"

And both of us, hugging each other tightly, overwhelmed by the same feeling of terror, listened, waited.

Another, longer shriek, like that of a person being murdered, reached us through the ceiling; and then another and even longer, even more heart-rending, which I now recognized, which I had heard before on a night long ago . . .

"Calm yourself, calm yourself. Don't be afraid. It's a woman giving birth upstairs. You know her? Signora Bedetti . . . Calm yourself, Ciro. It's all right."

But the howls continued, piercing the walls, piercing our ears, becoming more and more bestial. It was like the death-throes of a clumsily slaughtered animal. I had a vision of blood.

Then, instinctively, both of us stopped our ears with our hands, waiting for the agony to end.

The howls ceased; the pelting crash of the rain began again. Ciro lay down under the bedclothes again, shut his eyes. I repeated: "Sleep, sleep. I won't go away."

An indefinite amount of time went by. I was in the grip of my destiny, like a defeated man at the mercy of an inexorable conqueror. I was lost now, lost, inexorably lost.

"Giovanni, come. Wanzer's leaving."

Ginevra's voice? I was startled; I realized that Ciro had also been startled, but his eyelids had not moved. So then he wasn't asleep yet? —I hesitated before obeying. Ginevra opened the door to the room and repeated: "Come. Wanzer's leaving."

Then I got up, tiptoed out of the room, hoping that Ciro would not notice.

When I reappeared before that man I could read clearly the impression I made upon him. A dying man, still kept alive by some unnatural force—that is how I must have seemed to him. But he had no pity for me.

He looked at me, spoke to me in the same way as in the past. He was the master who had found his servant again. I thought: "During all the time I was in there, what did they say, what did they do, what have they *plotted* together?" I noticed a change in both of them. When she spoke to him, Ginevra's voice had a different accent than before. When it rested on him, Ginevra's gaze was covered *with that veil . . .*

"It's raining too hard," she said. "You must go down and find a carriage . . ."

You understand? It was an order given to me. Wanzer didn't object. It seemed quite natural to him that I should go and search for a carriage. Hadn't he already called me back into his service? —And I was barely able to stand! And certainly both of them could see that I was barely able to stand.

Inconceivable cruelty. But what could I do? Refuse? Begin a rebellion just at that moment? I could have said: "I don't feel well." Instead I didn't utter a word, I took my hat and umbrella and left.

On the stairs the lamps were already doused. But in the darkness I could see a multitude of flashes and gleams, and in my brain there appeared one after the other, with the rapidity of lightning bolts, strange, absurd, disconnected thoughts. I remained for a moment on the landing, thinking that I could hear madness coming through the shadows. But nothing happened. Distinctly, I heard Ginevra laugh; I heard noises from the tenants above. I struck a match; I went down the stairs.

As I was just about to go out on the street, I heard Ciro's

voice calling for me. I actually had a *real* sensation then, like the laughter, like the noises. I turned, climbed back up the stairs in an instant with inexplicable ease.

"So soon?" Ginevra cried, when she saw me reappear.

I couldn't speak because of my great agitation. Finally I blurted out desperately: "I can't . . . I must go in the other room . . . I feel sick."

And I rushed to my son.

"Did you call me?" I immediately asked as I came in. I found him sitting up in bed, as if he were listening. He replied: "No, I didn't call you."

But I felt he wasn't telling me the truth.

"Perhaps you called me while you were dreaming. Weren't you asleep before?"

"No, I wasn't asleep."

He looked at me, uneasy, suspicious.

"What's the matter with you?" he asked me. "Why are you panting? What did you do?"

"Come, be calm, Ciro," I begged, not replying to his questions, stroking him. "I'm staying here with you; I won't leave again. Now sleep, sleep!"

He let himself fall back on the pillow with a sigh. Then he closed his eyes in order to please me, pretending to go to sleep. But a few minutes later he opened them again, opened them wide. And he said, in an indefinable tone: *"Hasn't he left yet?"*

From that night on, the tragic presentiment was always there. It was a kind of vague, mysterious horror, which condensed in the depths of my being, where the light of consciousness can never reach. Among all the many abysses I have found within myself, that abyss remained inscrutable and seemed the most frightening of all. Continually I watched it, I would almost say that I craned over it with tremendous anxiety, hoping that a sudden flash might illuminate it for me, might reveal it to me completely. Sometimes I felt that I could hear this *unknowable* thing rise little by little and approach the zone of consciousness, almost touch it, graze it, then suddenly return to the depths, plunge back into the darkness, leaving me with an extraordinary perturbation. Do you understand? Imagine, my dear sir, so as to understand me, imagine that you are standing at the brink of an incalculably deep well. Down to a certain point the well is illuminated by natural light; but you know that in the lower darkness is hidden some unknown, terrible thing. You can't see it, but you hear it move around confusedly. And little by little this thing rises up, reaches even to the borders of the darkness where you can almost make it out. Just a bit more, just a bit more—and you will see it. But the thing halts, draws back, vanishes; it leaves you shaken, disappointed, terrified . . .

No, no . . . Childishness, childishness . . . You can't understand.

Well, *the facts*—here they are. A few days later Wanzer had taken possession of my house, he had established himself in it as a boarder! And as a result, I continued to be the trembling servant. Do I at this late date have to tell you how these things went? Do I have to explain them to you? Do they seem strange to you, perhaps? And must I enumerate all of Ciro's sufferings?—his silent, livid angers, his bitter words to which almost any poison would have been preferable; and his sudden cries and sobs in the night, which made my hair stand on end; and the cadaverous immobility of his body in bed, frightful; and his tears, his tears, those tears that sometimes began suddenly trickling down from his eyes which remained open and pure, which did not become inflamed or red . . . Ah, my dear sir, one had to see that child weep to know *how the soul weeps.*

We deserved heaven. Oh Jesus, Jesus, haven't we deserved Your Heaven?

*   *   *

Thank you, thank you. I can continue. Let me go on at once, otherwise I'll never get to the end.

We're getting closer—you understand—we're getting closer; we're already there. What is the date today? The twenty-seventh of July. Well, it was the ninth of July, this month! It seems a century ago; it seems yesterday.

I was in the back room of a grocer's, sitting at a desk working on the accounts, worn out from weariness and the heat, eaten up by flies, nauseated by the smell of the spices. It was most likely about three in the afternoon. I would often interrupt my work to think of Ciro, who at that time was feeling more unwell than usual. I was brooding in my heart over his constitution consumed by suffering, thin and pale as a candle.

Take note, sir, of one thing. From a tiny window—set in the wall to which my back was turned, and therefore above my head—slanted down *a beam of sunlight*.

And notice, my dear sir, these other things. A delivery boy, young and fat, was sleeping stretched out on the sacks, inert; and the flies were buzzing above him, countless flies as though around a carcass. The boss, the grocer, entered and went towards a corner where there was a basin. His nose was bleeding and, as he walked stooped over in order not stain his shirt, blood dripped on the floor.

Then followed a number of minutes of a silence so deep that it seemed a suspension of life. Not a customer entered; not a carriage passed by; the delivery boy wasn't snoring any more.

Suddenly I heard Ciro's voice: "Is Papa here?"

I saw him appear before me—in that squalid place, among those sacks, kegs, piles of soap, while he was so delicate, almost diaphanous, looking like a pure spirit!—I saw him appear before me like an hallucination. His forehead was drenched with sweat, his lips were trembling; but he seemed animated by an almost savage energy.

"What are you doing here?" I asked. "At this hour? What is the matter?"

"Come, Papa, come."

"But what's happened?"

"Come, come with me."

His voice was hoarse but determined.

I put aside the work I had been doing, saying: "I'll be back soon."

And I went out with him, terribly upset, my legs unsteady. We were on Via del Tritone. We turned up the street in the direction of Piazza Barberini which was a lake of white fire and looked deserted. I don't know if it was really deserted, for all I could see was the fire. Ciro clutched my hand.

"Well, won't you tell me? What's happened?" I asked for the third time, still fearful of what he was going to say.

"Come, come with me. Wanzer has beaten her . . . beaten her."

His fury made his voice choke in his throat.

He seemed unable to say anything more. He quickened his pace, dragging me along.

"I saw it," he went on. "From my room I heard them shouting; I heard what they were saying . . . Wanzer cursed her, called her every name you can think of . . . Yes, all the names . . . Do you hear? And I saw him when he jumped on her, his hands flying, yelling . . . 'Take this! And take this!' And he called her all the names . . . you know them . . ."

That voice was unrecognizable: raucous, shrill, sibilant, broken by the suffocation of so furious a hatred that I thought with terror: "Here, now he's going to fall; he's going to fall right here and lie stricken on the sidewalk."

But he didn't fall; he continued walking quickly, dragging me along beneath that ferocious sun.

"Do you think I hid? Do you think I just stood there and was afraid? No, no, I wasn't afraid. I went up to him; I began yelling at him; I grabbed him by the legs, I bit his hand . . .

that's all I could do . . . He knocked me down on the floor; then he jumped on Mama again, grabbed hold of her hair . . . Oh, what a coward, what a coward!"

He broke off, choked.

"What a coward! He pulled her by the hair; pulled her to the window . . . He wanted to throw her out . . . But then he let her go . . . "I'm leaving, if I don't, I'll kill you.' That's what he said. And he left; ran out of the house . . . Oh, if I only had a knife!"

He broke off again, gasping. We were on street past San Basilio, deserted. Afraid that I would fall, that I would see him fall, I begged him to stop: "Stop for a while, Ciro! Let's rest here in the shade for a little. You can't go on like this."

"No, we've got to get there quick, we've got to get there in time . . . Suppose Wanzer comes back to the house to kill her? . . . Mama was afraid, she was afraid he'd come back and kill her. I heard her tell Maria to get the suitcase, and put her clothes in it, so she could leave Rome right away . . . go to Tivoli, I think . . . to stay with Aunt Amalia . . . We've got to get there in time. Would you let her go? Would you?"

He stopped, only to look straight in my face and to hear my answer. I stammered: "No . . . no . . ."

"And will you let *him* come back in the house? Won't you say anything to him? Won't you do anything to him?"

I didn't answer. And he didn't realize I was dying of pain, of shame. He didn't see it; for, after an interval of silence, he suddenly yelled in a different tone from before, his voice shaking with deep emotion: "Papa, Papa, you aren't afraid, are you? You aren't afraid of *him*, are you?"

I stammered: "No . . . no . . ."

And we continued walking toward the house in the hot sun, over the plots of wasteland around Villa Ludovisio, through chopped down trees, piles of bricks, deep lime pits, which dazzled and attracted me. —Better, better to die burnt alive in one of those lime pits, I thought, than to confront the unknown event. —But Ciro had grabbed me by the hand again and was pulling me along blindly toward my destiny.

We got there; we went up the stairs.

"Have you got the key?" Ciro asked me.

I had it. I opened the door. Ciro went in first; he called: "Mama, Mama."

No answer. The house was empty, full of light and a suspicious silence.

"She's left already?" Ciro said. "*What will you do?*"

He went into a room. He said: "Here's where it happened."

An overturned chair still lay there. On the floor I saw a broken hairpin and a red bow. Ciro, who was looking at the same spot, stooped down and picked up some very long hairs and showed them to me.

"You see?"

His fingers and his lips trembled; but his energy was exhausted. His strength was gone. I saw him sway, then he fainted in my arms. I called to him: "Ciro, Ciro, my boy!"

He did not stir. I don't know how I managed to surmount the faintness that I felt too. One thought flashed in my head: "What if Wanzer comes in now?" I don't know how I succeeded in lifting the poor creature, to carry him all the way to his bed.

He came to. I said to him: "You have got to rest. Do you want me to undress you? You have a fever. I'll get the doctor. Now I'll undress you slowly. All right?"

I said these words, I performed these acts, as if nothing else was to happen, as if the ordinary things in life, the care of my son, were to occupy me for the rest of that day. But I felt, I knew, I was sure that it wouldn't be that way, that it couldn't be that way. But a single thought was actually digging into my brain, the anxiety of a single expectation was twisting my guts. The horror, already accumulated in my very depths, was now spreading throughout my being, was making my hair bristle.

I repeated: "Let me undress you and put you to bed."

Ciro said: "No; I want to keep my clothes on."

His new voice, his new words, also grave, did not interrupt within me the incessant repetition of that simple and terrible question of his: *"What will you do?"*

"What will you do? What will you do?"

I could conceive of nothing at all. It was impossible for me to settle on a course of action, imagine a resolution of the situation, reflect on an attack, a defense. Time passed, and nothing happened. —I should have gone to get the doctor for Ciro. But would Ciro let me go out? If he agreed, he would be left all alone. I might meet Wanzer on the stairway. *And then?* Or Wanzer might return during my absence. *And then?*

In accordance with Ciro's demands, I must not let him come back into the house, I must tell him something, do something. Well, I could have locked the door from the inside with the bolt. Not being able to open the door with his key, Wanzer would have pulled on the bell-rope, would have knocked, made a racket, furiously. *And then?*

We waited.

Ciro was lying in bed on his back; I was sitting alongside him and holding one of his hands, pressing my forefinger on his pulse. The beats were getting faster, much, much faster.

We didn't talk; we thought we were listening to all the noises and we weren't listening to anything but the sound of our blood. In the window's opening the blue sky foundered; the swallows swooped past, as if about to enter; the curtains swelled as though a gust of wind had filled them, on the tile floor the sun traced the window's rectangle exactly, and the shadows of the swallows played across it. For me all these things had ceased to be real, they were only an appearance; they were no longer life, but rather simulated life. Even my anguish was imaginary. —How much time went by?

Ciro said to me: "I'm very thirsty. Get me some water."

I got up to get him a drink. But the bottle on the table was empty. I took it and said: "I'm going into the kitchen to fill it."

I left the room, went to the kitchen, placed the bottle under the faucet.

The kitchen was next to the entrance hall. Quite distinctly I heard the sound of a key being turned in the lock. I was petrified *by the absolute impossibility of moving.* But I heard the door open, I recognized Wanzer's step.

He called out: "Ginevra!"

Silence. He took a few more steps. Again he called: "Ginevra!"

Silence. More steps. Obviously he was now looking through the rooms for her. *The absolute impossibility of moving.*

Suddenly I heard my son cry out, a savage scream, which instantly dissolved my rigidity. My eyes ran to a long knife gleaming on the bread-box; and, at the same moment, my right hand darted out to grasp it and a prodigious strength filled my arm; and I felt myself swept to my son's doorway, like a whirlwind; and I saw my son clinging with feline fury to Wanzer's huge body, and I saw that man's hands on my son . . .

Two, three, four times I drove the knife into his back, right up to the handle.

Ah sir, please, please, don't leave me, don't leave me alone! Before evening, I shall die; I promise you that I shall die. Then you can go, close my eyes and go. No, I'm not asking even for this; I, I myself, before I breathe my last, will close them.

Do you see my hand. It touched those lids; and it turned yellow . . . But I wanted to lower them, because every now and then Ciro would stiffen in his bed and cry: "Papa, Papa, he's looking at me."

But how could he look at him if he was covered up? Can the dead look through sheets, perhaps?

And the left eyelid wouldn't close, it was cold, cold . . .

*   *   *

All the blood! Can a man contain a sea of blood? One can barely see the veins, they are so fine one can barely see them. And yet . . . I didn't know where to put my feet; my shoes were soaked through like two sponges—it's strange, eh?—like two sponges.

One person, and so much blood; and the other, not even a drop: a lily . . . like a lily . . .

Oh, my God, a lily! So there are still white things in this world?

All the lilies, so many, so many!

But you see, you see, sir, what I feel? What good things I am still able to feel?

Yes, before evening, before evening.

A swallow flew in . . .
Let it come in . . . that swallow . . .

Rome, January 1892

LEDA WITHOUT SWAN

Leda Without Swan

I HEARD all this yesterday just before nightfall on the flat pontoon which the low receding tide was little by little leaving behind it, while all around we heard the rustle of the hidden life of the sands and from time to time the horned owl complaining to the brush along the shore, luxuriant with weeds and marine rushes. I heard it from Desiderio Moriar, most exquisite artist, innocent of works and fame, who knows as do I that in living even more than in reading nothing is as precious as attentiveness.

But his voice resembles one of those turbid days in March, all silver flashes, sudden gusts of wind, crashes of rain and hail, and pauses pregnant with melodiousness, when things not yet born seem even more powerful than those which have already come into life. And this voice flows from a mouth avid and dissatisfied like that of a greedy child who, clutching a crimped counterfeit coin, lingers before the window of a pastry shop. And at certain words his dark glance darts between the flickering lashes with a disquietude that seems to set fire to a drop of blood in the corner of the lid close to the nose, like that living touch of cinnabar one sees in certain Mannerist portraits. Sometimes, though, his eyes seem to retract their gaze deep inside themselves and to float on some remote dream-waters like two smooth hazelnut shells.

Nor is he, when seen fullface, the same man he reveals in profile. To an adventurous sensuality, intolerant of constraint but bent on discriminating despite desire's suddenness, he seems to oppose when turning to face you the abnegated will of one who unfailingly discovers the same dreadful emptiness behind both the most facile and the most difficult of life's caprices. His beautiful hands, now fluttering like those of a great violinist between bow and fingerboard, now boneless and soft like those of a famous couturier preparing to fit a *grande dame* for a dress, with a brisk gesture drew again and again a crepitating sound from their fingers as if to test the pitch of the concealed skeleton. Then certain rapid, sensitive quivers passed over his cheek bones, while his temples and chin reminded me of the extremely tender skin of a thoroughbred horse and, at times, even of a rabbit's comical, endearing nose.

What an admirable living instrument with which to assess by a gesture, an inflection, a pause, a look, the values of visible and invisible things!

Yesterday evening, prompted by the boyishness and magical that are mingled in him, he said: "Isn't the night omnipresent and perpetual? If I clench my fist under the full sun of noon, why, look, I create night in the hollow of my palm." And so, as he told the story, he constantly made me feel that miraculous darkness on which shapes and events are traced, those divine shadows that fill the fold of a skirt or the fissure in a heart.

I despair of reproducing even approximately his lively art, and so in recounting some of his stories I try to imagine that the incidents happened to me personally, that I am the protagonist.

I was going through one of those days of tedium which, they say, were invented by Nero's tutor for ambiguous temperaments, days when life's active goodness withdraws from the circles of the soul like water from the pond of a fulling press or mill, leaving behind the drained ditches cluttered with debris and with filth clinging to the inert mechanism.

One seems to scent an odor of fermenting slime in one's every thought. One's body is itself unsheathed, as it were, a broken stump: it tries to hold itself upright, to lean against something, to find respite in some enduring attitude, but it resembles those battered old crucified Christs stripped of the cross that in antique shops seem nailed to new torments, no matter where they stand and no matter what contraption they are put up against.

The season also contributed to all that misery, for on the barrens it rained and didn't rain. A sieve-like cloud sprinkled a stretch of sand with fat, sparse drops that were almost lukewarm and seemed to dribble from a ladle. But beyond the moist band you could make out bone-dry sand and farther on another sprinkled patch and farther yet another strip of dryness, so that the earth too seemed to be unwell, like those pregnant women whose skin feels hot and cold in spots while within at an indefinable depth something shapeless is startled.

I was standing at the gate of the garden, just about to part from one of those sweet tiresome creatures who, after encountering Dante's youthful vision, insist on carrying about on their sleeves, endlessly, their disappointed love—"wrapped lightly in a blood-red cloth"—for they cannot resolve to bury it and would have us feast on their dear heart as if it were pure spirit, and yet it is not consumed. *Vide cor meum.*

The sound of that well-known lamentation reached me like the drone left by quinine in the ear of a malaria patient after an attack, and I stood there neither in nor out, because the stone slab of the threshold lay between us strewn with yellow pollen. And I saw that wild dust cling to the fresh paint of the new gate, fill the interstices, envelop on a cross-bar of that not wholly dead pinewood a bubble of resin which swelled like a

157

blister rising on the palm of a hand before turning into a callus.

A small terracotta crock hanging from a stripped tree had suddenl received so much resin at the first upsurge of the sap that it had overflowed with long filaments of an almost sugar-like aspect; and seeing it I had the urge to offer her a mouthful of it, so as to besmear her vexatious tongue and glue the inopportune words to her palate. Here and there, beneath the limpness of a milky, irresolute cloud, the birds sang off-key like listless choirboys. And all of life had for me the quality of one of those allegories that long ago my rhetoric teacher used to propose to us at the long examination bench. And I had done such a shabby job of writing it that, by way of punishment, I was condemned to carry the sheet attached to my back by two pins.

Then, as I was heading towards the Ville d'Hiver along the paths through the woods, I thought with envy of the few shepherds left on the barrens—the last descendants of those extraordinary old men who, on their tall stilts, used to cross the ponds and marshes of that sandy wasteland and could, with their long strides, go as fast as a galloping horse in the Pyrenees.

I had met one of them in the brush a few days before. The legendary poles reduced in length to two modest stumps, his faded green umbrella and brownish satchel slung over his shoulder, his mushroom-shaped beret pulled well down over his ears, he spent the entire day absolutely immobile, leaning on his cane, busy with his knitting needles, as untouched by worries as his dog, as indifferent to the flight of time as an hour-glass, his tongue stored in the silence of his saliva like a sardine preserved in the oil of its tin.

Far from loved or no longer loved eyes, the light seems to be different. To enter our room, the sky waits for all the lights to be extinguished.

In between the freshly scarred pine trees (from a distance their trunks looked as though they had nailed to them those reddish goat-hides that usually hang in front of butcher shops) I made out the varicolored town of Phthisis smoldering beneath a clammy, oven-like warmth, just as repulsive as the air one inhales in certain Turkish baths transported to the West, where fat men sweat with zest and anguish, reading the newspaper of their persuasion spread out over their dripping bellies.

The villas seemed gracefully built of papier-mâché and perforated tinfoil by a mediocre, moderately republican architect with a goatee on his chin and a flourish in his tie, who has tried to blend together in his hospitable art the spirit of the Italian Riviera and that of the Lake of Lucerne, both equally soothing.

Inscribed in Art Nouveau letters each façade dutifully bore its name gleaned from mythology, botany, civic glories, or sentimental idiocy. Each interior undoubtedly contained its vase with artificial flowers covered by a glass bell, its large, warty conch, its statuette of Joan of Arc in black plumbago armor, and its cuckoo clock to summon happiness or death.

Mounds of shawls and blankets, stirred from time to time by a fit of coughing, rested on long wicker chairs behind crystal-clear windowpanes which, like the tanks of an aquarium, seemed to enclose a far-off world. Along the white roadway an interminable file of caterpillars descending from God knows where moved toward eternity with a slight and eerie contraction of its myriads of rings. Their fuzzy nests at the tips of numerous branches presented the image of a hurt hand swathed in shredded cloth. A piano up there which had inherited from a distant relation the soul of a barrel organ, played one of those pieces that carry a number printed above each note to guide each finger to the proper key; and an unknown romantic ancestor awakening somewhere inside me seemed anxious to know whether the sheet was adorned by a black gondola, a weeping willow, or an Ossianic harp, and whether the title of the song was "The Sigh of an Exile" or "The Last Day of Mary Stuart."

An atrocious and infantile thought flashed through my mind: "If I let out a scream, all the patients will rush to their windows and stay there showing me their faces, which are all the same and pocked full of holes like the cork floats dangling from a seine net hung out to dry after the day's fishing."

In the frame of a curtainless window, beyond the glass, flitted something that looked like a pale gesture shooing away a fly or beckoning to me. Surely nothing but a thin sheet of glass separated me from death—and that unknown hand was about to smash it.

I remembered how a cousin of mine at Nice had once had the good fortune of being splendidly loved for an entire afternoon by a canoness from Krakow who then expired that same night.

But my unique and doomed woman's door was closed; and in the small garden a maid servant wearing a bonnet and wooden clogs was washing a chestnut poodle whose color seemed to melt under the lather as if it were made of chocolate, while the dirty water crept down the narrow garden path and into the street towards me, like a crippled hand groping along the ground, growing larger and broader as it searched for something I had lost.

I could not imagine what.

I expected someone behind me to call out eagerly: "Turn around, Sir, look, you've dropped this" whatever it was. But nobody breathed a word; nor did that dripping hand rise from the ground to return to me whatever I had lost; it went on feeling its way until it reached the gutter, breaking up a seminar of caterpillars assembled at a sort of hemp stalk that looked at once like the sloughed-off skin of a snake and the tiny cells of an emptied, dried-out honeycomb.

Meanwhile a small cart shaped like a basket was moving

toward me on its three wheels, pushed by a mustachioed, gray-haired man who performed that office with the dignity peculiar to survivors of the nation's glorious battlefields and to professional rescuers assigned to drownings and conflagrations. Inside the basket lay an old woman who despite her moribund appearance retained some mysterious gleam of fury in a pair of eyes at war with the universe, eyes which bulged at the top of two wizened pouches, recalling the ferocity of the octopus attached to his melancholy sack, and it wasn't quite clear by what accident the eight tentacles stippled with suction cups were missing. At a few paces from me the cart came to a halt so abruptly that I was startled.

A line of grubs was crossing the street, and moved by some obscure impulse of compassion, revulsion or superstition, the worthy trundler was trying to find an ingenious way to avoid the holocaust. When, from behind, he pressed down on the rim of the basket to raise the front wheel, on feeling herself being bounced up and down in that manner the old woman rallied all her energies to spew the venom of her two feelerless polyps at the bumbling fellow. The wheel dropped and cut into the hairy, soft entrail. The two rear wheels and the two shoes followed, completing the resection.

I turned away in disgust and saw a boy laughing behind a fence. He had porcine eyes smothered in a face so huge and lustrous that it seemed to me on the verge of bursting open, as though, through a hole at the nape of the neck, someone were continually stuffing it with lard and ground meat.

Is not the maggot-ridden carcass of a mongrel dog upon a pile of garbage an almost enjoyable sight when compared to certain apparitions of human ugliness dressed up in clothes?

A strong gust of wind swept over my head, one of those sudden breaths that seem to come from the miraculous frontier of another life which can be perceived only at times through certain flashes of remembrance or incandescent flickers of anxiety, when the spirit, perhaps remembering, perhaps presaging, struggles in vain to escape from the habits, manias, lies, grimaces, fears—the innumerable contagions that make up our lives.

Pollen seemed to steam from the shaken branches and gild the lacerated cloud which suddenly allowed me a glimpse of the most angelic countenance among all those faces of the air, framed between two edges that looked like linen bands dusted with that sylvan gold.

And even before I heard the faltering note of a novice nightingale I felt that at the passing of that breath the pine tree, like a wind instrument, swelled with music from foot to crown.

And that gracile note sufficed to change everything.

So I hastened to the town, thinking that music was perhaps about to interpret the enigma of all those images introduced in me by an obscure, cruel sense superadded to my normal vision.

A young musician from the *Schola Cantorum,* trained to emulate the grace and power of the ancient Italian harpsichord players, had written to me with proud courtesy that at his concert that day he would play only for me.

An excellent precaution, I might add, for I realized upon entering the Casino that the greater part of the local swine— *more biblico*—were not attracted by pearls.

The audience was small, scattered through the vast hall which was entirely and lavishly adorned with murals in that Turkesque style which has the uncommon quality of inflaming the imagination of the lower ranks of the soldiery in brothel parlors. The only thing lacking was the scent of those famous aromatic tablets called "pastilles of the seraglio." The local Euterpe, a bony, brusque female, assigned to guide each of the rare auditors to his seat, thrust her hand from time to time into the pocket of her smock, arousing the hope that she might be reaching for one of those lozenges and would burn it in the small polished bowl meant for tips, but each time her gesture was followed by disappointment.

A fresh downpour splashed against the skylight; after which lo and behold, the agile spirit of the water seemed to suffuse the squalid gloom with the mysterious earthly fragrance of joy.

The walls opened up; the huge carcass of iron, wood, stucco and varnish was swept away by a single gust of wind, almost as though it were a little heap of pine needles on a beach washed by the Atlantic.

Clear, swift springs burst forth from all sides, as in the quiet remote corner of a park where, with a mysterious smile, the host leads his unsuspecting guests and, unseen, turns the key hidden inside a cupid's quiver to start the fountain's tricks and deceits.

From the shorn grass, from among the symmetrical shrubs, the trimmed box-hedges, from the Naiads' breasts, the Tritons' shells, the dolphins' backs, the cheeks of the bronze frogs squatting beside the benches or at the grottoes' thresholds, from the mouldings of the balustrades along the terraces and ramps, from the domes of the small rotundas and the arches of the covered walks, from every side the jets spurt, leap, whip out, pursue, smite, formidable as swords, as rapiers, as pikes in an ambush.

Ladies and courtiers shriek, laugh, run, shy away, recoil.

But in every shelter, every hiding-place lurks the cool insidious pursuer; here a diagonal dart finds the nape of a neck, an ear, the hollow between the shoulder blades; there a low spout plays beneath a hobbleskirt like the clapper inside a muted bell; here a rude burst of water snatches at a wig, tousles it, undoes it, turns it into a curlicue of its own foam.

Fleeing Amaryllis trips on a rosebush. Falling full length, she scatters the petals and pricks herself. The mischievous spurts overwhelm her like a swarm of transparent gnomes and ravish her defenseless charms. A plume, a veil, a ribbon, a bow, a silken beauty mark, a tortoise shell comb, a tiny slipper of golden cloth, each airy item dances upon a tip of nimble spray like a punctured, emptied egg shell; and also a green leaf, a white petal, a russet thorn.

"Help! Help!'

The gallant Palamedes does not tarry, or turn around, or hear; he runs off as fast as he can accompanied by a great tinkling of pendants and trinkets, his tassels askew, his stockings glued to his illustrious shanks, clutching the limp sheath of his dirk.

They all flee shrieking, panting, hugging the hornbeam espaliers, heading toward the pink marble stairs, looking like a mixed flock of goslings and swans chased from their lake by sudden fright.

The lovely fugitives now think they're safe and are shaking off the drops when the little marble sphinxes—flesh-colored, well kempt and prim like young ladies in waiting poised on their paws with harmless claws—from their unenigmatic lips begin to spew broad entwining fans of water along the entire length of the stairway.

The delightful rout resumes; and the stairway seems to grow like Jacob's ladder into the mild eastern sky where shuttling swallows weave melancholy's violet veil.

And lo! suddenly the first pearl necklace snaps, the grains come spilling off the string, flow tumbling down along the smooth roseate steps which the water descends in miniscule cascades.

There snaps the second necklace—of seven strands?—then the third—of twenty-one?—and another, and another yet, of strands beyond number.

The pearls multiply, imitate a mild hail, scatter in all directions, resplend, resound, rebound, mingle with the rivulets— now they look like precious bubbles of the water, now like drops scattered by drenched, pouring beauty.

And when the sphinxes cease puffing, the peacocks perched

in the hornbeam rise with a shrill cry, flock upon the path as if attracted by unexpected feed; they pursue the grains, trailing their folded ceremonial fans over the moist slabs of marble.

And suddenly arrives—no one knows from where—a supple pack of Angora cats as white as cream and as gray as smoke, with red eyes, with blue eyes.

And suddenly arrives—no one knows from where—a troop of Barbary Apes as black and sparkling as jet, with tiny, pale, wrinkled hands, a golden bell tied to their tails.

And the cats and the monkeys rush after the resonant pearls, stop them, seize them, fling them back and forth, laughing, gamboling, brawling, vying with turns and twists and gestures of always fresh and effortless grace.

And up there the necklaces keep on breaking, spilling, rippling, almost as though some miracle were transforming the carnal laughter of Youth into those scattering gems, fugitive and irretrievable. (And down there, what of Amaryllis? Has she swooned in the rosebush? Or surrendered her soul?)

He was playing Domenico Scarlatti's sonatas.

The young musician's shaven, angular face was dotted with any number of bristly warts *à la* Franz Liszt. He wore a pair of professorial gold-framed spectacles on his almost Grecian nose, flaunted Jacopo Peri's ancient shaggy fringe of hair and a double-loop cravat over one of those long velvet vests we see on elegant gentlemen in Gavarni's lithographs. But his fingers' prodigious artistry and his intuitions proved him to be a true "maestro of the harpsichord," worthy of the eighteenth century and the divine Neapolitan.

That music's vigor, audacity, elegance, gaiety, directness, and fickleness miraculously renewed and refreshed the sense of life in me. Each sonata with its single theme, developed by a two-part movement, seemed each time to draw the brief line of an ever-varying perfection and to embellish the lively strength of its most limpid elements with unexpected modulations.

During an intermission, while my lids were still lowered over one of my enchanted fantasies, I was reached amid a tenuous rustle by a woman's perfume which was like the scent loosened from a shaken rosebush; so that at first I thought I was being perturbed by my own dream. Was it Amaryllis?

However, on turning, I saw a young woman about to sit down on the chair next to mine; and the first thing I noticed was the quality of her eyes which did not seem to help her find her way. Instantly the world created inside me by that music crumbled and dispersed as if one of those crystal globes that represent the terraqueous globe and are poised on the palm of an English angel of creation had slipped from my hand. The water-spurts stopped their fencing match, the necklaces no longer broke and scattered. My soul, magically delivered from itself, leaped back over the intervening centuries.

Our life is a work of magic which eludes the reflected light of reason and the farther on it moves, the richer it becomes, realizing itself in mystery and often in conflict with the order of perceptible laws. Nor, when we are sleeping and dreaming, are we really asleep but rather the Magician rests and ceases to help our faculties grasp the virtue in things with his unpredictable and unfailing skill. Left for a short while to ourselves, we could perhaps spy on him, find out what he is like as well as detect our secret, if he did not arrest some mechanism in us—like some factory worker who jams a nail or some little wedge into his machine so that it cannot be used. But man is always awake, since the world's beginning; and in truth no Macbeth can murder the sleep that never comes to him.

Human sleep is an error, as are time and space.

Our bed is nothing but the symbol of an incomprehensible or misunderstood rite, like Adonis' ancient catafalque or the

bier of Jesus erected in the church's nave before Easter. It is
not man but the waxen image of a god that lies down in it.

The woman's eyes were of the kind that leave us perplexed
and desperate, as when confronted by a sheer granite wall
without an opening or foothold. The edges of her eyelids were
hard and clean, holding her eyeballs firmly gripped as bezels
hold precious stones, and they made me think of the eyes of a
god or athlete cast in bronze, eyes made of bluish silver or a
vitreous paste, poured or set into the metal sockets to become
immortal and perpetually demand offerings or praise, while
giving nothing in return.

But the color of the skin on her naked face was by contrast
so delicate that it moved me as hitherto I had only been by the
first small single blossom budding from the bare branch of a
peach tree. It was a pallor lit up either by some lofty quality
of the blood or by the powerful molding of the features, for I
had never before seen the planes of a living countenance
treated with such a plastic magnificence that, in the narrow
confines of a face, it could remind me of the stately sweep of
the earth in noble landscapes, the inimitable rhythm of valleys
and hills in the frailest, most silent season.

I covered my eyes with my hand and, my head lowered, I
listened for several moments to her breathing beyond the
music, or perhaps in the depths of that music which no longer
seemed to flow over the keyboard but rather to even out and
grow quiet like those pools of water left behind on the beach
by the tide at sunset, when my Mediterranean-fed imagination finds a cause for their sublime beauty by making believe
that some of the statues lost at sea below the Cyclades have
been washed ashore.

The sense of the human presence seems to me so prodigious
that I wonder by what aberration or what cowardice I have
chosen to live for so long among the trees and on deserted

shores. But it must be said that even the sturdiest, most alert spirit shies away from uninterrupted strain, and that an extraordinary charge of attention is needed to reach beyond the opaqueness of the blunting screen of habit and to perceive the secret rhythm of a stranger's life.

I was immediately submerged by a wave of sadness, as if that creature had retraced my walk among the homes of the sick, endured the gaze of those ferocious senile eyes bulging over wizened pouches, and were bringing back to me the ashen thoughts pawed by that filthy hand groping along the ground.

With the impact of an hallucinatiion as irrefutable as reality, I was suddenly, pervasively, vaguely overcome by a sense of misery and disaster, not connected with that face and that body but rather diffused—as when you climb a sinister staircase, hesitate along a drab, dingy hallway, and then enter a dimly lit room which still contains the traces of a crime that has been committed there. I think that in the semi-darkness I would have discovered some revealing object—had I not removed the screen from my eyes and turned to look at my neighbor with an involuntary rudeness which seemed to surprise rather than offend her.

Her beauty adhered completely to my senses as if it already had its proper place in them and were simply returning to occupy it, in the way a rare jewel fits smoothly in its case, a bas-relief slips back into its original mold. My mournful insight receded, delivering me completely to my new emotion.

The line of that form obeyed the law governing great plastic works; for wherever I might imagine its inception to be, there, by a sort of fluid necessity, it was brought to completion: departing from the nape of the neck it returned to the nape of the neck; departing from the knee it returned to the knee, with a continuity and fullness uniquely its own, with a movement that was suitable to it alone, like a specific musical form, like the three-quarter time of *andante*, like the six-eight time of that *allegro* by Domenico Scarlatti.

She wore a short chinchilla coat softer than the down of an ash-gray swan, over a narrow skirt of heavy gray cloth which clung to her unchastely. Beneath her hat, made of stiff and lightly woven horsehair, turned up on one side and adorned with two feathers like two knives, skeins of a golden chestnut silk, soft and shining, were held up by neither visible comb nor hairpin but rather by their own vivid thickness.

She was completely sheathed in the exquisite style of the fashion that in those years seemed to deck women out so they could lie comfortably inside the long narrow coffin of some pharaonic princess. On her chair she took up no more space than that provided by one of those Egyptian biers of painted wood. But even through her most up-to-date elegance, from the line that flowed from the curve of her cheek down to her toes, she was, for me, drawn just as artists must imagine the ancient Leda of the Eurotas. From the waist down her beauty seemed inflected toward the mystery of "the divine Olore," as Polyphilo would have put it.

And I thought again of that Leda by Leonardo which Cassiano del Pozzo, Poussin's friend, could still see at Fontainebleau in 1625 and which I always dream of rediscovering in some improbable manner.

"Beethoven?" I asked in a low voice, surprised by the accent of the music I was hearing again after the indefinite interval of my distracted silence.

With spontaneous curiosity, the woman glanced at the programme that lay on her muff and, as if prompted by my expectant pose, she replied: "Ferdinando Turini."

She had proferred the Italian name with a childish, almost affected shyness accompanied by a blush that seemed to wipe out the power of her features like the vermilion juice with which the virgins of Apulia used to tint their sad faces before preparing to embrace Cassandra's funeral statue.

"Would you say," I asked, thankful for the pretext, my heart pounding, "would you say he was acquainted with the early Beethoven manner? I can't really make up my mind. If we could be sure that he did not know it, what original and significant value this sonata in D flat would take on for us!"

I caught the profound, innate indifference of her spirit to this kind of subtlety and problem, just as from a single testing note a singer becomes convinced of a room's faulty acoustics. Between the precise edges of her lids her eyes once more became impenetrable. Instinctively I leaned slightly towards her, over the brink of her secret, but bewildered, no longer possessed of that gift which during the first instants had revealed in her a dark mass of obscure misery.

Her perfume dispersed the force of my scrutiny: and now I gazed at her like someone gazing at some supreme object for whose sake he has made an incredibly long journey. A flood of remote life, similar to the sudden breath I had felt sweep over my head and over the pine trees, was rushing toward me to overwhelm and submerge me. I felt as though a pathetic necessity were hovering over me and that I was already disposed to that sort of contrived folly of which the enchantment which precedes passion is composed.

And indeed I considered every detail in an indefinable light that seemed already enveloped in the past, like someone who studies and then with utmost care wraps objects to be put away, objects on the verge of turning into precious souvenirs from which he will derive a certain sure intoxication when in the future he chances to hold them in his hands. So past and future converged in that complex feeling of mine, and the present was merely a kind of leaven.

Inside myself I spoke to her as if on some future day to come: "Everything is clear in my memory. You were leaning a trifle forward as if to better receive the music. You seemed not to listen with your ears, covered by your hair, but rather with your full, swollen lips, as children sometimes do when entranced by a fairy tale. You kept your right hand inside your muff. Twice you took it out and then thrust it back in with strange haste as if to prevent something from falling out of it. The glove covered your wrist but your hand was bare, slipped through the slit, and the slough of soft leather dangled from the back of your hand, preserving the shape of the living fingers. Along the thumb I noticed an indentation, like the slight bruise produced by contact with some mysterious harshness . . ."

I don't believe she was really listening to the Italian sonata. I had the impression that her musical sensibility was very slight.

Music infuses an aerial quality in the bodies of women who respond to the innocence of the melody, like the air that fills the hollow bones in the wings of flying birds. Once, I don't know why, seeing my mistress bowed by illness and quivering with the sovereign lamentation of a famous violin, I thought of those air bubbles which the hunter sees rise through the warm blood of the wounded wing where the shot has broken the shoulder. A beautiful and profound image, which returned to my mind as I considered by contrast the density of that woman's life, the cohesion of her very substance, the sort of complete animality dissimulated by the volumes of so noble an architecture.

And yet within her dwelt an anguish that at that very moment must be pounding against the hull of her rib-cage as if to shatter it. And the sorrow that rose from time to time to swell her lower lip was so evident to me that I was almost surprised not to see its wave ripple over the delicate fur like certain shudders of agony that, shaped like a fishbone, furrow the pelts of sick animals.

"Are you suffering?" I dared ask her, in a changed voice that undoubtedly touched her.

She turned to me the enigma of that face of hers, with its broad planes strongly joined as in the head of some shepherd king carved from basalt.

"Not at all," she replied; and she laughed a dry, sharp

laugh without resonance, as whores will sometimes laugh at someone standing behind them, while the mirror reflects that fixed, curt expression with which they stick a long hatpin in their hats.

Then all my fantasies again disintegrated. She began to chatter like a little Parisian prostitute, with a soft, rubbery mouth that exaggerated the shape of the words and syllables to the point of grimacing. She poked fun at that Turkesque hall, at the shaggy pianist, the insipid audience; she aired her contempt for the petty, boring life in that awful town that had grown up around the shacks and sheds of a settlement of resin gatherers; she complained bitterly at being forced to vegetate there almost the entire year round.

"But why?" I asked timidly. "Because of your health?"

She laughed again, acrimoniously.

Here and there a throat coughed in the dim light, which seemed to grow gradually colder while a new downpour crepitated on the gray glass ceiling.

"No, of course not."

She sat up in her chair, straightened her torso with an abrupt, almost involuntary movement, like the harsh spasm sometimes sent through us by an inexplicable shudder. I noticed the breadth of her shoulders and her breasts, a solid structure that corresponded to the style of her head. Through the opening of her muff I caught sight of something shiny, ivory and steel, which looked like the butt of a revolver about to slip out.

"It's for my car," she said, smiling, almost in answer to my probable surprise at seeing her armed. "After the concert, I have to drive all the way to Bordeaux."

Truly now it seemed that those lips belonged to another woman, living another life in the middle of that face, those lips with their frivolous mobility which was in such conflict with the hewn firmness of the other features and the formidable mystery of her naked glance. I thought again of certain

Sardinian dances danced with a closed and darkly ominous expression, of certain Arabian dances in which only the belly moves, moves incessantly upon a body fettered by some unknown snake-like fascination. The artificial red of her lip-rouge was fresh, applied perhaps just before entering the hall, and with a hasty hand, for it was uneven, slightly smudged at the edges and corners. Her teeth were strong, the lower ones set a trifle irregularly, resplendant like chips of some precious substance, made of an enamel so dense and pure that you thought of the carats that measure perfection, as though they were gems to examine on a jeweler's tray.

"Listen," I said, stirred by some notes in a passage in the second movement of a sonata by Domenico Paradisi, the last on the program.

I watched her from under my lowered lids.

The force of dissimulation suddenly left those lips over which an emotion of unknown gravity seemed to draw a real band of gauze, woven as tightly as the one worn by Berber women in our white and crescent-shaped Ghadames.

And yet, the cadenza having almost come to its resolution and my heart dreading its end like a farewell, I looked at her again as one looks at a supreme thing for which one has journeyed the very greatest distance.

She was so smooth that it seemed she must not be marked by a single furrow in the palm of her hand. She was truly polished by the waters of the Eurotas, since in my memory brilliantly shone the flat stones of that swanless, laconic river, amid the narrow blue shadows of oleanders and reeds. "What are you, who are you?—you who certainly harbor a cunning serpent behind your low forehead, even though your heart is heavy with tears."

As many other times before, my whole being clung to the unknown which is at the root of life, because of the shadows the body contains, the darkness that fills the secret recesses of the flesh, the mystery of viscera and precordia.

I felt sorrow and death trickle toward me like drops oozing from the walls of a deep and gloomy cave.

Desperate poetry became my very flesh.

She stood between chair and chair while the audience left the hall like some fluent pulp swept toward the door by Euterpe's broom. Every human shape seemed to be bowed, deprived of backbone, faded and limply dragging along—save for the one standing in front of me, whole, silent, throbbing with a unique sickness similar to a truth or the profoundest lie, which in her took the place of life.

The most solitary places are not in deserts or mountains, not among sterile sands or rocks, but where the soul confronts its destiny, breathing for a few seconds an air that no one even nearby can breathe.

Now, looking at me, she slightly narrowed those lids which I had been so certain were immobile, like the raised ridges of bronze surrounding the eye-socket cavity in archaic statues. A horse-trader examining a beast put up for sale never had a colder and shrewder look in his eyes. But it seemed to me that in the depth of her pupils that scrutiny had the sheen of a deadly weapon by which I would soon be wounded. She kept only one hand hidden inside her pearl-gray muff, her ungloved hand; and in it she certainly clutched the small weapon to make sure it did not fall. But the darting light in her eyes was a much greater danger. I don't know why, but I felt more fragile, more mortal, tormented by an apprehension not unlike the one we experience when a doctor palps our body to discover our weak spot. And (I report this with absolute truthfulness even though later on it may appear unusual) a spontaneous image flashed through my mind, arising perhaps from a forgotten episode in my past: the bizarre and lugubrious image of an insurance company physician, intent on palping and probing a customer's stomach, liver, lungs, heart in order to estimate his approximate life expectancy. I realized that my spirit's craft could not prevail over this creature whom the divine, as in the myth, must approach in the guise of an animal.

Under her appraising glance I was only a miserable body, worn out by excesses, torn by restlessness, continually threatened by the collapse that inevitably follows extreme tension. "Yes, no doubt," my irony urged me to reply to that scrutiny, "it would be easy to finish me off. All my vigor is concentrated at the base of my skull. A sharp little blow would be enough, or a tiny puncture no bigger than that made by the weasel in a chicken's head . . ."

Now, from which feature of her face did that murderous aura come? Why was she herself revealing to me at that moment the evil and destructiveness of her secret depths?

And yet she was not simply lying in wait for prey, there was also an indistinct cry coming from her which did not yet reach my ear but already touched my soul.

"We must go," she said, moving with sudden haste toward the squalid maze of chairs.

Now, as when she had first arrived, her eyes did not seem to help her find her way. Brushing against a chair with her legs she tipped it over, then overturned another. She kept on like a blind person, running into an uninterrupted series of obstacles. To get through meant tearing them down. It resembled certain obsessive and ridiculous dreams.

I don't really remember whether the hall had gone dark, but to me it resembled an ugly church, reverberating with echoes in the service of Darkness. And the skeletal custodian came rushing up to us with the zeal of a sexton infuriated by desecrators. The offering of a coin placated her and roused in her an inexhaustible hilarity: the lady I was accompanying having laughed her false laugh out of flattery, the custodian echoed her without restraint, picking up chairs and convincing herself and us as well that this was the most amusing prank in the world.

Outside, the rain had stopped. A cool wind, thick with resin, like the rain water that fills the crocks hanging from the pines, cleansed my face. The crest of clouds in the West was like incandescent foam.

Something silvery, almost a shimmer of mother-of-pearl flickered in the unknown woman's eyes. The first quarter moon hung in the greenish sky as if Morgan le Fay had set it there to mirror the pallor of the barrens.

"Do you have a car to drive home?" she asked with a hesitation on which my shyness failed to seize.

Did this mean that she knew my way home and me?

"I'm walking home," I replied.

She looked at me, debating within herself something I couldn't see and which nevertheless seemed to affect the horizon and charge it with an energy akin to the lightning that flashes through the sky on certain summer evenings when our entire soul is ready to spurt in sparks from the apex of our heart, like a flame assailed by the wind. Her face was distorted by a muscular tremor that, becoming unendurable for me to watch, almost transferred to the joints of my jaws like the spasm that doctors call trismus.

My awareness was the axle of a wheel spinning at tremendous speed.

"Goodbye," she then said, walking over to her automobile with the short, jerky steps imposed by the hobble skirt.

What pathetic irony there was in the contrast of that dark will impeded by those stylish fetters!

"Shall we meet again?"

The hand holding the weapon still remained hidden inside the soft fur.

"Who knows?"

Amid the roar of the engine, beyond the glass in the door I glimpsed a gesture of the other, gloved hand, a white gesture similar to the one I had seen behind the curtainless window in the town of the sick and dying. A second later, on the road, between the two grooves cut by the tires, remained only the reflection of the dazzling cloud caught in the liquid slush.

The unknown woman had disappeared. Forever.

Certainly, for me, a hearse could not have taken her into a deeper mystery, a gloomier annihilation. Did not her absence and the night have the same countenance? I had to summon up her face from a darkness as impenetrable as that of a grave.

I walked back the same way, passing again through the Ville d'Hiver; but more than of my own direction I was aware of the distance traveled by that destiny made of flesh along the rectilinear road which the young moon was beginning to mark with shadows of a tenderness excruciating to a desperate heart.

It was already the hour when household lamps appear. And each time another lit up, my melancholy overflowed as if to feed them.

I could detect no expression in any of those houses: they no longer seemed to contain any life other than that concentrated within the luminous circle where the shadows flocked to imbibe light as at the quiet edge of a fountain. Beyond that circle everything was shrouded in a human mist as if, out there, the slight, obstinate fever that begins to smolder in the diseased colony after the setting of the sun were sending off its fumes.

The twilight was still bright enough for me to distinguish a starry cobweb spun between the bars of a garden gate or, among some blades of grass, one of those small downy spheres whose name I've never known, lighter than the first fluff of a cocoon, destined to fly away and vanish, driven beyond the borders of the world by the breath of a puff-cheeked arrogant boy.

A poplar quivered, solitary, clothed in iridescent silver, at the corner of a garden; and through the rippling rustle I heard: "Look, look—there she is."

Suddenly the one he had announced with such trepidation

appeared. But much whiter, and fresh, all nuptial jubilation, a modest bride, arrayed in her own virginity: the blossoming of an apple tree.

Every appearance was an apparition to the fervor of my senses; but each one was accompanied by a stabbing, blinding pain which seemed to me almost physical, similar to the one I experienced in the past from avidly inhaling marine air with a chest where three broken ribs were not yet healed.

I suffered the urgency of a force over which I had no control; and of which I did not really know whether I contained it or was contained by it.

That cinereous taste in my mouth as I descended to the unexpected encounter now returned to me commingled with a peculiar blood-like sweetness, against which a revulsion rose in me as bitter as nausea, and my thoughts had a hideous resemblance to those leeches that as a child I had seen placed in a dish full of ashes to make them vomit the blood they'd sucked.

When at last, having left behind the domain of illness and agony, I found myself in the wild wood and felt the invisible threads woven from branch to branch brush softly against my face, my neck, I understood that these were the caresses of spring and that perhaps until now I had been obscurely suffering the pangs of the new season.

A drop fell on my hand, another on my lashes; a brittle pine cone crackled under my heel; something flaccid hopped across the path, a toad perhaps; the scops owl played its oboe with a single note; the nightingale in the shadow picked up that note of dark brown velvet and transmuted it into limpid, voluble, crystal warbling. The entire wood was suddenly filled with lament and song, it dripped with rain, was drenched in resin, pungent as a dish of mixed herbs, ineffable as the sentiment of puberty.

But within that vast breath my anxiousness searched only for the memory of that perfume "similar to the scent that wafts from a shaken bush," which had come to me from the fettered woman. The eternal anxiety for adventure seized me again and agitated me again with mad violence. What further novelty of possession could I hope for? What other communion could I expect? What other disillusionment could I reap? Enraged regret bit and clawed me for not having been able or wanted, with an audacious initiative, to prevail over the unknown woman's momentary perplexity, when double sharpness of dilemma had shone in her fixed eyes. I was filled with contempt for myself as if I had let a magnificent prey slip away out of slackness or foolishness. I forgot how, amid that maze of chairs, her scrutinizing gaze had filled me with apprehension.

The ferment of the wood communicated to me an illusory energy, from which were born senseless resolutions. I tried to orient myself towards the place of the distant race, towards the highway. Would I have the time to get there, so as to be there waiting when she passed upon her return in the evening or night? It seemed to me that across the barrens a remote folly was calling out to the folly in me. I quickened my pace. Twice I lost the path and found it again, hastening through the thicket, broom and prickly bushes, my heart pounding like a bandit lying in ambush.

In my house too the lamps were lit. Having occupied the sky again, low-lying clouds now grazed the roof, in flight towards the Orient. When I entered, the ground-floor rooms were full of that indistinct fright which seems to fill deserted rooms until a familiar presence dispels it, for when man gets up and leaves it seems that a ghost takes his place and sits down where he was sitting just before. The tide was rising; and something like a female multitude clamored threatfully against the moon, resounding with a hollow sound out on the balcony.

"Did anyone come?" I asked the servant.

"The signora," he answered.

Although I could have no doubt to whom he was referring, in my heart I felt a thud as the other woman's image presented itself there.

"She looked very upset," he went on. "She waited here until six o'clock. She begs you to go to her immediately after supper."

There are hours of the solitary life in which the body's sensitivity seems to dilate all the way to the walls of the house, just as, at times, when lifting an arm we feel our heart throb all the way to our finger tips, and beyond.

The entire house seemed to be getting ready to receive something unknown. A silent event might enter through any door. The attention of the walls was turned wholly towards the night. No room retained its feeling of privacy, but harkened to what was about to happen outside and ceased to keep the warmth and to conciliate the thoughts of the objects gathered and arranged in it.

I looked among my prints for some of the known Ledas. The first I came upon was Ammannati's, which is at the Bargello. A very remote Florentine remembrance arose in me; I found it in the secret book of my memory, under the date of the twenty-second of September 1899.

I read, with a confused emotion which I did not dare examine for fear of dissolving it: "Yesterday, incredible to say, some attendants at the Bargello, wanting to move the Leda, dropped it; and the marble statue broke into seven pieces. Today the fragments have been taken to the stone workshop to be restored. I went today to see that dismembered voluptuousness. The parts that expressed pleasure most intensely are intact. The head is cracked, like mine . . . From the workshop I then went on to the Museum, to see the void left by the shattered group. My imagination has filled it with a more arduous beauty. Now, as I was standing absorbed in this fantasy, suddenly all those silent and abandoned bells that clutter the loggia—gagged mouths—began to toll in my head . . ."

The next page seemed to have been written in a slight delirium, nor did I know any longer because of what love, what absence: "It seems to me that, lifting my head, I could seize something of you in the space and pull you in through the distance, as a child pulls the string of a kite which the wind threatens to carry away beyond the clouds. The space lights up, and you open your mouth to drink in the coolness of the speed. You laugh. I hear your laugh; I touch it as one touches a necklace, grain by grain. One could weep . . ."

Never before had the magical sense of life become so profound in me. Just as the music of a forgotten score relives intact and again exerts its vigor, as if it were created that very moment when the musician touches the strings, so that rhythm of the past goes in time with the breath in my mouth. Some of the words appeared to me like those scrawled on a mirror by the little finger of a baby sister, in a distant past, which became visible only when the glass was misted over by a breath. At last I read: "There is an old burial stone in England that shows Lady Beauchamp's head resting not on a pillow or on her faithful greyhound, according to tradition, but on the back of a swan which seemed to be floating around Arthur's island. I am sure that if I could secretly return to the workshop tonight, this is how I would see the dead Leda . . ."

I closed my eyes; and on the face of the fettered woman, along the edge of her upper lip I searched for the tiny spot which, free from rouge, had looked slightly bruised during her nervous tremor, while the delicacy of her nose had seemed to grow thin and take on, around the nostrils, the smoke gray hue that usually accompanies a fainting spell.

My man came to tell me that the lantern was ready. I carried it to find my way between the puddles along the sandy path leading to the garden of my mistress.

The barrens were dark beneath the cloudy sky; but the air was mild, as in our nocturnal Maremma when the wind blows from the east or the south and amid long pauses you hear a quacking of mallards in the tamarisks, a chittering of foxes along the swamps tender with young green reeds, a crumbling of stones under the feet of boars making their way over the low stone walls, the lamentation that rises from the depths of the centuries.

Here I heard the faint cries of the sea birds beyond the dunes, similar sometimes to a sad whimpering, and the voice of the regretful, plaintive ocean, and the note of the owl which each time touched the most aching part of my heart as if it knew it better than I.

A sudden homesickness saddened me, engendering in my senses phantoms so ready that a torn part of myself seemed to rise from one of those grassy marshes and then plunge again into some pond, or issue from a low swamp, follow a track, and browse beneath a cork oak. Then the animal hallucinations broke off; and the lyrical feeling for my homeland was like the murmur of spirits who dream in the shadow of distant gods.

"I cannot see her, speak to her, hear her," I thought, coming to a halt and setting the lantern down on the sand inside the imprint of a man's foot.

I felt I could no longer endure the presence of the tortured mistress who was waiting for me, nor the contact or proximity of any other petty, troubled being that would remind me of myself, force me to return to my senses, force back again into the usual tracks that extraordinary life that flowed impetuously from my breast and embraced the entire horizon, lusting for remoteness, new things, creation.

The lantern stood on the ground before me; and from the footprint it occupied began other footprints that led in all directions and disappeared beyond the limits of the light. The furrow made by a wagon shone white as though strewn with flour that had fallen from a torn sack, and it was the pollen fallen from the cloudy sky; in another parallel furrow a chain of caterpillars crawled towards eternity with the light and frightful contraction of its myriads of rings; a broken, leafless branch lay aslant, forked at the end like those branches used to discover buried treasure. There was little light on the ground; but it seemed to me that, had I wanted to, I could have ignited at the summit of my spirit one of those all-seeing beacons that from the turrets of a battleship explore all the hostile space and shed light on the cautious advance of death. I could have scrutinized the depths of the night had I raised another lid that was deeper inside than the physical one on which I liked to feel the marine coolness, by closing it as though under a fleeting kiss. But the anxiety to create arrested at every moment the expansion of my spirit, my aspiration towards the infinite, my inclination towards the abysses, as though I had in me a kind of mysterious rennet that curdled the ideality of the world in specific figures.

A great silence had come over the Landes; which was nothing but the silent growth of night. Just as birds dive into the glass of the lighthouse, just as insects fly around a lamp, the life of solitude pressed to the brink of the dim luminescence, breathed towards me, spied on me without being seen.

I strained my ear for a singular sound, not without fright; for it seemed now close, now distant, now in the air, now under the ground, like the rhythmical beat of two sticks striking against each other with the tinkle that needles make as they clash when one knits. Was it the shepherd?

It was certainly the immortal shepherd of the Landes, on his stilts, there in the shadows, leaning against a scaly pine tree, at his feet his wild dog with its eyes that throbbed like the flickering lights of a glow-worm. Was he clothed in leaves? Was his beard a swarm of bees hanging from his chin? Did there issue from the assiduous activity of his fingers panicles of corymbs?

The shape and its metamorphosis were so alive in my imagination that, had I doused the lantern, I would certainly have thought I saw the man and the demi-god with the pupils in my head.

Again I strained my ears, anxious; because the strange beat continued without interval. Following the sound, I entered the shadows with an inexpressible emotion; as if leaving the circle of brightness I issued from myself to assume I know not what nocturnal nature, and perceived the throb of my own pulse in the substance that was about to engulf me. It was nothing but the wind playing with the hard, tapered leaves of a certain liliaceous plant that grows densely along the beaches.

And inside me there was nothing but the dark monster of love, not yet subdued, not yet bound, which still changed and changed again, taking on a thousand shapes, tempting me and deceiving me through a thousand images, tormenting and renewing me with a thousand wiles.

Just as inside me, so outside me everything was travail and change, anguish and frenzy.

I walked forward at random, holding the lantern low, dangling and swinging to cast light on the edges of a world prodigious as the world a diver sees through the glass opening in his helmet. As on the bottom of the sea, plant life and animal life had the same appearance. The bushes were bristling with horror, an alert voracity strained through the branches. And I was urged on by the fate of the man who, having glimpsed the shadow of a mermaid at the threshold of the cave, could no longer find his way back to the surface.

Where was the woman of the myth at that moment? Were the headlights, preceding her speeding wheels, lighting up the deserted road down there, the muddy ruts, the heaps of pebbles, the rim of the ditches? Had she been totally shattered by her secret pain, like that marble statue which was restored to its former shape?

Suddenly there fell like lead upon my heart the severe sadness which had overcome me when, having covered my eyes with my hand, I had listened tensely to catch her breath through the music. In an instant that sylvan delirium of mine faded away. I felt exhausted, as when a fever falls. To walk on the sand became painful. Nothing was left in me that was not human, sickly, miserable.

I found my way back to the path of habit.

A dismal sultriness slackened the vividness of the air. From the dense overcast a few almost lukewarm drops began to fall. You could hear the crackling in the bushes grow little by little. A scops owl complained in the thicket: and it seemed to recall to me the words written in the secret book of my memory: "One could weep . . ."

At first through a windowpane I saw a pink lamp burning in the house. For some reason my heart was pounding, almost with fear. Near the gate, as I stooped over to put out the lantern, I was called by name by an anxious and hoarse voice, a voice of disaster which chilled the blood in my veins. I approached, I too called out her name. I saw my mistress's shadow inside the gate, agitated, all white, who, both her arms bare, was shaking the slats of the gate, trying to open it.

"What's wrong? What happened?"

Her hands passed through and touched me, trembling, already wet with rain, as if to feel me alive.

"Push!" she said in distress. "Push hard! I can't get it open."

I pressed with my shoulder, but the gate would not budge. The new wood had swollen in the dampness and fresh paint had welded the edges together. My repeated attempts to push it open were in vain. Crushed bubbles of resin made my fingers sticky.

"We'd better call the servants," I suggested, trying to laugh, as seemed appropriate.

"No, no," she cried, vexed and greatly upset, her voice already stifled by tears, clutching the slats again. "Try, try some more!"

I tried. Her hands reached through again, touched my face, dismayed.

"What did you do? What did you do?"

The rain fell harder, crashing down. The scops owl continued to complain. The entire barrens seemed oppressed by an inexplicable despair.

And love sobbed as if I had nailed it against the dying wood and flogged it.

The figures of that afternoon and that night were soon stripped of all reality, even by the time I awoke the very next day. The remembrance floated like the shadow of a dream over the uneasiness of spring. All desire to obtain information and to investigate was immediately stymied by the habitual discipline of my withdrawn life, by the rule of monastic seclusion devoted to study, by the wise resolve not to give way to temptation again. Chance favored neither another meeting nor the discovery of any sort of useful information. To these causes for renunciation were added the suspicions, the vigilance and the constancy of my tenacious mistress. Then followed the torments of our break, an illness of a nostalgic order, a long convalescence in a country of hills and meadows, a diligent renewal of meditation and contemplation.

Nevertheless I had a frequently recurring image of Leda without swan, a living breath issuing from lips that the game of dissimulation could no longer distort, lips never perfectly closed but always slightly parted, like lips that must allow more than one soul to breathe.

It visited me sometimes at the hour of the lighting of the lamps, when the servant prepares and lights them in the room below and they seem present already owing to a divine something which seems to precede them on the already darkening stairs, that interval becoming the occasion for those divine thoughts which accompany the departure of the other light from each of our friendly objects as it returns to the West.

Then, since for the solitary man the whole long day is nothing but a construction of the will, he likes towards evening to leave a small door open through which may enter beggar or witch, herbalist or poisoner, in short an emissary of the Unknown; and he likes to tremble again in expectation of the unexpected. Most times nothing enters but some harmless ghost.

That guest of mine was tied to life by a great number of knots and enchantments, fettered by more than just her hobble skirt; and each time she leaned towards me she seemed to be pulling at a chain, to have to snap a thong, break a rope. To encourage her I would say: "Don't be afraid. Come forth. I am ripe for your coming. I understand everything, I sense everything."

It seemed that my consciousness strained toward the glorious moment when it could accept and render everything safe and immune, like those cities of asylum where the accused without guilt or beyond guilt sought shelter, those sacred places that in ancient times welcomed "the dregs and knavery of the world." But its acts were not without ambiguity and contradiction. At bottom, it toiled in the hope of creating a new emotion, one capable of guiding the most turbid energies of instinct and rising higher than voluptuousness. In this art, justice and compassion are worthless. Other guises, other rules, other rites are required.

Meanwhile, with the new spring, the anniversary of the strange day approached, almost brought back by the long procession of caterpillars upon the road again yellow with pollen. And, almost on the same date, the young maestro of the *Schola Cantorum* returned with the nightingales to give his Italian concert. This time he had brought along his companion: a small Spanish woman from Cuba, golden as an exquisite leaf of tobacco, and who, in promising to sing arias and ariettas by Carissimi, Caldara, Antonio Lotti for me alone, made me think not without regret of that breed of dogs that do not bark which the Conquistadores discovered on her miraculous island where today the breed no longer exists, even its memory being lost.

However, the harpsichord's honors were for Domenico Scarlatti. Like a magic formula his sonata in A Major conjured up from the past the mysterious hour whole and alive, as if the unknown woman had come again to sit beside me and I with all my acuteness were again leaning over the brink of her secret.

Although the audience was more numerous, the chair next to mine remained empty.

I saw a shadow approaching along the row.

From second to second my disquietude increased so fervently that I turned, with my soul in my eyes and my heart leaping in my throat, as if to receive all at once that beauty which already had its place in all my senses. Two thin, bony hands with spatulate fingers were held out towards me, and my name was pronounced by an unforgotten voice.

I immediately recognized a friend of mine from whom I had not heard for some time: a musician of great talent and high reputation, who more than once had been a guest of the sad Ville d'Hiver, hovering between getting worse or better.

"I didn't know you were here. Since when?"

"I spent the whole winter here with my mother—not too well."

"But you look wonderful."

To sink his teeth into his pain he still had a lean jaw from which the razor seemed to have scraped away layers of dead skin replaced by the greasy sheen of glycerine.

"No, I got burned."

His cheeks were red and veined like the leaves of a wild vine hanging from a wall in autumn, not without some greenish remnant and a few traces of snail-slime. For his wretched condition I had—alas—the same implacable eyes that would have noticed the slightest wave in the opulent silk of a certain woman's hair or the gap left by a single fallen lash at the edge of certain eyelids.

"Burned by what?"

He made an almost brutal gesture of indifference, but fixed on me the kind of stare that from man to man delves deeply and seems to search in your heart for a point of support, the place of masculine sympathy.

His eyes now also seemed to me deprived of their outer skin, as if they had been brought into direct contact with external ruthlessness, as if they were the exposed apexes of his sensitivity and there was no medicament that could soothe them. The look in them pained me.

"Are you staying any longer?" I asked. "Would you like to get together?"

"I'm leaving in two or three days, Saturday perhaps. My mother is tearing me away."

He had the smell of port wine on his breath, but his white teeth still gave his mouth a youthful quality.

I felt his humanity with unusual force as if I had for some time been his nurse and had endured the smell of his sweat and knew all his petty troubles and manias.

And from him too I was already expecting the unexpected.

"Come and have lunch with me tomorrow. I'll send the car for you."

"Very well. I'd like to."

And he grabbed my hand and squeezed it with his convulsed fingers. The Sonata in F Minor was beginning, and we fell silent. It seemed to me that the music did not bring us closer but separated us, for I thought that as a craftsman he must hear it in a very different way. He sat there unable to restrain his restlessness, and he communicated it to me.

"What's troubling you? Whom are you looking for?"

Since he had twisted around, I turned too. In the back, standing to the right, leaning against the wall, was the unknown woman, facing our way, nodding. My inward commotion made her features waver and then wiped them out, like a pastel dipped in water.

"Do you know her?" he asked me, with one of those exclamations that seem to hiss in a breast suddenly emptied of everything.

"No. I just saw her once. Who is she?"

He said the name, that did not adhere to the person but remained suspended in the air, an extraneous, meaningless sound, like that imposed upon the beauty of a distant hill which for a long time has been living nameless and ideal in our feelings.

"Till tomorrow," he added, getting up as the cadenza was ending.

Just as the flame bursts from the ember veiled with ashes, so the fever lit up his ruined face. I saw him go towards the woman, his shoulders faintly hunched but with an anxious solicitude that permeated even his clothes and the prematurely gray hair over the collar of his coat. I saw him stop in front of her, exchange a few words of greeting, and then leave with her. Behind me I heard the vicious comment of two people in the audience. I restrained the tumult inside me, shook off the impurities of my solitary fantasies, regained the sharpness of my vision, braced myself to plunge my hands again into the living substance. I forgot the play of the water, the broken, rippling necklaces, Amaryllis' tiny shoe dancing at the tip of the jet, the merry chases over the pink marble stairs, and heard again sorrow and death trickle towards me like drops oozing from the wall of a deep, dusky cave.

My friend came, as agreed. I still pitied him; but I realized that I now looked at him rather as an instrument I must tend to, a tool for dealing with this episode with a delicate or rough hand. And my kindness, as is often the case with me, was only an aspect of my energy.

Lucidity sometimes accompanies an almost animal hideousness which seems the punishment inflicted on those who break the spell of illusions, flout convention.

When eating he had the bad habits of an ill-mannered

invalid; he chewed noisily, drank with his mouth full, smacked his lips, displaying a voraciousness and a thirst unchecked by the least civility. And this gross behavior in that monastic room furnished with books and prints, where I was in the habit of taking my brief meals while reading or following my thoughts—this behavior that I found unbearable was worsened by my insidious emotions; for I kept loading his plate, refilling his glass, intent on stuffing him, making him drunk as you do with a chum when you want to have him at your mercy.

It really seemed he had to fill huge vaults or to appease the appetite of the one inside him who threatened not to leave him either cartilage or bones. Next to that shriveled face, flushed by a touch of intoxication, framed by long hair and a fluttering bow tie, still with a certain resemblance to Henri Mürger, I set the enigma of that other face with its broad planes strongly welded together as in the head of a shepherd king carved in basalt.

And I asked almost silently: "So, she is your mistress? Do you know the shape of her knees? Do you touch her with your spatulate fingers? Eat, drink up."

A breath of monstrous creation stirred within the walls thickly lined with books, where my soul was vibrant as the air imprisoned by the dry wood of a well-constructed violin. That which from immortal books mingles with the fluidity of life in the silence, the eternity which is fixed in the pathetic fragments of masterpieces, the myth which burdens an invisible temple with the wine-colored flower of the hyacinth, the transparent splendor of the wine similar to the corporeal presence of the god it dissolves, bread, fruit, a knife, a strip of meat transformed by fire, the rim of a glass touched by the grace of a ray of light, everything before me and around me expressed myself to myself. Full of meanings, I played with love and with death. With the figure of my guest, with the figure of the absent woman and with my sober intoxication I composed one after the other the scenes of a new *Danse macabre.*

"Who is that?" he asked, looking toward the fireplace.

It was a complete cast of one of the eight hooded men who carry the burial stone of the Great Seneschal of Burgundy. He stood near an andiron, stooped, but his shoulders unburdened, his face hidden inside the hood, only one long-thumbed hand exposed.

"Really," he said, "this isn't a very cheerful place you've made for yourself."

And, fixing a murky stare on something only he could see, sadness overtook him, as the soul does when it curls up on a stuffed bag.

"Come, come," I said, suddenly standing up and taking him familiarly by the arm, with a bold cheerfulness. "Tell me about your new love affair."

"What love affair?"

"I'm dying of envy. She's a magnificent beast."

I made him sit down in a comfortable armchair, while the servant brought liqueurs and cigarettes. I went and stood in the shadow of a bookshelf, away from the light, as if lying in wait.

From a small wooden box he took out his tobacco mixed with opium and rolled it in the paper between thumb and index stained yellow as if with iodine. He was affecting that vain, effete smile of his which I knew so well, that disgusted smile of a womanizer who sees no difference between one affair and the next. As he sat there with his weak legs outstretched, one of them trembling while he stared at the tip of his shoe, there arose again in my memory the image of a peasant I had seen in a field looking calmly at his bare foot, to which the head of a viper seemed stuck forever like a sixth toenail.

"Why do you call her a beast?" he said. "Do you know her story?"

"I know nothing. Who is she?"

He smeared her with a filthy word; and then turned his tongue in his mouth as though it had suddenly dried out.

"So you are in love with her?"

He began to talk—rancorously, dismayed, talked about revenge and spells; there was something unbearable about it, like the sight of an agony; something false, like a clown's routine, alternately pitiable and odious, tragic and ridiculous.

Now Leda without swan was there, so smooth that it seemed she could not even have the mark of a furrow in the hollow of her hand, truly polished by the waters of the Eurotas. And her life was something else.

She came from one of those mixed races whose tragic quality is the product of an obscure confluence of blood and destinies, like the potency of those stimulating concoctions in which mandrake root is boiled in the urine of a mare. Her father, a great lover of horses, had kept a famous racing stable; then he had lost all his money, had lived by expedients, as a swindler, sinking lower and lower, stumbling more than once into the arms of the law. After living in daily contact with grooms, jockeys, trainers, giving rein to her innate, hereditary recklessness and to her exhibitionistic tendencies by riding three-year-old colts on the public bridle paths, at the age of eighteen she had married a French gentleman. She had divorced him at twenty and had found herself first with a lover who was a cold calculating scoundrel and then alone, in straitened circumstances, at loose ends, harassed by her father who would have liked to turn her into the source of a good income that not she but he would pocket. Unable to cope with poverty, ready for anything, at a spa she had run into some sort of procurer in search of accomplices and victims, who, through a sequence of lucky moves, managed to get her engaged to a foolish young man just barely come of age, an orphan, already very rich and about to inherit an even more lavish fortune. She, the fiancé and the matchmaker had lived together for two years "hitting the high spots," roaming from hotel to hotel, from pleasure to pleasure, from boredom to boredom, from one sleepless night to the next, from one gambling table to another, in unconfessable promiscuity; for the bride-to-be enforced the rule of fasting and abstinence until the ascent of the nuptial couch, and the best man had managed to maintain complete domination over the dupe, something akin to a perverse spell, with the help of that philtre which is offered in a golden syringe. The morphine, administered by his skilled hand, had generated such a rosy feeling of benignity that with no trouble at all and no suspicions an insurance policy for one and a half million was obtained for the austere bride-to-be, as a nuptial guarantee. After the first payment was made as prescribed, foresight advised getting rid of the benefactor. One day, on a twisting, dangerous road in the Pyrenees, a stronger dose of the drug was followed by an accident prepared with exquisite caution. After a casual halt, the car was started and then plunged headlong into the ravine, with the murderer left behind unharmed on the road.

Was I not listening to things I had heard many times before? Undoubtedly, similar cases abound in the judicial annals and the scarlet thrillers consumed by janitors, washerwomen, housemaids. But underneath that vulgar hodgepodge meandered I know not what dark track along which my soul had traveled before and was traveling once again, confusedly recognizing the signs of its first passage. And those depths filled me with eagerness to delve even deeper into myself, to reach in myself a more real me that would not fail when confronted by what was about to take on substance and manifest itself.

"How do you know about all this?"

From time to time, enlivening his tale, he injected here and there personal confidences which can be entrusted to another person only by someone recklessly confessing in order to incriminate himself.

"I know it from her."

"She accuses herself?"

"She does not accuse herself; she talks. She has no idea of right or wrong. First she tells you something dreadful, without looking at you, with a kind of timid smile, like someone testing the strength of a plank laid across a stream before venturing over it. Then she bends you under a weight, piles on a guilt that crashes down on you and you've got to support with main force."

"Are you sure that with all these things she wasn't and isn't putting together some sort of imaginary life?"

"She wears the shackle of reality well fastened to her foot."

"What do you mean?"

"She lives with the murderer."

"Where?"

"In this town."

"How long has that been going on?"

"For two years."

"Was she already his mistress before the accident?"

"She was, yes; but in payment for his mediation, and afterwards because of their complicity. She loathes him."

"Then why does she put up with him?"

"The circumstances surrounding the prospective bridegroom's death aroused some suspicion. And the insurance company seized on this to challenge the validity of the policy. There was no evidence or it was too vague. Nevertheless the case was taken to court and is still dragging on. Consequently the man holds the threat over her head of a wild denunciation that would destroy them both. I believe that after the trial, whose favorable outcome is by now assured, the two of them will divide the money according to some kind of agreement they have already made."

"Just what sort of dregs from old detective stories are cluttering your imagination?"

"It's all true, and it is only a particle of their everyday

reality. Just picture it: they live together on the Basin over there in one of those rackety little villas with thin walls and ceilings where you can hear a heart beat or a lung dilate in the next room, where it is impossible to escape the smell of the person you hate or the splash of his wash water."

"And what kind of a man is he?"

"Think of a head the shape of a truncated pyramid, a real python head, exact like a geometrical creation, rigid as a problem or a condemnation, with two colorless eyes behind a pair of lenses as thick as the glass in a dark lantern . . ."

"And who pays the bills?"

"His background is just petty bourgeois, his father owned a china factory near Limoges. She still has something left from her dowry. But that little would not be enough to pay for her elegant, expensive habits, at least externally. Belief in the trial's favorable outcome makes available to her a ruinous credit with the money-lending wine-dealers of the Gironde. And for those extortions too the cold python willingly acts as go-between."

"And what does he think of you?"

"I'm the chosen victim for the usual swindle. Two or three times, while I was at the piano there, in the villa over by the Basin, I saw him appear in the doorway, snicker silently, then leave hurriedly like someone rushing off somewhere to enjoy his mirth to the full. And every time he appeared he had for me the look of one of those phantoms produced by certain dissociations of a mind on the brink of madness, which terrify the patient with their intermittent presence. A colleague of mine, poor man, before entering a clinic, was assiduously visited by such a caller; and he never dared turn his head for fear of discovering him at his side. Now something of this sort is happening to me too . . ."

"But it is quite obvious that you are dealing with a tolerant, even obliging ghost, my dear friend."

"He does not interfere with the workings of chance and of

fantasy, the caprices of boredom and cruelty, he merely watches them from nearby or from a distance. Only one thing interests him: to keep his accomplice tied to him, on a long leash he can slacken at will, if convenient. His one fear is of flight, of her escaping, her "giving him the slip,' let's say. Now, the arms he uses against her and the threats you can imagine leave her no earthly way out. But there is a possibility of escape toward darkness, there is the possibility of escape to the nether world. And this is the only threat she can oppose to the threats that oppress her."

"Do you believe she would be able to kill herself?"

"At any moment."

Again I saw the steel and ivory weapon gleaming through the opening of her pearl-colored muff. Again I saw the woman with the concealed hand, standing before me, intact, silent, her evil sickness filling her like a truth or like the profoundest lie, which in her took the place of life.

"At any moment, just like that—as you might open a door, cross a threshold, go down a step."

Until that point the things he had told me were no less alien to her ideal figure than, for example, to the cast of the Piombino Apollo resting over there on a square revolving bookcase beside the piano. I was unable to understand or even feel that such could be the true substance of her life. Her mystery remained as untouched as the obscure divinity of the statue which, glowing like gold in the afternoon light, attracted my gaze. Such definite acts were as unlike the unhappy creature I'd met as an Homeric hymn or a chapter of mythology differed from that intent form inhabited by a spirit no less unknowable than the vigor of a tree which provides its fruit.

Where was the hand that had shaped above the god's brief brow that symmetrical, double row of curls? No less forceful seemed to me the power of a past in whose unyielding mould her soul must be imprisoned. My spirit found nothing coherent in that mass of cheap, distasteful facts, but was possessed by a poetic emotion that contained, mysteriously combined with it, what comes into existence under the protection of man's silence. That is why instinct so often guided my eyes toward the Apollo that, finished in every detail like the work of a goldsmith, expressed through every line an infinitude of poetry. Once again form became for me a clairvoyant faith; and listening to so many degrading details, I believed only in that which the beauty polished by the waters of the Eurotas signified for me.

But then suddenly that beauty appeared to me to cling to death like one of those cameos engraved in the white vein running through a dark agate. The contrast was so fierce that everything else vanished. I could hear my heart pound so violently that I was surprised my friend did not hear it. But he was certainly deafened by his own agitation, on which every so often he poured a fiery gulp.

"Why?" I asked him. "Is it because she alludes to it cunningly; because, like so many other women, she uses it as a charming bit of bravado . . ."

"Two years ago, during a period of particular exasperation and rage, she defied death almost every day. She used to have one of those light speedboats you see at the races in Monaco, equipped with a sixteen-cylinder engine, the gift of an Argentine admirer. A daredevil mechanic was always with her, at all hours of the day or night, when that damned North wind would whip up a storm in the Basin and the ocean channel became murderous, and nobody dared venture out past the cape. Through monstrously clever ruses she eluded the closest surveillance and every impediment. She almost always returned just when all hope of seeing her reappear seemed lost. For hours on end the foaming waves would have lashed at her as at a figurehead. Whoever kissed her then must have got a good long taste of the salt on her dried lips."

I could see her so well . . . as if the mooring-place were within me—I could see her wrapped in her waterproof slicker, her face hidden inside the oil-cloth hood, diaphanous as the light of the floating Portuguese man-of-war. And I had waited for her only in order to set off with her again in the dusk.

"At a fasionable Normandy seaside resort, shortly after her divorce, she was assiduously courted by a young polo player who let her ride his delightful horses. Without ever granting him anything, she was able to arouse such an insane passion in him that he asked her to marry him. She laughed him off and tortured him with such subtle perversity that one day he summoned the courage to leave and perhaps went off to play his game on some good English polo grounds in India. She was not in love with him and she had grown accustomed to him only as to a slave she could use for inventing and experimenting with different tortures; but she dearly loved one of the polo horses, a young bay roan that had been given the Shakespearian name of Petrucchio. When she found out they had gone she poisoned herself the same evening, swallowing a number of pellets of corrosive sublimate, and hovered for days on end between life and death. From the bed where she lay in terrible agony she kept holding out the palm of her hand, repeating the gesture she made when she offered lumps of sugar to her Petrucchio."

Now, before my half-closed eyes, I could see that naked hand, freed from the glove; that long strong hand with its lean polished knuckles, grazing the thin delicate lip of one of those small Phidian horses that gallop on the plaster reproductions of the Frieze hanging along my wall. The slender, elegant Athenian riders lacked only the wooden ball and the mallets with the long flexible handles, the hooves of their neatly poised animals lacked only the shorn, springy meadow grass. I could see the slanting sun strike the lush green meadows of Normandy; and a sheaf of light like a golden blade sever with a clean stroke two nervous feet digging into the ground in a sudden, abrupt halt. But my rival's heart leaped with wild joy to the words: "She was not in love with him."

"A year ago, actually around this date at the beginning of April, one evening . . ."

My heart stopped. Inside me I could again hear the overturned chairs banging noisily to the floor, down there, in the dim hall filled with echoes, like a church during the Tenebrae office.

"One evening?" I said, encouraging the voice that had broken off as though intimidated by my anxiety. I could again see the uncontrollable tremor affecting the unknown woman's features, and in her eyes the reflected shimmer of mother-of-pearl.

"One evening, at Bordeaux, for a similar reason, while she was sitting in the car arguing with the uncle of some poor boy that the relatives wanted to prevent her from seeing anymore, she suddenly shot herself in the breast with the revolver she was carrying in her muff. The bullet grazed the lung and lodged under the shoulder blade. Once again her life was in danger for weeks and weeks, again the horror of a hospital confinement, the disconsolate python at her bedside . . ."

All the appearances and all the premonitions of that distant spring evening streamed through me with increased vehemence, giving birth to a kind of immense sorrow with which I would become thoroughly acquainted only at a later time. There was no doubt in my mind; nevertheless I asked:

"What day was it? Do you know?"

"Yes, it was the fifth of April."

"Because of some hopeless love affair?"

An obscure jealousy tormented me.

"Because of some imagined love. And out of weariness with life's stupidity. That Paolo, the youngster she had corrupted, was the nephew of a wine merchant with whom the python had made some usurious deals, borrowing at exorbitant rates against the hoped for bundle—against the devil's own harvest, so to speak. Just see how strangely everything worked out! Almost by way of retaliation against the crook who had fleeced her, she took possession of the boy who was quite charming physically and had rather delicate feelings. In no time she transformed him, made him into her belonging, which she held on her fist like a young hooded falcon. Become aware of the danger, the boy's family decided to put a stop to it, taking at once the most effective measure. They sequestered Paolo, dragged him away, hid him who knows where. This was enough to turn her thwarted whim into frenzy. She asked to see him once more, to talk to him one last time. Their answer was no. Almost every evening she drove to the street where his relatives lived and sent a message; but nothing came of it. That night, having received an imperious and threatening note, the uncle ran out to speak to her, to try and persuade her to give it up. She was sitting in the car; he talked to her standing on the running board. Obstinately she kept repeating: 'I want to see him.' Obstinately he refused. From beneath the fur the gun suddenly went off, almost as if by accident. The usurer took her wounded body to the hospital. When she regained consciousness and could whisper a few words, she begged them to let her see Paolo just for an instant. In vain. The law those merchants laid down was implacable. Only the python remained beside the white bed, with spring clinging to the windowpanes. The bullet was extracted. The scars . . ."

"Ah. Please, describe those scars to me."

I could no longer control my agitation. At those words he had broken off to gulp down yet another drink, to pour yet another dose of liquid fire into the cavern where his tired heart was gasping. His spatulate fingers enveloped the glass completely, so that index and thumb surrounded the rim which he touched with his lips to inhale the aroma of the lukewarm liquor. His nostrils twitched, limned against that worn mask of vice. Everything about him now repelled and irritated me. Between his deformed fingers and the almost crushed glass, I could see the glint of some strangely loathsome smile. I thought of the demonic pigs that often inhabit that particular kind of artist, waiting to be expelled by the exorcism of inspiration.

"So tell me, tell me. How did she finally come to you?"

He laughed brutally into the circle of glass.

"She smelled the carrion, perhaps."

"It would be more graceful, funereally, to say to hear the song of the swan. Doesn't she remind you of a Leda? Look at this group by Ammannati."

He heard the hostility in my voice.

"My dear friend," he said, violently agitated, staring at me. "Tell me the truth. You weren't putting on an act yesterday, when you asked me who she was? Didn't you know her before me? Didn't you too go through it all?"

"No."

"Then why are you jealous?"

"I am not jealous, but perhaps a little annoyed. You know it: I do not conceive of life save in the guise of expression. Now, with your opaque stories, you have denied, line by line, her expression in me. I must rediscover it and recompose it at the cost of love and pain."

"She'll come to you, and you will love her, and you will suffer because of it."

"Are you bequeathing her to me?"

"I assure you, I would like to die at her hands. But I'm being wrested away, like Paolo, I'm being snatched away from that enviable destiny. And this is her peculiar fate: at the crucial moment, each one of her chosen victims escapes her. Even she escapes from herself."

"To a lung already injured by a bullet, weren't you afraid to communicate your disease?"

The air in the room seemed to have become harsh, like that which fills places without laws and without lies. I was no longer capable of forbearance or kindliness. On one side I saw that stupendous figure moulded with a magnanimity as severe as that revealed by the examples of ancient art through whose presence my sense of the world continues and is confirmed; and on the other side I considered that human hotbed of infection, that species of ignominious sensuality which I could not separate from an image of filth and fraud. Their commingling seemed incredible. Deep down my question contained a malevolent curiosity, for I knew he was a braggart and quite incapable of admitting that he'd been jilted, like Petrucchio's rider.

"Did you really hold her in your arms? Did your breathe your breath into her?"

My eyes bored into him. An involuntary contraction of his lips seemed to me the clue I was waiting for; but he canceled it with a strident burst of laughter, rising to his feet with a slight stagger.

"Careful of you to collect information beforehand. And impudent too. But the contagion that attends succession would be my revenge. What time is it? She'll be here at five o'clock, to pick me up and take me back home. You'll see her. She wants you to show her your dogs. I am leaving with my mother tomorrow morning, that's definite. One might say I'm handing you the torch on the run."

I opened the glass doors to the verandah, with the haste of someone on the point of being stifled by some evil emanation.

The tide, which is female, was mounting toward the dune bristling with reeds. The entire surface of the sea trembled and glittered, submerging the sand banks, pale and languid like the bodies of shipwrecked sailors sucked dry by sirens. There was a murmur deep as must be that which announces the spring breaking through in countries that winter covers with ice. The declining sun left behind it a resplendent path upon which it seemed its great white horses, unyoked, must descend. The myths of my race were rushing to invade the deserted places without history. My spirit was fervid, fecund, irresistible as at the beginning of love. The fulfillment of a prophecy was near, and the blood's oracular utterance had been rightly interpreted.

I no longer had the strength to turn and see again that ravaged face, the horrible skull, the harsh, bony mask covered by worn skin. Something stronger than I and that miserable presence was being born right now; and would soon resemble me. A spirit voice said: "Only that is that does not yet exist, and you are living in the future, you have no memory but of the future." My heart said: "I take all upon myself. She is guiltless. I absolve her. Look, there she stands."

It repeated the words of that evening's lone poplar, clothed in irridescent silver, at the corner of that garden. Returning, my twilight and nocturnal visions flowed through me and vanished.

I heard the sharp sound made by the raised piano lid; and I did not turn but waited, shivering as if his hand were touching my shoulder and not the keyboard.

The soul of the instrument vibrated as if shattered by sorrow. The doomed man spoke his true language. His despair seemed at times to reproduce the cry of a terrible happiness and seize his fate by the throat with a claw as powerful as Beethoven's. All that had been or thought before, all became small, empty, and distant. The light of the sun became a kind of blindness.

I turned my face to the jamb, I laid my hand high against it and against my hand I laid my brow, my eyes closed. I created night inside me, to see the dazzling light which the music intermittently poured into the vacuous bottom of life. A pause suspended me over my own annihilation. It was as if that silence would last eternally. The lament resumed; then fell silent again. Resumed a third time, as if halting before the threshold of a door that might remain closed; then it ended. We did not move.

Suddenly we heard the roar of an engine at the garden's gate.

And he rose, and I turned; and I saw myself discolored in him, deadly pale and with bloodless lips, breathless like someone returning to the surface from the bottom.

There are emotions of some curious plastic quality which almost seem to knead human nature and remold it into a momentary appearance.

As we were walking down toward the gate, still under the influence of the musical power, it seemed to me that we were a single being, greater than either of us, inhabited fully by a primitive soul, and that that fantastic, unearthly creature was staggering along, limping in the same direction. It was only an instant, inexpressible, which faded into the immensity of spring, and fled beyond the boundaries of the world. Had the woman's eyes possessed a magical power, she would have seen coming to meet her that lopsided embodiment of Love, like an evanescent chimera. But with each step we separated more and more distinctly. I felt my companion's emotion rise confusedly through his hazy intoxication, through the toxins in his blood, the impediments of his diseases. I felt mine flow like vigorous lymph through the lightness of my body almost completely empty of food, grow with each step as if my heel's contact with the ground enriched me with the fervor of the earth.

She had remained in the car, in front of the gate. When she saw us draw near, she jumped out, with a movement that provoked innumerable waves in me, as in the waters of the Basin the leap of a certain fish, golden and arched like the young moon, sometimes does.

She no longer wore her fetters. That inflection of her beauty from the waist down, which I had noticed earlier, and made me think of Leda in the act of embracing the swan, seemed enhanced by her skirt draped and somehow rolled up toward the front over her legs in a manner that suggested the tightly curled petals of those large gloomy irises called lilies of Susa.

Every fold and the shadow within every pleat and the light on the flounce and the yielding cloth and the recurrent pattern were expressions of her fresh life, which moved me like the outline of her chin stretched taut by divine youth. I took her in, simple, single and manifold in the way that the mass of the air presses against us and simultaneously penetrates each of our pores. Everything in her was known and unknown to me, for that fleeting moment and forever. And she certainly read this wondrous discovery in my eyes.

Inside me a spirit repeated "More! More!"—the word of those who are never satiated and know that after something beautiful there is something more beautiful still.

Visible and invisible things passed through the light, as if carried along by a current, with that precipitous onrush we see near a cataract.

The large garden was transformed into a cradle of warmth by one of those sudden flashes of heat that on the barrens seem the deception of the Western Morgana intent on simulating the breath of summer. The gold of the sun and the pollen of the trees mixed the same dust with the pulsating wind. At their tips the pine trees each bore a drop of vivid blue.

We talked. Each of us three had the air of listening to the other and of answering him. But it was as when in a dream we see the lips of the dead or the living move and do not hear any sound. A silent vortex formed from the fluid substance of two lives; and the third life was like one of those pieces of flotsam that a vortex attracts, spins round, then rejects. Everything was hidden and everything was manifest, everything took place at the deepest root of the soul and at the ends of the nerves, it resembled initiation and final perdition. And assuredly one of us was lost and perhaps two were lost and perhaps three, as in the Greek song of Charon.

"What are you doing!"

Seeing his instinctive gesture, I could not hold back the

exclamation but I was able to muffle it: he had seized the woman's arm and was clinging to it, almost beside himself, imploring and frightened. And nothing could be sadder than the manner in which by managing to control his feelings, he tried to give his involuntary gesture the appearance of an innocent familiarity.

She flushed, then she moved away, and began to run toward the kennel where the young dogs were already in a turmoil. We entered together, as if into the foam of a breaking wave. He did not dare, wary of the onslaught he remained outside, against the bars of the iron fence.

"Leda! Leda and the swans!"

She seemed recaptured and re-fashioned in juvenescent nature, inhabited by a spring welling up behind the crystal of her eyes. She was the source, the river, the banks, the plane-tree's shadow, the quiver of the reed, the velvet of the moss. Huge wingless birds assailed her; and certainly, when she stretched out her arm toward one of them and held it by its plumed neck, she repeated exactly the gesture of Testio's daughter.

"Leda and the swans."

She was leaning against a tree to resist the assault; and, when I tried to chase the frenzied animals with my stick or voice, she cried: "Oh, don't! Don't!"

It was a litter of borzois born in August from my pure white Thamar; but the divine image of sea-foam was linked to their birth as it is with the Hellenic name for Venus. They came racing to my call as the waves rush to the shoal; and I must say that each time I was astonished not to hear water crashing at my feet. Certainly they were made of the most precious substances; and no sea-shell was so delicate as their muzzles in the transition from the roseate hue of the gums to the white of the teeth. Some in their variegated, clear eyes had all the ramifications of marine flora as though concentrated in an incorruptible gem.

"Don't!"

Rearing on their hind legs, they were trying to lick her face and neck, seeking the touch of her hand; but one more than the others, dazzling, though touched here and there by a mark as light as the shadow of smoke—one dog more than the rest pursued and pressed her.

"Oh! This one!" she said with a loving voice, electing him.

I managed to lead the others away and leave her only that one.

Oh imagination, omnipotence of all-powerful desire, insight of poetry!

My heart brimmed with an unknown voluptuousness. Leaning against the tree, she was covered by the quivering beast; and she spoke to him with those words tenderness dissolves into empty sounds. The long, slender muzzle lay against her cheek; and both the feral and the human mouth had the same youthful freshness. Her naked fingers burrowed into the beautiful coat as into the downy feathers under a wing.

There are looks which as they meet celebrate a mystery with each flutter of the lashes. There are others, or even the same ones, that exchange such gifts that the value of all the rest is impaired.

The straw of dry pine needles made a dry, crackling sound under our feet as the three of us walked back to the gate in silence. The trunks to one side shone resplendently like copper armor, on the other they looked dark as if smeared with pitch. The edges of the path were yellow with wild floury dust. Seminars of caterpillars were assembled under what seemed a ragged bit of canvas that bore a resemblance both to the slough of a snake and to an emptied and dried-out honeycomb. I shivered on suddenly hearing close to my ear the sinister tinkle which in that distant night had evoked the figure of the silent shepherd intent on knitting his interminable garment. It was the vespertime breeze among long leaves shaped like iron spears.

"Goodbye then," said my friend, when we got to the car. "Are you really leaving tomorrow?"

"I am."

"Perhaps I'll be at the station when the train leaves, to say goodbye to your mother."

He twisted his mouth as if it had suddenly filled with gall. He climbed into the car with an effort, sat down next to the woman of the myth.

It was as though she no longer recognized either of us. Now, between the hard, sharp edges of her eyelids, she had those eyes that leave you perplexed and desperate, like a smooth granite wall without an opening or a foothold. The same slanting glow, which transformed the scales of the tree trunks into red armor, set fire on her temple to the metal of her hair.

"Goodbye," my friend repeated, waving the hand that had drawn the nocturnal lament from the keyboard.

"She does not love you, she does not love you."

Amid the roar, the wheels spun, cutting deep into the sandy road, leaving between the two furrows some of that fascination which my lantern resting on the ground had illuminated in the distant night.

The roar died down, faded away. Yet I stood there still listening. Now I only heard the beat of my heart drumming at the nape of my neck. An anxiety like a melting blast of fire dissolved every thought in me, and vehemently brought back to my mouth the taste of ashes and blood that had been under my teeth during the walk interrupted by that filthy hand trickling and groping as it searched for the thing it had lost.

I returned to the kennel, as you would return to the place where a miracle of life or art was accomplished, to ask again the questions that remain unanswered.

The long, slender, moist muzzles strained towards me through the bars, and the eyes darkened by the oncoming night stared at me like those of swans when one walks along the water in a garden already invaded by shadows and sleep. I went inside; I spoke, with those guttural sounds dogs understand. They were all around me, imitating on their four paws the crest of the wave when it forms a volute, or rearing up like dancing goats to commemorate the satyrs. One, however, apart, was in the throes of a wild happiness, as puppies are when they find a bone, tossing it into the air and then seizing it again between their teeth, although what he had hold of I was unable to see clearly. He was in fact the one Leda had liked best.

I called him several times. He stopped playing, looked at me with wily distrust, hesitated for a few seconds, more sinuous than a wave in a Japanese drawing; then went off again, leaping and cavorting on the pine needles. A sterner order made him obey. He came over, stealthily, almost crawling, with pleading grace; he took the last few steps bending to one side, then rolled over and lay on his back at my feet, as if he were about to faint or breathe his last. But between his teeth he still held the object with a careful strength which gripped it without breaking it.

"What have you got there? What is it? Let me see."

He pawed the air in supplication. To force him to release it I pressed my fingers on the articulation of his jaws. Thus I managed to take away his find; it was a comb of light tortoise shell, a small comb that had slipped out of Leda's hair!

I felt it moist and sticky with slaver. As I held it upon the palm of my hand I felt it live with a secret life. It weighed no more than a starfish. The dog was still there, stretched out, as if waiting to be forgiven for a transgression; and between his half-closed, fringed lips his fangs shone vividly, evoking in me the phrase "carats, measure of perfection."

I had a single, tormenting thought, generated by an obscure anguish: to try to see her again before night. The lost comb was a plausible excuse. Perhaps she had returned home, after having accompanied her lover. I thought, trembling: "If I could only find her alone; if I could talk to her!" Every delay seemed to me to favor some hostile power and lessen my chances. Anxiety cannot breathe unless things move swiftly. I jumped on a bicycle and went down the road at top speed. The first steep slope cost me no effort at all. A strange vigor ran through every muscle in my body, and the evening breeze played in my chest as through young foliage. I crossed the Ville d'Hiver, the town of the diseased. Here and there I glimpsed a lamp lit behind a glass pane. I thought I could see, to the right, before a bend in the road, the silvery raiment of the apple tree once again covered with blossoms. The bell tolled above the chapel. At the end of a tree-lined avenue, past a tall crucifix, the Basin glittered.

I knew that the house was close to the pier: the fourth on the left. To find it I dismounted and walked slowly, my courage ebbing. There was darkness in all the windows. I followed the garden wall, where the glossy leaves of shrubbery were still glistening. French doors into the entrance hall stood open: at the far end I also saw a balcony open onto the pale sky; and the breeze swelled the curtains, scampered along the arched, vaulted ceiling. The house seemed deserted. The waves' backwash resounded through it, as underneath a wharf. "Perhaps she is over there, sitting quietly in the dark. Now she'll recognize me, she'll jump to her feet, she'll cry out."

I waited immobile in the current of air which carried my life away with it in sparks. Now she was no longer before me; she was behind me, like a block of ice.

At the sound of a footstep I turned around. Someone was coming into the garden. Some unfathomable, instinctive revulsion and then the glitter of the thick spectacles warned me that the man with the head shaped like a truncated pyramid was approaching.

"Who's there?" he asked, in a sharp, penetrating voice that cut through the murmur of the tide.

I told him my name; I briefly explained my presence; I

handed him the small package containing the comb, asking him to return it to the person who had lost it.

"She has not come back yet," he said.

And, with a clipped, cold courtesy, he invited me to wait for her.

My eyes now accustomed to the darkness saw the unmoving head of the python as if I were in the midst of an incoherent dream where, unsuspectingly entering a room, in a corner one suddenly discovers an enormous snake, escaped from its cage, erect on the heap of its coils and staring fixedly from eyes at a man's level.

"Thank you," I said, unable to dominate my strange feeling of terror. "I must go now."

I left; I resumed my race; I reached the end of the promenade bordering the sea, hoping to meet her. I turned off over the dunes. I returned home; among my books and casts I was met again by the odor of tobacco blended with opium; I saw again the open keyboard and the shadow of the Immortal on the mute ivory.

I lived part of that night like someone who knows he no longer possesses his entire self. I stayed there listening to catch the cry which did not yet reach my ear but already touched my soul.

The lethargy due to my exhaustion had lasted for I cannot say how long when my spirits revived with the vehemence of a suddenly alarmed multitude. I found myself propped up on my elbows, shaken by a clamant pounding of the blood, my eyes staring into the dark, with no sense of time, place or what was to happen, like the man who wakes up to die in a house that is crashing down upon him. As always, my window was open; and I sensed the approach of dawn from the color of the starry sky. The cool air soothed me. I lay down again on my back, and stayed awake.

No shore is so lapped by the melancholy of the world as

this westernmost shore at the beginning of each new day. The cock on the barrens crows hoarsely, as though remembering his descent from a cock consecrated to a divinity begot of Night and unaided by any other god. Man, whom that crow awakens, knows he is a shadow before resuming the burden of his body to drag it again to its pain.

Again exhaustion overcame me.

When the full morning light roused me, I at once remembered my promise to pay my respects to my friend's mother. I hurried so as to be on time, and I took a bunch of violets with me.

The North wind had sprung up in an intrepid sky, laden with fecundity, with migrations and returns.

"Perhaps he won't leave," I thought, seeing before me his bitter mouth, hearing again his strident laugh. "No, he won't leave."

But another spirit, mindful of the burst of shattering pain that had torn the fibers of the instrument, told me: "He is leaving. He won't stay. He is vanquished."

And I had drawn a veil over the enigma of that ancient and new face with its broad planes strongly welded together as in the head of a shepherd king carved from basalt. I was expecting some occult message from some horizon, to expose it and to contemplate it without fear.

I walked onto the squalid covered platform. The train stood motionless on its tracks, black, stupid and massive. On a long counter were stacked certain cages made of cane full of dazed chickens. The face of every human creature seemed to be branded by servitude and infamy. The cock of the barrens had already crowed for them.

I was walking past the cars in search of my friend and of myself, when I saw him leaning broken against his mother's shoulder, waxen, as if stupified by a drug, with his legs sagging limply, a bit of the whites of his eyes showing through his partly lowered lids. A gesture of the old lady forestalled the inopportuneness of any word, any act on my part. She leaned with the greatest cautiousness towards me, making sure not to disturb her son, and whispered:

"Last night she killed herself."

This is what Desiderio Moriar told me.

Since his story seemed to have reached its end and he remained silent, staring at the arched sand bank in the middle (pale slope without asphodels and without relics, belonging to the world of the depths), I asked:

"Did you see her on her deathbed?"

"I saw her," he answered.

"Was her face intact?"

He nodded affirmatively, lowering his head, and his hands trembled slightly on his knees.

I added timidly, in a low murmur:

"And how was her face then?"

He made night inside himself, covering his eyes with his open hands, and remained silent.

The ebb-tide had left the immense beach bare; and the low water no longer breathed but immobile mirrored the immobile sky. The canals, the sand banks, the dunes, the long thin spits, the thrusting promontories, the low undergrowth, all the internal lines went in accord with the line of the ocean's horizon, obeying a rhythm of sublime perfection granted to man only during the hour that follows his passing.

In a silence the same as perfect nudity, the beauty of the Occident lay there supine.

In the Landes, June, 1913.

NOCTURNE

Nocturne

Aegri somnia.

I HAVE bandaged eyes.

I lie in bed on my back, my torso immobile, my head thrown back, a little lower than my feet.

I raise my knees slightly to tilt the tablet resting against them.

I write on a strip of paper wide enough for only one line. Between my fingers I hold a soft lead pencil. Thumb and middle finger of the right hand set on the edges of the strip make it glide as the words are written.

With the last phalanx of the little finger I can feel the lower edge and I use it as a guide to keep a straight line.

My elbows are motionless against my sides. I try to impart great lightness to the movement of my hands, so that their play will not go beyond the articulation of the wrist, so that no tremor is transmitted to my bandaged head. In my whole attitude I sense the rigidity of an Egyptian scribe carved in basalt.

The room is utterly emptied of light. I write in darkness. I scratch my signs in the night which presses solid against either thigh like a nailed board.

I am learning a new art.

When the doctor's harsh decree plunged me into darkness

and in the darkness assigned me the narrow space my body will occupy in the grave, when the wind of action grew cold on my face, almost cancelling it, and the ghosts of battle were suddenly excluded by this black threshold, when silence reigned in me and around me, when I had relinquished my flesh and recovered my spirit, from my first confused anxiety arose once more the need to express, to signify. And almost immediately I began to search for some ingenious way to elude the rigors of the treatment and to trick the stern doctor without transgressing his orders.

I was forbidden to speak and in particular to sculpt my sentences; nor could I overcome my old aversion to dictating, and maintain the secret modesty of art that rejects intermediaries and witnesses which stand between the subject and him who works with it. Experience advised me against approaching the page with closed eyes. The difficulty lies not in the first line but in the second and those that follow.

Then there rose in my memory the way of the Sybils, who wrote their brief sentences on leaves scattered to the winds by fate.

I smiled a smile that no one saw in the shadow as I heard the snicking sound of the paper which Sirenetta,* stretched out on the rug in the next room in the light of the low lamp, was cutting into strips for me.

Her chin must be lit up as it was by the reflection from the burning sand when in the time of joy we lay next to each other on the beach at Pisa.

The paper makes a regular, rustling sound which in my imagination evokes that noise of the waves' backwash at the foot of the tamarisks and junipers scorched by the southwest wind.

Beneath the bandage the depths of my wounded eye flare like a high noon in summer at Bocca d'Arno. I see the sand

---

* D'Annunzio's pet name for his daughter, Renata.

corrugated by the wind, streaked by the waves. I can count the grains, bury my hand in them, fill my palm with them, let them stream through my fingers.

The flame grows, the great dog days rave. The sand glitters in my vision like mica and quartz. It bedazzles me, fills me with vertigo and terror, like the Libyan desert on that morning when I rode all alone to the tombs of Memphis.

I have the protection neither of eyelids nor of any other screen. The dreadful fire is inside my forehead, inescapable. The yellow turns to red, the plain convulses. Everything becomes bristling and sharp. Then, as a creating hand molds figures from the yielding clay, a mysterious breath lifts from the glaring expanse the reliefs of human and bestial shapes.

Now the solid fire is carved like chiseled stone.

I have before me a steep wall of red-hot rock sculpted with men and monsters. From time to time it flutters like an immense sail and the apparitions writhe. Then everything vanishes, borne away by the red maelstrom, like a huddle of tents in the desert.

The rim of the torn retina burns and curls up like the Dantesque papyrus, and darkness effaces the words on it one by one.

I read: "Why have you twice deceived me?"

Salty sweat runs down into my mouth mixed with tears from my compressed lids. I am thirsty. I ask for a sip of water. The nurse refuses to give it to me, for I am not allowed to drink.

"Thou shalt quench thy thirst in the sweat of thy face and in thy tears."

The sheet clings to my body like the sheet that envelops a drowned man dripping with salt, pulled ashore and laid out on the sand until someone will come to give him a name, close his foaming lids and howl over his silence.

It is no longer an apparition; it is a continued presence that repulses whoever draws near. But the first apparition comes back to me with an aura of terror.

It is the evening of the burial.

My sorrow is nevertheless still entangled in his decayed flesh.

It is the night of St. Stephen. His fire is lit. I sit where he always sat. Again and again he annihilates me. I lose myself in him.

I can no longer hear what the living at my side are saying.

Cinerina is there, with that strange inspired face of hers which reminds me of the young Beethoven, with her extraordinarily large eyes whose gaze is enriched by melancholy and irony mixed together like a mysterious cosmetic. Manfredi Gravina is there too, to comfort me, to convince me that there are still friends in the world, that there are still comrades sworn to war.

"How is the weather outside?"

Cinerina says that when she arrived at seven o'clock the sky was clear and full of stars. Manfredi says that now there is a thick fog.

It is ten o'clock. It is time to go. Renata is tired.

I put my large gray cape on over my thick aviator's sweater. We make all the gestures in the entrance hall that we did when he was there. But his small black cape is not hanging on the gilded hook, nor do we hear his gracious, ironic voice.

We go outside. We chew the fog.

The town is seething with ghosts.

Men walk noiselessly, shrouded by the mist.

The canals steam.

From the bridges one sees only the white stone edge of each step.

The singing of a drunk here and there, a shout, a sound of shrieks and uncouth laughter. Blue steel lights in the haze.

The cry of the air raid look-outs hoarsened by the fog.

A city of dream, a city of another world, a city washed by Lethe or Avernus.

Ghosts pass by, graze us, vanish.

Renata walks in front of me as she did *then*, and Manfredi walks at her side. They speak as Renata and my comrade spoke. From time to time the fog separates me from them. We cross the bridges. The lights shine like will-o'-the-wisps in a graveyard.

The piazza is full of fog, like a basin filled with opalescent water.

The ancient Procuratil Palaces are almost invisible. The top of the belltower dissolves in the haze.

The Basilica is like a rock in a misty sea.

The two columns in the Piazzetta are like two columns of smoke risen from two identical heaps of ashes.

On the Riva degli Schiavoni, the lights of the boats at their moorings.

The gay music in the Café Orientale, behind the frosted doors; a dance rhythm.

The song of the drunks.

The wandering ghosts.

Tonight the dead are abroad; roaming the streets, as on the night between All Saints and the second day of November.

We say goodbye in the lobby of the Hotel Danieli. I hope Renata will be able to sleep tonight.

I start back to the Red House, alone. My friend is with me, in spirit. A profound regret trickles from my heart.

I look at the edge of land where his small boat used to lay to, where every night we shook hands and said, "See you tomorrow."

In the Piazzetta a man turns around at the sound of my steps. He turns again, walks away, becomes a vaporous shadow, is engulfed.

I enter the arcade of the Procurator's Palace lit by blue lamps. I am astonished when I hear a large family talking about the usual things with the sluggish stupidity of people returning from a night of guzzling. Are they alive? Are they dead? I pass ahead of them. They become shadows.

Beyond the Ponte San Moisé, while I am thinking with a shiver that I will have to pass in front of the alley of Corte Michiel, I catch sight of someone walking at my side, noiselessly, as if he were barefoot.

It is someone of the same height as my comrade, with his identical figure, his way of walking.

He wears a sweater, an indefinable suit of a grayish color, and a cap, also grayish.

He is silent, his is a singular silence, as if no voice at all or breath ever lived inside him.

He walks without heels, without shoes, without sandals. I have an instinctive sensation of terror. I slow down. I see him ahead of me.

He walks like my comrade. Shortly afterward he is again at my side, there, in front of the passage which leads into Corte Michiel. The street is deserted.

I switch on my flashlight at the corner and slow down. I manage to keep a distance of two or three yards between us. He never turns his head.

His step is so soundless and so strange that the rare passersby look at him, stopping for a moment. We have reached the church of Santa Maria del Giglio. The fog is in my mouth, fills my lungs. Toward Canalaccio it fluctuates and accumulates.

The stranger becomes grayer, evanescent; a shadow.

Now I walk faster, so as not to lose him.

In front of the house where every evening one hears the sound of a piano, in front of the house where the antique dealer is, he disappears, suddenly.

He did not fall into the canal, he did not cross the bridge, he did not go through a door. Doors and shops are closed. I examine them with my light. I retrace my steps to make sure.

Then I run up the bridge and all the way down the *calla* to make sure I am not mistaken and that he is not still in front of me.

The *calla* is deserted. Campo San Maurizio is deserted. Perhaps I shall find him again in the narrow *calla* that leads to the Red House? My heart falters. A tatter of fog brushes against my cheek. A swarm of drunks brawl down there at the end of the ferry.

We hear somebody come up the wooden stairs and knock at the door, calling my name.
It is Renata's voice. I open the door.
Renata is pale, beside herself.
"Come, there's been an accident."
"What accident? Miraglia?"
I think of him immediately.
"Come, Genua is downstairs. He will tell you."
I go, my heart in turmoil. I find Memmo Genua at the door, very disturbed. He tells me that he has found out from telephone calls from the air defense look-outs that the plane piloted by Miraglia has crashed into the sea and that the pilot's condition is serious. The mechanic, Giorgio Fracassini, our Fracassini, cannot be found! Perhaps he went to the bottom.

I rush back upstairs, I say goodbye to Cinerina, who is dismayed. I run back down.

Genua, Renata and I start running along the Zattere, looking for a gondola, any sort of boat.

Miraglia has been taken to the Naval Hospital. I keep questioning Genua to find out the real truth.

My knees shake. My tongue is mired. I leave Renata at Campo San Maurizio. I continue down Via Venti-Due Marzo. I pass Miraglia's house, at the entrance to Corte Michiel. People stare at me. I am unable to master my horrible fear.

We run into a sailor who is walking quickly. Genua stops him. I cannot hear what he says to him, I come closer. The sailor was on his way to my house. I learn that the body has been taken to St. Anna's Hospital.

The body! He is dead.

Genua steadies me.

I begin to run, looking for a way, any way, to get to our destination and escape the curiosity of the passers-by. The sailor catches up with us and offers to take us in a launch waiting near Santa Maria del Giglio. We go.

The small bay in front of Saint Mark's—bright blue.

The sky everywhere.

Bewilderment, despair.

The immobile veil of tears.

Silence.

The throb of the engine.

The Giardini.

We turn into the canal.

On the right, the bank with its naked trees; it looks funereal and remote.

Ahead of us, in the low sky, close to its shelter, the foolish and obscene shape of the anchored blimp, the color of silver.

It is about three o'clock in the afternoon.

We arrive. I jump onto the dock, I go inside.

I ask the officer on duty for Giuseppe Miraglia. He points to a door. I enter.

The corpse lies on a trundle bed.

Bandaged head. The lips tightly closed. The right eye injured, livid. The right jaw broken: beginning to swell. The skin dirty olive in color: an expression of unusual serenity. The upper lip slightly protruding, slightly swollen. Cotton plugs in his nostrils.

The look of an Indian prince wearing a white turban.

Hands yellowish, crossed over his chest. Both feet swathed in white gauze bandages.

The right foot is broken. The thumb of one hand is broken. One leg broken. Several ribs broken.

He wears a blue jacket with gold buttons. The jacket he had on yesterday.

They try to drag me away. I refuse. I remain on my knees. Beg them to leave me here alone.

When I am alone, I bend over the dead man, call him several times. My tears rain down on his face. He does not answer, does not move.

I fall on my knees again.

The sounds of the day.

The throbbing of engines on the canal.

The thud of steps on the boardwalk.

A sailor enters with a sheaf of candles; sets four candles at the four corners of the bed.

Luigi Bologna comes in, Carlo della Rocca comes in. I cannot move, cannot get up.

Somebody places a bunch of flowers at the feet of the corpse. I think I recognize Silvio Montanarello, the youngest aviator.

Two sailors come in with fixed bayonets and take up positions at the head of the bed, standing there immobile. Another sailor attaches a ship's flag to the rear wall, facing the window. A flag is placed at the head of the cot.

After a period of time that I cannot reckon a sailor arrives with another bundle of candles and opens the door in the wall opposite me.

The door has been closed.

I hear shuffling feet. On a stretcher two sailors are carrying in the body of Giorgio Fracassini, found after two hours amidst the torn canvas and twisted wires, when they were taking the plane's wreckage back to Sant'Andrea.

They cross the threshold, put him down in the other room.

I get up to go and look at him. I bend over him.

Memories of the flight over Trieste, his advice about the gasoline pump, his cleverness in stowing away all twenty-one of the small green-white-and-red sacks . . .

225

He looks as though he were sleeping. His face is composed, severe. He is wearing his leather suit.

He looks like a monk to whom the crossing has brought beatitude. His manly face, almost always shiny and dripping sweat, with its pale, daring eyes, its broad open forehead, its hooked nose, has become peaceful, ennobled. He is truly at rest.

I return to the adjacent room and find my comrade's body covered by the black cloth with the golden cross.

His face, too, is covered with gauze.

A sailor is about to remove the flag from the head of the cot and replace it with a small Red Cross flag. I stop him. He was taking it to put up on the wall in the other room.

I arrange the red and the green, right and left, over the black cloth.

The magnetic life of the Navy's battle colors.

The white roping as on the border of a sail, the slip-knot . . .

They go to find another flag for Giorgio.

Admiral Umberto Cagni arrives, accompanied by other officers. I see him dimly through burning eyes. He approaches, uncovers the dead man's face, murmurs a word, what word I do not know. He also goes to look at the mechanic. Then he comes over to me as I lean against the wall and make an effort to control my horror. He takes my hand, clasps it, saying in a rough, soldierly, almost violent tone: "Goodbye!" He leaves.

The boat's crepitating sound. The launch moving away.

Here is Manfredi Gravina, then Alberto Blanc. I do not move. A sailor puts a black cushion under my knees, the cushion from the *prie-dieu*.

Night has fallen. I hear the first call from the look-outs: "Over the air keep watch!" I think about Renata, I think about the flowers she has put in our vases for him.

I get up, go outside on the pontoon dock.

Low, opposite me, the golden moon shines in the sky.

I step into the boat, go back down the canal.

The walls of the Gardini, the shore with the bare, stark trees, the blimp's black bulk.

Genua accompanies me, to pick up the parcels I had prepared and give them to Alberto Blanc who was supposed to take them to Rome.

With me I carry death, the smell of death. Renata is waiting for me: she knows everything. We embrace, weeping. She wants to come and see him.

I go into the dining room to get the flowers. There are three settings! I gather all the flowers from all the vases. I take them with me in a sheaf.

Again I enter the mortuary chamber.

The candles burn. The small flames waver, reflected by the blades of the bayonets. The two sailors are at attention, on guard, rigid.

I arrange the flowers on either side of the corpse: I feel the shape of his thighs, his legs.

I put the white jonquils on the red and green of the flag.

I uncover the pitiful face. The right cheek is swelling out and turning black. The mouth seems closed.

Again and again reality escapes me. I reflect. I close my eyes. I imagine him alive as he was yesterday. Then I look at him and see him inert, bloodless. Is it true?

The vigil begins.

Opposite me is the door to the other death chamber where Giorgio Fracassini lies, illuminated, filled with wavering shadows.

The two stock-still sailors; the stiff gleam of the naked bayonets.

The plash of the canal below the window.

The shout from the sentinels on guard outside.

A singular atmosphere, like a block of impenetrable crystal, surrounds the corpse.

Around ten o'clock the Commander-in-Chief arrives. He

enters with a firm, energetic step. Dominates his emotions.
Kneels, prays. Rises, goes into the room where Giorgio Fracassini lies. Shakes my hand in silence, leaves.
I hear the throb of the launch. Then everything returns to
silence.

Faces faces faces, all the passions of all the faces flow
through my wounded eye, innumerably, like hot sand through
the fist. No one stops. But I recognize them.
Is it not the enormous Roman crowd in May, in the evening
at the Campidoglio? Enormous, fluctuating, howling.
I feel my pallor burn like a white flame. There is no longer
anything of me in me. It is as if I were the demon of that
turmoil, the genius of the free nation.
My perseverance over thirty years, my love and my worship
for Italy the Beautiful, the courage of my solitude, the song in
the desert, my contempt for obscurity and vituperation, the
patience of my waiting, the restlessness of my exile, are transformed for me into a single mass of incandescent force. The
whole past flows together toward the whole future. I live my
Credo at last, in spirit and blood. I am no longer intoxicated
with myself, but with all of my race.
Faces faces faces, shaped in the smoldering flesh, printed in
the blood-red fire.
The turmoil has the breath of a furnace. The gasp of a
voracious crater, the crash of a savage conflagration.
I lead and am led. I ascend to crown and I ascend to crown
myself.
An epic spring uplifts and carries me off as if this ancient
triumphal stone were melted by scarlet lymph.
Riots of swallows graze Marcus Aurelius' green horse,
which at each shrill cry seems about to unseat the emperor
and rear up towards the ultimate fate.
The confused delirium of the multitude becomes a clear
voice within me.

I speak. Each of my words echoes under my skull as if cast back by domed metal. Each breath strains the circle of my breast. I suffer and am proud that my joy is mixed with pain. It is like the suffering of creation, like the anguish of a birth. The crowd howls in labor. The crowd howls and writhes to engender its destiny.

Beyond the lead-covered ledge I see thousands and thousands of faces, and only a single face. A face of passion and expectation, of determination and redemption, which burns in the center of my breast like a generous wound.

Like a sudden *chanson de geste*, my words separate into ample loops which the clamor completes and lofts on high.

Overwhelmed by a cry higher than any other, I lose my voice in the pause. The imperious cry seems to demand more than speech.

Before me on the leaden ledge an unknown hand sets down a large sabre, curved like a scimitar.

I grasp it and draw it from its sheath. That cry demanded that gesture. A flash of lightning seems to pass over the turmoil.

It is Nino Bixio's sabre, the weapon of the slashing hero, with the names of victorious battles etched on the honed blade.

I press my lips against the unsheathed sabre. It does not feel cold because my lips are bloodless. All the blood flames in my heart.

The silence of the crowd is like a maelstrom that attracts me, surrounds me—like a vortex that drains and destroys my life.

I fling away my life, abandon my soul to delirium. The last words are like those blows of the founder's mallet struck to open the tap out of which the molten metal flows into the mold.

The crowd is like an incandescent pouring of metal. All the mouths of the mold are gaping. A gigantic statue is cast.

I turn. I descend. I sway, prey to a slight dizziness. Thirst devours me. I beg for water. The women of the people crushed in the crowd surround me with compassion while I wait. A rough hand gives me a glass of lustral water. I quench my thirst and purify myself. I drink and spill the libation that precedes the sacrifice.

I descend. I am carried down, I do not know by whom. All is ardor and clamor, creation and inebriation, thirst and victory, beneath a sultry battle-like sky through which shrieks a flashing of swallows.

We suffer because we are defenseless. We suffer because we are not fighting, because we are not transformed into a thrust of swift legions crossing the unjust frontier.

Dishevelled youths with wild faces, dripping sweat as if after the struggle, throw themselves at the wheels as if to shatter themselves.

Workers darkened by the dross of labor, bent by concentration, gnarled by effort, workers of all works, who it seems to me have all wielded the hammer, pounded the boiling iron on the anvil, reach toward me with their strong hands as if to seize and crush me in their sudden love,

Women, powerfully carved like the mother of the two tribunes, with the same gesture throw me a flower and give a son to the war.

The fold of a flag blindfolds me. It is the red flag of Trieste. It is continually over my head. At times it waves, drops and covers me. I pour my yearning into its folds.

In the red shadow of its folds I hear the first chime of the Capitoline bell. My heart cracks. I rise. The wheels stop. The crowd falls silent. It is nothing but the chain of vertebrae traversed by an identical shiver.

The bell tolls. The roar of the bronze penetrates every marrow. An immense shout drowns it, rises above it. To war! To war!

Does it ring from the depths of the dead centuries? Does it ring from the depths of centuries to come?

We are carried by the twentieth wave of the centuries—ten and ten—by the second decennial tide.

The bell of the people proclaims war. It no longer is a call of bronze. It is a call of red fire at the summit of the Latin sky. The entire Fatherland hears it and leaps!

To war! To war! The splendor of the evening is defeated by these thousands of flaming eyes, by this stirring of flags and threats, by this sublimation of the free populace once more possessed by its true god.

Faces faces faces, all the passions of all the faces, flow through my wounded eye, innumerably, like hot sand flows through a clenched fist.

It rains wildly on the evening of Ash Wednesday. A cloudburst in March. I listen intently to the crash of the water.

My ear now—it seems to me—is more sensitive than when it composed the music of the poem "Rain in a Pine Grove."

I distinguish all the strings on the great harp of the meteor, and I almost test them.

If only I could open two holes in the wall facing the garden, and push my dessicated hands outside!

Won't the downpour be too violent for the fuzz of the small, delicate, new leaves?

Nerissa sends her little maid through the rain to bring me an armful of flowers she had found in Padua this afternoon.

The moist air comes into my room, cool freshness spills onto my sheets.

Speaking about the maid, the nurse says to me proudly: "She has come without an umbrella! She is dripping like an eave. The flowers are all drenched. We must wait until they dry."

My relentless thirst sniffs out the moist smell that immediately impregnates my darkness. My heart throbs. I beg the compassionate one to come close, to let me touch the flowers.

NOCTURNE

I beseech her. I threaten to rip off my bandages, to throw myself from the bed to the floor. I get my way.

The flowers are placed on the counterpane. I have them under my seeing fingers. I palp them, separate them, recognize them. There is the hyacinth. In small bundles tied with thread. The stems are uneven. Together they form a thick cluster. As I inhale, their perfume grows like the pain of a small cut.

There is the zagara. It is the Arabic name which Saracen Sicily gives to orange blossom. I learned it as an adolescent on my native beach, from a cabin boy off a schooner. It pleases me so much that if I utter the name, I can smell the perfume.

There is the hot-house zagara: a bunch of leaves which vibrate under my touch and, at the center, the hard buds. I feel them one by one. Some are closed, some are split, some are half open. Some are delicate and sensitive like nipples, fearful of a caress. The scent is candid, unripe, infant-like. But one must seek it out among the ice-cold, dripping leaves which wet my chin and enter my mouth.

There is the rosemary. It is the most rain-swollen, completely saturated with water from the clouds. It smells most strongly at the apex, like the last phalanx of a finger putting on eye-shadow and rouge. There is at the bottom of its scent something of the milky fig, the small, green fig. There is also, if I persist, something of the ripe greengage plum. More the smell of grass than flower, more of fruit than flower.

Most of all I like the zagara, both name and thing. It is more tenuous, rarer; not nuptial but virginal. I search for it again, inside the leaves. It pales the fire in my eye. It is hard and white like the sclera.

I remember the large orange groves at Villacidro on the island of the Sardinians. I was a lissome animal. My ankles were slender. I used to take off my shoes and walk with my young feet on the snowy flower which wove over the ground.

I remember a walled-in orange grove at Massa, in the direction of the Amalfi coast, if my memory does not deceive me. I had not quite recovered from an evil potion. I was bewildered, as though I had entered an unimaginable labyrinth. The trunks of the trees seemed carved from the stone of secret grottoes. The flowers were like the foam of which immortal flesh is born. The shade was almost aquatic, modulated by the dying song of some mysterious Siren banished from the sea.

The rain does not cease. I hear it splatter in the garden, on the embankment, the small piazzas, the alleyways. My generous friend will not dare to venture, as her maid did, through the deluge which has submerged gloomy Venice. I had thought the flowers were to announce her.

The tedium of immobility oppresses me. Dull anger tautens me from the nape of my neck to my heels. I am getting up, I will throw off the bandages and walk under the eaves.

My melancholy pleasure is already exhausted. The nape of my neck throbs. From the stems of the hyacinths oozes a disagreeable fluid which glues my fingers.

And where does this scent of violets come from? Are there violets in the room? Who has hidden them from me?

I reach out with cautious hands, groping around. I find a bunch that had slipped from the counterpane to the top of the bed. My heart flutters. For nothing at all, my heart is startled!

It is a bunch of violets. Wet, they had no perfume. The warmth of the bed gives life to them again. It is an exquisite surprise. I am delighted by them as if I myself had gathered them at the edge of a strange meadow. They are no longer violets from Padua—for me they are wild violets from golden Pisa.

I remember a March cloudburst in Pisa. We were on Piazza del Duomo. We took shelter under the architrave of the main portal, shaking off the drops. There we lingered, waiting for the rain to stop. *Imbres effugio*, said the speaking emblem on the door.

The rain fell on the short grass with an even crepitation which to us seemed as intimate as the sound of a shell held against one's ear. Leaning back against the bronze of the doorjamb, we began to possess it, merge with it. The dampness seemed to augment the preciousness of the material. Like curious children, we stuck our fingers in the metal foliage, fondled the tiny wreathed head which gazed out from among the olives and branches. Above us spoke the symbols: *Fons signatus, Hortus conclusus.** Astonished, amid the leaves we kept discovering lizards, snails, frogs, birds, fruit—endlessly. In our fingers we felt the pleasure of the artist who had shaped those forms, his wisdom and his whims. The more we looked at the bronze, the richer, more powerful and deeper became its patina. It was enhanced by our loving eyes and returned love for love. Above us spoke the symbols: *Onustior humilior, Tantumodo fulcimentum.*** The crashing downpour slowly diminished. The sound seemed to reach us and be stilled within us like the harmony produced by the interior echo of the Baptistry; the empty meadow had a sense of derelict gentleness along the walls in the direction of the old town. Archbishop Ubaldo's graveyard was closed and meditative, withdrawn around its fifty-three shiploads of soil from Calvary.

Then we descended from the smooth threshold. We left the bronze and marble for the grass. Dusk was falling. We were alone. And life led us by the hand, indulgently.

It was said that from channels and canals beyond the Camposanto a silent fever would rise toward evening and come to roam the holy meadow. Yet we felt nothing but the shiver of the soggy, softish spring.

We walked between the Camposanto's wall and the side of the Duomo, where there was a mystic space for our music. In our fantasy the interior frescoes shone through to the outside.

---

* Sealed fountain; closed garden.
** More burdened are the humiliated; Only a support.

And our music had the face of that robed woman whose cheek rests upon her psalter.

I was vigilant and attentive to my desire.

I was what I am when my nature and my culture, my sensuality and my intelligence cease to struggle and are wholly renconciled. I was a musical mystery, with the taste of the world in my mouth.

When I halted, my companion, who for me bore the name of Ghisola, would ask: "What are you seeking?"

Dusk was falling. The marble's shadow was cerulean. It is a marble that at sunset exudes blueness like lapis lazuli. It blued the grass almost like a brush-stroke of ultramarine.

The silence opened up before us, divided to right and left, flowing along our sides as the river polishes the swimmer. Our feeling was simple and ineffable. We were poor and unburdened, we were rich and unburdened. We were like two beggars without wallets and like two sovereigns without diadems.

"What are you seeking?" beautiful Ghisola asked me at intervals, as if in cadence.

Was I a magic seeker for treasures or wells of water? All my wells and all my treasures were within me.

I sought for my desire. And suddenly I had found it.

I stopped, closing my eyes to keep my happiness beneath my lids. I was no longer anything but a single sense. My entire brain throbbed in unison with my knowing nostrils.

I stooped in the watery shade, deftly probed the moist grass with my fingers. My lowered face also felt suffused with ultramarine; even my hands turned a faint blue.

"But what are you trying to find? What?"

I had discovered a clump of violets.

Sirenetta has a voice that soothes, that lulls. When she speaks my heart is assuaged, my pulse slows. It reminds me of the young voice of my mother who every evening made me fall asleep in a small boy's bed with a fairy tale.

NOCTURNE

Sirenetta reads the poets, and the stream of dreams carries me into the shadow of the laurel groves.

She stops reading, and immediately pain bites into me again. Her speech is Tuscan, with a Siennese purity. This is how St. Catherine spoke as a young girl when she tended her garden. A bee has left sacrificial honey in her mouth.

Through her mouth the sonnets of *Vita Nuova* touch me deep inside as when, at sixteen, I read them on Affrico's grassy banks, around the time of the Resurrections.

And as I dwelt with bitterest sorrow "like those who cannot stir," I too saw faces of dishevelled women who said to me: "Your youth is dead!"

And also, after those women, I saw faces different and dreadful to behold, which said: "You are dead."

Having a beautiful voice, the dear child is sensitive to beautiful voices. She tells me which one she loves most among the people in our family. She speaks about them as about the taste of water from different fountains.

Then she tells me about a night of full moon when she was a pupil at Poggio Reale and was taken with several other girls to the observatory at Arcetri. In her memory she sees large terraces whitened by the moon, large terraces piled one above the other, leading to the stars as to the abode of an astrologer invented for a poem of chivalry.

And there she heard the world's most beautiful voice.

It was that of a modest assistant, who while at the telescope spoke of the lunar mountains and valleys, of Saturn's rings and Mars' reddish glow. All the young girls hung from his lips, entranced by the spell of the full moon.

The pure voice was like a note of the celestial harmony. And the crown of virgins pulsed like a humanized constellation, encircling the student of the stars.

My daughter has dark Oriental eyes, those Saracen eyes which blossomed in Sicily at the time of Frederick II.

236

Sometimes, when she suddenly bends over me, they seem set in her temples like those of palfreys which gaze out of ancient miniatures.

A head, white in color or rather the color of peach blossoms, with a dark tightly curled mane difficult to divide into braids.

Sometimes, when she sits on a low cushion and cuts for me the strips of paper which rustle slightly like dry palm leaves, the poem "The Flower of Soria" written by Frederick, comes to mind.

She had gathered small olive branches in the Garden of Gethsemane; and was braiding them with the skill that adorns Palm Sunday and she had learned in our region.

With them she made a mat the length of my body, for me to lie on.

Entering the shadow, "The swallows have arrived," Sirenetta says, in a restrained tone which seems the shadow of a cry.

I recall, I don't know why, the sound of my voice of long ago, when as a boy I lifted the ironbound cover of the well and, leaning over the stony rim furrowed by the rope, flung a shout to its bottom where I glimpsed my face in the shimmering water.

In my eyes I see that muffled, silvery sound in which the levity of maidenhair fern shivered.

I would lower the cover cautiously, so that the clang of the iron latch would not drown my secret cry.

And it seemed to me that I had imprisoned in the cool dark well something living, like a bird that continued to fly and sing, fluttering its wings against the damp bricks.

Sirenetta speaks, remembering that one evening I took her to see the staircase of the Bovolo* and, to prepare her for the delight, blindfolded her lovely eyes with my hands in the

---

* A winding staircase in Palace Contarini del Bovolo in Venice.

narrow alley there, before coming out in Corte Contarini. Sirenetta says: "Don't you think there must be nests hanging in the Bovolo stairs? I want to go and look at it again to find out if the swallows go to live there, as I would if I were one of them!"

O child, unnail me from here and then take me with you.

I am immobilized by two nails in my armpits and two in my feet.

I remain silent. But a leaping instinct of my tired flesh imitates the flashing swallow.

Her tiny wild eyes open beneath my bandage.

She enters Corte Contarini. A cry, two cries.

She comes from Riva degli Schiavoni.

She passed over Chioggia.

She flew to San Francesco del Deserto.

She circled around the Oriental belltower on Isola degli Armeni.

Alighting for an instant in the mouth of the Lion on the column of the Piazzetta, she was tempted to build her new nest there.

She enters Corte Contarini. A sharp cry, a white flash.

She descends toward the dry wells, set apart by iron fences.

Then she brushes against the loggias spiralling one above the other, with the musical rapidity of a hand executing an arpeggio on the strings of a sculptured harp.

She shimmers and flutters around the last balustrade.

Then I see her disappear, hear her shriek under the low ceiling.

Then I see her dart like an arrow, cross the roofs, pierce the azure.

I hear her cry of pain, cry to the sun of my suffering.

While my body is being washed and perfumed part by part by compassionate hands, like the body of someone dead, a faint drowsiness comes over me. All the apparitions of my sleepless night have dissolved in the light of morning. My left eye is allowed to see a little light.

The shutter is almost closed so that the sun cannot enter, but down over there the old rose-colored silk of the wall turns golden. The glimmer touches my naked lid together with a mild warmth which is nothing but its own sweeetness. I feel my wasted knees rub against each other, I feel them as polished as the knees of graveyard statues.

The sleep which the spring equinox brings me is like the sleep of Ilaria in her tomb at Lucca. This glow resembles the glow of the stained glass window which there in the Tuscan duomo illuminates the reclining statue.

This musical tone of fatigue brings back to my joined feet my love for the most beautiful of my young borzois.

I surrender to sleep with reluctant slowness, and know that I may never wake again.

Compassionate hands cover me with a fresh sheet which gives my blind eye a vision of whiteness.

I have escaped from the night.

The sad soul seems "purged in the fire of suffering," as the mystic says.*

My sleep is no longer a flaming of formidable phantoms, but rather a quiet, even lightness.

The nurse said: "The front of the house is already dressed in green *like Ornella*."**

The wall dissolves without dust and the small new leaves tremble against my face. My breath stirs them.

How long did I sleep? I immediately feel my sick eye lacrimate under the bandage. A tear has reached down to the joining line of my lips.

The tears expressed by the soul and those shed by the irritated lid—are they bitter with the same salt?

---

* A quotation from *Le Poesi Spirituali* of B. Jacopone di Todi. (Tr.)
** She is quoting from D'Annunzio's play *La Figlia di Iorio*, act 1, scene 1, verses 6-7. (Tr.)

I sense the afternoon. There lingers in my puny body almost a golden hue from the diurnal sleep slept in the light. I call. It is three o'clock in the afternoon. I have slept for a long time. The nurse smiles and says that the musicians have come to play music. From the small adjacent room I hear the tuning up of the cello and violin.

Sirenetta appears on the threshold. She wears a striped dress and her beautiful dark head rises from a white collar moving on her bare neck with that grace which is peculiar only to birds and therefore seems dictated by the singing instinct.

She is an angel in a tunic stepping out of a Florentine singers' gallery. She precedes the music and announces it.

The first notes of the Fifth Trio by the Flemish Beethoven truly touch my heart, physically, as drumsticks strike the kettledrums in the living marble of Lucca.

It is the trio also called "The Ghost Trio."

I listen to it as if after death.

The musicians are hidden, they are in the other room. The small, enclosed room acts like a soundbox. Harpsichord, violin, and cello are three voices which speak as though in a religious drama, a sacred mystery.

I have pulled the bandage down over my living eye too.

When, after a long pause, the instruments begin the *largo*, I see a yellow stripe blend into a purple stripe. Then I see a purple cloth with a yellow border over a shape which is that of the crucifixion. The ravaged knees protrude, lifting the cloth in the center; and when the violin resumes the theme, at the center the cloth turns scarlet.

And then each time I feel a deep, piercing agony.

From vein to vein all the way to my heart each note drives the dregs from the cup of life, what I have not as yet tasted, what I have prayed should be kept far from my lips. Each note drives them closer to my heart, and the heart will not open to receive them but twists and rejects.

They have suddenly reached the rim, it is near. The heart falters, and is suddenly possessed, filled, replete.

I discern the shadow of my childhood bending over my face. Her light fingers touch my cheek beneath the bandages, become wet with my tears. Over chilled, sticky tears, warm weeping gushes from my lost eye.

The soul's life drenches the bandage.

I do not deceive myself. I am certain that the tide has poured first from the blind eye socket, then from the other.

Now both eyes are alive with the same sublime life. They are two living founts.

I no longer know where my misfortune is. My misfortune is a blessing that is unknown.

The tears overflow. My child has immersed her fingers in them but does not dare to dry them.

I feel her head close to the pillow.

And my daughter, the daughter of my flesh, says a material word to me on the threshold of old age, the tender word that mothers say to children!

I feel that with that word she takes me upon her lap like the ancient Pietà and assuages my wounds.

Once more the demon has kindled all the fires deep in the depths of my eye; and he blows on the sinister pyre with all of his madness, as during the most desperate hours of this remorseless martyrdom. The burning in my eye reduces my whole wretched body to a bundle of brushwood just at the edge of the flame.

The fern leaf I have inside my eye multiplies, rises, thickens. And now I am like that clump of ferns, the color of copper and gold, which I saw in the burning forest of the Landes, untouched at the borders of the fire.

The flame had grazed it without burning it. And I was filled with wonder and superstition at seeing that fragile, so burnable thing on the rim of the fire, intact. It was ready to flare up in an instant, turn to ashes in an instant, and the voracity of the fire had spared it for a miracle.

Who is swathing me in searing ashes? The heart's apex sparkles and traverses the ashes.

I am my ashes and I am my phoenix. I am opaque and I am refulgent.

I survive the pyre, intoxicated with immortality.

Who has lifted me onto my horse with such an imperious hand?

The spirit of attention invades me like a god armed with a thousand eyes.

Attention creates that which it contemplates.

I create ardor.

My intimate fate is this.

Oh woods of the westernmost shore! Oh forest of fecund wounds! Oh exile of my power drained in tears like resin.

I ride through the already burnt stands of pine.

I ride through the already parched pine woods. I roam through the young pine plantings without a future, sacrificed like prime adolescents on the idols' searing bronze.

The ground is hot and smoky and here and there blackened, streaked with whitish ash.

The pine trees are dark, scorched to the crown, without needles and only naked branches; but all standing straight like unvanquished martyrs. Some are charred; the fire still smoldering in the mutilated trunks seeks out the roots, gnaws away underground.

Some carry their blackness covered by impalpable flakes of ashes all along the craggy trunk.

The hoof of my horse could sink into an empty trunk as into a smoldering sheath. I never relax my vigilance. I am all eyes and all acumen. The black twigs threaten to pierce the sole, strewn like those iron tridents which once lamed the enemy's chargers.

The smoldering ashes are burning hot. I perceive the smell of the burnt nail, as though I were at the door of a blacksmith's shop. I breathe in the flame, I hear it interspersed with gasping, crackling, scraping. I am drenched and I pant.

Who is that man who, the skin of his face burnt, his clothes in flames, rolls in the sand of the fireguard and shrieks?

I continue across the ashen barrens. I ride over ash and sand through the dark wood.

Now and then a silent gust lifts the ashes to great heights.

In the silent sky I see the slender twirl of a waterspout that wavers.

It casts a spell.

I turn my horse toward it to observe it from closer by.

As I approach, it disappears.

And another rises farther away.

And casts its spell.

And I approach. And it fades away.

And another rises still farther off; and then another; and then another.

Silently they vacillate in the burning air; beckon; dissolve and disperse.

They are like the ghosts of holocausts.

I cross the ditches; pass beyond the wide, sandy roads, which in the Landes are called fireguards, which did not suffice to preserve the adjoining woods. The sand on them is mixed with a dust of ash and ground charcoal.

Beneath a landslide a knot of roots burns and smokes, hissing, squeaking, crackling.

Here and there amid the carbonization and incineration I see a dry blade of grass intact, an untouched leaf of fern. I discover here and there along the edge of the ditches where the fire has reached, a tuft of grass, a stem laden with small rosy or purple flowers.

The astonished soul alludes to itself.

No longer ghosts of ashes, but gloomy columns of smoke.

And a sinister roar, which seems to rise from the heart of the earth.

Among the burnt pine trees I urge my horse toward the expiatory abyss.

The serpentine fascination of danger encircles my breast.

The ground smokes and splutters under the hooves.

The fat cloud of smoke swallows the flames farther away.

The acridness of the resin bites into my throat.

The world grows larger, pounds at me, deafens me.

From deep inside me a song bursts forth against this when suddenly between the tree trunks living flames appear.

Beauty of the fire, you are newer to me each time than the time of spring.

The multitude of flames is deployed on the field before me like an impenetrable enemy.

Higher than the splutter of the turf, above the sizzle of the resin, above the crashes and bursts, they sing.

They are deployed in a single line which advances, voraciously.

They eat away at my eyes, devour my face.

They have an orange color, which receives again and again an admixture of blue and green and gray. They darken at times like embers; dazzle at times like lightning. Their very diversity perturbs me, like the looks of an enchanter.

They have left behind the carbonized, smoking forest. They advance in a long, endless chain. Deploy a battle front which disappears into the distance, diving into the cloud of black smoke.

Their violence is such that it does not seem to spring from

the surface of the ground where the stubble is rooted, but erupts from the depths, surges from the abyss, like the vomiting of open craters.

They have violence and tenacity, impetus and perseverance. They teach us how to fight.

Here are the modes of the flames' artfulness.

They assail the trunks, first testing the evident roots, the exterior outcrops. Then they glide upward over the scales.

They seem to fondle, they seem to search for the place into which they can sink their fangs most effectively.

They stroke where a branch was pruned, where there is a resinous wound, an aromatic sore, and then they dig in there.

In a lull of the wind they fall lower.

But the one that has bitten into the trunk at the vital spot, that flame does not let go. She remains alone, suspended, intent on biting, intent on devouring, detached from the others, alone with her hunger and her fury, obstinate.

I think—I don't know why—of those naval battles, those boardings and assaults when fists and jaws seize the ship's rails and enemy axes chop through wrists, sever necks; and the dreadful hands still remain clinging to the wood, the teeth remain sunk into the wood, while the bodies plunge down and sink below the water. Thus the red claws of the flame, thus the red maw of the flame cleaves to the trunk severed from the body, which subsides.

Oh inert combatant, remember the brother of Aeschylus.

Certain tree trunks burn only on one side, bursting out from inside through the vertical incision made by the resin spike.

The fire is like a tattered flag hoisted on the tree.

Now the wind grows stronger.

All the victorious flags snap and unfurl and tear into shreds which dissolve in flight.

A great salty squall comes from the open sea.

With the roar of a tempest, the fire bounces up again and

again, drives past the tree tops, envelopes whole trees, reddens them from root to crown.

Flaming scales of bark and blazing pine cones spurt far out like crystals of solidified lava from a volcano.

The innumerable nests spun by caterpillars' larvae catch fire and fly even farther and propagate the fire even down there in the safe wood.

The resin sizzles, bubbles, splutters. The clay resin jars, boiling, searing, brimming over, leap, fall down again, explode like hand grenades. Every explosion hurls myriads of red needles.

Within the clamor a mysterious melody takes shape, stretches, uncoils, flows.

Are the salamanders singing?

The flames flee with the smoke into the sky. A vortex of dark, sinister smoke fills the air, attacks the sun. Through it I see the sun like a reddish disk about to turn cold.

I no longer see it. It is swallowed.

The wind makes a truce. The smoke thins out.

I see the disk again. Little by little it turns from red to russet orange, from russet orange to blond. But in the shadows the fire surpasses the splendor of the sun.

Then suddenly all around their edges the smoky clouds turn blond, resplendent.

Is the sun triumphing?

For an instant it blazes in the blue, while the huge flame collapses and crawls.

But up there, in those high knots of the trunks, the small flame survives and gnaws. But up there, in the eaten-out trunks, already abandoned to death, the small obstinate flame searches for the last morsel.

And, during a respite in the attack, the mysterious melody becomes more distinct. It is light like a soprano voice. It enraptures me in a way that is beyond all ardor.

Are the salamanders singing?

*   *   *

The Ocean once again hurls its powerful volleys between the bold dunes. The thunder and crash cover the magical voice which releases the burning victim from his suffering. The thunder and crash change into the lowing of buffaloes; the roar of lionesses. Infuriated again, the flames advance taller and thicker, in battle order.

"The fire is mine!" shouts the implacable leader who has my warlike mask. "The entire forest and all of its aroma!" He leads the charge; and is the first to seize the bristling mane with his red hand.

"Men with me! With me, people of the forest!" shouts the audacious adversary who has my warlike countenance.

Fire will overwhelm fire, flame will kill flame, so that from the two hostile ashes the earth may be made fertile.

Who is this man with the scorched face, the burning vestments, who flings himself on the sand and burrows into it as if to bury himself?

And he is not extinguished.

Against the chain of flames is set the human chain. Against the front of flames is set an opposing front.

The counterfire flares up.

With long branches of fresh pine, the young, the old, women and children strike the savage red beast to force it to advance against the other advancing savage beast.

Help! Help!

The beaten flame writhes, the gusts of wind drive smoke over the fire-fighters. The increasing heat from the flame singes lashes—eyebrows—beards—clothes. Throats become dry, eyes begin to tear.

Help, help!

The counterfire advances. The enemy approaches. In turn yellows, reddens. Shatters into myriads; recomposes; dissolves; disintegrates. Roils, shrieks, croaks, squeaks, hisses, crashes.

Help, help!

From what bowels rise this howl of pain and terror which splits my soul open?

It is no longer the voice of the element; it is the voice of the creature.

Caught between fire and counterfire the crazed beasts try to find a way out.

The fire drives them from behind, the counterfire is upon them.

Blinded by the glare, they ram into trunks that crackle in the growing blaze.

Down the long torrid corridor of the labyrinth without exit they plunge on, howling; and the lugubrious howl shatters the sooty suffocation into a turbulence of blazing scales, chips and burning pine cones.

Help, help!

We trample on embers, pound the smoldering bits of wood, swallow sparks.

Are these tenacious fire-fighters a phalanx of martyrs compelled to fight the fire of Our Lord? Each has looming before him a flaming angel and a thousand swords. The children weep; the old fall to their knees; the women howl as if in the throes of a bad childbirth.

And who is the Lord of this scintillating battle?

And which of the far centuries does this battle redden?

I see the ancient Sybil without her turreted crown and without her lions.

I see her robes variegated by water, earth and fire.

I see her pine bearers, hirsute teams of her *dendrophori* that resemble the sacred tree.

Who howls? Who roars? Who calls from the abyss and from sleep?

The sun is obscured.

Is this the thunder of the Last Judgment which dominates the collision of the two roaring adversaries?

Where they clash, everything is already devoured. Everything is black char, embers and hot ashes. There is no more fuel for it. There is nothing more to catch fire.

The fire dies.

The fire is dead!

Sorrow is dazed, and terror falls silent.

But, suddenly, a quiet vortex seizes the ashes which still throw off sparks and lifts them to the sullen clouds which are thinning out.

I see the tall, frail vortices rise, sway, go off.

It is the ghost of the holocaust.

To be a beautiful Italian pine tree
on a Roman hill
when the moon is full
and hear the wind of night
move the tender pinnacles
which are reborn among the old needles
at the summit of the ancient branches
rosy as children's fingers.

To be the tallest, darkest cypress tree in Villa d'Este
after the twilight
when the fountain
removes the veil of maidenhair
from its dripping ear
to spy on the remote drone
of the Tiburtine waterfall;
and fondle the grace of evening
with the light, sensitive green
that edges the funerary leaves.

To be in the Forum
the spirit of a blind herb
and toil patiently
to discover the fissure of aged stone

over which the Triumphs clattered
and at last find it
and strain up with the slender head
and burst forth, and bloom, and delight in the sun
which saw nothing greater than Rome.

Horses, horses without number, as at Versailles during the first dog days of the French war.

They are tied to a line strung between tree trunks, under trees which still display the adeptness of the pruning shears; and hay, straw and dung befoul the polished surface of the noble avenues.

But a large bunch of roses rests on the shoulder of that wounded man; and that other man, whose ravaged legs were black with blood and flies, is covered by a shawl of Flemish lace.

The regal city is transformed into an equine city.

I see the horses around the abandoned basins greenish with floating putridity. The palace is a dead thing, inexpressibly dead. The sweep of the broad canal, like a Styx compelled not to twist, thrusts into the melancholy of an infinite Hades.

I see other horses around an even sadder pond. They neigh towards the doleful, grim water which reminds me of Lake Nemi's face beneath a cloudy sky. Their makeshift troughs, shaped like black boats, stand in the shadow of the elms. A heartbreaking odor of stable has invaded the King's delights.

Now they are dead; they are all killed, slaughtered en masse.

The Battle of the Marne leaves them behind, reclining in the grass strewn with empty bottles and unexploded shells. They all hold the same pose, all the way to the horizon they all make the same lugubrious gesture, with a swollen belly and a hind leg rigid in the air.

In the sweet meadows of erba medica, swollen bellies, lifted legs, yellowed gums, whitish eyes, flocks of ravens, swarms of flies; and in the valleys and the fields and the streets, everywhere—slain horses; and the horror of that always identical gesture; and the glint of iron in that petrified underbrush beneath a jet of lacerating sunlight.

In a field of sugar-beets, behind a pile of wrecked guncarriages and large ammunition caissons, I come upon a surviving horse. He is alone. He cannot walk. One of his fetlocks is smashed, there is a deep wound in one of his haunches and another in his withers.

But he is quiet. His eye is tranquil. The clamor has ceased. The inferno is ended. All is silence. The birds do not sing. A man walks down the path in the distance beneath the drizzle, a folded burlap bag on his head. Close to a ruined house a threshing machine sprawls, toppled over, belly up, like the carcasses. The grassy knoll curves so gently that it seems to express some arcane tenderness of the earth. The weathervane on the bell tower rules over the silence, which the fine rain soothes. At rare intervals the wind raises a damp gust. The smell of death chokes his breath off.

Stretching his neck, the survivor tries to eat the grass near his mouth. He is alone. Soon night will fall. A lost, voiceless swallow grazes his flank.

> Oh sadness sadness
> why bring back to me
> from so far away
> what you already found
> so heavy to bear?

And now you are also leading me back to him who was the favorite of my childhood in the comfort of my home when my mother was the pensive flower of my healthiest youth in Pescara, my native city.

He comes to me, moving through the dense crowd of my memories, as when he parted the tall, not yet scythed grass with his chest.

He opens a furrow through my life which bends from side to side, touching the good soil with its pliant, grassy tips.

He was a small Sardinian horse. A tawny bay, with a white fringe above his hoofs and a white muzzle. His mane and tail were long and rich. His name was Aquilino.

In the stable, between his stall and that of the pair, there was an empty stall where I would have liked to put my small wrought-iron cot. Whenever I was able to slip away, I went downstairs, my heart beating with excitement, and went inside from the courtyard. Aquilino, recognizing my light step, neighed softly as if to prevent anyone from hearing and finding out. Each time my joy was so great that the corners of my smock in which I carried the booty slipped out of my hands.

Then his neighing trembled with impatience; and while I gathered up the bread, apples, everything I had been given for my afternoon snack, and whatever I had been able to filch from the pantry for my sweet-toothed friend, I stilled my hunger with a smile which had a nourishing quality I have never tasted again.

One of the stable doors opened on the coach room. This room was almost always empty, lit by a chapel-like light that shone down from the colored panes of the fan-window. There stood the large, covered wedding coach, lined with blue cloth, silk curtains behind the glass, and silver handles on the doors. There was a gig with its collapsible hood, and a wicker basket on two wheels. And hanging against the wall there were the harnesses which I never grew tired of contemplating: collars, pectorals, cruppers, straps, traces, bridles, buckles, loops, rings, always sparkling, and the long whips for which I yearned.

That child stooping over the floor to gather the bread and fruit he had denied himself for the sake of his love, that child already avid for a singular life and mysterious communions, entranced by that neighing as by a magical voice, illumined by his own smile as by a subterranean lamp, leave that child within my reach. Let me recognize in that act of his, in that pleasure of his, an image of fleeting happiness which is peculiar to me and which from time to time flashes through me even on this bed of sorrow.

Was I already then possessed by the lyrical daimon that exalts and transforms my whole being? Was the magical sense of life already awakened in me?

And just as Aquilino neighed to me softly, so I spoke to him in a whisper. Just as he understood me, so I understood him, happy to stand with my two feet on the straw on a level with his four hooves.

He took the pieces of bread from the palm of my hand, the slices of apple, the squares of sugar, with a careful grace which tickled and sometimes made me burst into convulsed and smothered laughter or yelp unrestrainedly. But I was intimidated by the two large coach horses that continually rattled the wooden balls attached to the ropes of their halters; and I tried not to be seen by them.

And little by little that trepidation and cautiousness and understanding created in the closed stable a mysteriously fantastic sense of remoteness. And that black gaze which Aquilino kept fixed on my face as he chewed and that face of his marked by his lips' white and rosy spot, mobile as the muzzle of a hare, and that way of demanding with a greedy quiver of his nostrils when he had finished, and his teasing way of nibbling at my shoulder when, to goad him, I hid what was left behind my back, and all his ways of pretty duplicity gradually merged in me both his species and mine and bewitched me.

"I'll give you the rest if you'll let me take a hair, if you'll let me take two hairs, three."

I remember that when I ripped them out I had to overcome a slight feeling of shame, of remorse. Did it hurt him? Did he know that I wanted them to make snares for the swallows that lived in the eaves?

My sister Ernesta was the one who had put me up to pulling them from his mane and suddenly I felt sick at heart, perhaps for having given on condition, bartered, perhaps for having thought of bringing death and mourning to the small mud nest.

When I pulled, many more than three were left in my fist.

The stable boy who was an accomplice of my secret forays came in. And he lifted me up and set me astride "the Sardinian."

I liked to ride in a dream without moving. But I did not like to be watched.

I would say to the stable boy: "Go away and come back later."

I closed my eyes. I was bewitched. The door opened onto the edge of the woods. Night was falling. It was impossible to see the end of the path.

But that day the manger remained fixed against the wall, and the wall did not open up; and the horse did not move, even though I talked to him in whispers.

I still had those hairs in my fist and that shadowy regret in my heart.

A sudden sharp cry, a white flash.

Had a swallow entered through the broken pane, the crack? Was there a nest attached to the ceiling of the stable? How long had it been there?

I shivered with astonishment.

A light feather descended through the enchanted air, wavering: the one feather I needed to put in the mane as a lure.

I did not wait for the boy to come back and take me off. I lifted one leg over his back and let myself slip down onto the straw.

"I'll be back, Aquilino. Before evening, I'll be back."
And I went straight for the hearth with a brow on which the
vertical furrow of willfulness was already being scored.
And I threw that fistful of hairs into the magical fire.

Oh sadness sadness
why bring back to me
from so far away
what you already found
so heavy to bear?

I, my brother, and my three sisters, had gone downstairs
into the coach room, we had climbed into the old wedding
coach where the blue cloth lining smelled of dried rain and a
cushion was still warm from the cat who had slept on it.

The door to the stable was open. Aquilino lay on the straw
in the agony of death. My father knelt at the side of the dying
horse between the coachman and the whimpering stable hand
who held the cup full of medicine and the wooden spoon.

Through the window of the coach, huddling together in
dismay we watched without crying, with hearts so pinched
that neither a drop of blood nor a tear of grief could flow. We
watched death for the first time, we who had never thought
about it except on the eve of All Souls, waiting for the gifts it
would bring us.

I could see the convulsed movements of the hoofs, and the
one leg marked by the white fringe hurt me most; and the
tremor of the poor white muzzle hurt me even more.

But I could not cry; and, alone, I kept back the grief of all
five of us.

The stable boy burst into sobs. I pushed mine back into my
throat with a feeling of indignation that I cannot describe. I
saw that the poor legs had stiffened.

We huddled even closer together and together turned to ice
beneath that dark sky formed by the carriage, in that feeble

light from the fan-window. And for the first time with ten fixed eyes we looked at death. But I received its mark for all of us.

Then my father rose, crossed the threshold, halted, turning toward us in our dismay; and, over the icy silence in my breast, said in a tone that now rings vivid and precise in my ear and soul: "Gabriele."

> Oh sadness sadness
> why bring back to me
> from so far away
> what you already found
> so heavy to bear?

I ask one of the musicians to show me his cello. He brings it to me with a modest smile.

This Alberghini is a very clever hunter of instruments, scouring the mountains and valleys in search of them. Whenever he hears about a violin hiding away somewhere, as others when they hear about a boar or hare, he sets off and will not abandon his search until he has found it.

This cello of his was made by Andrea Guarneri. He came upon it in Egypt, in Cairo. I smile, thinking that under my hand I have a thoroughbred like El-Mar, and that even its coat resembles that of my sorrel.

The varnish is intact and rich, of a beautiful reddish-brown color which allows the gold beneath to shine through. The golden sheen comes through more frequently on the back in streaks, in patches, and here and there on the sound-holes which smell of amber. The back of the neck is pale, polished by the sliding hand. But the true miracle of gracefulness is at the back's center: there a bird of paradise has once mirrored the brief treasure of its throat and the reflection is still there, captured in the everlasting varnish.

The musician tells me that, in Cairo, he traded instruments

with a colleague whose hand was short, giving him a small
Gagliano.

The cello had been bought near Cremona. A rustic had
been playing it in the choir of a country church. One day,
during a solemn service, the chancel had collapsed, along with
organ, cello, musicians and singers. The cellist broke a leg.
The back of the instrument was damaged but not its sound-
post. A few days later it was rescued from restoration by an
inexperienced mender.

"Don't you think that with its delicate bridge and its sound-
holes ending in large open tear-drops, it looks like a beautiful
face with a beautiful voice? It is alive. There is no need for a
bow. It plays by itself, sings by itself. In Mexico City the
women used to draw near, fascinated by its angelic timbre,
and wanted to touch this skin, more precious and sensitive
than their own."

So says the artilleryman from Emilia, dressed in his gray
uniform.

"A woman's skin eats into the varnish. At Nice I saw a
Stradivarius almost completely stripped by the violinist's bare
arm and shoulder.

"But then in Ferrara I saw another Stradivarius under a glass
bell. It is one of the earliest, when he was still an apprentice to
Amati. The wood has turned almost all to dust but the strength
of the varnish alone holds it together. And I remember that I
was afraid to breathe in the presence of that relic.

"Who can say anything absolutely certain about varnishes?
Red varnish? Yellow varnish? To be so impregnable it must
contain the dust of diamonds."

My hands rest on the shoulder of the cello while the soldier,
seated, holds it by the fingerboard. And before they reach my
ear, the things he says seem to travel through the sensitivity of
the strings and the wood.

"There exists a strange similarity between man's structure
and that of the instrument. There is a definite relationship

between the player's physical condition and the quality of the sound. Earlier they played without a ferrule, resting the cello on their joined ankles. Movement of the legs stopped any vibration that might reach the sound-level too forcefully. Bones are musical, you would say that a good musician's bones ought to contain air rather than marrow. Both tibia and femur exert a continued influence on the sound. Each note can be corrected by expert pressure.

"The bow is also very important. Depending on the kind of bow the sound is more or less full. Between the wood of the bow and that of the instrument there must be a vital correspondence. The fiber of the wood, not bent by firing, immediately transmits the intention of the hand.

"This is a Tourte, it is nervous, the rod is octagonal, the heel ebony, the eye is mother-of-pearl. Here is another, its round rod covered with black leather tooled with the design of small hoofs, the heel is dark tortoise-shell, the eye is gold.

"Here is a Dodd, it's English, it has an entirely different gracefulness or perhaps it has none, with its whale-bone sheath, its ivory heel, its octagonal pommel made of ivory and silver.

"And here is another one, nameless and unadorned, indeed, poor thing, a truly Franciscan bow that would suit *Il Cantico delle Creature*, and there is nothing to recommend it but for the reddish-brown color of its wood, attuned to my Guarneri.

"And only this bow, who knows why, suits my cello; and only this bow, who knows why, can extract from its soul all of its voice.

"They understand each other. From what you see by examining the two woods closely, you might even believe that this bow was extracted from the cello's rib just as Eve was from Adam's."

The soldier laughs openly like a child and plucks the first string.

I say to him: "It could be. Instruments have a demonic nature. Sometimes, at the end of the neck, instead of the scroll, the old masters carved the image of the splendid Enemy. I saw a tenor viola with a neck ending in a horned head. In my hometown in Abruzzi, I saw a viola d'amore with a kind of screech-owl, its very long neck bending toward the player to tempt him and instill its perfidious fascination in his heart."

The soldier no longer speaks in jest: "There is no doubt," he adds. "The great violin-maker is a magician. Only magic can illuminate him in the choice of woods. Why does a Testore go and pick the soft wood which immediately becomes saturated with sound, and so that the sound circulates through it uninterruptedly like a dry lymph? And why, on the other hand, does a Guarneri del Gesu not attach too much importance to the choice, feeling able to transform any wood by his mysterious influence? There you have the true occult poet. He does not work unless inspired. He cuts two imperious sound-holes into the violin's face; and the face lives, expresses, speaks, is anxious to sing.

"So then, what is the sound-holes' influence on the harmonic plane? Guarneri's sound-holes resemble neither Amati's, nor those of Stradivarius, nor any others. How did he find them?

"And is he not a magician, that Gennaro Gagliano the Translucent, who hurls his small striated tigers at the throat of Music?"

I admire the animation of this exquisite cellist attached to a heavy artillery unit, who feels and expresses with such lyrical intensity the life of living things.

He says: "There was no such thing as a muted cello for practicing. So I decided to build one, with a very narrow sound-box to fit the extended strings. And by chance a new instrument was born, which has a delightful English horn sound, perfect for dance melodies."

I say to him: "Let's call it an *Alberghina*."

He goes to get his Alberghina. He returns, and plays a jig, a courante, a galliard.

Halfway through the galliard we hear the lugubrious howl of the siren followed by the roar of canon.

Beauty of the night, how many times have I lost you?

To see, to look, to know: I was avid, always. Insatiable, always. And yet, my restless eyes, you have not seen enough, you have not looked enough, you have not been able to take in all the faces of the manifest deity.

And one of you is already extinguished, and the other grows turbid and tired and is perhaps fated to be obscured.

"Look! Look!"

Under the full moon echoes that voice which knew how to match every tone of misery and every note of happiness: the voice of Giusola.

"Look! Look!"

She was rousing me from sleep. I had drowned in sleep as in a black river. It felt as if, her hands under my armpits, she was trying with all her strength to lift me up from that torpid whirlpool.

"Look! Look!"

Thus she pulled me to the window. And I lifted my heavy eyelids; and saw the tall sapphire peaks, the supernatural summits of a planet without men.

"Look!"

I saw the transfiguration of the Tuscan Alps in a lunar night arisen from the depths of some ecstatic god's millennial memory.

I closed my lids again, pressed down by inert sleep.

"Look!"

I opened them again and closed them again. The divine spectacle was erased by the wave of the forgetful stream.

I descend the stairs with infinite caution, carrying my eye inside the reliquary of my lifted head.

Sirenetta is there, ready to support me.

Here is the last tread.

Here the downstairs room.

Here the green dazzle beyond the panes covered with lace.

Here the living air which like an unaccustomed potion fills my greedy mouth with its new taste.

Here the garden, here the leaves, the flowers.

My hand rises to the blindfold. It is a sterner bandage than usual. It is not white but dark. It is not of linen but of silk. My eye is dressed in mourning, clad in weeds.

With her childlike grace Sirenetta seizes the mad hand, draws me toward a rosebush trained to a tall, slender trunk, and says to me: "Look at this little rose."

Mystery of an intonation which can make of a young girl and a rosebush a single creation.

As she holds the stem between her middle and ring fingers, the little rose seems to have sprouted in the hollow of her hand, almost the beginning of a vernal metamorphosis.

She wears a striped dress, white and green, which seems patterned after one of those silvery poplars that shiver with all their tender branches in the wind from the river bank.

The little rose is grafted into her, it is the flower of her tenderness.

It is so pure, so fragile, so delicately constructed that no corporeal thing can be compared to it but perhaps only a chaste, ineffable thought.

There is no form of infancy equal to it.

One must kneel and worship it.

Its perfection is so shortlived.

I think I see its petals open with each instant.

By early evening it will already be open, and in vain.

The inertia of so many days had imprisoned me in the feeling of solitary transiency amid inanimate things. Now once more I regain the ear of the poet, resting on the bank of time's stream; I hear again the melody of the perpetual flux.

Sirenetta minutely knows the garden's brief fairy tale. She

knows where to find the caterpillar, the bee, the spider, the scarab, and what they are doing. She knows the sick branches, the number of buds; what is late, what is about to open. She complains about the gardener's laziness and fetches a small bellows to blow a healing dust on a rosebush that crawls with greenish insects. With hesitant compassion she leads me to a large white rose whose deepest heart is being devoured by a scarab.

"Why don't you shake it off, why don't you get rid of it?" I ask her.

"The rose is done for by now," she answers. "And if the scarab does not get enough of this, it will go looking for another."

I sense that her compassion is divided between the insect and the flower, just as the heart of St. Francis included the famished bird and the pecked worm, the burning fire and the burnt garment, the ailing flesh and the herbs crushed to heal it.

I halt before this spectacle of devastating passion.

The insect is nailed into the flower's sweetness with a craving which resembles both perdition and rapture. It is dazzling, like a gold lamella shining through a polished emerald. It is a stupendous jewel and a savage force.

It is forgetful of everything, oblivious of all risk, all surprise, all threat, submerged in its delight as in a crime that fears no punishment.

I sense again, as in my early youth, what there is of the divine in thirst and hunger.

The entire heart of the rose is spoiled and, surrounded by a crown of still intact petals, appears yellowish like a trace of honey.

The sore oozes nectar, the murder is sweet.

Unsatiated love does not know guilt.

Who feeds on beauty grows in beauty.

I would like to linger and catch the instant when the scarab will extend its wings outside its carapace and fly away along a ray of sunlight.

The afternoon wanes. Even the slightest breeze is gone. The new leaves breathe and hope, the old meditate and remember.

A vast flowering of wisteria, which covers the entire wall up to the roof, issuing from a trunk similar to a tangle of ropes, calls forth the image of a net that I saw pulled up on the Atlantic shore filled with futile, almost violet jellyfish.

The swallows riot and screech furiously, and I suffer ancient wounds as if they were stabbing me through and through like lightning bolts.

In a corner I see two overturned watering-cans and, I do not know why, they give me a sense of silence, create a pause amid the lacerating shrieks.

"Here is your speaking laurel," says Sirenetta.

It is a rounded laurel on a slim, bare trunk, as tall as a man. It has a certain allegorical air: it seems transplanted from a grove in the dream of Polyphilus. It lacks nothing but the flutter of a scroll wrapped around the middle of its trunk. Its foliage is somber, harsh, thick, so that the Muse cannot reach into it without the cutting edges injuring her hand. And from the perennial foliage, at rhythmic intervals sway the small new leaves, so lively that they seem to chatter like small impatient tongues filled with "the will to speak."

Sirenetta's fresh young soul has immediately heard the soundless rhythm.

The laurel speaks. It says: "So as not to sleep?" or does it say "So as not to die?"

Never was sleep more alien to me, nor was I ever so deep in death, filled with so much eagerness for immortality.

I still have a deep song in my tempered heart.

The sun sets beyond the bend of the canal which now is as green as the speaking laurel. The bells are silent, but the air seems to quiver with the expectancy of their angelic sound. My bandaged eye brims with luminous wisteria; yet the other eye, disaccustomed, is lost in reverie.

Outside of time a slow harmony unfolds. Core's house is nothing but a vast garland supported by the heads of lions bent over the water. From Palazzo Doria to the church of Santa Maria della Salute, brick and stone, under the rose-colored light, become almost carnal. The two façades support each other, like women leaning one toward the other so as not to fall, overcome by the sudden languor of April.

A huge black boat loaded with resplendent sulphur, propelled by long oars, glides by like an apparition from beyond the millennia and memory.

Along with the broad ram it has the ancient rudder with its long tiller, held by a man who resembles a Phoenician helmsman.

As it enters the shadow, the sulphur takes on a color for which there are no words. That yellow has the power of an unexpected theme which suddenly raises a waning symphony to sublimity.

A strange silence falls within me.

I no longer hear the swallows.

And my heart trembles for fear that a knell interrupt this tacit music.

Liz Poulson
0763 - 241604